PRAISE FOR
CHARLIE N. HOLMBERG

SMOKE AND SUMMONS

"[An] enthralling fantasy . . . The story is gripping from the start, with a surprising plot and a lush, beautifully realized setting. Holmberg knows just how to please fantasy fans."

—*Publishers Weekly*

"With scads of action, clear explanations of how supernatural elements function, and appealing characters with smart backstories, this first in a series will draw in fans of Cassandra Clare, Leigh Bardugo, or Brandon Sanderson."

—*Library Journal*

"Holmberg is a genius at world building; she provides just enough information to set the scene without overwhelming the reader. She also creates captivating characters worth rooting for, and puts them in unique situations. Readers will be eager for the second installment in the Numina series."

—*Booklist*

THE PAPER MAGICIAN

"Charlie is a vibrant writer with an excellent voice and great world building. I thoroughly enjoyed *The Paper Magician*."

—Brandon Sanderson, author of *Mistborn* and *The Way of Kings*

"Harry Potter fans will likely enjoy this story for its glimpses of another structured magical world, and fans of Erin Morgenstern's *The Night Circus* will enjoy the whimsical romance element . . . So if you're looking for a story with some unique magic, romantic gestures, and the inherent darkness that accompanies power all steeped in a yet to be fully explored magical world, then this could be your next read."

—Amanda Lowery, *Thinking Out Loud*

THE GLASS MAGICIAN

"I absolutely loved *The Glass Magician*. It exceeded my expectations, and I was very impressed with the level of conflict and complexity within each character. I will now sit twiddling my thumbs until the next one comes out."

— *The Figmentist*

"*The Glass Magician* will charm readers young and old alike."

—Radioactive Book Reviews

THE MASTER MAGICIAN

A Wall Street Journal *Bestseller*

"Utah author Charlie Holmberg delivers . . . thrilling action and delicious romance in *The Master Magician*."

—*Deseret News*

THE PLASTIC MAGICIAN

"The everyday setting with just a touch of magical steampunk technology proves to readers what an incredible job Holmberg does with her world-building. Fans of previous Paper Magician books will love this addition to the world, and readers new to it will quickly fall in love with the magic-wielding characters."

—Booklist

THE FIFTH DOLL

Winner of the 2017 Whitney Award for Speculative Fiction

"*The Fifth Doll* is told in a charming, folklore-ish voice that's reminiscent of a good old-fashioned tale spun in front of the fireplace on a cold winter night. I particularly enjoyed the contrast of the small-town village atmosphere—full of simple townspeople with simple dreams and worries—set against the complex and eerie backdrop of the village that's not what it seems. The fact that there are motivations and forces shaping the lives of the villagers on a daily basis that they're completely unaware of adds layers and textures to the story and makes it a very interesting read."

—San Francisco Book Review

"Holmberg weaves a skillful story with an elegant touch for character and detail, one sure to please lovers of modern fantasy."

—AuthorLink

"Quite clever, and the character work is endearing."

—RT Book Reviews

"Entertaining."

—Publishers Weekly

SIEGE & SACRIFICE

ALSO BY CHARLIE N. HOLMBERG

The Numina Series

Smoke and Summons

Myths and Mortals

The Paper Magician Series

The Paper Magician

The Glass Magician

The Master Magician

The Plastic Magician

Other Novels

The Fifth Doll

Magic Bitter, Magic Sweet

Followed by Frost

Veins of Gold

SIEGE & SACRIFICE

THE NUMINA SERIES

CHARLIE N. HOLMBERG

Text copyright © 2019 by Charlie N Holmberg LLC
All rights reserved.

No part of this book may be reproduced, or stored in a retrieval system, or transmitted in any form or by any means, electronic, mechanical, photocopying, recording, or otherwise, without express written permission of the publisher.

Published by 47North, Seattle

www.apub.com

Amazon, the Amazon logo, and 47North are trademarks of Amazon.com, Inc., or its affiliates.

ISBN-13: 9781542092593 (hardcover)
ISBN-10: 1542092590 (hardcover)
ISBN-13: 9781542092579 (paperback)
ISBN-10: 1542092574 (paperback)

Cover design credit: Ellen Gould

Cover illustration credit: Marina Munn

Printed in the United States of America

First edition

To Sharlene Beck, my first writing teacher and the voice of my internal editor. Thank you for your guidance and your passion.

Chapter 1

The eruption was like being submerged in a vat of boiling iron. Like blood and fire and *power*. It happened so fast. One moment Rone was running for his amarinth, and the next he was on his back, staring at a smoke-filled sky, breathing in sulfur and ash.

Except the smoke wasn't from the city. It was black, thick, and curling, and it smelled like singed hair and rotten eggs. It spewed from a monster as tall as the Lily Tower. But where the tower stood tall and white, elegant in its structure, the monster hunched, its skin the mottled red and black of volcanic stone splitting from the pressure of the magma beneath. Its body was humanesque—legs, arms, torso—but its face was that of a bull. Great horns on its head pierced the sky even as black smoke poured from them. Red slits revealed large, narrow eyes, and rows of obsidian teeth jutted beyond split lips. Arms stretched heavenward, ending in hands spiked with bleeding talons. From its back jutted spiny wings, curved and hard like overgrown fingernails. They were the color of river silt and looked more like claws than anything meant for flight.

The red cracks in the monster's armor brightened to near white, sending hot wind gushing over Rone. It dried him out instantly, sucking moisture from his mouth and nose.

Kolosos. This was Kolosos, the numen that had terrorized Sandis. The being that had struck fear into Rone's father, the unfeeling Angelic.

And to think Rone had once found *Ireth*, the fire horse, terrifying. He couldn't move. His brain floated elsewhere. His body was lead. He lay there in shock, staring at the monster that had consumed his amarinth, even as its smoke burned his lungs. On its blackened shoulder, Kazen—was that Kazen?—laughed and ranted, but Rone couldn't hear his words over the hissing of Kolosos's joints. How could the madman perch there without being engulfed? All the while Kolosos watched them, feral, awaiting command.

It was Sandis's scream that pulled him back to himself. She knelt a few paces behind him, her knees and palms bleeding, her eyes wide, her lips forming a word over and over. A word he couldn't hear.

Run, you blasted idiot.

Rone's limbs were awkward and heavy, but he found his feet and stumbled toward Sandis. Grabbing her shoulders, he hauled her up. Had she always been this light?

"Anon," she wheezed. Her brother's name. "Anon. Anon. Anon."

"Sandis, *run!*"

She shook her head, somehow managing tears despite the heat radiating from the monster. "Anon. Anon. He . . . Kolosos . . ."

Rone paused, staring at her, then shot a look at Kolosos, which stood still as its mad owner continued to yell, unaware that the few people who'd lingered couldn't hear him. A priest ran, limping, past them, sweat drenching his white-and-silver robes as flames devoured the holy tower behind him.

Rone didn't see anyone else. No dead brothers. No—

He stared at Kolosos's hooves. The vessel . . . she couldn't mean the *vessel*, could she? The adolescent who had clutched the amarinth before . . .

A grumble from Kolosos's throat shook the earth beneath their feet. The numen lifted a smoking hand.

"Run *now!*" Rone grabbed Sandis's wrist and yanked her toward the half-crumbled gate to the city. She complied, following his tug.

Rone's legs burned with fear-spiked energy. They had to get away. *Faster, faster—*

The sound of marble and wood breaking barreled into him as though it were a physical thing. Rone stumbled, his knee hitting the path hard. Sandis tripped over his leg.

He dared to look back.

The top two floors of the Lily Tower were shattered chunks around Kazen and his monster. Kolosos lifted a hoof and stepped on one of the smoking remnants. The stones hissed under the contact and exploded into ash.

Kolosos's molten eyes lowered, its gaze finding Sandis and Rone.

Rone cursed hard enough to make any god wince. Sandis was already on her feet, pulling at *him*. He leapt up and ran, his fingers tight and clammy around hers. His vision tunneled as though shadows swirled around his path. There was only the wall. Only the entrance to the city. They had to run. Hide. *Run.*

The ground shook. Rone didn't need to turn around to know the enormous numen had taken a step toward them. It shook again, harder this time, pulsing as though it contained a heart the size of Dresberg. The third time, the ground bucked enough to throw Rone off his feet. He pushed himself up and sprinted, still holding on to Sandis. The fourth step, the path cracked.

Sweat poured down Rone's face as the heat increased. He could just make out Kazen's voice, though his words were a jumbled mess. The bastard would finally have his revenge. The wall was so close, but not close enough.

Sandis was saying something to him. Rone's legs pumped as he turned toward her, trying to understand.

"Can you carry me?" The question was a desperate plea, hoarse and loud. She was too tired to go on. They were already dead. But Rone nodded, regardless. He'd rather die holding her.

Sandis yanked her hand from his grip, causing him to trip over himself. He turned around only to see her throw her dress at his feet.

Then she erupted into pure flame, a bonfire of white and orange that barely reached Kolosos's knees. A pale halo surrounded her and spun like the loop of an amarinth.

A ball of fire the size of a carriage shot upward, headed right for Kolosos's face.

No. She had aimed for *Kazen*.

Kolosos reared back to protect its summoner, and the flames exploded against its mouth. The ground shook twice under two retreating steps.

Sandis fell in a naked, extinguished heap.

Rone didn't think, only acted.

He grabbed her and her dress, threw both over his shoulder, and bolted into the city.

Of course she only takes off her clothes when we're about to die. The thought was hardly serious, but Rone's mind was spinning in a million directions, and the pathetic humor helped him focus. His body was putty, his shoulders and feet numb, but he kept loping through the city, over broken bits of wall and road, around abandoned wagons and empty buildings. The city, usually packed to the brim with people, looked abandoned. The bell towers failed to ring, and even the smokestacks' polluted whispers had hushed.

One of his rampant thoughts repeated, *Where to hide? Where to hide? Where to hide?* His mind jumped from Kolosos to his mother—safe in Godobia—to Bastien. Kazen's lair. They'd left the ginger vessel in Kazen's subterranean lair, under the care of the priest who'd brought them to the Lily Tower earlier that day.

It was as good a place as any, and close.

The ground shook again, causing buildings to bow and tremble, cobblestones to knock together. This quake wasn't quite as strong—perhaps Kolosos had turned around to finish wreaking havoc on the tower. How had Sandis known where Kazen would strike?

Rone's toe caught on an unleveled cobblestone, but he managed to stay upright. He shifted Sandis's unconscious form on his shoulder and kept running, passing two men cowering behind a street cart.

The dilapidated buildings that surrounded Kazen's old lair were probably the last place Rone would want to be during an earthquake; already he saw one that looked to have crumbled from the impact of Kolosos's footsteps. But he trudged forward, lungs and calves burning. Sweat stung his eyes. Air stung his nostrils. His dry tongue was a wadded sock in his mouth.

He got inside the hidden door, half slid down the stairs, and collapsed at the start of the white corridor that led to Sandis's old prison. Rone's back hit the wall, and Sandis fell into his lap. Hugging her, he closed his eyes and desperately gasped for air. His entire body tingled as his muscles unwound. His joints ached like deep bruises.

"What's going on?" Cleric Liddell, the Angelic's messenger priest, bellowed down the corridor. "What—by the Celestial!"

Rone opened his dry eyes and turned his stiff neck so he could look at the cleric, whose white robes looked too pristine. The cleric stared at Sandis.

Moving his arm lower to cover her breasts, Rone croaked, "Water. Now."

The priest dumbly nodded his head and retreated.

Rone didn't move. He couldn't. He managed to unclaw his hand from Sandis's dress, but he didn't have the energy to lift it over her head. He could fall asleep right now, his foot crushed beneath his backside, his body stiff with drying sweat, his insides sore and strung out. When Liddell came back with the water, the priest had to hold it to Rone's lips to get him to swallow. Half of it poured down the side of his neck. It felt too cold, like Rone had a fever.

The lair trembled softly, like it purred. Liddell inched toward the exit, muttering something about "another one." Only then did Rone piece together that the priest might have been staring at the brands on Sandis's back more than her nudity.

"Be careful if you go out there," Rone rasped. The cleric paused for a moment before giving a grim nod and continuing up the stairs to witness the carnage for himself.

Despite his fatigue, Rone tightened his arms around Sandis. The lair rumbled again, but Rone closed his eyes, exhaustion weaving through his blood.

When he opened them again, Cleric Liddell hovered in front of him with a lamp. "The beast is gone," he said, his voice too high, too weak. "But so is the tower."

Chapter 2

Sandis woke with a start, the bland colors of a too-familiar ceiling swirling before her eyes. Between the coils she saw fire, darkness. A slit red eye.

Kolosos.

The monster had stood before her, close enough to make her sweat steam. Enormous, angry, *powerful.* Even in her visions, she'd never seen it whole, and yet the pieces alone had terrified her. When put together, they inspired a fear unlike any other.

She blinked, eyelids dragging. She was parched, hungry, gritty. Her bones felt hollow. Her fingers, stiff. But she was alive. When she'd summoned Ireth, she hadn't known if she'd wake up. If the mind-splitting pain would be the last thing she ever felt.

As if her thoughts had called the numen, a warm pressure formed behind her forehead. Closing her eyes, Sandis allowed herself to savor the sensation. *Ireth.* He was back. He was hers again, thanks to Bastien. The world was coming apart, but Sandis was finally whole. And . . . *it* wasn't there anymore. That looming cloud, that feeling of being watched. It was finally gone.

Kolosos was alive, solid, and in the world, but its presence had left her body completely. It was strange to feel relief at such a moment—the demon was a true threat now, to all of Dresberg and beyond—and yet she did.

Sitting up slowly, Sandis waited for the headache she knew she'd have, though half summoning didn't take as harsh a toll. A blanket slipped off her bare shoulder. She caught it, wincing as the scabbed scrapes on her hand pulled. She recognized the blanket, the cot, and the room around her. This was where she and the other vessels had slept at night. The room with the door that locked from the outside. For half a second, she believed herself trapped again, but a voice cut through the panic, dissipating it.

"Sandis?"

She turned, the edge of the blanket still clutched in her hand, covering her nudity. Rone had pulled a cot—Dar's—closer to hers. He sat on the edge of it, looking tired but uninjured. Another wave of relief swept through her, cool as a winter wind.

A smirk tempted his lips. "I didn't look. Much." He tilted his head, indicating the off-white dress folded at the foot of her cot.

Sandis didn't reach for it. "What happened?" Her voice sounded like sand. Surely Bastien would have made a joke about that. But Sandis had summoned on him to get Ireth's blood to repair her tattooed bond. He likely hadn't woken yet.

"You exploded, I grabbed you, we ran."

She swallowed, then coughed against a dry throat. Rone leaned over to grab a cup of water sitting on the floor and handed it to her. She drank greedily, and her belly throbbed in protest.

When she finished, she asked, "Kolosos?"

"Gone, for now." Rone rubbed his hand down his face, and for a moment he looked ten years older. "Liddell said he could see it from the top of the building we're under. Kolosos leveled the Lily Tower and started destroying the east wall. Then it ran off and winked out of existence. Or something."

Sandis processed this, and a new memory hit her like a sledgehammer. "Anon."

She hadn't meant to say his name out loud.

Rone didn't speak. Only waited.

She gripped both cup and blanket in white-knuckled fingers. She would have wept if her body had the tears. "It was him. Kolosos's vessel. Rone, that was my *brother*."

Her own words pricked her like rusted needles. Shaking her head, she tried to believe what she already knew to be true. She may not have seen Anon for four years, but there was no mistaking the curve of the nose he'd broken when he was ten, or the way his lips had formed her name. He looked different, older. Broader. But the boy—almost a man—holding that amarinth had been Anon Gwenwig. Her brother, back from the dead. And he had recognized her, too.

She'd finally found him, only to lose him again.

"You said he was dead."

"He . . . He was . . ."

Kazen had said Anon drowned in the canal. Sandis had questioned the claim before—Kazen was, after all, a consummate liar—but Anon had vanished *three days* before the summoner's slavers captured Sandis. He'd never come home, never shown up to work. What else could have happened to him, save the worst? Besides, wouldn't Kazen have killed anyone who might come looking for Sandis? He'd certainly thought nothing of slaying Heath and Rist's parents.

Which brought her to a different question. *Had* Anon searched for her?

So many thoughts plagued her. Closing her eyes, Sandis winced, trying to sort them out.

Rone's warm hands touched her arms, then took the edges of the blanket and carefully wrapped them around her shoulders. "Are you sure, Sandis?"

She nodded, letting her mind wander back to that moment. Anon. She'd been only yards from him before Kolosos . . .

"I feel sick," she whispered.

Rone tucked her dark hair behind her ears and kissed the top of her head. "I'll see if I can find you something to eat."

Sandis nodded her thanks. She sat there awhile after Rone left. When she finally released the cup, her knuckles ached like they were centuries old.

Kazen. Anon. Kolosos.

Standing, she let the blanket drop and pulled on her dress and the familiar vessel underwear tucked beneath it. Tugged her hands through her hair. Paced the length of the room and back, though her bones felt hollow as flutes.

Rone returned with some meat and root vegetables. He must have found Kazen's cold storage, or Bastien had shown him where it was.

"Bastien?" she asked as Rone set the plate on her cot.

"Still out." He sat down. "You were asleep for about five, maybe six hours."

She nodded. Since he'd had a full summoning, Bastien would sleep for six to twelve hours more.

Rone said, "Liddell is beside himself—"

"Kolosos will be back." She didn't apologize for the interruption, but Rone didn't seem offended. He focused on her, silent and intent. "Kazen probably guided it away so Anon could revert to himself without being caught by soldiers or police. A vessel's body can only be possessed for so long before it tires too much, and that monster must take so much energy . . ."

"Sandis."

She took a deep breath.

Rone crossed the room, then gently wrapped his arms around her. Sandis buried her face into his chest. His shirt smelled like smoke, but rain scented his skin. The clean kind that came after a storm cleared the sludge from the sky.

"We'll figure it out. One step at a time." He sighed, and Sandis let herself take comfort in the rise and fall of his chest. He held her like that for a moment, the food forgotten, until he finally asked, "How did you know?"

Sandis didn't move, only made a muffled sound of question against his shirt.

"Where Kazen was," he clarified.

She pulled back. "The sphere."

Rone's brow crinkled. Taking his hand, Sandis led him from the sleeping room to Kazen's office, where Bastien still slumbered on the table Sandis had been strapped to twice, once to receive her brands and once when Ireth was stripped away. Liddell perched uneasily in a chair beside Bastien, shoulders hunched, feet shaking, reading a book from Kazen's shelf. He stood when Sandis and Rone entered, but didn't say anything.

Sandis moved to the cupboard in the back of the room and opened it, revealing the two etchings of the astral sphere on the inside of its door.

"This." She traced the first sphere. "I was looking at this, thinking about Kazen and what the Angelic said about him being a cleric. He always talked about proving 'them' wrong. Proving himself right. I thought . . . I thought there must have been a reason Kazen left Celesia. There must have been something he wanted to prove. He once called Kolosos a god."

Rone exchanged an uneasy look with Cleric Liddell.

She pressed her finger to the base of the sphere. "This is Kolosos. And this"—she pointed to the top—"is the Celestial."

Cleric Liddell gasped and dropped his book. "Blasphemy!" Lines contorted his forehead in what looked like a painful manner. "You dare insinuate that the *Celestial* is a *numen*?"

Ignoring him, she said, "There has to be some sort of power to balance out Kolosos. Even the Angelic hinted at that." She traced the Noscon symbols at the top of the sphere. "If I were to take out my

11

revenge on those who had wronged me, I would do it where it hurt most. The Lily Tower."

Rone looked almost as incredulous. He ran a hand back through his hair, snagging one of his fingers on a tangle. "He *was* at the Lily Tower."

"*Everyone* saw Kolosos at the tower!" Cleric Liddell threw his hands into the air. "She hardly predicted it with this . . . this *witchcraft!*"

Rone's expression darkened. "We were there before the beast was summoned, Liddell. You saw us run from this lair before the screams. Before the quakes."

"The fact that this woman, who *lived* with Kazen for *years*, knew where he would strike does not prove your heresy." Cleric Liddell shook his head and sank back into his chair, staring at the floor. "The Angelic will have—" Pausing, he covered his face with his hands. "Celestial, save him. Please let him live."

A soft growl sounded in Rone's throat. Sandis was sure only she heard it. She searched his face, though he didn't meet her eyes. The likelihood of the Angelic having perished . . . did it hurt Rone? He claimed to have no special feelings for his father, and whenever the two were together, they argued bitterly. But she understood the power of family. Hadn't she hung on to hope about her great-uncle until the very end?

Sandis touched his wrist. Rone replied with a shrug.

She waited for him to do more, say more, but when he didn't, she turned back to the astral sphere and stared at the Noscon writing. She had been right, hadn't she? She felt it with an unshakeable certainty. And yet to believe her god was a *numen*, no different than Ireth or Kuracean or Isepia . . .

Surely an unbound numen couldn't hear her prayers. Could neither help nor condemn her.

Cleric Liddell didn't know this secret history, but did other priests? Did the Angelic? If they did, they condemned her and the other vessels for being exactly what the numina needed—what the Celestial needed—to enter the mortal plane. Wasn't that hypocritical?

If the Celestial was a numen, did God even exist?

Her stomach twisted. This was too much. This revelation, Kolosos, Anon. Too much.

Warmth crept up her neck, as though trying to comfort her. *Thank you, Ireth.*

If only the fire horse could speak to her directly. Maybe he could answer her questions.

She took a deep breath. "Kolosos will return."

Cleric Liddell lifted his head.

"Then we need to be ready." Rone leaned against the wall. "I don't know how long this place will hold. Should we leave the city while we can?" If there was ever a time to escape Dresberg without papers, now was the time to do it. Though in truth, it was crossing Kolingrad's borders that would prove tricky.

"With Kolosos gone," Cleric Liddell said each syllable with care, "the people might not think they *need* to leave. They'll think it's over. Even so, surely the triumvirate will rally its forces to hold the peace."

"You mean hold its citizens in a walled death trap." Rone's voice was low and dark, and it raised gooseflesh on Sandis's arms.

Cleric Liddell retorted, but Sandis didn't hear his response. The heat in her neck became nearly painful, and new pressure pounded behind her forehead. *Ireth?* She searched inside herself. Touched her neck. The skin was oddly cool against her fingers.

The pressure in her skull seemed to *tug* before dissipating, as if Ireth were trying to guide her but had lost his grip. The heat faded as well. Looking up, Sandis saw Bastien.

Had the numen been trying to direct her gaze to him? Did Ireth want to go *back*?

The thought panicked her until she glimpsed again the etchings of the astral sphere. Her gaze shifted between the cupboard door and Bastien.

"Do you really think," Rone was saying, "those bastards give a slag about what happens to—"

"We need to bind Bastien." Sandis waited for both men to look at her. She swallowed. "When Bastien wakes up, we need to bind him again. We need to be ready to fight."

Cleric Liddell's color left him completely. Rone let out a long breath. "To whom? Or *what?*"

Sandis touched the etchings on the cupboard door, feeling the looping symbols beneath her fingers. For a moment, she thought she could read them. "Ireth is going to tell us."

Bastien stood beside Sandis the following morning, more rested than anyone else. His strawberry-blond hair flowed in crimped, loose locks down his back and shoulders, and he twisted a section of it around his fingers over and over, giving away his nerves. He had awoken knowing nothing of Kazen and Kolosos, and now he had agreed to let Ireth somehow pick a new numen for him to be bound to.

At least, Sandis hoped that's what Ireth intended.

She'd tried meditating the way she always did before summoning, listening for the fire horse who had been too long separated from her. Nothing happened. And so they had waited, and in the interim, they'd used Kazen's tools and tinctures to carefully remove the remaining symbols of Ireth's name from below Bastien's neck. Sandis didn't voice it, but the ink vials and razors made her think of Rist. Her brother wasn't the only one under Kazen's power. Kuracean had been at the Lily Tower with them, and in her heart, she knew it was Rist. Unlike Kaili, his script had remained intact. Fixing the *Kuracean* tattoo at the base of his neck would have been a simple matter. He had fled with both a broken heart and Rone's amarinth, and now was a slave once more.

How much of his fate was Sandis's fault?

If only she could have saved Kaili. If he hadn't lost his love in such a horrific fashion, he'd still be with them. They both would.

Sandis and Bastien loomed in the back corner of Kazen's office, staring at the etchings of the astral sphere on the inside of the cupboard door. Her eyes passed over the words again, pausing on the figures she knew: *I, Reth, Koh, Lo, Sos, Kur, A, Cean, I, Sep, I, A, Hap, Shi, Duh, Rang.* She didn't know the Celestial's real name; it was three figures, but from what Sandis knew about Noscon writing, it would have to be four, maybe five, to read *Celestial*. Though *Celestial* was a Kolin word.

She found a few patterns in the lines of ancient text: symbols that repeated themselves or that always preceded or followed each other. She was tracing her finger over one of them when a familiar pressure began to warm the base of her skull.

She straightened. Bastien noticed and asked, "Ireth?"

Rone, who sat in Kazen's chair, looked up at the name. Cleric Liddell had wandered off half an hour ago, still digesting Sandis's revelations, but she suspected he would be back.

Sandis nodded. Closing her eyes and focusing on that warm pressure, she thought, *Ireth, will you help me? What do I do?*

The pressure increased, and heat that reminded her too much of Galt's sacrificial blood trickled down her right arm. She lifted her hand and pressed her index finger to the etchings, following them by feel only. She slowly traced the first half of the sphere with her finger, then finished the loop. Again, slower.

The pressure increased, then decreased. Pausing, Sandis drew her finger back one syllable, and Ireth responded with a burst of heat. Even as she opened her eyes, she could feel him retreat. He was never able to stay with her for any dependable amount of time.

One syllable. The ones to its left and right were wrong, from what she could sense. She'd never known a numen with a single-syllable name.

A small smile grew on her lips. "It's hidden."

"What?" Bastien asked.

She tapped her finger on the rounded syllable. "Have you ever known a numen with a single-syllable name?"

Bastien shook his head.

"This one isn't bound because, maybe, no one knows about it. It's hidden among the longer names." One row above Ireth's name.

Bastien must have noticed, too, because he stopped playing with his hair and took a step back. "Sandis . . . it's a level eight. I'm only cleared for sevens." Reaching back, he ran his fingers over the skin above his golden brands. It was probably still sensitive and sore from the ink removal, but they didn't have time to let him recover.

Sandis bit her lip. If a numen was summoned into a vessel too weak to hold it, the vessel would die. She'd watched it happen to Heath, who'd been strong enough to hold a level-seven numen, just like Sandis and Bastien. When Kazen had tried to summon Kolosos into him, he'd been turned inside out. Ripped to bloody pieces.

Sandis closed her eyes and pinched her nose. She could still smell his corpse, a scent that had been amplified by the closed walls of that horrid room. That incident had finally given her the courage to run from Kazen.

"We'll find something else," she whispered after the silence dragged on too long. "We have the ledger; we'll find a level seven, or a level six—"

Rone turned toward the desk to grab the ledger filled with Kazen's handwritten notes on the occult. Those notes did not, they'd noticed, include any of the three symbols Sandis believed to be the Celestial's true name.

"No."

Sandis and Rone both glanced to Bastien, whose pale eyes had locked on the inscription on the cupboard door. After reviewing the ledger, Rone interpreted the name as Mahk.

Bastien let out a strained breath. "No. Ireth once inhabited my body. He knows it, right? If he thinks I can do a level eight . . ."

A small lump formed in Sandis's throat. "But if you can't—"

Rone finished, "We'll be down a man when Kolosos returns."

Yes, that was true. But Sandis would also lose a friend. She had few enough as it was.

Bastien collected his hair over his shoulder and began braiding it. "Which of you has the steadier hand to make the mark?"

Sandis exchanged a glance with Rone. "Rone will draw it. But I need to summon it first, get its blood. And I'll need yours." And she would give him hers. It would create a bond between them, giving her the ability to control the numen once it was summoned.

Rone shifted his weight to one leg. "Why don't we go to that big, creepy room? You know, in case this Mahk thing is . . . big. Or in case Bastien explodes."

Neither Sandis nor Bastien laughed at the joke.

Chapter 3

Mahk was a whale.

A *whale*.

"This is perfect." Rone picked himself off the floor, pretending his hip didn't hurt from being slammed into a wall the moment the beast appeared in a flash of light. "A fish without water. Tell Ireth he picked a real winner."

Sandis ignored him. She stared in awe at the numen filling nearly the entire room where Kazen had once attempted to summon Kolosos into her body. She stepped toward it slowly, raising an arm that was bandaged around the elbow from the blood transfusion between Bastien and herself.

Rone dared to step closer, too, but not by much. The creature looked so wildly out of place, but the lack of sea didn't seem to bother it. Its large eyes, like marbles of dark amber, watched Sandis with calm interest. Its slate-colored body was twice as long as it was wide, and its mouth took up half of that length. It breathed through a blowhole that engulfed almost the entire top of its head, far too large to be normal. Then again, nothing about this was normal.

The two fins on the sides of its body—one of which had hit Rone when the numen had successfully morphed the Godobian—looked like an odd cross between a fern branch and a fly's wing. And an old feather duster. Simply put, they were weird.

"Easy now," Sandis crooned, though with Bastien's blood in her veins, Mahk had no choice but to obey her. She held a thin tube ending in a needle in her hand. She had to get Mahk's blood to create the tattoo that would bind the incredible monster to Bastien, which would allow Sandis to summon it at a moment's notice, no sacrificing of mice and cleansing with purified water needed.

Though how a land-bound whale would help them, Rone hadn't any idea.

When Sandis finally dismissed the creature, leaving Bastien naked and prone on the floor, Rone felt like he could breathe again. The room seemed bigger than before, like the beast had stretched it out. Sandis averted her eyes, and Rone took to dressing the unconscious Bastien. Once he was done, they lugged him back to the table in Kazen's office.

"This will be hard on him," Sandis said once Bastien was settled. "Summoning so close together. He'll be sick when he wakes. The more water and broth we can get him to swallow while he's asleep, the better he'll fare."

Cleric Liddell appeared in the doorway. "Is he . . . all right?"

"He will be." Rone eyed him. He'd expected the priest to return. His robes were dingy. "Where have you been?"

"The roof." The priest wrung his fingers together. "The part that's still there. Watching."

A shiver ran up Rone's arm and into his neck; he swatted at it as though it were a mosquito. "Anything?"

Liddell shook his head. "Not yet." His voice was strained, his eyes circled by shadows.

Sandis said, "You should get some rest."

The man merely shook his head and disappeared back into the hallway.

Rone watched the doorway after Liddell had gone, an earlier thought churning to the front of his mind. Turning, he glanced to the cupboard, its door now shut.

"Sandis."

"Hm?"

"If the Celestial *is* a numen"—*that* was still hard for him to swallow. How had his people come to worship a monster from the ethereal plane? Had his father left them for a false god? Or were all gods simply contorted creatures one could summon into another's body?—"would it be . . . bound?"

He knew Sandis hadn't thought that far, judging by the unease that wriggled into her features. She leaned hard against the table where Bastien slept, and folded her arms—more in a way that kept her warm than in contemplation. "I don't think so. It can't be." She paused for a moment. "It took an amarinth to bring Kolosos here. No one could be strong enough to summon the Celestial. There's no possible host."

Rone's hand moved to his pocket, the one where he usually stowed the amarinth, only to find it empty. "Unless"—the hairs on the back of his neck rose—"the Lily Tower has an amarinth."

Sandis started.

"If there was only one, would there even be a record of it? There must be more," Rone said, more to himself than to her. "You said Kazen knew about them—maybe he learned about them through his connection to the tower." He paused, then added, "And if the Celesians had one, it would be in the Angelic's possession."

Sandis shook her head. "It was a transcription of an old text. Something Kazen kept records of, talked about. He'd sketched pictures, theorizing its shape. A few looked very similar to the real thing." She met his eyes. "You don't think . . . the Lily Tower keeps a vessel for the Celestial, do you? But looking at Kolosos . . . *if* the tower had an amarinth and could summon the Celestial, we would know about it. I don't think someone could hide a numen like that."

He thought of the Angelic . . . but he couldn't be a vessel. He was too old and wasn't a virgin.

"If Kazen was a priest," Rone said, "that could be how he knew about amarinths."

She looked uncertain. "He would have used one from the beginning if he knew. He would have hunted you more than me."

"Didn't he?" He offered a half smile.

Sandis's shoulders relaxed. A small victory, that. Yet a frown tugged on her lips. "Cleric Liddell didn't know the truth about the Celestial. Maybe none of them do."

He breathed out a frustrated sigh. "How did Celesia start in the first place?"

"I don't know, Rone." She dropped her arms, voice laced with defeat. "I don't know. I don't even know how many of them are still *alive*."

That word drove into his gut like a nail. *Alive.* Could his father have died when Kolosos and Kuracean attacked the tower? If Kazen wanted revenge on his former religion, wouldn't he kill its leader first?

Why did that even bother him? His father was such in biology only. The Angelic had rejected his family the moment he donned his mantle. A requirement of the office, yes, but one he'd accepted with equanimity.

The sensation of Sandis's fingers sliding between his broke his thoughts. Her thumb ran up and down the side of his knuckle.

Rone let out a long breath. "I don't know if we can win this."

"We have to try. We're connected to this. I am, at least."

"We."

She smiled. "We. We have to try. And if we can't . . . we'll run. Kolosos can't take on the entire world. We'll find your mother."

Her voice shook, and Rone knew why. Run for his mother, at the expense of her brother. He smoothed hair behind her ear, trying to imagine leaving Dresberg and Kolingrad behind, finally reuniting with his mother in Godobia, Sandis at his side. It felt too good to be true. It probably was. Even if the borders were too overrun for the guards to stop them from passing without papers, they would be leaving behind a monster. The thing about monsters was that they didn't care much about arbitrary borders. If they left Kazen to ravage the country, who was to say he'd stop at the Fortitude Mountains? But Sandis . . . He had an uneasy feeling that leaving Anon behind to be consumed would break her, and that would break him.

Lowering his head, Rone touched his lips to Sandis's. Their warmth, their softness, made it easier to dream. He could almost picture a little cottage with laundry on the line. Sandis in his bed, his mother humming in the other room. But it was only a dream. Right now, they had to at least *try* to face reality.

It was the best they could do.

<hr/>

Kolosos returned before Bastien woke. Near midnight, Liddell ran into the office, where Rone and Sandis had dragged two cots, and raved about fire across the city.

Then the first quake came.

The ground shivered with it. It was a soft rumble, like the start of hunger. Rone, who'd been dozing prior to the priest's intrusion, leapt to his feet and ran up the stairs to the lair's entrance. His eyes had grown accustomed to kerosene lamps—lights that wouldn't last much longer if they didn't find more fuel. It took a second for them to adjust to the depth of night.

A slight tremor rolled under his feet once more. He might have thought it a factory explosion on any other day.

Rone climbed the dilapidated building, nearly losing his footing twice before he reached the top. It impressed him that Liddell had been up and down so many times without killing himself. The man practically wore a dress.

The darkness illuminated Kolosos's path of fire.

At least it's far off, Rone thought, gaze following the flames. The growing destruction pointed toward the center of the city. The Innerchord?

No, the cathedral. He'd bet half his savings on it.

When he climbed down, Sandis was waiting for him at the foot of the building, her white skirt blowing softly in the smoke-scented breeze. A long shadow hugged her back; it took Rone a second to realize it was her rifle. Liddell moved closer to Rone, huddling into his vestments, silently seeking refuge with the one person who, while hardly holy, at least was not a branded heathen.

Rone nudged him back with his elbow.

"What do we do?" the priest asked.

The skin around Sandis's eyes tightened. "I don't know enough about it. Ireth . . ." She paused, staring at nothing. "Ireth is trying to tell me something. I don't understand. Maybe I can understand if I get closer to Kolosos. But Bastien is still unconscious."

Rone snorted. He couldn't help it. "I don't think we can get much closer than we were before. Seems like the only thing it'll get us is a quicker death."

Sandis nodded. "Kolosos is . . . invincible." She winced at the word. "But Kazen is not. If we hurt Kazen, Kolosos disappears." He heard what she didn't say—*and my brother will be back.*

Rone nodded. "Liddell, watch Bastien."

The cleric bristled. "I am not some dog to be ordered around—"

"Fine," Rone snapped, "then go back to the tower." He raised a finger to his chin. "Oh wait, it's gone."

"Rone." Sandis's tone was one of warning.

But Liddell's fire went out like a match in a hurricane. "I'll watch him."

"We don't have much time if it's like before." Rone moved away from the lair, scanning the dark streets ahead. "Do you want to steal a horse, or try the roofs?"

"Roofs," she answered without hesitation. "I want to be able to look Kazen in the eye."

It was harder to jump roofs at night. Dresberg was generally a well-lit city, but where it wasn't, the lip of a building could blend into the black gulf beyond it. Rone was used to this, but Sandis wasn't. He had to be careful to make sure neither of them fell. The immortality bestowed by the amarinth, however brief, was no longer an option.

It wasn't hard to see their destination, even from the southeast corner of the city. Kazen wielded Kolosos like a madman, and with every roof Rone and Sandis crossed, the fire grew brighter. Once Rone's legs started aching, he could hear the screams of fleeing Kolins. Sandis breathed heavily behind him, but she never complained, even when they had to climb down to the street and run on foot. The Innerchord, located at the center of Dresberg, was the only part of the city where buildings weren't close enough to leap between roofs. The bureaucrats liked their space.

Once they climbed up again, Rone felt his joints lock. Not necessarily because of fatigue, but because he could *see* Kolosos's enormous wings and fiery snout. The monstrosity of the being. Not even Mahk had been this huge, this terrifying. This numen was like something out of a macabre fairy tale—the exact kind he imagined Kazen loved to read.

Rone was leading Sandis right toward it, and part of him reeled at the fact. That part wanted to flee with Sandis, away from the danger and carnage. It wanted to secure her in the shadows, hold her close, make love to her, and wash away all the guilt, fear, and memories that weighed them down.

But the larger part of him knew Sandis was stronger than he was, especially when it came to the occult. She'd never forgive him if he subverted her will a second time, even in an attempt to protect her. And in his heart of hearts, he knew she might be the only person capable of stopping Kazen. So he didn't try to stand in her way. Not yet.

The sounds grew louder—some screaming and shouting, but most of the Kolins had already fled from the scene, taking their terrified voices with them. Below, scarlet-clad policemen and soldiers garbed in steel blue clustered together like ants around a crumb. Gunshots punctured the sweltering air, bullets racing to see which could strike the six-story demon first. Kolosos ignored the onslaught; Rone imagined the volcanic monster merely absorbed the metal and made it part of itself. A new vein here, an extra claw there.

Rone didn't know what kind of building they stopped on, only that it had a smokestack beyond the numen's reach. He hunkered behind the stack, and Sandis dropped to her knees behind him. Neither of them spoke as they caught their breath. The space between Rone's lungs burned hotter than the demon ransacking the city. Sweat gathered on his brow and soaked his hair. He pulled off his jacket. The night air was hotter than noon at the peak of summer.

Sandis cleared her throat. "Do you . . . see him?"

Creeping to the edge of the smokestack, Rone peered around. The monster was two blocks away. *Too close.* But that had been the point of coming, hadn't it? To get close.

"I don't see Kazen."

Sandis was already on her feet, creeping toward a roof to the east. She found a board near the lip—Rone wondered if this was one of the places he'd crossed before, and if the board was one he'd left behind— and he helped her use it to bridge the gap. He held it steady as she crossed, then bounded across it himself.

From this angle, he could see the cathedral. Or rather, what was left of it.

"God's tower," he cursed. "It's . . . nothing."

Where the Central Cathedral of the Celestial had once stood, there was now a carpet of orange embers, like someone had taken a broom to a dying bonfire. Steam billowed from the west side—the fire brigade? It seemed ridiculous to worry about the embers when a practical god continued to wreak its destruction on the surrounding buildings, but in a place built as packed together as Dresberg, an uncontrolled fire could demolish the entire city.

A whistle blew somewhere behind him. Perhaps a scarlet calling for retreat, or backup. Maybe the triumvirate had finally released some of the hundreds of guards standing watch over the broken prisoners at Gerech to fight Kazen. Kolingrad was the northernmost country in Meletarr; it was surrounded on three sides by frigid ocean and on one side by nearly impenetrable mountains. It was a risky place to conquer, so no one did. The place didn't have much of an army, and yet it had border guards in the thousands. All its three leaders had to do was pull them in and teach them how to march in a straight line.

How much destruction had to happen before they cared enough to do it?

"He's there, on the thing's horn," Sandis said. "It must be able to control its heat." She didn't need to whisper; Rone could barely hear her over the chaos unfolding around them. Sure enough, the place where Kazen stood was black as though cooled.

She pointed ahead to their next destination, a building far too close for comfort. One wrong turn by the monster and the thing would crumble like the Lily Tower. If that happened, they would be caught in the fallout. But Sandis crept forward, so Rone didn't hesitate to follow her.

Brilliant orange light burned one side of his body and blinded his left eye. "Stay low." The last thing they wanted was for Kazen to see them.

They made it to the next roof, and Sandis knelt again. Rone went one step farther and dropped to his belly. She took the rifle from her back and pressed its butt to her shoulder. Squinting, Rone tried to find her target, his eyes watering from the raging light of Kolosos's inner fire. He caught a flash of pale skin on one of the beast's horns, which had blackened to dead rock. Kazen's face? The grafter always wore black, and in this case, it allowed him to blend in with both the numen and the night sky.

Sandis just needed the beast to turn, and she'd get a shot. Could Rone help, somehow? Get onto another roof and start yelling, draw Kazen's attention? Would the old man even hear him?

Another round of gunfire erupted from the south. *What good is it? Save your bullets!* None of the shots came close to Kazen. Did the scarlets and steels even know this monster was a numen? That killing its summoner would ultimately kill *it?*

Except . . . Rone's mind shot back to Kazen's lair, to the night he'd found Sandis chained up, standing in a pool of blood. Isepia, the one-winged witch. Kazen hadn't controlled her, and she'd run rampant. Surely Sandis knew that killing Kazen would allow Kolosos to do whatever it damn well pleased . . . but only until its vessel tired. Then it would go back to the ethereal plane, and the nightmare would be over.

It was a necessary risk.

Kolosos turned toward the gunfire, one of its wings crumpling the corner of a building. The movement exposed Kazen.

Sandis pulled the trigger, and the explosion of the releasing bullet hit Rone's ears like a hammered nail.

At that exact moment, Kolosos raised its lava-laced arm to strike at the police brigade. The bullet hit its wrist instead of Kazen. The grafter must have noticed, for before Sandis could ready another shot, the demon whipped toward them.

"Run!" Rone grabbed Sandis by the back of her dress. "Run, run, *run!*"

They bolted toward the opposite end of the building and jumped just as Kolosos's clawed hand slammed down on the roof; Rone heard the structure buckle as a wave of heat collided with his back, propelling him to his target. He landed and fell hard on his knees.

"Rone!"

Whipping around, he saw Sandis hanging on to the lip of the roof—her hands clasped the edge, but the rest of her body dangled against the side of the building.

New energy spiked through his body. He rushed for her and grabbed her forearms, pulling her up with a heave. They ran to the next roof, which was a little closer, and climbed down the fire escape. Rone didn't miss the irony.

Sandis still had her rifle—which may have impaired her balance on that last jump—and when they reached the ground, she turned around, back toward Kolosos. "I have to touch it."

It took Rone half a second to realize the *it* was Kolosos. He snatched her hand. "Are you out of your mind? You'll be incinerated if not shot!"

"But I know the words!" she shouted as a puff of cinder-laden wind blew over them. "If I can touch Kolosos, I can send it back into the ethereal plane."

But Rone shook his head. "There's no way, not without burning to a crisp. Remember the tower?"

The closest they'd been to the demon so far. The heat of it . . . the memory burned in Rone's skin. It would never work.

"I have to try," she pleaded, her voice barely audible over a nearby crash punctuated with screams. "If not, maybe I can shoot Kazen from the ground."

Rone gritted his teeth. *No one else has been able to.* He didn't say the words aloud—it wouldn't change her mind. Besides, if anyone could do it, she could.

The two of them ran into the heat, toward the embers, to the heart of the fire. One block away from Kolosos's hooves. Half a block, and the moisture in Rone's mouth and nose evaporated, leaving him half a husk. Sandis must have felt it, too, for she readied her firearm instead of venturing closer to the beast to touch it. They passed a line of soldiers who shouted at their backs but did nothing to stop them.

Rone didn't know why he noticed the lone man ahead of them. Maybe because he didn't wear a uniform. Maybe because he was unarmed. Probably because he stood closer to the numen than anyone else, even the soldiers. A thin silhouette, robes wild in the heat-stirred wind.

Rone noticed him, but not the falling chunk of building. Not until Sandis screamed.

It was right over them, a tumbling mass of shadows that blocked out the stars. It would crush all three of them. They'd never run fast enough to clear it.

Just before it struck, a light brighter than the glowing coals of the cathedral erupted to Rone's left. He knew even before he looked that it was Sandis. Ireth. A beacon to both Kazen and the world. Their salvation—and perhaps their ruin, too.

Her fire exploded like a storm, knocking Rone into the stranger and disintegrating the falling rubble into raining dust.

For a moment, the world diminished to soot and darkness. Rone's hearing came back to him first. Thunder. No, that was marching feet. The soldiers ran past them as Kolosos trekked deeper into the city. Or was it retreating, its time in the mortal world running out? Rone wasn't sure. Right now, he didn't care, so long as it was going *away* from them.

His voice was lost, so he merely dug in the ash. First he found the stranger, who burst from the pile like a dolphin from the sea, gasping for air. "Good heavens! What just . . . Oh my!"

Rone ignored him and rushed to the next lump in the ash. Just debris. The next, Sandis. Naked as the day she was born, again. Unconscious, again.

"This will be hard on him," she'd said earlier, referring to Bastien. *"Summoning so close together. He'll be sick when he wakes."*

How bad would it be for her?

"Is she . . . all right?"

The man stepped toward them, his voice pitched high, but Rone didn't think it was from fear.

Rone scooped up Sandis and held her close to his chest before addressing the man. "If you want to live, I suggest you get out of here."

Taking his own advice, Rone sprinted back the way he and Sandis had come.

Much to his chagrin, the stranger followed.

Chapter 4

Her eyes were sand. Her bones glass. A pathetic mewling sound touched her ears. It took Sandis a moment to realize it came from her own throat.

"Sandis?" The name was far away. Something caressed her. Fingertips like barbed wire. She shied away from it, only to discover a dozen sore muscles.

Water splashed over her lips. She half choked on it. The moment her mushy brain realized what it was, however, she came alive.

Muscles and joints protested as she sat up and gulped water down her parched throat, letting it hit her empty stomach like an avalanche of jagged rocks. The fingers brushed her arm again, but this time they weren't so uncomfortable. Just warm, calloused. The water ran dry, and Sandis mourned the empty cup.

Rubbing the heels of her hands into her eyes, Sandis blinked, trying to banish the gritty feeling clinging to her eyelids. The light around her was too yellow to be natural. It striped the walls in between the assortment of shadows. Lamplight. Her old room. Her old cot.

"Are you all right?" It took her a moment to place that voice. Cleric Liddell?

"Does she look all right to you?" Rone.

She tried to speak, but her voice crumbled at the back of her mouth like burnt bread. To her relief, someone refilled her cup with water. Her stomach protested every drop of it as it went down, but her vision and head began to clear.

Ireth. She didn't feel him now, but she remembered summoning him again. Why . . . ? Oh yes, the collapsing building. Did she still have her rifle?

Blinking, Sandis looked down. Her hands were clean, but dirt lingered under her nails. She recognized the material covering her front—it was a vessel's shirt, a little too large for her, its back left open to reveal the golden brands of her script. The kind Kazen had made her wear so his associates would know she was a weapon.

She didn't like it.

"Take a break from combusting, all right?" Rone's voice was half-tender, half-irritated, if such a thing was possible. He sat on a chair beside her cot, wearing one of his old shirts. Was he laundering the one he'd worn to the cathedral?

The cathedral. Ashes and embers. In the moment, she'd been too intent on her mission to take in the destruction of the sacred place. But was it still sacred, knowing what she knew? And yet if the numina weren't gods, and weren't mortals, *what were they?*

She cleared her throat and rasped, "I don't know if I'll survive another one so soon." She felt terrible, worse than after awakening from a full summoning. Her body was dried out like old paper. Her head throbbed.

Cleric Liddell hovered at the foot of her cot. Where was Bastien? Still unconscious? He would feel worse than she, when he awoke.

Oh Celestial, Anon, she thought, ribs squeezing tight. How terrible must it be for him? The amarinth kept him alive, protected him from the lethal part of the summoning, but it wouldn't be able to heal the damage of hosting such a monster, would it?

Who was *that?*

He stood off to the side, a couple of paces behind Rone and Cleric Liddell. He looked to be in his midthirties, with long, wavy brown hair tied at the nape of his neck. Only his light-gray eyes signified he might not be a Kolin. Did he hail from Ysben? His face was narrow and a bit feminine in shape. He looked . . . excited.

"That was magnificent," he said once Sandis made eye contact with him. "I am so grateful to you, Miss Sandis. Truly. I've never seen such a spectacle! I didn't know such a thing was possible."

Rone set his jaw, and Sandis had a feeling that during the hours she'd been recuperating, Rone had determined he did not like this newcomer.

"I'm sorry," she spoke carefully, "but who are you?"

The man practically jumped forward, bumping Rone's shoulder as he did so. He extended his hand. "My name is Jachim Franz. It really is a pleasure to meet you and your associates."

Sandis tentatively took his proffered limb.

"This sack of ashes was standing at Kolosos's feet like he was stargazing." Rone folded his arms.

Sandis perked up. "I remember you." She'd seen him, a silhouette against Kolosos's glow. The one who'd stood under the falling building. She smiled. "You survived."

"Oh yes, a little dirty, but quite well." It was then that Sandis noticed the dirt stains on his clothes. He wore a long, formal shirt that hung to his knees, tied with a belt around his waist. She recognized the symbol on it—a four-pointed star with a line slashed through it—but didn't know what it meant.

As if sensing her thoughts, Rone said, "He's a scholar. And an imbecile. And he refused to leave until he talked to you." He sighed and stood, gesturing to his chair as though it were some won prize. Jachim—Sandis was sure that was a Ysbeno name—sat in it as though it *were* some great reward, and he leaned close enough to Sandis to make her uncomfortable.

"I'm a student of Noscon anthropology," he explained, overeager with a voice pitched higher than that of any grown man in Sandis's acquaintance. "A historian, and a linguist, if I may boast." He grinned. "Of course, I've studied the occult as well. Its roots are entirely Noscon, did you know that? I've never seen it practiced anywhere outside of Kolingrad, where we live over the ruins of their civilization. At least, the practice hasn't been documented anywhere else. There are certainly people in Godobia who have taken an interest in—"

"She's ill," Cleric Liddell said, as though uncomfortable with his own interruption, "and the city is under siege. Surely you can get to the point?"

The smallest smile tugged at Rone's mouth. And least he and Cleric Liddell were getting along.

"Oh yes, yes." Jachim pushed his finger up the bridge of his nose as if he wore invisible spectacles, then seemed surprised to find nothing there. He shrugged. "I couldn't help but notice the symbols on your back, Miss Sandis."

The statement alarmed her, but Jachim looked so *friendly*, the panic receded. "It's . . . Gwenwig. Miss Gwenwig."

"Your colleagues failed to tell me your surname."

Rone rolled his eyes.

"I, of course, could not pass up the opportunity to study what must be the greatest numen of our time! I suspected it to be the one called Koh-Lo-Sos"—the way he said the name was foreign and jarring—"and your colleagues here confirmed it. To think such a demon, described so briefly in Celesian texts, could penetrate our mortal realm. I had to study it. Which in turn leads to my gratitude to you for saving my life. But oh! My dear Miss Gwenwig, I did not think it possible to do what you—"

Jachim jerked back suddenly. Or rather, Rone had grabbed the back of his collar and hauled him to his feet. "You said you wanted to give your thanks," he growled, turning him around roughly, "not interrogate her."

Jachim appeared unfazed. "But surely that was the power of a numen! And she is no summoner. She did it herself, she—"

"Out." Rone shoved him toward the door.

"Oh, please, let me stay!"

For a moment Sandis felt sorry for him. But surely it would be safe enough for him to leave the lair. The ground wasn't shaking, and Kazen relied on the amarinth to summon Kolosos. It could only be used once a day and wouldn't reset for several hours. And yet, the last time she'd ventured outside had been so . . . frightening. It had been dark, burning, lightless. Screams and gunshots had filled the air. Shivers coursed down her arms—

"It's for the sake of knowledge!" Jachim pleaded as Rone bullied him into the hallway.

"Rone, wait," she rasped, stretching her hand toward the two. Rone paused in the threshold while Jachim scratched his ear.

Sandis took a deep breath. If the man merely wanted to study her, he was welcome to leave. But he claimed to be a Noscon scholar, didn't he?

"Mr."—what was it?—"Franz," she said, rubbing her throat. "Do you perhaps know the true nature of the Celestial? And its connection to the numina?"

Cleric Liddell visibly tensed.

Rone's grip on the scholar slackened as the man said, "The Celestial's connection to the numina? Surely everyone knows Celesia detests the occult—"

Rone didn't let the man finish before shoving him out of the room.

Sandis rubbed her dry eyes and sighed. *He doesn't know.* Reaching back, she traced her fingers across the ridges of her brands. It took a moment for her to remember Cleric Liddell. Looking up, she met his gaze. The priest turned away.

If the Celestial is a numen, surely a Noscon scholar would have heard whispers of it. Perhaps I am wrong. Yet in her gut, she felt sure she was right. Would Ireth be able to confirm either way?

"I would shun you," Cleric Liddell said after a moment, "but I'm not sure what is right anymore."

Sandis pulled her hand from her brands. She wasn't sure, either. She started to stand, but dizziness swept through her, so she remained seated. "We'll have to focus on what's right outside of religion. On working together, being kind, looking out for one another." A dry itch wormed up her throat.

Cleric Liddell offered her a weak smile. "I suppose that is true."

Sandis mirrored his smile as she lay back down on her cot, giving her weary body a little more time to rest.

Sandis was feeling more herself by the time Bastien woke. He threw up over the side of his makeshift bed, and Sandis cleaned it up without a word while Rone made him a plate of something to eat. Once he was sitting up and sipping water, Sandis told him all about Mahk, the fantastic numen whale Ireth had chosen for him.

"Wh-What does it do?" Bastien asked after finishing his second cup of water.

"Do?"

"You know. Ireth spits fire and runs fast, Isepia flies, and Kuracean has impenetrable armor . . . What does Mahk *do*?"

Sandis rolled her lips together. Her mouth still felt dry, despite her belly being so tight with water. "He swatted Rone into the wall."

Bastien snorted.

"I didn't test any of it. I called him just long enough to get the blood for the bonding tattoo. I'm sorry."

Reaching back, Bastien ran his hand over the new symbol pricked just below his neck, wincing. "It's fine. Better to wonder than to destroy the place, right? *Mahk* a real mess of it?"

Rone groaned at the pun before leaving the room.

But Sandis barely heard it. *Destroy.* The word brought her back to the smoldering patch of embers where the cathedral had been. How much more would Kazen destroy before he was satisfied? Or would he never stop?

Holding her breath, Sandis waited for the ground to quiver. It remained still, but her stomach formed a loose knot of anticipation.

She told Bastien about the destruction in District Three, summoning Ireth again, and the scholar who seemed far more interested in the occult than anyone Sandis had ever met outside of grafters. Perhaps he *was* a grafter, but Sandis was fairly certain she knew of all the grafters who dwelled within the city. And he seemed too nice, too honest, too . . . clean.

"Good that he left." Bastien picked at the stale bread on his plate. "With Kazen unleashing K-Kolosos over and over, these scars on our backs will see us dead faster than you can say 'Gerech.'"

Sandis rubbed gooseflesh from her arms. *Anon.* Kolosos didn't even register on the numina scale. Was hosting it painful for Anon, or did the amarinth somehow protect him beyond the initial summoning?

Sandis knew Kazen. He wouldn't run her brother ragged for his revenge. Not until it was complete, at the very least. He had always taken care of his vessels, physically. Except . . . perhaps Kazen's success was solely due to the amarinth, and not because Anon was a strong vessel. If that was the case, the summoner would feel no need to preserve his health.

Her mind revolted against the idea. Vessels like Sandis and Bastien were hard to come by. They had been the strongest in Kazen's collection. Bastien could hold a level *eight*, and Sandis . . . Sandis could actually communicate with Ireth, something no other vessel—as far as she knew—could do. Anon had to be a strong vessel, or Kolosos would burn out too fast, limiting Kazen's destruction.

Even so, Kazen couldn't keep Kolosos out for long. Ireth could be summoned for hours, given a full summoning. Hapshi had lasted the entire night. The damage Kolosos wrought was appalling, and it had only been out for less than an hour.

Something cracked down the hallway—a splintering door?—and a ruckus of footsteps followed. Men's voices filled the air, too many for it to be just Cleric Liddell and Rone. Sandis and Bastien exchanged a wide-eyed glance. Shooting to her feet, Sandis barely had enough presence of mind to help Bastien to his before rushing to the door. She could see nothing from the doorway, but the voices grew louder.

"We have nothing you want." That was Rone.

Sandis and Bastien exchanged another look and then, in silent agreement, rushed to the next turn in the hallway. Sandis's heart leapt into her throat when she saw them.

Scarlets.

Four of them, all well-built men, wearing the scarlet uniforms of Kolingrad policemen, the symbol of a boat without sail marking their chests. Men who, if they knew what Sandis and Bastien were, would arrest them and take them to be executed. They might do the same to Cleric Liddell and Rone for merely associating with them.

And Sandis's shirt had an open back.

Her thoughts grew thorns and spun in a frenzy. Should she and Bastien run? Could Rone fight the scarlets without the amarinth? Perhaps they could hide? Or maybe—

"We mean you no harm," the scarlet at the front said, sounding . . . tired? He was perhaps in his midforties and had thinning hair starting to gray at the roots. Though his arms were thick with muscle, his uniform stretched over a well-fed gut. "I presume you're Rone? Rone Comf?"

Rone took a retreating step, but his shoulders didn't relax. He started to glance behind him, toward Sandis, but stopped himself. Sandis knew he didn't want to draw attention to her. "What do you want?"

"We're here for you and your company. Miss Sandis Gwenwig, I believe. And a priest and another man?"

Sandis bit her knuckle. How would they know—

Jachim. The scholar. Panic feathered under her skin.

"You are not under arrest. Quite the opposite," the scarlet continued. "My name is Tomm Esgar; I'm the chief of police in Dresberg."

The name sounded familiar to Sandis's ears. Chief Esgar was the one who'd been unwilling to further investigate the disappearances of several youths in Dresberg. The ones Sandis had linked to Kazen. The newspaper journalist who'd written about the kidnappings had said as much.

Rone's hand inched toward his boot, where Sandis knew he kept a knife. "You're not helping your case."

No, Rone, Sandis internally pleaded. Maybe, *maybe* he could fight them without the amarinth's aid, but then the entire force would be looking for them. Sandis was tired of running.

Chief Esgar rolled his eyes. "You're being summoned by the triumvirate."

Rone's hand stopped. So did Sandis's breathing. Bastien sputtered.

"The triumvirate?" Cleric Liddell clasped his hands together. "What? Why?"

Chief Esgar's shrewd eyes whipped to him. "Because there's a monster tearing down our city and one of their chief scholars believes you can help stop it. Let me make this clear. If you *don't* come, I *will* arrest you."

Rone scoffed. "I'd like to see you—"

"We'll come."

The two words surprised Sandis, especially since they came from her mouth. All four policemen looked over, noticing her and Bastien for the first time. Straightening, feigning a confidence she didn't feel, Sandis said, "We'll come." If the scarlets wanted them dead, they could have managed it by now. They could have at least restrained them. "On your honor that we will not be harmed in any way, and we can leave at will."

Thoughts of her uncle passed through her mind. She didn't want to be under another person's thumb again. But she also knew they were painfully outnumbered and without direction. They needed allies, information. Even if those allies had been her enemies mere days ago.

But Kazen was enemy to all.

Chief Esgar scanned both Sandis and Bastien. Evidence of their vesselhood was hidden from his eyes, yet Sandis felt the man could see it. She tried to read his face—was that a twitch of disgust? A glimmer of curiosity? Fear, as her uncle had once expressed?—but his countenance remained neutral.

"You already have the words of Triumvirs Holwig, Var, and Peterus. You do not need mine." Perhaps noting Sandis's frown, or the tension flowing off Rone in waves, he added, "But you will have our protection as well."

Rone retreated toward her, never taking his eyes off the scarlets. When he reached her side, he mumbled, "We don't have to do this. *You* don't have to do this."

"But how much can we *do* if we don't work with them?" she whispered back.

He met her gaze. His expression was easy to read. He was unsure, frustrated, and something else. Something she didn't often see on his features. It took her a moment to decipher the emotion, and when she did, the knot in her stomach pulled tight.

Rone Comf was afraid.

Chapter 5

Rone didn't trust any of them.

He'd handed Sandis his jacket the moment the scarlets turned to escort them to the Innerchord, and she'd taken it without comment, using it to cover her criminal brands. Bastien had unbraided his hair, using the long, wavy locks to hide his own brands. Granted, these men *had* to know they were vessels. How else were they supposed to "help" fight Kazen? Rone didn't think they were walking into some sort of ill-timed trap to be shipped off to Gerech—the triumvirate needed all the help they could get—but the truce wouldn't last. If they managed to nab Kazen in between summonings, how quick would these officers be to slide their swords between their new allies' ribs?

His fingers twitched, aching to touch the coiled loops of his ama-rinth. It had always given him confidence, even when stationary. He'd have to fake it for now, if only for Sandis.

As they left the dilapidated neighborhood and started down the abandoned streets, passing shuttered houses, Sandis reached for his hand. Her fingers knit between his own and clamped down hard. Seemed Rone wasn't the only one seeking courage. He pulled her close, as though he could shield her from the cracked world surrounding them. Bastien followed half a step behind, wide eyes darting around as though a grafter would jump out at any moment. Cleric Liddell licked the heels of the scarlets, seeking his protection among them.

None of them spoke as they followed the scarlets to the center of the city. The silence hanging over them was so complete Rone could hear the voices of people hunkering in flats or alleyways still unaffected by Kolosos's destruction. It struck him viscerally that the roads, usually packed with people, were nearly empty. The city had become a completely different place overnight, and it made his skin itch.

Rone had been to the Innerchord before. He'd yelled at a secretary in the Degrata and even broken into the citizen records building. But for some reason it felt different now—the buildings looked too big and too far apart. It was as if they were leaning in to inspect him as he passed, debating whether or not to allow him passage, or whether they should lift a boot and end his pathetic mortality.

They chose the former. Chief Esgar led them into the Degrata, past a thick row of guards. Ah, so they hadn't restationed Gerech's men to fight Kazen. They'd just moved them here to protect their own sorry hides.

The first floor was empty save for a few more guards, most of whom lingered by the stairs. They looked over the shabby group as they ascended, and Rone made a point of making eye contact with one until it became uncomfortable. Once they were trapped in the stairwell, guards before and behind them, Rone found himself thinking about his old master, Kurtz, who'd taught him all he knew about martial arts. Odd, the way the mind worked. He hoped the man was all right.

Bastien was winded by the time they reached the third floor and passed more guards. Chief Esgar whispered to one of them. Sandis looked around, taking in her surroundings like they were in some sort of palace. The place was nice, yeah—marble tiling on the floor, strips of red carpet, dark oak panels on the walls. Frosted windows tinted pale blue. And oh, look, a plant. It was even alive.

The chief led them around the corner and into a larger seating area with a couple of sofas and a smattering of upholstered chairs. At the end of the space stood a tall middle-aged man speaking to a soldier with biceps the size of Rone's thighs. A sheaf of paper occupied the soldier's hands.

The middle-aged man looked up as Rone and the others approached. His dark-brown hair boasted streaks of gray and pointed into a severe widow's peak. His facial features were stern: narrow eyes, pointed chin, a hooked nose not dissimilar from Kazen's. He was dressed in finely tailored clothes, his shirt sage green and possibly velvet. For a second he looked angered by the interruption, but his eyebrows lifted when he recognized Esgar.

"This is them?" he asked.

Esgar paused and bowed. So this guy was important. One of the triumvirs? They didn't exactly have their portraits hanging in public areas. "Yes. We found them without problem, just where Franz said they'd be."

It took Rone half a second to connect "Franz" with the scholar. He had an intense desire to punch the academic in the eye.

Esgar turned toward them. "This is Triumvir Boladis Var."

Liddell bowed immediately, and Sandis followed suit. Bastien, hesitant, awkwardly repeated the gesture. Rone shoved his hands in his pockets and leaned his weight onto his left foot.

"Wonderful weather we're having," he said.

The chief of police scowled, but held his tongue.

Var appeared unfazed by Rone's lack of respect. "You're the last ones we're waiting for. We've gathered our city's experts in hopes of bringing this war to a quick end."

So it was a war, then. All of Kolingrad against a single man armed with a demon and an amarinth. Seemed fitting.

"Come," Var said, moving to a pair of double doors behind him. "We have much to discuss and little time." He said something under his breath to the beefy soldier before leading the way in.

Sandis hesitated, glancing at Rone. He squeezed her hand. She offered him a small smile. She took Bastien's hand, too, but had to release it when they reached the doors so they'd all fit through. There were over a dozen other men in the room, but Cleric Liddell's eyes shot straight to a pair of white-robed men in the far-left corner.

"Praise the Celestial!"

The cleric immediately bounded around the long oval table at the center of the room, making his way to where the Angelic, a high priest, and a familiar priestess stood. Rone's blood vessels immediately constricted. His father's gaze met his for a second before turning to Cleric Liddell. Only a second. Why had he wasted a moment's worry for the father who hadn't felt any concern for him? Or for his mother? The Angelic couldn't know Adalia Comf had already fled the city.

The Angelic and Liddell clasped each other's shoulders and bowed their heads together, a warmer welcome than Rone had ever received from his father.

"Rone," Sandis whispered, but Rone merely shook his head and turned his attention elsewhere, ignoring the urge to shout across the room, *Guess you should have listened to us the first time, eh, Pops?*

Esgar made quick introductions, starting with the two men who sat across from the double doors, wearing sage uniforms similar to Var's. The younger man, perhaps in his early forties and with an unfortunate haircut, was Triumvir Mirka Holwig. His father had also been a triumvir before his death, and rumor had it that Mirka had ridden his coattails to get where he was today. Kurtz had complained nonstop about it for the week following Mirka's initiation. The older man, perhaps in his midseventies, was Triumvir Gunthar Peterus. He was stocky with a stern face, along with jowls and a stomach that said he ate better than any other man in Dresberg, if not the country. His white hair stuck out in tufts over his ears. Surveying Sandis and Bastien, he leaned over to whisper to the man beside him, who was none other than the scholar Jachim Franz.

If Rone leapt over the table now, how many times could he punch the scholar before someone pulled him away?

Franz smiled stupidly at them and waved when Esgar needlessly introduced him.

Bastien shifted closer to Sandis, his gaze glued to the far-right corner. But Esgar went the other way with his introductions.

"This man"—he referred to the oversized soldier with the impressive biceps—"is General Istrude, head of the Kolingrad Militia." He swept his arm to the left. "And of course you know Angelic Adellion Comf, head of the Celesian Church, may God ever smile on him," Esgar said. He was either devout or a sycophant. The Angelic nodded his approval.

"Rone, you're hurting me," Sandis whispered.

Blinking, Rone realized he was crushing Sandis's hand. He immediately let go and pulled away. Sandis offered him a sympathetic smile as she took his hand again. Rone could no sooner meet her gaze than he could his father's.

Esgar introduced the high priest as Dall and the priestess as Marisa, which made him glance up. Yes, he knew her. On their last visit to the Lily Tower, she'd pulled them aside and read them a passage from scripture about Kolosos. The Angelic had sent them away, ignoring their message, but at least *she'd* tried to help.

And now they were here.

"And"—as the chief of police turned, his tone dropped to that of indifference—"lastly, we have—"

"Oz," Bastien said.

Rone turned to the Godobian in surprise. His blue eyes met the dark gaze of the middle-aged man in the far-right corner. Three adolescents sat at his feet, oblivious to what went on around them. They played with a tied piece of string, passing it between one another's hands. All were dark haired and dark eyed, and looked between the ages of fifteen and seventeen.

Rone lifted his gaze back to the man Bastien had called Oz. The man tilted his head and smiled in an oddly familiar way.

The truth struck him just before Esgar made the introduction. Bastien had spent the last several years as a slave. There was only one reason he'd know this man.

The adolescents at his feet weren't his children. They were his vessels.

"Yes, this is Oz, who still refuses to offer us a surname." Esgar's voice had shifted from indifference to frustration. "And his slaves, of course."

"Such a harsh word." Oz had the kind of voice you'd expect from a comedic actor. "If I didn't keep them, my good man, you wouldn't have the information you have."

Sandis perked up. "Bastien. Is he . . . ?"

"My old master, yes." Bastien tipped his head in acknowledgment.

Rone ran his free hand back through his hair. "This is awkward all around, isn't it?" All they needed was Talbur Gwenwig to complete the circle, and it'd be one horrible family reunion.

"What information?" Sandis asked.

Triumvir Var, whom Rone had temporarily forgotten, said, "Let's be seated. I need order to think."

Everyone who was not sitting moved to do so, although Oz's vessels remained huddled in the corner. Var took a seat opposite Triumvir Peterus, and Rone sat next to him, followed by Sandis, Bastien, and Liddell near the end of the table. The general sat on Var's other side. Chief Esgar moved around the room and between lingering guards to sit beside the loathsome Franz. Rone noted he left an empty chair between himself and Oz, while two empty chairs islanded Oz from General Istrude.

Var spoke first. "What Oz means is that we have better knowledge of predicting when this man, whom we've identified as Kazen Dalgar, will summon Kolosos and strike again. A vessel needs twelve to eighteen hours of rest after hosting, and so we expect—"

"Sir?" Sandis's voice was a mouse's.

"—that Kazen will return by nightfall."

"Sir?" Sandis asked.

Thick lines creased Var's forehead as he turned toward her.

"It won't be eighteen hours. It will be twenty-four."

Oz shook his head. "I don't know if Kazen starved you, lass, but the standard sleep for a vessel—"

"She's more familiar with the situation than you are," Rone said, meeting Oz's eye.

The grafter was silent long enough for Sandis to finish.

"It will be twenty-four hours minimum because Kolosos cannot be summoned without an amarinth," Sandis finished, gaining more confidence with each word.

Jachim perked up. "What was that you said? An amarinth?"

"You know it?" asked Peterus.

Jachim nodded. "I've heard of it, yes. It's part of Noscon legend, mentioned in the Yokhosho Temple . . . what's left of it. A device that spins—not like a top, mind you, but like a gyroscope—and grants its owner immortality."

"A minute of immortality," Rone added.

"A minute?" Peterus asked.

"A minute," Rone repeated. "Sixty seconds."

"Fascinating." Jachim leaned back in his seat, then flung himself forward. "Wait, you believe it to be *real*? And that Kazen *has* one?"

Sandis nodded.

"I know it's real because it's mine," Rone said. "All of us"—he gestured down to Bastien—"have witnessed it. It's real, and Kazen has his vessel use it every time he summons that monster here."

A soft sigh passed through Sandis at the mention of her brother. Rone shifted his hand over and rested it on her thigh, under the table, where the others couldn't see.

"So that's how the bastard did it." Oz set his chin in his palm.

The priests whispered to one another.

The other triumvir, Holwig, said, "Noscon goods can't simply be owned. They're property of the government—"

Oz interrupted, "I don't think that's up for debate at the moment, chap."

"They shouldn't be owned at all, but destroyed," chimed in High Priest Dall.

"Well," Rone said, "why don't you march up to Kazen and tell him about the miscommunication? I'm sure he'll hand it over."

Priestess Marisa frowned.

"We have no need for vitriol here, young man." The Angelic folded his hands together on the table.

Rone folded his arms. "And I'm sure you told the triumvirate that you had advance warning about Kazen's plans and did nothing, right?"

"What?" asked Var.

"Rone," Sandis hissed.

Peterus slammed his fist onto the tabletop twice. "As my comrade said, we don't have time for this! We'll deal with legalities *after* the city is again safe." Despite his words, he cast a hard glance at the Angelic, who seemed unaffected by Rone's accusation. Rone thought about pointing out that the triumvirate could have had advanced warning, too, if they had a means of actually listening to their citizens, but he kept his mouth shut. For now.

"An amarinth," Jachim murmured as though completely oblivious to the argument. He pulled out a clean sheet of paper and began rapidly writing.

"Would it not be easier"—Marisa treaded carefully—"to follow Kolosos when it runs? After it diffuses, Kazen could not carry the vessel *too* far—"

"I would love to try," General Istrude replied, "but the crab numen picks off my men like weeds. And last night, before vanishing, Kolosos shot out a wall of fire so bright it blinded the soldiers it did not kill." He set his jaw as though trying to stifle emotion. "The beast leapt the wall, and we've yet to discover where it went, despite its size. We will try again tonight, if it returns."

Peterus took a moment to collect himself and rubbed his wrinkled forehead hard enough to leave red marks. When he looked up, his eyes shot to Sandis. "It's my understanding you're a vessel."

Rone tensed. Sandis jolted enough to move her chair. Bastien's lips pressed into a white line.

They all stared at her. Rone shifted forward, trying to block some of them. Was it such a shock to them? Did these people sleep with their heads under their pillows, ignoring what really went on in the world around them? In the city they professed to run?

After a long pause, Sandis answered, "I am."

"Were you, perchance, in Kazen's employ?"

Rone scoffed.

"I was not employed, sir. I was taken against my will." Her voice was even, her gaze level.

You're doing great.

Peterus and Holwig exchanged a brief glance. "Be that as it may . . ."

"Yes, I was one of Kazen's slaves." She licked her lips and dropped her eyes, taking another moment before lifting them again. She glanced at Bastien, who nodded. "As was Bastien, but for only a short time."

"Do you know anything about Kazen that could help us?"

The room grew deathly quiet as Sandis went on to describe Kazen in minute detail, so much so that no one could believe her to be lying. Most of it Rone knew—she'd shared some of it when they were on the run and whispered the rest to him in the dark when she couldn't fall asleep, curled against him as though he could absorb her stories and give them happier endings.

And he wanted to. God's tower, he wanted to.

Jachim sat upright in his chair hard enough to shake it. "Could it be Kazen knows how to harness the power of the amarinth not just to *bring* such a colossal numen into the mortal realm, but to *keep* it here? It could be acting as some sort of power reserve even after the minute passes, not for him, but for the vessel!"

"Franz," Triumvir Var hissed. *"That* is not what you're supposed to be taking notes on!"

Jachim blinked. "Oh, right, yes." He returned to his original papers and, after shaking out a hand, began writing down what looked like Sandis's testimonial. Holwig encouraged Bastien to add his information as well, as though the account of a single woman wasn't enough to satisfy him. Rone decided that he didn't much like the man.

Var spoke next. "And how did he come to get the amarinth?"

Rone got to relay that one, albeit in far less detail than what Sandis had provided.

"And how did *you* obtain it, my boy?"

The endearment rankled him, but Rone repressed his annoyance. He didn't love giving away all his secrets, but he supposed his days as Engel Verlad were over. Truth be told, he'd known that before Rist ever stole the amarinth. "I used to work sewage. One of the tunnels collapsed. I found it in the rubble. I presume it fell from a Noscon burial ground or some such."

Var raised his eyebrows and looked to his fellow politicians.

"It's a viable story," Jachim said with a nod, accidentally smearing ink on his chin. He didn't seem to notice. "Much of the Noscons' abandoned city was destroyed by our ancestors, but portions of it were merely built over. Some of their streets merged with our sewer system. I highly doubt it was a burial ground, however. My studies indicate the Noscons burned their dead."

"I suppose your studies can also tell us where they ran off to?" Rone asked.

Jachim's lip quirked. "Wouldn't that be useful? To have one of them here to guide us. This is all their mess, really. Their gods, their magic. I have not yet cracked that egg, but I dearly wish to. I have a theory involving barges—"

"Franz," Peterus groaned.

The scholar shut his mouth as quickly as he had opened it and scribbled something in his notes.

"It is clear," General Istrude finally spoke, "that we need to strike Kazen between summonings. If I could have more men—"

"You cannot have more men," Var interrupted.

"With all due respect, Triumvir, border patrol is not critical at this time. If this man and his numen are not taken care of, you will have no citizens left."

Finally, a man with sense.

Oz chuckled.

High Priest Dall narrowed his eyes. "Tell me, sinner, what causes you such mirth?"

The Angelic's brow furrowed in a familiar way that gave Rone more nostalgia than he cared to admit. "Do not condemn him here, brother."

High Priest Dall drooped. "My apologies, Reverence."

Rone sighed. Sighed, because he was growing tired of being angry.

"Kazen is a smart son of a whore," Oz said with a radiant grin. "He makes sure Kolosos always runs before it changes back, even if the work is left unfinished. Does it in a great sea of fire, too, flushing out any spies who might try to follow. Kazen also knows where to hide. He knows this city better than any of you."

Triumvir Holwig said, "We have lost many good men trying to pursue him. Those who survive the fire are hindered by the fallen buildings and broken streets left in his wake. Others are picked off by the crab monster." He closed his eyes and grimaced. "At least, those who have not deserted."

Unfazed, Var asked Oz, "Do you have a similar knowledge of the underground?"

Oz shrugged. "I'm an ant compared to Kazen. The reason this one"—he gestured toward Bastien—"isn't with me anymore is because I don't have the old bird's savvy." He chuckled, as if that were some great joke. Sandis's hands formed fists, so obviously it was a joke she understood. "He will never hide in the same place twice. He will never hide where you can find him. If you get close, he'll hunker down. You get closer, he'll summon one of his monsters and kill you."

"He has Rist."

Sandis's voice was reverent, but the table heard her. "The other vessel with him doesn't need a full day to recuperate."

"Aye," Oz agreed, "but neither do we."

Bastien, twisting his hair around his fingers until they turned purple, said, "S-So you plan to use us as your army?" Not so different from what Sandis had intended with Kaili and Rist, but it felt different.

"We will use all the assets we have." Var rubbed the stubble on his jaw. "I would like General Istrude to continue rallying his men in the city. Search, and try to maintain some degree of normalcy. Enforce the Citizen Action law."

"The what?" Rone and Bastien asked simultaneously.

Jachim answered, "It's a law that requires citizens to continue working in times of crisis if their immediate vicinity is not in danger."

Rone's brows drew together. It made sense, yes, but to require men and women to work their factories when a monster could rise up and crush them at any moment . . . and then to use the border patrol to prevent them from fleeing? *Who are the real monsters here?*

"Can any of your numina fly, Oz?" asked Holwig.

One of the lads with him looked up suddenly. So they were paying attention after all.

Oz nodded. "Jansen here is bound to Pettanatan. It's a flyer."

Rone mouthed the strange word. He heard Bastien whisper, "It's like a sandstorm on legs. Level five."

"But," Oz continued, "none of my vessels, and none of the numina I know, will best that monster. I'm aware that grafters are the cockroaches of your wonderful city"—a wry smile played on his face—"but the actual number of summoners and vessels is much smaller than you may think. Vessels are hard to come by. They don't always survive the . . .

51

process. We have some powerful ones"—Oz looked in their direction, but Rone couldn't tell if that look was for Sandis or Bastien—"but even together . . ." He shrugged. "I don't think so."

"I will use the resources we have," Triumvir Var repeated, not dissuaded. "But I want you to take your boy as close as you can the next time Kolosos strikes. I want you to follow it. Our soldiers have yet to succeed on foot; perhaps you can find it from the air."

The smile faded, and Oz turned an almost paternal glance to Jansen. A moment passed before the grizzled man nodded. "I'll do it."

Jansen averted his eyes.

"Once the monster is gone," Triumvir Var continued, "Kazen will be far less of a threat. We have three options." He paused, looking around the room slowly, meeting everyone's eyes. "Kill Kazen, take his amarinth, or kill the vessel."

"No!" Sandis jumped up on her seat.

Every head turned toward her. Rone grabbed her fingertips and urged her back down. They had to be careful around these dogs. Keep their cards close.

A vein protruded on Var's temple. "Were this any other situation, Sandis Gwenwig, I'd have you tossed out for that."

Sandis squeezed Rone's fingers. He felt her shake. She was losing her nerve. "I-I only mean to say that . . . that killing the vessel is unlikely to fix the problem." She swallowed. "Kazen has others. With the amarinth, he'd be able to summon into them as well."

Rone ground his teeth together.

Var nodded, albeit with a frown. "Regardless, I want to know where Kazen is. And Oz"—he focused on the summoner—"if you have *any* opportunity to end his life, *take it*. You will be rewarded handsomely."

The corner of Oz's mouth ticked into a half smile. "I'm sure adequate compensation could be arranged, Your Grace."

"But I want an excavation team assembled." Var turned first to the other triumvirs, who nodded their consent, then shifted his focus to Jachim. "I want you to direct it. And take this lot." He gestured to Rone, Sandis, and Bastien. "I want to know more about this amarinth, and I want to know if there is more than one."

Jachim considered. "It's very likely. I have little documentation on the artifact, but the plural form of the term is used just as often as the singular. There could be more than one."

Really? Rone sat up a little straighter. *More than one? How many?*

He was not the only one interested in the scholar's claim. Whispers rose up around the table.

"As helpful as that may be," Triumvir Holwig said, "I don't believe Kolosos can be defeated in a minute." He glanced to Rone, who nodded. "And not by a single person. It's my understanding the amarinth works only for the individual, not the group."

"It's a start." Var sounded defeated.

Sandis squeezed Rone's hand harder, drawing his attention to her. Her jaw was tensed, as were her shoulders. He was about to lean over to ask what was wrong, but she blurted, "There's another way to defeat Kolosos."

Everyone in the room straightened. Was she going to say what Rone thought she was? He peered in Cleric Liddell's direction. The man was pale and bug-eyed.

Sandis swallowed. "There's a numen I believe is equal in strength to Kolosos."

Now the Angelic and Dall stiffened. Did Marisa?

Interesting. Perhaps they *did* know.

"What do you mean?" demanded Var.

Oz touched his chin. "I wondered . . . the poles?"

Sandis nodded.

Cleric Liddell sputtered, "Perhaps now is not a good time—"

"The Celestial is a numen, sir."

Rone could feel the collective intake of air at Sandis's words. Felt it grow stale within their lungs.

The Angelic slammed his fist on the table. "This is blasphemy."

"Indeed," murmured Peterus with interest.

But Var held up a hand, silencing further outbursts. "What on earth are you talking about?"

Sandis talked about Kazen's time as a priest, his rants about the church, and her discovery about the astral sphere. Hearing the secrets spoken out loud, among so many, made Rone shiver.

Var's reddening eyes turned toward the priests. "Is this true?"

"It is blasphemy," Dall echoed.

Cleric Liddell stared at his lap.

"Regardless," Oz chimed in, "whether it's the Celestial or not, there is a name on the top of the astral sphere. One I cannot translate. Perhaps your scholar here can help."

Jachim worked his mouth, but didn't answer. He looked defeated.

"*If* we had an amarinth," Oz went on, "we may be able to summon this numen and mimic what Kazen has done. We'd be able to fight him on his own ground."

The high priest continued to mutter about blasphemy.

"Then that is an avenue we will pursue," Var said. "Jachim?"

"We'll start where you found the first amarinth." Jachim's eyes sought Rone. "If you can remember the location."

Rone licked his teeth under his lips, and for a moment, he thought he felt a twinge in his once-injured shoulder. "I think I can. But you're going to get wet."

Chapter 6

They all filed from the room, Bastien practically thrumming with eagerness to get away. Sandis didn't think it was because of Oz—Bastien had never seemed particularly fearful of his previous master, whom he claimed was kinder than Kazen. She assumed it had to do with the four walls, made to feel closer by the sheer number of bodies between them. Bastien didn't like tight spaces.

Jachim and two of the triumvirs descended upon Rone, carrying him out of the room on a palanquin of inquiries about the sewer where he'd found the amarinth. Chief Esgar and General Istrude followed them. Oz took his time gathering his vessels, who seemed oblivious to their surroundings. But it was the priests Sandis waited for. The Angelic, specifically. And though his three attendants huddled around him like bodyguards, they all stopped when Sandis blocked their path.

She looked straight at Rone's father's face and said, "I need to speak with you."

The Angelic's eyes narrowed. "You have spoken enough."

"Please."

Sandis expected him to push her away, as he had always done before. But something had changed in his countenance. Changed in Dresberg, and changed in her as well. Glancing around the room, likely to ensure it was indeed empty, the Angelic said, "Leave us."

"But—" Cleric Liddell began to protest, but the Angelic silenced him with a raised hand.

High Priest Dall leaned in. "We'll be just outside the door." He gave Sandis a look cold enough to freeze before he pushed past her, guiding Cleric Liddell and Priestess Marisa to the large foyer beyond the room. Rone, shoving Jachim aside, started toward her, but Sandis waved a hand, urging him to stay put. He glanced once to his father before nodding and turning back to the scholar.

Sandis looked the Angelic in the eye without flinching. "I want to know the truth. I want to know about the name on the top of the sphere."

In a low, quick voice, almost a hiss, the Angelic said, "You should have *only* spoken to me. To say such a thing aloud in this company . . ."

"Then it's true."

"You do not know what powers you toy with—"

Sandis cut the air with her hand, interrupting him. Matching his tone, she said, "I will shout it to all the world if you do not speak to me as an equal, sir." She'd had enough of being talked down to from Kazen and her great-uncle. She had value here, and she wouldn't let this man, however she'd once respected him, take it away from her. "I spoke out because I want my city to survive. I want the people I love to live. Now"—she leaned closer—"I need answers to very specific questions, and we have very little time to speak privately."

Sandis didn't dare take her eyes from the Angelic. She waited for him to refuse her demand for equality. Never before had a vessel been anywhere near *equal* with the head of the Celesian Church. Anything but. Yet Sandis knew the secret at the heart of their religion—a secret that meant she and the other vessels were more entwined with Celesia than she'd thought possible.

The Angelic let out a great, deflating breath that aged him twenty years. He pressed a hand into the wall as if to support himself. When he spoke again, it was with a sliver of voice. "The last thing this country needs is a trial of faith."

Sandis gritted her teeth. *A trial of faith? What about* my *trial of faith?* "Am I not a sinner, then?"

She hadn't planned to ask that. Yet now that the words hung between them, her heart constricted, desperate for an answer.

He contemplated the question only a moment. "The occult is what it is."

Her mouth soured. "That is not an answer."

"You tread very delicate ground, Sandis Gwenwig."

Sandis straightened. She was a few inches shorter than the Angelic, who was a few inches shorter than Rone. She could see traces of Rone in his father's face—not the shape of his eyes, but the color, the faint star around the iris. The nose was the same, too, the curl of the hair. That was it. Perhaps age had skewed the Angelic's features, but Sandis suspected Rone's looks took after his mother.

"I need a straight answer," she whispered, focusing on the black circles in his eyes. "Do you have an amarinth?"

Genuine surprise widened his features. "No."

She nodded. "Then how could you summon—"

"The Celestial has never stepped foot in the mortal realm," the Angelic said, clipping his words. "It is too powerful."

"You once said that of Kolosos."

The Angelic shook his head. "I do not have one. I did not know what one was until this meeting." He weakly gestured to the long table surrounded by empty chairs. "If I did, I would forfeit it. I would do whatever it takes to crush the evil that grafter has unleashed on this city." His face fell, and he rubbed his forehead. "But I cannot stop him. Not yet. I am . . . too weak. I fear we all may be."

Sandis rolled her lips together. Were they too weak?

Adellion Comf's heavy hand settled on her shoulder. "I admonish you, Sandis. Swallow what you know and keep it safe. Before today, I could count on one hand those who knew the nature of God. You will destroy the people's spirit if you treat the truth lightly." Pulling himself to full height, the Angelic walked away, joining the others from his retinue.

Count on one hand, she thought, her gaze seeking the nearest window.

And one of them was Kazen.

This wasn't the first time Sandis had been in the sewers beneath Dresberg, but this time the cool darkness made her uneasy, despite all the people with her. Perhaps *because* of them. Rone and Jachim were the only ones she knew by name; the rest were excavators Chief Esgar had rounded up.

She splashed into the water, though here it only reached midcalf. Rone's hands were warm around her waist, which was the only pleasant thing about the tunnel lit by handheld kerosene lamps. The water looked relatively clean, but it smelled of mold and excrement. When Sandis put a hand on the wall to steady herself, her fingers slid on the slimy surface.

"Careful, it's splintering," Rone said, holding his own light high, studying the wall. Sure enough, not far from the manhole, the concrete had cracked. He guided her away from it, farther down the narrow passageway to make room for the remaining excavators. The street was about nine feet above them. The sewer narrowed up ahead, unless that was a trick of the shadow. As they trudged forward, Sandis noticed a connecting branch of the tunnel had crumbled in on itself.

She eyed the concrete ceiling and prayed.

"Here?" Jachim asked, his light swinging with his excitement.

"Up a little ways more." Rone offered his hand to Sandis; she took it with both of her own.

In the past, she and Rone had traveled through the sewers in near darkness. The lanterns brought to her attention colors and textures she hadn't noticed before. Things she didn't *wish* to notice—filth and splintering concrete and foul slime—so she kept her eyes on the water and listened for rats. They dropped down a small incline, the current growing louder as they went. The water deepened, but concrete lips on either side of the tunnel gave them something to walk on. Everyone's shoes squelched with their steps. Sandis stumbled, but managed to right her footing without impeding the others' progress.

They trudged for twenty minutes before Rone said, "Here, I think," and pointed. Sure enough, a quarter of the tunnel up ahead was cluttered with debris. Jachim instructed the men with pickaxes to tear at the wall beside it. Sandis watched for several minutes as stone and concrete splashed into the water and the hammering of steel echoed through the sewer.

"Hey." Rone's voice drew her away from the sight of destruction and scent of burning kerosene. He clasped her shoulders and lowered his face until it was level with hers. "What are you thinking?"

She hadn't had a chance to tell him about her conversation with his father. She would when they were alone. Of course, Rone knew she'd spoken with the Angelic.

"They won't hurt you," he tried.

Shaking her head, she said, "Not thinking about that."

He pressed his lips to her forehead. They were warm, soft, assuring. She wanted to pull his mouth to hers, forget her worries for a few seconds, but there were so many people—

"Here!" a man called, and he set aside his pickax to haul a great stone brick out of the wall. "Hold up the light!"

Sandis and Rone exchanged a glance before pushing closer, Rone literally elbowing excavators aside. A man held a lamp near the excavated hole, and Jachim stepped up to it, peering inside.

He turned toward Rone with a wan expression, as if he'd seen a ghost. "By the Celestial, you were right. These are Noscon ruins."

Rone shrugged. Sandis's muscles tensed like they'd been tightened with a corkscrew.

The men made quick work of the wall until there was an opening roughly the size of a short doorway. Jachim went in first, followed by one of the excavators.

"Mr. Comf, Miss Gwenwig, come in here!" he called out through the hole. An excavator peeked in, but Jachim said, "There isn't much space. Hand me your light and wait there."

Taking Sandis's hand, Rone led the way into the exposed cavity.

It smelled like mold and stale water inside, and slime grew over the walls. The ground was covered with two inches of water. The excavators had set up four lanterns to illuminate the space, which was about twenty feet long and twelve feet wide—or would be, were the far corner not collapsed in a jumble of rock and concrete. Sandis wondered if this was the same collapse that had injured Rone's shoulder three years ago.

Jachim moved to a stone tabletop and set his lamp upon it, running his hands over the surface as if oblivious to the slime. "Look at this workmanship," he said, stepping back to examine the legs. "This is Noscon make." His grin stretched ear to ear. "A new secret to explore."

Rone took up his lamp and walked the length of the room. Sandis began following him, but something on the far wall caught her eye.

"Jachim," she said, "come over here."

The scholar crossed the room, humming excitedly under his breath as he saw what she had spotted. When he held up his light, Sandis gasped.

Swathes of stone were covered in Noscon writing—fat, looping symbols like the ones branded into her back. Jachim reached forward and touched one of them, then traced his fingers higher to a line etched in the wall.

"Tablets," he said, mystified. "Look, they slide—" He pushed his hand into the side of one, grunted, and the tablet moved over an inch, colliding with its neighbor. Sandis saw what he meant—the thin stone slabs were held between tracks in the wall.

"Can you read it?" she asked.

Jachim pressed his lips together, studying. He moved between tablets. "I need to dry these off and take etchings . . . but yes. Well, almost. Noscon writing is so complex; no living man can comprehend the various levels of meaning. I'm familiar with many of the symbols, of course, but I cannot translate the language verbatim. Hardly." He shook his head and squinted, spouting random syllables as he recognized them, moving slowly across the tablets. There were six in total. Behind him, Rone had set his lamp on the floor and was examining the fallen rubble in the corner.

"Here." Jachim paused at the second tablet, holding a pale finger to its center. "This says something about a portal. A portal? How interesting. A portal, and . . ." He dragged his finger past several symbols. "Light? And this arrow has an *X* on it." Jachim turned toward the opening. "Gula! Get me my pack, quickly!"

"I think this is gold." Rone's voice tightened with excitement as he swept aside some of the rubble. His lamp gleamed off a yellowish metal shaped to the divots in the stone floor. Lifting his lantern, Rone inspected the rest of the rubble, reached forward, and dislodged a stone from about head level.

When he did, part of the ceiling came down. Rone stepped back just in time to avoid injury.

Sandis ran to him, assessing his condition, but he coughed and waved his hand. Despite the wetness around them, the rubble still spat up dust.

"Thought maybe there'd be a hallway or something," he said. He picked up his lamp, and its light rocked back and forth in his hand. The bit of gold he'd found on the floor was buried now, but wouldn't take long to dig up. "But I don't think so."

Sandis was about to chide him for not being careful, but a glimmer in the rubble caught her eye. She turned toward it, searching.

"Rone, light."

Rone stepped closer and stretched out his arm, letting light spill over the pile. He must have seen what Sandis did, because he swore.

A gold loop, peeking out from between uneven rock.

Handing the lamp to Sandis, he carefully climbed up the pile until he was high enough to stick a finger under the loop. He pulled gingerly, and Sandis, with her free hand, dug at the stones around it.

The gold came free, and sliding rock forced both Rone and Sandis to backpedal to avoid crushed feet.

Rone cursed again. Sandis held the light aloft.

It was the loop of an amarinth, curved and twisted just like Rone's. But it was only one loop, broken at the end. It lacked the glowing center that had mesmerized Sandis on more than one occasion.

"It's broken," she whispered.

"It's . . . off," Rone agreed. "Like it wasn't right to begin with. See this?"

He gestured with his pinky at the edge, where the core would sit, but when Sandis leaned in to study it, heat exploded in her head like a fire stoked by bellows. She bit down on a scream and dropped the lamp, clutching the sides of her skull. She fell backward, slamming her tailbone into the stone floor. She smelled iron and . . .

Heath. It smells like Heath.

"Sandis?"

She blinked spots from her eyes. Rone crouched before her, pushing hair from her face, his expression full of concern for her—not the broken amarinth. Jachim loomed above them, turning the gold piece over in his hands.

"I . . . I don't know what happened." She swallowed, throat dry. Something similar had happened to her when she'd stared at the amarinth in Helderschmidt's firearm factory, where she and Rone had hidden from Kazen's men. *Ireth? What's wrong?*

"It's a prototype," Jachim said reverently. "I'd swear it. And this"—he lowered the amarinth and turned, taking in the stone room—"this is a workshop. The structure, the design . . . it has to be."

One of the excavators had joined them in the small space. He'd cleaned the tablets and was meticulously copying them by pressing paper against the stone and running a charcoal nub over it. He finished and handed Jachim the papers just as Rone helped Sandis to her feet.

Jachim didn't smile this time. His face was slack and serious, his eyes twitching in deep contemplation. "We must return to the Degrata and retrieve my reference books," he said, his voice pitched lower than Sandis had ever before heard it. "I think . . . I think these are instructions for creating an amarinth."

Rone's mouth drooped into an O. Sandis shivered.

Ireth blazed, and amid the pressure and heat, Sandis felt his fear.

Chapter 7

Rone could not stop twitching.

He couldn't remember the last time he'd been so nervous. His fingers kept quivering of their own accord, as did muscles in his neck and back. He tried pacing, but it didn't help. He was going to get a crick in his neck if he didn't stop looking at the table where Jachim Franz sat surrounded by books and ledgers. Glasses perched on the tip of his nose, the scholar hovered inches above the etchings they'd taken from that room, despite the fact that the tablets themselves had been laid out on the far end of the table. Every so often, he'd write something down. A small something. A single word, maybe a single letter. Then he'd start riffling through the pages and pages surrounding him, and Rone would twitch and pace and rub eyelids that felt too thick. But he couldn't sleep. He'd tried, but he couldn't stop thinking about that room, that broken amarinth, and the promise of what Jachim had said.

Could he really be unraveling the mystery of how amarinths were created? If so, how many could they make? Could they take down Kazen? Would the magic get out of hand, and soon everyone would be immortal? What would *that* be like?

Regardless, they still had nothing to protect them from Kolosos's next rampage. If Kazen kept to a twenty-four-hour cycle, the monster could appear anytime now. And Rone had no idea where he might attack next.

He turned, gazing at Sandis, who lay across a leather bench with a blanket draped over her. She'd been given a change of clothes after the sewer: a long-sleeved navy dress, simple in design. Both hands were tucked under her head, but she lay awake, staring straight ahead.

Rone let out a long sigh. She'd pulled him aside earlier and told him about Ireth, plus everything his father had said to her. His father who'd disappeared along with his priests. They couldn't have gone far. Both the Lily Tower and the cathedral were rubble and ash.

He moved to the bench and sat in the space beside Sandis's stomach. When he touched her forearm, she took his hand, but her eyes stayed unfocused. God's tower, she looked like a doll thrown aside by some self-important kid.

"Anything else?" he murmured. They had an audience; Triumvir Var lurked in one corner, reviewing ledgers of his own alongside the general. Bastien, perhaps the only one of them who wasn't tired, thanks to his numen-induced sleep earlier, hovered near Jachim, seemingly fascinated by everything the scholar touched. Whether or not Jachim noticed Bastien's presence was up for debate; the scholar was hyperfocused on deciphering those tablets.

Sandis shook her head. She'd said Ireth could only make his presence known on occasion; he had not done so since their visit to the sewers, where an excavation team continued to dig in hopes of finding something more.

They'd sure as hell better get out of there before Kolosos returned. One well-placed stomp, and the tunnels could collapse.

Rone's pinky twitched. He needed to do something. Cheer Sandis up somehow. But he was at a complete and utter loss.

"Celestial, save me," Jachim whispered.

Rone stiffened, but it was Var who dropped what he was doing and crossed the room to the scholar. "What? What have you found?"

Jachim shook his head, his eyes darting between three different references. "I'm not positive, I need to examine—"

"Damn it, Franz, we've been waiting for hours. Tell me *anything*." Var's fingernails were leaving dents in the padded back of the scholar's chair.

Jachim nodded, even as he read. Then he swallowed. Clasped his fingers together, unclasped them, played with his hair. "I . . . well, how well do you understand the occult?"

Rone interjected, "I think we've all got it down pat. Tell us what you have."

Sandis sat up, life returning to her features.

"It . . . I was correct. Whoever owned that workshop did indeed create the amarinth." Jachim spoke carefully, never looking up from his work, cross-referencing even as he relayed his inflammatory information. Gooseflesh trailed down Rone's arms and back. "I . . . I can't translate all of it. But I believe . . . I believe this"—he touched his finger to the shaded transcription of the fifth tablet—"describes . . ."

"Out with it," Var growled.

Jachim took a deep breath. "It details how to kill a numen."

Sandis squealed, both hands flying to her heart. She closed her eyes, sweat beading on her forehead.

"Sandis?" Rone whispered, dropping to his knees in front of her. "Sandis, are you all right?" Her body was warm through her dress. Too warm.

Bastien croaked, "B-But they're immortal. You can't kill a numen . . . I mean, y-you only kill the vessel."

Rone stroked Sandis's knee with his thumb. When she opened her eyes, her pupils were dilated. "He's right," she whispered. "Ireth . . . Ireth wouldn't react this way if he wasn't right."

The fire horse was listening, then?

Rone ignored the unease building in his chest and glanced over his shoulder. Jachim moved some books around, then pulled out the ledger he'd been using for notes. "I still don't understand a lot of this, but Oz's contributions have helped me interpret some of it. You see, a

summoner—like Oz—summons a numen into a mortal body. A vessel."
He nodded toward Bastien. "Numina are spiritual in nature. They'd
have to be, for such a summoning to work. But this . . ."

He gestured to something in his ledger. "This is a mark for the plural. It's not used anywhere on the tablets. A single person summoning
into the same body."

Sandis stiffened. Rone's mind whirled. Could he mean . . . Were
there others, like Sandis and Ireth?

The scholar jumped into action suddenly, throwing his chair backward and crossing to the edge of the table, where the tablets had been
arranged in order. Var followed him, watching as he stabbed his finger
at different symbols on the tablets. "Same, heart, light, death. Life." He
tapped the last one. "Eternal life, but it has a line crossed through it.
Temporary eternal life? It must be."

He glanced up at Rone.

"Do your best to put it in simple Kolin, if you would," Var said,
voice low.

Jachim licked his lips. Looked at his papers, the tablets, and his
papers again. "There is a method of summoning into oneself. I *believe*
the amarinth . . . is made from the heart of a numen. And its vessel.
Taken at the moment when the two are one and the same."

Rone's limbs turned cold. Did he mean . . . the glimmering center
of the amarinth was formed from the *heart* of a numen?

"There is a crucial moment"—he tapped something else on the
tablet—"where it must be done. A flash of light. I admit I've never
witnessed a summoning, but . . ." He glanced to Bastien.

Bastien was white as an overboiled soup bone. "Th-Th-There's a
flash. A-At the moment of trans-sition."

Jachim's eyes lit up. "Then I'm correct."

"It's not possible," Var said, rubbing his widow's peak. "Oz has said
as much. A summoner summons into a vessel. There are always two.
You're reading it wrong."

Rone's body tensed hard as steel.

Jachim brightened. "No, my liege, it's correct! Sandis Gwenwig *has* done such a thing. I've witnessed it!"

Rone didn't remember moving. Didn't remember thinking. One minute he was beside Sandis, and the next Jachim Franz's collar was taut in his hands. The scholar's glasses lay shattered on the floor, and a bruise was forming over his eye. Rone's right knuckles stung.

"Control yourself!" Var shouted, trying to separate the two. General Istrude was halfway across the room.

"You piece of hell slag!" Rone shouted, throwing Jachim against the table. "She *saved your life*, and you're going to throw her under the wagon?"

Two impossibly strong arms grabbed Rone and wrenched him away from the scholar. Rone jerked one arm free, but General Istrude twisted and blocked him from Jachim. Said something Rone couldn't hear.

Jachim looked at him wide eyed, holding his injured face. "I-I didn't mean to—"

"Didn't mean to *what*, you son of a whore?"

"Rone."

Her voice was so faint, so distant.

Rone backed off, pulling clear of the general. "No," he said, then turned to Sandis. "No. It's out of the question."

"I hate to interrupt," Bastien said, his voice tight with nerves, "but I've been thinking."

"Not now," Triumvir Var snapped. "Jachim, hypothetically, do you think—"

"Kolosos will be summoned soon, if Kazen keeps to his pattern," Bastien continued. "He's struck the Lily Tower and the cathedral. I-I think . . . I think it would make sense if the Innerchord were next."

The room went silent. All turned to Bastien, except Rone, who hurried to Sandis's side. She didn't look scared or worried, just exhausted. Just . . . sad.

"I won't let them," he whispered, taking her in his arms and pulling her tight against his chest, more to reassure himself than her. "I won't let them hurt you."

"That is an unfortunate point," Var said to Bastien. "General, round up the guard and see that the tablets are transported. We'll move to my home in District Two to continue this discussion."

"There is nothing to discuss," Rone snapped.

Var turned on him, pointing a long, bony finger at his nose. "We may be in a time of crisis, Comf, but the doors of Gerech are not sealed. Control yourself, or I will control you. Is that understood?"

So much for letting us leave freely, Rone thought, remembering the demand Sandis had made of Esgar. But whether they were allowed to do so freely or not, they were *leaving.*

"Move out, quickly!" Var barked. "Istrude, prepare your men! Get Oz ready with his vessel!"

Rone waited for him to yell at Sandis to prepare Bastien, but he didn't. It struck him that these men still didn't understand what she could do—that she was both summoner and vessel. That she was worth the lot of them.

Something else struck him. The triumvirs would be preoccupied with protecting themselves, the scholar with his tablets, and Oz would have to stay close to this flying Pettanawhatever if he were to control it.

It would provide just enough chaos for them to escape.

Jachim pulled his hand from his bruising eye and rushed to gather his papers, clutching them to his breast like they were his children, while guards from outside came in to collect the tablets. The scholar shouted at them to treat the slabs carefully, seemingly more concerned for the millennia-old stone than his own life. Var was gone in an instant.

Sandis was listless, lost inside her own thoughts, and Bastien began to hyperventilate. He spun on his heel twice, as if forgetting where the exit was. So Rone took Sandis's fingers in one hand and Bastien's elbow in the other, pushing them out of the room, down a flight of stairs, and out into the cool night. But as he wrapped around the building and chose his own direction, two armed men in blue uniforms stopped him, hands on their rifles.

"The carriages are that way, Comf."

He could take them. The fight played out in his mind; he'd attack the one on the left first, hitting him in his left side and forcing him to lose hold of his gun. Then he'd turn and crumple the second soldier quickly with a blow to the nose before smashing his foot into the left's stomach—

Sandis squeezed his hand. He barely heard her murmured words: "We can't afford to have more than one enemy, Rone. Let's go with them. For now."

Rone gritted his teeth under the scrutiny of the two soldiers, bristling at the suggestion. *No.* If he attacked them now, he could drop them. Carry Sandis if he had to, slap some sense into the panicking redhead next to him. They'd run.

And go . . . where?

Damn it.

A long, tight breath left his throat. Tugging Bastien's elbow, he allowed the guards to lead them in the opposite direction. "For now," he mumbled, repeating Sandis's words.

It would be easier to run from a house, anyway. Not as much room for guards.

Rone hated everything about Dresberg, especially its government, but as he approached the carriages, even *he* had to admit it moved efficiently. Already guards were prepping the vehicles; the first took off with Triumvirs Peterus and Holwig, along with Chief Esgar. Rone shoved Bastien into the next, then carefully lifted Sandis in.

"I won't let them hurt you," he whispered as he settled beside her. She didn't seem to hear him.

Chapter 8

"Vre en nestu a carnath."
    Suffer as I have suffered.
    "Ii mem entre I amar."
    You did not seek truth, so I will force it upon you.
    "Vre en nestu a carnath."
    And punish all who wouldn't listen.
    "Kolosos epsi gradenid."
    Come to me, my monster.

A great punch of red light accented the soft whirring of the amarinth before swallowing it whole. Kazen reached forward and grabbed
the tip of one of Kolosos's great horns as the beast formed on the mortal
plane, its brilliant red-and-black body a bloody star against the shadows
of night-choked Dresberg.

Up, up, up Kazen flew, until he stood above the great wall of
Dresberg. He commanded the horn to cool, but heat billowed off
Kolosos, burning his skin and drawing sweat from his pores.

Kazen stroked Kolosos's horn. *Do not harm me.* The blood bond
between them pulled taut, and the heat diminished. Good.

Below, Kuracean looked little more than a roach, awaiting his command. And to think Kazen had once believed it powerful. But the
armored monster had its uses, even if it was merely a distraction for
soldiers who thought themselves brave.

He had a great deal of work to do, and if his calculations for the last two summonings were correct, he had limited time. His monster had survived in the boy's body nearly two minutes less the second time than the first. Was it happenstance, or was Kolosos simply too powerful, even for an amarinth-powered vessel? Only time would tell. Allowing Anon to rest longer could help, but Kazen didn't want to lose his advantage. He also didn't want the lad to try and run.

Their efforts would pay off handsomely, soon enough.

Kazen pictured his destination in his mind's eye. Kolosos turned toward the center of the city, then paused. Dug its hooves into the earth, gripped the wall with its great talons. Its wings folded. Smoke sputtered from the numen's nostrils.

"Go." Kazen voiced the command aloud this time. Still, he met resistance. It had come as an unpleasant surprise, this numen's reluctant obedience. None of the others had been able to thwart his will. Kazen had taken more blood than usual before this summoning, but he dared not take *too* much, for fear of damaging his vessel further. Already Anon Gwenwig showed increased signs of wear, and not even the amarinth would keep him alive if he faded away in his summoning slumber. *"Go!"* Kazen repeated in a shout, pouring his will behind the word.

Kolosos trudged forward, crumbling the Dresberg wall with its sheer size. Stone hissed as it gave way to the numen's powerful legs.

He didn't hear screams this time, even as Kolosos's shoulders crumpled the corners of flats and crushed abandoned carriages underfoot. No, their terror was silent. Like a prayer. And it was *him* they should be praying to.

Kazen allowed glee to form on his face, pulling his mouth into a tight smile. He'd already destroyed the homes of the two men who had betrayed him. The ones who'd refused to accept the truth of the Celestial. The ones who'd so faithfully served the Angelic who'd cast him out. That man had long since died, replaced by another, and another. But the taste remained bitter in Kazen's mouth.

Celesia and its priests were not the only ones who needed to be taught a lesson. He would punish its supporters, too. The men who thought they could control him in a city *he* owned.

The Innerchord came into view. *Destroy it,* he commanded. *Start with the tallest building.*

He heard the whiz of an arrow and smelled smoke when it hit too low and burned against Kolosos's half-molten skin. The fools. Did they still think *mortal* men could best him? But here they were again, faced with Kolingrad's little army, noticeably smaller than before. Lining up a . . . was that a cannon? How quaint.

"Crush them," he crooned.

Kolosos lifted an enormous hoof and slammed it down in the middle of the battalion, forcing the soldiers to scatter like mice. Something exploded beneath its weight—perhaps one of the cannons. There was a *crunch* as Kolosos shifted forward, swinging out his other hoof, but whether it was concrete or bodies, Kazen couldn't tell. He also didn't care.

"Don't let them get in your way, my pet." He patted the side of Kolosos's massive horn. "Let's finish our business, shall we?"

Kolosos growled and shifted forward, splaying its bloody talons. The Degrata crumbled beneath the beast's fiery claws.

The carnage was glorious.

Chapter 9

"You will comport yourself appropriately, Rone Comf, or you will be dismissed from these proceedings, and we'll make the decision without you." Triumvir Var's whiplike voice was at odds with the delicacy of the room. The crystal chandelier and its small candles, the floral wallpaper, the leather-bound books on the shelf against the far wall. A room in a house finer than that of Talbur Gwenwig.

It was an almost dizzying contrast to the destruction they'd felt beneath their feet as Kolosos's steps shook the city. Kazen's latest rampage had stopped not half an hour ago, and traces of fire still rose from the city's great center. Now it was up to General Istrude's scouts, Oz, and Jansen to track the monster. And Sandis didn't mean Kolosos.

She began a prayer for their success, but it was cut short by the thought that she no longer knew whom she was praying to. But surely, if Ireth could sense her, the Celestial might as well.

It couldn't hurt. She uttered the final words and fell silent. She'd missed a portion of the ongoing conversation.

"Surely not." She felt the Angelic's eyes on her. "She has such a bond? To which numen?"

Sandis curled her knees to her chest, careful to let her skirt fall over them modestly. She sat on the window seat in front of drawn curtains, leaning one shoulder against the edge of the alcove. Rone seethed beside her.

"I'd never read of such a thing myself," Jachim said, sporting a purple eye, "but I witnessed it with my own eyes."

Sandis really should pay attention. Listen to what everyone was saying, not just the louder snippets that wriggled past her knotted thoughts. But her mind was fragmented, lost in different parts of the city. Her consciousness bounced between them.

The lair, where Sandis had uncovered Kazen's truths.

The sewer, where they'd found the broken amarinth.

The Degrata, where Jachim had voiced his revelation.

The cathedral, burned to ash.

The Lily Tower, where she'd watched, helpless, as her lost brother transformed into the greatest horror the world could offer.

"Theorize then," someone—Triumvir Peterus?—said. "Both of you. Tell me how it could possibly work."

In her mind's eye, Sandis stood in front of the stone tablets in the Noscon ruins at the heart of the city, staring at them as though they'd speak to her at any moment. A special bond to a numen. A flash of light. Two hearts, merged into one. Ripped from their shared body to form the glimmering core that powered an amarinth.

Was that why Ireth had been so afraid? Did he know these men would learn how to kill him?

Or was he afraid for her?

"You cannot fight evil with evil," High Priest Dall countered. "You cannot possibly want to go through with this. Even to theorize about it is blasphemy!"

Sandis's thoughts shifted again, and this time she found herself in Kazen's office, peering at the diagrams of the astral sphere. *Is it blasphemy, when all of it is the same?* she wondered. Celesia, the occult . . . Where did one draw the line?

Did Ireth worship the Celestial, too?

"She is an innocent woman," said the Angelic.

A long, tense breath squeezed from Rone's chest. "For once, we agree. Consider our options! Sandis is powerful. More powerful than anyone here. You'd sacrifice her on a whim?"

Could they hear the anger lacing his voice, the sorrow? Rone's hand touched her back, his thumb tracing one of the symbols embedded into the skin there.

"You'd sacrifice this city?" asked Chief Esgar.

He glanced at Sandis, but she couldn't escape that moment at the Lily Tower. She was looking at Anon, his dark eyes glimmering with recognition. Watching that flash of bloody light. Seeing that monster rear its head in her brother's body.

Pressure rose in her head, warm and familiar.

Would it save them, Ireth? she asked. *If we gave ourselves up, would it save them? The city? Rone? Anon?*

Wouldn't it be worth it, to die so the people she loved could live? So that the children hiding in their flats could see another day? So that mothers could take their shifts and put food on the table?

"I don't know." Jachim's voice was oddly serious. "I . . . Both are excellent arguments. Lose the woman, or gain our salvation? Surely there are others who might be made vessels in the city . . . but from what I understand, it takes some time to recover from the branding."

Was it too high a price to pay?

Warmth trickled up her spine. It wasn't fear. Was this Ireth's confirmation that their sacrifice would end the violence?

Could this be what he'd been trying to tell her from the beginning?

"That is the other side of the coin," chimed Triumvir Holwig. "If we want an army capable of fighting this numen, then we must raise it, now, especially if it takes time for the vessels to recover from the branding. We can mandate all people between ten and thirty to come in for inspection. Oz could inspect them, couldn't he?"

"N-No!" Bastien's voice was wet with fear. "Y-You can't just force them into slavery!"

"It's not slavery," countered Chief Esgar. "They will be free to leave when the city is reclaimed."

In a rare moment of speech, Inda, one of Oz's vessels, said, "Funny how you persecute us, until you need us."

"Without you," hissed Triumvir Holwig, "we would not have this problem in the first place."

"I cannot listen to this!" shouted High Priest Dall.

"We are desperate, you fool!" Triumvir Var matched the priest's volume. "You must either bend your faith or die by the hand of a demon!"

Rone stood, adding his voice to the fray, followed by General Istrude and Triumvir Peterus. They shouted, pleaded, and coerced well into the night.

Sandis was still at the Lily Tower, frozen in the moment of her horrific reunion with her brother.

Var needed to take his own advice. None of the council was "comporting," not anymore.

They screamed at one another like little kids. Rone stared at the ceiling, feeling tired, wishing he could just whisk Sandis *away* and pretend the scarlets never found them in the first place. Bastien had his hands planted over his ears, and his face was scrunched like he was about to explode. No one else noticed. They didn't actually *care* about the others in the room, just about making their opinion the loudest.

This was getting out of hand.

It was too loud to hear the door open, but Rone spied it from the corner of his eye. Oz appeared in the gap, his clothing singed, his body ragged. Rone squeezed Sandis's hand, drawing her attention to the grafter. Bastien noticed, too, and turned in his chair.

"Hey!" Rone shouted, but his voice didn't carry above the cacophony. "Would you shut up for a minute?"

Both of Bastien's hands tore from his ears and slammed onto the table with shocking strength. *"Oz is here!"* He shouted so loudly Rone felt it in his chest. Beside him, Sandis tensed. Thankfully, the others finally shut up and noticed the new arrival. Var and Peterus even ran over, taking the summoner's elbows and helping him stay upright.

Shaking his head, Oz coughed and said, "I lost it. I followed Kolosos halfway across District Four and lost it. I . . . I lost Jansen, too."

A small gasp emitted from Sandis, and Rone squeezed her hand harder. But it was Bastien who worried him. The Godobian's expression cracked. His pale skin blanched to white. His lips formed the name *Jansen.*

Bowing his head, Var had the audacity to say, "That is unfortunate."

Bastien hid his face in his arms and sobbed.

***

Triumvir Var's house was large and divided into many rooms, most of which were modest in size. Even the very wealthy in Dresberg could only take up so much space. Like everyone else, they had to fit inside the circular stone wall that enfolded them.

Sandis was starting to see why Rone thought of the city as a cage.

The vessels and grafters had been assigned two of the rooms—Rone, Bastien, and herself in one, Oz and his remaining vessels, Teppa and Inda, in the other. Sandis should have talked to the younger women. Seen how they were faring. Learned what they had in common.

If you think it will replace them, you're wrong.

The thought came unbidden, but it struck like a crowbar. Heath, Kaili, Alys. Gone. Gone. Gone. And what of Dar? Rone had seen him working construction in the city. Was he still here? Was he hiding, or had he been injured in one of Kolosos's attacks? Did he have work and money, or was he starving in an alley somewhere?

Rone kicked the door to the room closed; Bastien had stayed with Jachim, asking him questions and answering the scholar's many, many queries in return. Celestial knew he was in need of the distraction.

Sandis sat on the edge of the bed, her body leaden and exhausted, her mind twisted like stripped wire.

You can still save him, she thought. *Dar. You can save all of them, if you give them the power inside you.*

"Sandis?"

She blinked and looked up. It seemed to take too long to move her neck and meet his eyes.

Rone frowned. He'd been unbuttoning his shirt, but paused on the fourth button down. "This is going to sound like a stupid question, but are you all right?"

She took a deep breath, thinking of how she should respond. But all her thoughts were aligned the same way, so the truth came out. "I could save them, couldn't I?"

Rone's eyes widened, and his face blanched white. "Sandis, no."

Her gaze fell to her knees. "No, I can't save them, or no, I shouldn't try?"

"Sandis. Sandis." His voice was weak yet urgent. He dropped to his knees on the floor in front of her and grabbed her hands. "They don't even know for sure, all right? Please don't think like that."

But Sandis shook her head. "Jachim knows more about the Noscons than even Kazen does. He would know—"

"No!" His response was sharp, and the bump of his throat bobbed. "No, Sandis. And so what? Even *if* we could *make* an amarinth, then what? We can't beat Kolosos in sixty seconds."

"We could summon the Celestial."

Rone's hands turned to ice around hers. The look of horror and pain etched into his face made her heart squelch. Her eyes burned.

Setting his jaw, Rone shook his head. His grip on her fingers tightened nearly to the point of pain. "Please." His voice was hoarse. "Please don't,

Sandis. If you give in now . . . everything we've done is meaningless." The last word pitched high, and Rone swallowed again, waiting a moment before continuing. Even then, his voice trembled, and the sound of it crumbled something inside Sandis. Something delicate and necessary, and it hurt. "What's the point of surviving, if you're just going to leave?"

The image of his face—his beautiful face—blurred. Sandis blinked, and a single tear traced the length of her cheek. She whispered, "I don't know what to do."

"Not this." His own eyes watered. The only time Sandis had seen him this emotional was in that underground tunnel on the evening he'd apologized so genuinely to her. The memory only spurred more tears. "Please, Sandis, not this. I can't . . . I *can't* without you, don't you understand?"

Sandis pressed her lips together to contain her own emotion. She pulled her hands free and cradled his face, sweeping a curl from his forehead. There was so much she wanted to say. Those unspoken words warred inside her, and inside him, too. She knew him well enough to feel it. They stayed like that a long moment, barely containing their words and their sobs. Sandis's throat ached. Her chest ached.

Pushing himself off the floor, Rone kissed her, sending spikes of heat through her skin that clashed with the sorrow. She welcomed him, tilting her head to the right and parting her lips. The taste of salt and sadness washed through her, and she gave him her worries and fears in return. He took them eagerly, tracing her mouth with movements both familiar and new. Replacing them with a fire so very unlike Ireth's.

Sandis tangled her fingers in his hair—hair she loved touching for the softness of it. Rone pulled back just enough for a quick breath, and Sandis nipped at him, needing him. Needing to feel him and not her doubts.

His hand pressed into her lower back. The kiss deepened, his tongue slowly, softly seeking hers. He tasted like the ocean and rain and winter storms. And then the mattress was at her back. Rone's weight on top of her was tantalizing and wonderful. Their mouths danced, and Sandis's fingers explored his hair, his jaw, his shoulders. He broke away, placing a kiss just below her ear, making a trail of them down her neck. He supported himself on one forearm by her head, while his free hand slid up her thigh—a touch that stoked the flames growing in her belly.

She whispered his name, and his mouth returned to hers. She cupped his face, guiding his lips where she wanted them, taking the lower one for her own. A soft moan escaped him, and he pressed harder into her.

Regret spiraled slowly, starting in her navel and working up to her throat. She wanted all of him, but her script began to itch, reminding her.

She slowed her movements, forcing him to slow as well. When he paused for another breath, she pressed her fingers into his cheeks and said, "Rone . . . Ireth."

She barely recognized her own voice. It was half air and strangely low. The regret broadened and filtered into her limbs.

Pressing his lips together, Rone rested his forehead against hers for a moment, then kissed her jaw and slid to the side of her, lifting his head so that his chin touched her hairline. He kept her close to him, and Sandis snuggled into the hollow of his throat, kissing the skin there.

She needed to keep her connection to Ireth now more than ever. And a numen could only be summoned into the body of a virgin.

As she lay there, entwined with Rone, her mind finally gave in to fatigue. She curled into his warmth, resting her head on the inside of his bicep, and drifted to sleep.

She dreamed of Anon.

Rain drizzled around her, gray and thick with pollution. Dresberg's wall was gone, its towering buildings far away. Beneath her feet looped overgrown, trampled grass and mud. But it didn't smell like rain. It smelled like chloride lime.

Anon lay on a tarp ahead of her, pale and glassy eyed. Soaking wet. Somehow she knew it wasn't from the rain. It was from canal water. He'd drowned, just as she'd believed for all those lost, lonely years.

Men without faces, little more than shadows, grabbed the corners of the tarp and heaved him upward. They swung him back and forth three times before letting him go. He fell into a giant square-shaped pit behind them. Sandis ran to it, arriving at the crumbling edge too late to stop them.

It was a grave. A mass grave, with bodies strewn together without grace or sentiment. An arm here, a broken leg there. Anon rested at the edge, his lifeless eyes staring up into the storm, unblinking even when raindrops pattered against the whites. The corpse beside him was face-down, but Sandis would know it anywhere. The exposed spine glistened despite the clouds. Kaili, harvested for her golden script. Next to her was Rist, curled around a bloody pile that could only be his brother. Below him, Alys, the bottom half of her body covered by other corpses, her blonde hair matted and stained red.

Sandis tried to pull away from the sight, but she couldn't. Her eyes locked onto each face, one after another. Triumvir Var, Jachim, Chief Esgar. They were bloated and pale, unmoving. Bastien lay at the far edge, his braid a noose around his pulseless neck. Near him were a little boy and his mother, the strangers who'd offered her help the first night after she'd run from Kazen. And there, half-buried in limbs, was Dar, a great scar cutting through the symbols branded between his shoulder blades.

Then she saw him. At the very center of the pit, at the crest of all that death, lay Rone, on his side as though he were sleeping. Yet his chest didn't rise and fall, and the faintest trickle of blood flowed from the corner of his mouth.

Sandis awoke with a start, her skin covered in sweat, her heart pounding and head aching. It took her a moment to orient herself, to sit up and recognize the bed and the room, the sleeping form beside her. He was on his side just like he'd been in the pit of horrors. She held her breath, listening for the intake of his. When she heard it, relief cooled her and left her shivering.

Just a dream, just a dream, just a dream. Sandis was accustomed to nightmares. She wasn't sure why they still affected her so.

But she'd never had a nightmare like *that*.

She searched the room for Bastien, but he hadn't joined them. Turning back to Rone—carefully, as he was a light sleeper—she watched his serene face for a long time, as if convincing herself that he really was alive. She lifted a hand to touch his curls, but dropped it again. She didn't want to wake him.

She couldn't watch him die, either.

Will the Celestial save us? she wondered, unease snaking through her middle. *Does it even have the power to?*

Perhaps it had given *her* that power.

Steeling herself, Sandis carefully slid off the bed, gently tugging her skirt free where Rone's knee pinned it to the mattress. The faintest light glowed under the door; she turned the knob silently and slipped into the hallway, fingers trembling when she closed the door behind her.

Ireth? she thought. There was no answering pulse of warmth. He'd been there earlier, however. Not afraid. Warm and resolute. Surely it had been a message. Encouragement.

The house was eerily quiet. The entire city was. Stopping at a window, Sandis drew back a curtain to peer into the night. The faintest orange glow illuminated Dresberg's center. How many people were fighting that fire at the Innerchord, while the triumvirate snoozed safely in soft beds?

How many had already died?

She closed the curtain and kept a hand on the wall, feeling her way through the darkness. Found the staircase and took it down. The soft glow of lamplight beckoned her to the right, to the study with its door ajar. The politicians, priests, scarlets, and soldiers had left, leaving the make-shift meeting room quiet. Jachim sat at the table, poring over his books, rubbing his neck as he stooped. Bastien sat beside him, studying a ledger. He murmured something to the scholar, who glanced over and nodded.

"Jachim." Sandis's voice was quiet, but so was everything else, so both he and Bastien lifted their heads when she spoke. "I need to speak with you."

Bastien said, "You need to . . . book an appointment?" He picked up a ledger. His voice was strained, but he was at least trying to lighten the mood.

Jachim chuckled. Sandis managed a sliver of a smile. "I do. But . . . alone, if you don't mind."

The humor faded from Bastien's freckled face. He glanced between Sandis and Jachim twice before standing. "I should probably go to bed anyway." He shrugged.

Sandis stepped aside to let him pass, but before he did, she pinched his shirt sleeve in her hand and, in a hushed voice, said, "In the morning . . . tell Rone I love him."

Bastien met her eyes, confusion lacing his blue irises. "What do you—"

"In the morning," she repeated, firm. Turning sideways, she gestured for Bastien to leave. He did, hesitantly, and Sandis closed the door behind him before she could lose her courage.

Nerves pricked her limbs as she crossed the room to Jachim. His eye was still swollen; Rone hadn't held back when he hit him. She pulled out the chair across from him, but couldn't bring herself to sit. Jitters danced through her body and stiffened her spine. Anxiety ballooned in her chest as though she were about to confess her greatest secrets. But she supposed everyone already knew those.

"You look worried," Jachim said.

She nodded. "We all are."

He rubbed his jaw—it was so smooth Sandis suspected he didn't grow facial hair. Shaking her head, she brought herself to the present. "I want to do it."

Jachim blinked. "What?"

"The amarinth," she specified, toes curling against the carpet. "I want to make a new amarinth."

Chapter 10

Jachim stared at her a long moment. "You're . . . willing?"

Pinching her lips together, Sandis nodded.

The scholar removed his glasses and rubbed his eyes. "I'm certain I know how it's done. I've been translating as much as I can . . . but . . . are you sure?"

Sandis filled her lungs with a deep breath and forced herself to study the table between them. "Do you really want me to change my mind?"

Jachim looked at her, his gray eyes so different from her own. After a moment, he shook his head. "No. No, I don't. I quite like you, Sandis. And that brute of yours is right—you saved my life. But I can't find any other way to stop Kolosos—"

"Neither can I."

He nodded, stood. "Then we are in agreement."

"We need to do it now." Fear began to coil beneath her ribs, but Sandis pushed through it. *It's the only way.* Surely an immortal could best an immortal.

"Let me wake—"

"Only who is necessary, please." The thought of Rone's tears sent an ache lined with barbs spiking down the center of her being. But it did not banish the lingering image of him in that open grave. "Quickly and quietly."

Then he could finally see his mother. His family. Rone would still have a happy ending.

The set of Jachim's brow told her he understood. "Stay here. I'll be right back."

Bastien's fingers fumbled with the candle at the bottom of the stairs. He dropped it twice before lighting it. He didn't like walking through dark places without a light. Especially the narrow hallways of this place. He didn't like not knowing what was there.

Clutching the candleholder in one hand and the stair rail in the other, he began to ascend into the darkness, but stopped halfway up. Not because his candle went out or because he'd forgotten where his bedroll was, but because of Sandis. The tension around her eyes and the sadness to her voice. *In the morning.* Why in the morning? And why should Bastien be the one to tell Rone? Did the two have a fight or something?

He took two more stairs. Paused. Something gnawed in his gut, like he was hungry but not. His candle shook. He was holding it too tightly. One by one, he forced his fingers to relax. Then his arm, his shoulders, his neck.

He wasn't athletic like Rone or brave like Sandis, but he was a good thinker. Oz had always told him so. That's why his old master had confided in him so often. And something wasn't right.

Rone would be mad if he woke him for nothing.

But the last time Bastien had failed to act, Rist had stolen the amarinth and their worst nightmare had stepped into the mortal realm. Continued to step into it. Trample it. In a way, that was Bastien's fault, wasn't it?

Glancing back down the stairs, Bastien thought. Hard. Reached for his braid and gave it a good tug. He was glad Kazen had never gotten around to cutting it off.

Footsteps upstairs. Chewing on his lip, Bastien returned to the main floor and tucked himself beside a closet. Steeling himself, he blew out his candle.

And listened.

***

Should she have said goodbye first?

Jachim, General Istrude, and Triumvirs Peterus, Var, and Holwig stood with her in the basement of Triumvir Var's home. Unlike the rest of the house, it was unfurnished, its walls and floor made of smooth concrete. The wooden beams of its ceiling were exposed. A large, plain rug took up the middle of the room, and a stack of carpet squares sat beneath the stairs.

For a moment, Sandis wondered where the man's family was. Not here. Surely he had one. Were they already outside the city walls, running for safety?

The floor was cold beneath Sandis's bare feet. She hugged herself against the chill, against the fear. But alongside the fear was hope. *We'll make it better, Ireth.* Their power could be turned into something great.

Closing her eyes, she sought confirmation from the numen, but felt none. *Where are you?*

Would they give her time to write a note? She didn't write often, and her penmanship was poor, but she knew how. Would it be better for Rone if she wrote him a letter?

Would he understand if she did?

Her heart ached. From the beginning, she'd only wanted him. She'd always feared that he would leave her, but now it was the other way around, wasn't it?

But Anon. *Anon.* Her brother was alive and being brutalized by that demon. She could save him, too. All of them. *Right, Ireth?*

"Just . . . cut it out?" General Istrude gave her a sympathetic glance.

"The body changes," Jachim explained. "In the moment between forms, it should be . . . soft. I don't think a weapon will be necessary."

Sandis touched her chest. They were talking about removing her heart. They'd already sent for a smith to form the gold loops of the amaranth. Sandis didn't know if they needed to be gold, but both Rone's amarinth and the prototype were gold. They couldn't make any mistakes. Sandis would *not* die in vain.

Neither would Ireth. Again she felt for him. His presence was always fleeting and seemingly random, but if there was ever a time for him to make himself known, this was it. So why hadn't he?

"Sandis." It was Jachim. "Do you want . . . some opium or something? For the pain?"

Sandis shook her head. It wasn't the loss of her heart that would hurt. Summoning itself was the worst physical pain a person could experience, and nothing tempered that.

"You're sure that's it?" asked Triumvir Holwig. Dark circles framed his eyes.

Jachim nodded.

Sandis lifted her head. "Then let's proceed." Before her own fears made her condemn the entire city. Then, to Jachim, she added, "Don't let the Angelic stop you from saving the others."

Closing her eyes, she thought of Rone and Anon, of Bastien and Rist, of the people in this room and in this house. She thought of Sherig and the Riggers, of the bankers, of all of the strangers she'd never met. She'd failed to save Kaili and Alys and Heath, but Sandis could save the others. She *would* save them.

Taking a deep breath, she pressed her palm to her forehead.

"Rone."

Someone jabbed him in the ribs.

"Rone."

Rone startled awake, shooting up to sitting, only to have his forehead collide with another's. He cussed and winced, his hand flying to the bruising spot.

"Ow," Bastien whined.

"The hell?" he asked, blinking. Only a single candle illuminated the room. It took him a second to recognize his surroundings. Var's place. Sandis? She wasn't there.

Rubbing the side of his head, Bastien said, "I think something's wrong. The others . . . they're with Sandis. In the basement."

Rone's hand dropped. "What? Why?"

Ice crystalized sharp in his belly as he recalled what Sandis had said before they fell asleep.

"Sh-She didn't want me to hear," the Godobian went on. "She told me to tell you she loved you. Only . . . in the morning."

Terror seized Rone's chest.

He pushed past Bastien and bolted for the door, flinging it open hard enough for the handle to break through the wall behind it. He tripped on a table, and something ceramic crashed at his feet. It bit into his big toe, but he kept running. Took the turn in the hallway. Sailed down the first flight of stairs and nearly fell to his knees when he reached the bottom. Basement. Where the hell was the basement?

His heart thundered as he turned around in the darkness, the only light coming from a lamp left in Var's empty study. He raced down the hallway behind the stairs, only to find a privy and startle awake Chief Esgar. Whipping around, he flashed the other way. Through the kitchen. Yanked open a door—a mop fell onto him. He hit his hip on the edge of the dining table as he soared for another door. Locked.

Rone backed up and kicked it right beside the handle, sending all his weight and strength down his leg and into his heel. The thing splintered and flung open, and the momentum nearly sent him headfirst down a set of wooden stairs.

He descended them in two leaps.

"Ii mem entre I amar."

God, no. That was Sandis's voice. *No, no, no, no—*

He ran into the room, shoving Triumvir Peterus aside. General Istrude's big body blocked her, only a foot away, his right hand lifted and clawed in anticipation, his left clutching a knife.

"Ireth."

Rone flew toward her.

"Epsi."

Shoved Istrude aside with strength born of desperation.

"Gradenid."

White light filled his vision, then snuffed out all at once. He fell hard to the ground, scraping palms and knees, blinded. Cold.

"Sandis!" he shouted, whirling around, blinking spots from his vision. But she wasn't there. Neither were the general, the triumvirate, the scholar.

The basement.

Rone stared at the blackness around him, hovering like a shadowy fog. Indigo like an empty night sky loomed high overhead. Where were the stars?

There. He saw one, then another as his vision adjusted. Dozens of stars. Hundreds . . . *thousands* of them.

Beneath him.

Wide eyed, Rone rolled onto his hands and knees and looked down into the heavens. Gooseflesh rose on every inch of skin he had.

He heard three things. The first was his breathing grating up and down his throat. The second was a growl, low and feral, somewhere behind him.

The third was a voice in his head, one that was decidedly not his own, pushing out a single word.

Run.

Chapter 11

Sandis blinked, the memory of pain raising the hairs on her arms. She knelt in the basement on the cold cement floor, staring straight ahead. Her heart beat heavily in her chest. Still there. As was she.

Still alive, and still dressed.

Ireth hadn't come.

"Good God," Jachim uttered.

Triumvir Peterus picked himself off the floor. "Where did he go?"

"What happened?" asked General Istrude. The knife in his hand dropped to the floor.

Sandis searched inside herself, trying to orient her thoughts. Ireth had been right there. Right there, and then—

Celestial, save me, what have I done?

But before her panic could mount, she felt a familiar pressure inside her head. *Ireth.* Relief consumed her until she felt a pulse of fear that was not her own.

A hand appeared before her face—the general's. Sandis took it, and he helped her to her feet. Her body trembled—she couldn't help it. She had begun a summons, and then . . . it had stopped. Snapped her out of the transformation before it'd even happened.

All five men stared at her. Sandis glanced at each of them before settling on Jachim. "What happened?"

"Uh," Jachim said, pushing up glasses that weren't there. "R-Rone. He came running in—"

Sandis turned around, but all she saw was an unadorned basement wall. Spinning back, she said, "Where?"

"He ran for you," the general said, his eyes more white than brown, his brows nearly reaching his hairline. "He ran for you and disappeared."

"Portal," Jachim whispered. "I need my notes!"

He hurried for the stairs, but Triumvir Var grabbed his shoulder and halted him. "Tell us what you know *now*, Franz!"

Jachim shook with . . . excitement?

"Where's Rone?" Sandis repeated. Why was it so hard to breathe?

"There was something in the tablets I didn't understand." He waved a hand and shook his head before rushing on. "Something about a portal. Light. That's . . . surely that's what happened! The portal appeared in the flash of light before the summoning. And to think it just nullified it! I wonder if it would work again right away, or if the traditional resting period is still needed—"

"Franz!" Triumvir Var shook him.

The scholar focused. "Oh, yes, sorry. It's a portal. Has to be. How else could the chap have vanished like that?"

"Vanished?" Sandis whispered. She turned around again, hoping against reason they were wrong. That Rone was hiding somewhere. But there was nowhere to hide. "He was here?" she asked, even as Jachim spoke over her. "He was *here*?"

Her heart hardened and sank all at once.

"He was," General Istrude finally answered, his brow lowered and his voice soft. "Right as you finished . . . I saw him as he shoved me away. He went . . . he went right into that light and . . . he's gone."

Tears sprang to Sandis's eyes. Rushing past the general, she ran to Jachim, slipping under Triumvir Var's arm to get to him. She grabbed the front of his robes. "*Where?* Where would the portal go?"

"I—" The scholar glanced from her to Triumvir Var and back. "I can't decipher that part of the tablet. The writing is so old, and there are so many symbols we don't have context for—"

"Jachim!" she shouted, hurting her own ears. *Where did he go?*"

Jachim pressed his lips together, thought, and said, "M-My best theory is . . . well, the only place I could think of . . .'"

Sandis gripped his robes tighter, her breath reduced to a thin trickle of air.

Jachim sighed. "The ethereal plane, I suppose."

Sandis's grip went slack at the same time Triumvir Var spurted, *"What?"*

They talked, argued, but Sandis couldn't hear them anymore. She stumbled away from Jachim, away from the others, and stared into nothing. Grappled for Ireth, but he, too, had vanished. Her fingers and toes chilled. A thin lock of hair stuck to the corner of her mouth, but she didn't brush it away.

Rone had tried to stop her, and he'd been taken . . . *there?*

"Celestial help him." Sandis fell to her knees. Almost instantly, warm arms surrounded her. She didn't need to look up to see who it was; his red braid fell over her shoulder.

"I'm sorry, Sandis," he said, voice hitching. "I had to tell him. I-I didn't want you to d-die."

Her hand found his wrist and she squeezed. This was all a dream, wasn't it? She blinked her eyes as dry as she could get them.

"How do we get him back?" The words were too faint to be overheard by the arguing men. She tried again, a little louder. "How do we get him back?"

"She's hale enough," Triumvir Peterus said. "Let's try again."

"No!" Sandis jolted to her feet, knocking Bastien onto his hip. "We will *not* try again, not while he's trapped there! Jachim!" She moved for him again, hands pressed together in pleading. "How do we get him *back?*"

The excitement drained from the scholar's face, making his mouth go slack. "I . . . I don't know, Sandis. I can't even theorize . . ." He bowed his head in apology. "I simply don't know."

Sandis shook her head, running back to the corner where she had meant to die, putting distance between herself and the others. "I'm summoning again. I'm getting him out."

"S-Sandis," Bastien said.

"Not for the amarinth." She shot a hard look at each of the men. "I'm summoning Ireth and getting him out."

"Sandis," Jachim hurried to her, clutching a ledger. "We don't know how the plane works—"

But Sandis's hand was already in her hair. "Don't let them kill me," she told Bastien. Then, before anyone could react, she rushed through the summoning and cried Ireth's name.

Flames engulfed her, pain radiated hot and vicious through her body, tearing her in two, burning her to ash, searing blood and flesh. She looked for him, but saw only flames and her own blistering agony.

Then everything went dark.

Rone ran.

Where he ran, he didn't know. It was dark, and vastly empty. No sewers to wade through, no buildings to vault, no garbage bins or fences to climb. Just smooth nothingness. And stars. So many stars.

And something huffing behind him, its claws chiming like bells against the whatever-surface beneath his feet. Rone swore he could feel hot moisture from its mouth at the back of his neck. He only dared look over his shoulders once, but it was so dark he couldn't make out what it was. But it was large and hunched and ran on all fours.

And it was getting closer.

His lungs and legs burned, but he pushed himself faster, faster, nearly losing his footing on the smooth ground. Even curses left his mind. He just had to run. Run. *Run.*

Duck left.

That voice again, strangely accented, pluming up from somewhere in the middle of his skull.

He didn't question it.

Rone dodged left, his shoulder hitting something—a block of some sort. He tried to stand, but a ceiling appeared over him. About four feet up. So he crawled, his knees burning through his trousers. Crawled until there were no stars, only black.

He was going to die.

The thing behind him howled and began scraping against the block—blocks?—behind him.

Fall.

"What?" Rone's voice was hoarse. He kept crawling. He could hide in here, he could—

The ground suddenly gave out beneath his left hand. He nearly toppled forward into the abyss.

Blinking sweat from his eyes, Rone peered down. He couldn't gauge the distance well. Everything was black and deep blue, but there were stars down below. So many stars. He'd never seen so many stars in his life.

Something thudded against the roof over him. He cursed.

Fall, Rone. Trust.

Rone's racing heart trembled. "How do you know my name?" he whispered. "Who are you?"

Fall.

Swallowing, Rone reached forward, feeling the hard lip of the surface beneath him and the nothingness beyond it. It wasn't so much a hole in his path as a ledge. His gut told him he was very high up. Higher even than the roof of the Lily Tower.

Maybe it was only a few feet. Maybe he was crazy.

The ceiling shook.

Damn it, damn it, damn it, damn it. Gritting his teeth, Rone leapt. And fell.

His stomach surged up into his rib cage. Cool air flooded his mouth and ballooned his cheeks. He spun, geometric shapes above him, stars below him, above, below, until he was disoriented and sick and *falling*—

A rush of wind slowed him, so hot it made his every pore sweat. But he slowed, facing the stars head-on.

The wind faded, and he hit the glassy ground with a thud.

He spat Sandis's least-favorite curse and rolled onto his back, cradling his nose. He poked it gingerly. He was screwed if he broke it again. He had no amarinth.

Amarinth. Sandis.

He sat up, gasping like he'd swum from the bottom of a pool. His body was whole, but his mind was fragmented, spinning.

A burst of light glimmered to his left, brilliant against the dark. Something hissed as the light expanded, and Rone thought he heard the flapping of wings. A hawk? A monster?

Monsters . . .

Carefully, Rone stood, his legs shaky, muscles exhausted. He squinted at the bright light and moved toward it. Not just light, but a mass of flame. Orange, red, and white. Shaped oddly. He moved closer. It remained stationary. There was something weirdly familiar about it. As he neared, the shape of the white became clearer. It was a giant ring. A wreath, or a halo.

Rone's lips parted. His feet picked up speed. *It can't be.*

But it was. He came closer, closer, until the body around the flames took shape. Fire danced around hooves of dark bronze and tarnished silver. The flames highlighted four separate horns and reflected off black darker even than the expanse above him.

Rone stopped four paces away, rolling heat warming him. "Ireth?"

The fire horse lifted its head. *Hello, Rone. You are unexpected.*

The voice. It was the same.

And Rone knew exactly where he was.

Chapter 12

Sandis awoke with a start, the lamplight around her brilliant and sharp. Her mouth, throat, and eyes were dry as ash, and her bones sang with the memory of utter agony.

She sat up anyway, brain sloshing inside her skull. Bastien, beside her, shouted, "She's awake!" His voice drummed in her ears. He moved to the door of the room—the bedroom—and bellowed, "Jachim! She's awake!"

He returned and poured her water in a crystal glass, an extravagance that struck her as ridiculous. Clutching it in her hands, Sandis croaked, "Rone?"

Bastien shook his head. Sandis would have wept had her body not been so parched.

She sipped at the water, forcing it over dry and rising sobs. She was halfway through the glass when Jachim and Triumvir Peterus pushed their way into the room.

"You fool woman," the latter said. "We are in times of peril! You cannot just—"

"Please," Bastien interrupted. "She's sick."

Sandis couldn't bring herself to utter an apology. She hugged herself with one arm, only then noticing she didn't wear her dress, but a shirt—Rone's shirt. It still smelled like him. Her chest ached like it was collapsing in on itself.

"Where is he?" she asked.

Jachim pushed in front of Triumvir Peterus, causing him to throw up his hands in silent protest. "I . . . I think my theory is right. At least, I don't have another hypothesis to go on. You see"—he opened the book in his arms and pulled out a copy of one of the tablets—"there are a large number of numina, which leads me to believe the ethereal plane must also be quite large. Even if Rone remained rooted to the spot after porting over there . . . I don't know how he'd know when the portal would reappear, if it even does. He wouldn't know where it would be, or when to jump—"

"What do you mean, 'if it even does'?" Sandis rasped. She forced her grip on the glass to lighten, lest she crush it in her hands.

Jachim pressed his lips together until they turned white. Turning the etching toward her, he said, "This one was the hardest to interpret. I didn't understand before." He pointed to a rounded, fat symbol. "This is portal. Doorway. I want to say this means the ethereal plane"—he pointed to another symbol—"but I have no context for it. And this. This isn't a Noscon symbol, just a picture."

His index finger tapped on an arrow with an X drawn on its flat side.

Sandis tried to swallow, and sipped water to relieve the struggle. "What does it mean?"

Jachim sighed. "My best guess is that the portal only works one way. Sandis . . . Rone might be trapped. Indefinitely."

Sandis dropped the glass onto the blankets, the water seeping through.

Sandis sat on the balcony outside the room she, Rone, and Bastien shared—had shared—as the dawn bloomed. She pressed her face against the painted iron bars and looked out over the city. Smoke puffed up from two different factories in the smoke ring. The triumvirs really were forcing people to continue working. She'd overheard Triumvir Peterus talking about a rebellion in District Three. He'd ordered Chief Esgar to double the police presence there.

Sandis didn't know which was better: letting the people give in to their fear and run to safety or keeping the city and its resources operating for as long as possible.

At least everyone would be safe during the day, while Kolosos, and her brother, slumbered.

She knew the bars were leaving dents across her forehead, but she couldn't bring herself to straighten. Fatigue clawed at her, but she couldn't sleep. Her stomach rumbled, yet she couldn't eat. Rone was gone. It was her fault. And she had no idea if a mortal could even survive in the ethereal plane, let alone how to get him back.

Ireth had not attempted to communicate with her.

She blinked to keep her sore eyes dry. *If I hadn't gone behind his back, this wouldn't have happened.*

And now they would have no amarinth, because Sandis would not chance abandoning Rone. *Come back, Rone. Please. Come back.*

Nothing answered her. Yet she could not accept that he was truly gone. If only Ireth could speak to her. If only she could figure out how to decipher his language—

She sighed. Sighed, because she couldn't cry anymore.

He's not dead. I'd feel it if he were dead.

Wouldn't she?

Time ticked away, though the bell towers refused to ring. Kolosos would come again. Then what would they do?

"Sandis?" Bastien's timid voice sounded behind her. She hadn't heard the window open.

"Hm?"

He stepped beside her, folding his legs under him as if they were starting another session of meditation. Perhaps that's what Sandis needed. A moment to clear her head, to reconnect to the ethereal plane. Maybe, even, she would be able to communicate with Rone. Doubtful, but she should try.

Bastien gingerly touched her shoulder.

Sandis finally sat up, wincing when her skin pulled free of the iron. She rubbed the prints it left in her forehead.

"You need to sleep."

Sandis shook her head. "I slept after the summoning."

"Not true sleep," Bastien insisted. "Your body needs rest."

She sighed. She would be of no use if she withered away, like her mother had after her father died. "I will. I'll find something to eat and—"

Bastien handed her a roll.

A small smile touched her lips as she accepted it. "Thank you."

"I thought it'd be breader than nothing."

The smile stuck, and Sandis shook her head. "That was terrible."

"It's the best I could come up with on short notice." He looked out over the city, his mirth fading as quickly as it had come.

Sandis sighed. She took a nibble of her bread, chewed it until it was too soft, and swallowed. Took another, staring out at the city. Trying to guess which factories were in operation, and how many more smokestacks would be sputtering by noon.

"They're all . . . talking." Bastien tugged at a loose thread on his shirt. "The triumvirate. Oz, the priests, the chief, the general."

She nodded and took another bite.

"Sandis, while we wait . . . can you do me a favor?"

She studied his self-conscious expression. "Whatever you need, Bastien."

The crinkles in his forehead relaxed. "C-Could you teach me how to read? I know it'll take a long time, but I have to start somewhere . . ."

The simple request was unexpected. "Of course."

Bastien drew in a deep breath. "I know a lot of the letters. I mean, I see them everywhere. But . . . I don't know how to put them together. I feel useless."

"You're not useless, Bastien."

"Not in some ways," he agreed, staring at his feet. "I know a little bit about Noscon symbols. Jachim liked that. But I couldn't read any of his notes. I couldn't *help*. And sometimes . . ." He paused, biting the inside of his lip.

"Sometimes?"

"Sometimes . . . I-I want to say something to them, you know? The triumvirs. But I want to be right first. I mean, I want to know the histories better, and I can't even read them."

Know them better, Sandis thought. Would that help her, too?

Taking his hand in hers, Sandis stood—her hips protesting—and pulled Bastien up beside her. This was a blessing, really. Something useful she could do that would help her keep her mind off Rone and Kazen.

"There's paper in the library down the hallway." Sandis led him back inside. "Find that, and something to write with. I'll meet you in the library in just a bit. I need . . . I need to talk to someone first."

Bastien smiled. "Thank you, Sandis. You're a good friend, to the letter."

Sandis let out a single, stale chuckle, but it made her feel a little lighter. She followed Bastien out into the hallway, but when he turned for the library, she descended the stairs to the study.

If anyone slept less than she did, it was Jachim Franz.

He was in the exact same chair she'd found him in before the first failed summoning, though a plate smeared with the remnants of food rested beside him. His left hand was stained with ink, and so was part of his chin—he must have left the smudge without realizing it. His eyes were alert, but his lids were heavy.

"Jachim?"

He startled, then examined his writing, perhaps to ensure he hadn't scribbled out anything important in his jolt. "Sandis! Yes." He rubbed his eyes under his glasses. "How can I help you?"

Stepping into the room, she closed the door behind her, then chose a seat to Jachim's right. "You're well versed in everything Noscon. Does that include the history of summoning among the Kolins?"

The scholar set down his pen. "Well, yes. That's how it all started, really. One day you're sitting in history class, and the next you're fascinated by a bizarre, impossible magic in the country up north . . . that is, that's the reason I came here. Your history is much more fascinating than Ysben's. Ours is literally centuries of people sitting around a table, talking about politics, and never doing anything exciting. There was a naval battle once. But everyone studies that, and I'll admit I'm scared of the ocean." He shrugged. "Sharks and the like."

Sandis smiled. "Would you tell me how the occult came to be?" Reaching back, she touched the skin just above her highest brand, where Ireth's name was inked into her skin. "I want to understand." If she knew more, maybe, *maybe*, it would help her bring Rone back.

Jachim pushed out his chair and stretched his spine. "I could talk about it all day—"

"The basics will be fine, to start." Bastien was waiting for her.

Jachim rubbed his chin, smearing a little more ink across it. "Well, it started with the discovery of the Yokhosho Temple. The original discovery, not the scholarly one."

"What do you mean?"

"I mean a group of Kolin settlers, fairly early in your history on this continent, found it and kept it secret for a couple decades. They don't teach you this in school?"

Sandis flushed. She'd never gone to a formal school. She shook her head.

Jachim shrugged. "Celesian superstition, I suppose. But yes, some second-generation Kolins found the ruins of the Yokhosho Temple, a place where the Noscons used to worship. I wonder now if any of the carvings there spoke of the amarinth, but there's no way of knowing. The temple was destroyed long before Kolosos ever became a problem. That's why these tablets are such a remarkable discovery." He ran his hand over them reverently. "But they did manage to translate some of what they found. There may have been illustrations in the stone; we can't be sure now. That's where they first learned about Noscon magic. And that's where the experiments began."

Sandis leaned back, a shiver coursing through her. "Experiments?"

"They formed a bizarre cult. If only we knew precisely what they'd read! What artifacts they'd discovered. Perhaps they translated something wrong." Sandis grew sick, but Jachim only became more animated. "Thinking of it now, perhaps there was a connection between their cult and the creation of the amarinth. We have records of their work with twins. They performed ritual sacrifices with magic now lost to us. I now believe those rituals were to shoot a spirit into the ethereal plane. Not too dissimilar from what happened with Rone, though his body went in as well. At the time, I thought the stories mythical, but . . ."

Sandis knitted her hands together. Perhaps she shouldn't have asked, but Jachim didn't notice her discomfort, and she couldn't bring herself to stop him.

Jachim shrugged. "I'm not sure where it went from there. Their dark practices were only stopped when one of their own reported them to the authorities. The Celesians lost their minds and 'cleansed' all of it, destroying *millennia* of history in their 'quest for righteousness.'" He scoffed. "If they had stayed their hands, if that place had been preserved . . . we might not be in the predicament we're in today. But it is what it is." He glanced at her. "But it started there, at the temple. Most of the cult was executed, but not all of them. They continued to practice their magic in hiding, turning it into what it is today. I'm sorry I don't know more."

Sandis swallowed against a tight throat. *Then it* is *evil.* She tried to imagine ritual sacrifices involving siblings, but her mind shied away from the thought. It could only handle so much brutality in so short a time.

"Thank you," she muttered, pushing back from the table and finding her feet. Her stomach felt like a raisin. "I'll . . . leave you to your work."

Jachim nodded, happily returning to his notes.

On her way to the library, Sandis bit the side of her cheek. *Ireth, you're good, aren't you?*

The fire horse didn't respond.

⬩⬩⬩

Rone studied the enormous horse's face. The fire whisked off its charcoal skin as if in a breeze, yet the air was still. Everything about this dark, geometric place was inert, except for the monsters.

The *numina.*

So many questions blurred together in his head. He stood there like a puppet with a cut string, trying to process everything. Trying to orient himself.

The first question left his mouth with little thought. "You can speak to me?"

Ireth nodded his head, an oddly human gesture. *In this place only, I can. Apparently. Forgive me for the delay. I was called.*

Called? Summoned. By Sandis. His gut sank. "She's alive?"

The horse nodded, and relief nearly made Rone lose his footing. He gave himself a second to breathe, to right himself, before turning around and taking in the expanse of nothingness around them. "Apparently? You haven't spoken before?"

You are the first with mortal flesh to come here. I did not know it was possible.

"Here. The ethereal plane."

Another nod.

Rone whistled; the sound was loud in the silence. "And that was a numen chasing me."

Ireth stepped back, short flames stemming up from his large cloven hooves. He looked upward, toward the blocky cliff Rone had fallen from. It was the silhouette of a perfect rectangle. Only then did Rone realize his sight had improved. The deep blue of the strange sky overhead was lifting. Dawn?

Where was Sandis?

Most have lost their minds. Ireth's voice brushed over Rone's like a wet feather, strange and foreign. It didn't touch his ears, yet he could *hear* it. It was a man's voice, old and slightly weathered, with a hint of an accent he couldn't place. But the words were entirely Kolin. *Some still remember.*

"Where is Sandis?"

Ireth hoofed the ground, and the fading stars beneath them split to reveal Dresberg. Rone gasped, stepping back as though he might fall through the vision that crept outward like spilled oil, but the ground remained solid. The city rose up toward them so quickly Rone stumbled, nausea threatening to empty his stomach.

She is here. She is safe. There was a touch of familiarity, close to adoration, to the words.

Once Rone got control of his body, he looked. Their perspective hovered right over her. She sat in the triumvir's library beside Bastien, scrawling out the alphabet on a piece of paper illuminated by a candle.

Reaching forward, Rone tried to touch her, but the strange glass encasing this place blocked him.

"Sandis?" he asked. She didn't react.

He is a good seed, Ireth said, referring to Bastien. *But unable to listen.*

"You talk to her sometimes." He focused on one of the horse's pitch-colored eyes. "Sandis. She feels you. Can you do that now? Can you tell her where I am?"

Ireth snorted. *Not yet. It is difficult.*

"Difficult *how?*"

Ireth looked at him with an almost human expression. One that reminded Rone it might be a bad idea to piss off his only ally in this place. Especially since that ally could incinerate him in seconds.

I can push the boundaries of this plane. Only with Sandis, he explained, ever patient. *But not often, and not for long. It drains me, spiritually. And when I am drained, the boundaries resist. I have not yet recovered enough to try again. But I cannot* speak *to her. I can only send her impressions, and hope she understands. As far as I know, there is only one other who can do the same.*

Rone stood, studying the numen's long face. "Who?"

Hepingya.

Rone hadn't heard that name from either Sandis or Bastien. "And where is he?" She? It?

Hepingya is reclusive.

Rone breathed slowly, deeply. "Can *I* do it?"

Perhaps. Ireth back-stepped, and the vision of Sandis vanished into the brightening sky.

"Wait! I have to try—"

Rone.

He paused, waiting.

You must try, yes. But not with her. You are mortal and, as such, have a natural connection to the mortal realm. You must try to bend that boundary and reach down to your world, but not for her.

Ireth took a few long strides to the left and hoofed the ground once more, revealing a small lake down below. Rone could have sworn he had passed something that looked just like it on the way to the Fortitude Mountains with his mother.

You must reach that.

"A lake? Why?"

Because if you are unable to reach it, you will die.

Despite the heat emanating from the fire horse, a chill coursed up Rone's body. "What?"

You are mortal.

"Yes, I got that part."

There is no sustenance in the ethereal plane.

The chill looped around when it reached his skull and tingled down to his feet. "No food. No water."

Another nod.

His heart beat too quickly. He swallowed against a dry throat, suddenly thirsty now that he knew there was nothing to drink. Clearing his throat, he said, "Tell me how to do it."

You must look down. Keep the destination in your mind.

Rone knelt and stared at the lake so far below him. "How am I supposed to reach it?"

The distance you see is not true. The ethereal plane is not stationary; it is everywhere. It is where you need it to be.

Which explained how he could see all of Dresberg in one moment and then Sandis in the library at another. He . . . sort of understood, but it made his mind hurt. The ground was solid beneath him, wasn't it? So how could it be everywhere, untouchable by those in the mortal plane?

Ireth didn't give him time to think it through. *Push out with your spirit.*

Spirit. Right. He'd listened to his father's sermons. He'd watched Sandis meditate. Even Kurtz had drilled spiritual nonsense into him. He got the gist of it. Closing his eyes, he pictured the distance between himself and the lake vanishing. Pictured his spirit.

Desire it. Strongly. Reach for it.

Rone did. Eyes still closed, he reached down and pressed his hands into the cold glass. It didn't warm beneath his touch, like real glass would. But he tried not to dwell on that. *Water. Water. Water.*

The glass bent, almost like he'd pushed his hands into putty. The movement startled him, but he kept his mind focused, his eyes closed. *Water. Water. Water.*

He reached deeper, deeper, until he felt wetness around his fingers. This time, he could not ignore his shock. His eyes shot open. He was at the lake, and water seeped up through the bowl he'd formed in the glass. Filling it up to his knuckles, his wrists, his—

It stopped, and the glass surface snapped back into place, leaving a puddle against its smooth surface.

He thought he heard Ireth sigh. *I am glad. You have a physical body and are able to touch the other world, influence it. Drink.*

He bent down to drink, only then noticing the numbness in his fingers, toes, and nose. His thoughts and senses were so sluggish—

Drink, Rone. The spiritual fatigue will fade in time. But for now, you must drink.

Clinging to that one simple direction, Rone bent down and drank, not entirely understanding why.

Chapter 13

Oh yes, there was fire in the boy's eyes. Even in the dark of night, Kazen could see it. So familiar. Sandis had once looked at him like that, long ago. Before he'd trained her to do better.

It was no matter now. If the lad wouldn't spin the amarinth, Kazen would do it for him. He forced Anon's fingers around the amarinth and spun it, savoring the soft, crooning whirl of its golden loops. Almost like a lullaby.

"*Vre en nestu a carnath. Ii mem entre I amar. Vre en nestu a carnath. Kolosos epsi gradenid.*"

His monster grew inside the mortal body, Kazen taking hold of its fiery horn as the beast's great body unfurled, shooting up, up, up in the city, pressed against the north end of the wall.

Forward, Kazen beckoned.

The numen resisted.

"Forward, damn you." Kazen pressed a finger into the bruise inside his elbow, where Anon Gwenwig's fresh blood flowed through his veins.

A deep growl sounded within Kolosos's red throat. Its body trembled.

Kazen scowled. "You cannot fight me, Kolosos. Our work is not yet finished. *Move.*"

Kolosos took one step, then stopped, resisting.

Chapter 14

Kazen's monster was punctual.

Sandis stepped close to Bastien, their sides touching, when red light highlighted smoky clouds far to the north. She couldn't see the monster, thanks to the numerous buildings separating it from the rubble of the cathedral it had destroyed, but Kolosos's light was unmistakable—just like the shudder that ran through the earth and the inhuman roar carried on the wind.

General Istrude had chosen to take their stand in the ashes of the cathedral. Chief Esgar had suggested hiding within Gerech Prison's fortified walls, but Istrude's plan had won out. Triumvir Var didn't want to draw Kazen's attention to what he considered one of Kolingrad's greatest resources, so their battalion had instead congregated on the ruins of a building already destroyed.

Sandis was fine with staying away from the prison that had always haunted her. The place she would have ended up if the government had found her *before* they needed her. The place that had nearly driven Rone mad. The place that might still hold her great-uncle captive, if it had not yet already killed him.

Soldiers in steel blue clustered together ahead of her, waiting for a signal, a strike . . . Sandis didn't know what was planned. General Istrude didn't invite the vessels to his war meetings.

In the distance, the demon's red light brightened.

"Wh-What's north?" Bastien asked, eyes locked on the sky. His teeth chattered, but from cold or from fear, Sandis wasn't sure. Maybe both.

What *was* north? What did Kazen want to destroy this time? The homes of priests? The wall itself?

General Istrude, mounted on a horse Sandis swore could challenge Ireth in size, rode in front of his men. "Lieutenant Martal, your men with me." He turned to Oz, who lingered several feet away, standing beside Teppa and Inda. He looked haggard, older than before. Kazen, too, hated losing his vessels, but he saw them merely as assets. Oz behaved as though he'd lost family.

Family. The word hardened in her chest, hurting her. She thought of Rone. Tried not to think of him. *Celestial, anyone, please, please protect him.*

He wasn't dead. He couldn't be.

"Are you ready?" Triumvir Var asked, and Sandis felt as if she'd caught Bastien's shivers. Kazen had used her as a weapon to frighten his enemies, but now she would be an actual soldier. Under Oz's direction.

She didn't like the thought of someone else controlling her. Didn't like the bruise on the inside of her arm, where Oz had taken her blood—along with Bastien's—earlier. She didn't know Oz. Didn't trust him. Bastien said he'd been a good master, but he'd been a master all the same. Sandis hadn't been used like that for so long . . . her stomach clenched at the thought of bowing under Oz's hand and disappearing until afternoon. If she came back at all. But Ireth was more useful in a separate summoner's hands. Sandis, by herself, could only hold on to the fiery numen for mere seconds.

She glanced back to that red light. It hadn't moved. The ground, too, remained still.

"I'm ready," Oz said, catching Sandis's eye. He gestured to the carriage pulled by a team of six horses—another extravagance of the triumvirs. It would give them the speed they needed, so long as the roads held up. Many had been crushed or buckled by Kolosos's trampling.

Taking Bastien's clammy hand in hers, Sandis pulled him toward the carriage as General Istrude's small cavalry headed north. Each step was a struggle. She wanted to fight Kolosos. Truly, she did. But if they won . . . didn't that mean Anon would die?

Her fingers grew cold at the idea. Could she stop Kazen and also save her brother?

Inda entered the carriage first, followed by Teppa and Bastien. Eyeing her, Oz slipped in. Sandis moved to follow, and—

Warm pressure filled her head and shoulders, strong enough that she gasped. *Ireth.* He was hale, he was *present*, he was—

A strong impression pushed through their connection. One Sandis had never felt from him before. *Safe.* It was clearer than Ireth's usual messages, almost like he stood behind her, breathing into her hair. *Safe.*

Then, all at once, the warmth and the impression faded, winking out like a dying star.

"Sandis, hurry," Oz said.

She blinked. Touched her heart. Turned that word over in her mind. She wasn't safe at all. None of them were. Why would Ireth—

Warmth of her own bloomed in her chest. *Rone.* The moment she thought it, she knew. *Rone* was safe. He and Ireth were in the same place. Did Ireth watch over him? Tears sprang to her eyes. She could have laughed. *Thank you, Ireth.*

"Sir."

Sandis turned, spying a scout jogging up to Triumvir Var. Several had been stationed atop buildings throughout the city. Sandis stepped away from the carriage, trying to listen.

"—stagnant, sir. It's just . . . not moving."

Kolosos?

"Sandis!"

She whipped her head back toward the carriage. Oz didn't need to explain; Kolosos only existed for a short amount of time each night, and Celestial knew what kind of destruction Kazen had planned for tonight. Sandis hurried into the carriage, which took off before she even closed the door behind her.

The horses sped into a gallop, and the dark city passed in blurred shadows.

"He's employed Kuracean to keep back soldiers." Oz spoke as though in the middle of a conversation, and Sandis realized she may have already missed something. Not that it mattered; Oz would make her and Ireth do whatever he pleased. "If there's no clear shot for Kolosos, I'll aim for Kuracean. It has a soft spot under its neck. It looks up, it's done for."

Sandis stiffened. She had sat right beside Oz on the carriage bench, their hips touching. Now she moved as close to the shaking carriage wall as she could, craving distance. Bastien sat across from her, his eyes wide. His thoughts must have matched her own.

Rist.

"B-But Mas—Oz, that will kill the vessel." Bastien was barely audible over the thunder of horse hooves and spinning wheels.

Oz's dark eyes narrowed. "We've all had to make sacrifices."

Jansen, he meant. But was that really *Oz's* sacrifice? Did he know the meaning of the word?

Rist hasn't volunteered for any of this. Ultimately, none of them had.

Sandis closed her eyes, listening to the cacophony of sound as the carriage dashed closer and closer to Kolosos's light. They took a turn, and Sandis slammed into the carriage wall. Anon. Rist. How many more people would be crushed in their pursuit of Kazen? What would Rone do in her place?

Save him.

Sandis's eyes opened. She stared at Bastien's pale face. Right now, Anon was beyond her grasp, but Rist . . .

She could save Rist, couldn't she? Didn't she owe him to try, after Kaili . . .

She winced and hugged herself, her dark hair flowing forward and catching on her eyelashes. Rist had already lost his brother *and* his love. He shouldn't have to lose his life, too.

Sliding her foot across the narrow carriage floor, Sandis pressed it against Bastien's toe, urging him to meet her eyes. She stared at him, hard, begging him to read her expression. Some of his blood still remained under her skin. Together, they could save Rist and take back Kuracean. Then strike back at Kolosos tomorrow night.

She couldn't do it without him.

Bastien's light brows drew together as he studied her face. He didn't speak, didn't nod, but his lips pressed into a thin white line, and Sandis knew he'd support her.

The air in the carriage grew hot, and the dark city lightened. Multiple horses whinnied, and the carriage came to an abrupt halt.

"Out! Move!" Oz shouted.

Sandis threw open the door and leapt out, Bastien right after her. Red and orange light glowed hot and deadly between stacks of flats to her right.

She ran.

She aimed for the shadows ahead of her, relieved when she heard another set of footsteps following—Bastien. Almost immediately Oz shouted after them to stop, but Sandis ran until her lungs hurt. Turned a corner and stepped into a pile of trash overflowing from a garbage bin.

A moment later, Bastien stumbled through the garbage, wheezing. He bent over and put his hands on his knees, then recoiled as the smell of refuse assaulted him.

"We find Kuracean first," Sandis said. She didn't have her rifle— Triumvir Var had made her leave it behind, as a numen had no need for firearms. She regretted her obedience. "Mahk is too large to fit through these roads."

"And if we don't?" Bastien huffed. "Find him? We need to go back to Oz so he can fight."

Sandis gritted her teeth. She didn't truly believe four numen, even if two of them were Ireth and Mahk, could defeat Kolosos. Its power was too great. She'd felt it in her veins, seen it in her nightmares.

Even so, she knew part of her hesitance was because of Anon. Because she wanted to save her brother. Given the choice, could she kill him to save the rest?

She didn't want to consider the answer, so she nodded her agreement. Kuracean first, and barring that, she would submit to Oz.

"Let's go." She took Bastien's hand, in part to lend him courage, in part to help him keep pace.

They ran toward the light.

Its brilliance and heat were nearly overpowering. An explosion sounded nearby—a cannon? Sandis rounded a bend, seeing silhouettes of the gathered soldiers. Gunfire exploded. Kuracean was not here, else the enormous crustacean would be picking them off like weeds.

"This way," Sandis urged, pulling Bastien past the soldiers and behind another building. A wail drew her attention to a trash heap and a young girl half-buried in it, tears streaming down her face.

Sandis cursed and released Bastien, running for the child.

"Get up, get up!" Sandis urged, grabbing her shoulders and hauling her from the garbage. She couldn't be more than eight years old. Dragging her back to the road, Sandis said, "The soldiers will keep the monster at bay, but you must run as fast as you can, until you can't run anymore."

The girl cried, "My father . . ." She raised a quivering finger and pointed toward the red light.

The words were like a spear through Sandis's middle.

"The police are in the other direction," she said, not sure if she spoke the truth or not. "Run away from here until you find a grown-up. They'll help you. Go. *Now!*"

The girl took off down the cobblestones on bare feet, not once looking back.

Still no earthquakes, falling rubble, roars. *"Stagnant,"* the scout had said. Why wasn't Kolosos moving? Was Kazen making some sort of stand?

Sandis darted back the way she'd come, Bastien a step behind her, and then hastened down an alleyway barely wide enough to fit them both. They climbed over a short fence near its end, and she caught a glimpse of a hoof. Kolosos faced south, toward the soldiers. Another cannon fired, but still the beast didn't move.

Why? And where was Rist?

Hunching, Sandis crept closer to the monster, the temperature rising with every step until sweat stung her eyes. The monstrosity towered above her, six stories tall, black and red and every bit a monster. It leaned forward, as if straining against invisible chains.

"What—?" Bastien asked. Sandis grabbed his arm, watching. Confused.

Seconds later, Kolosos lunged forward, as though those invisible chains had broken. Sandis nearly dropped to her knees as the ground bucked under the numen's footsteps, and shouts from the nearby soldiers spiraled through the city. A scream wove between them.

In one swoop, the numen's lava-dripping hand crossed its body and snatched a black form from its head. Its summoner. Kazen.

And crushed him.

Chapter 15

Sandis felt as though *she* were the one in Kolosos's curled fingers.

Bastien gripped her arm, his short nails digging into her flesh as he slumped against her, ready to be sick. But Sandis didn't look away. Her eyes were fixed on that closed hand, the slits marking red knuckles. It couldn't be. Kazen was always so precise, so smart. He'd never summon without Anon's blood in his veins. He'd never—

Kolosos opened its hand, and ash tumbled from its palm. It was all that was left of Kazen. Her master and tormentor. Her kidnapper and abuser. The man who had imprisoned her and her friends. Killed people she loved. Chased her across the city and back. The man who had been so ready to sacrifice her to the beast that stood before her now. The man who had always been one step ahead of her. Always.

And yet watching his charred remains catch on the wind did nothing to heal her.

Because Kolosos had done that *against Kazen's will.* Sandis didn't understand how, but she knew what it meant. The numen was even stronger than she'd feared, and it no longer had a leash.

Kolosos couldn't—shouldn't—come into the world without a summoner, and yet Sandis felt in her bones that something about that knowledge was incomplete.

Something was very, *very* wrong.

A bellow screamed far to Sandis's left—a scream she recognized. A *numen's* scream. *Kuracean.* He was rampant now, too, without a summoner to control him. He was a free numen inside a mortal body.

Another cannon fired, shaking the buildings around them. Sandis glimpsed one of Oz's numina, a frogish, plantlike thing with cricket legs—just as Kolosos's smoking, bull-like head turned and focused on the army. Something feral yet *intelligent* flashed in its eyes.

"B-Bastien." Sandis's voice was little more than a hiss of steam. "Bastien, we have to get to—"

Kuracean came out from behind Kolosos's brilliant light, running on four legs hooked like talons. Two massive, hardened arms stretched from its narrow body, ending in armored claws, the right twice the size of the left. Its turtle-like head was dry and peeling, its eyes wild and glassy. Kuracean's beak dripped crimson. It had already found a victim.

The whole city shook with Kolosos's footsteps as it advanced on the army, the creature still bent on its mission of destruction.

"Now," Bastien said beside her, pulling her focus from the two numina. "Now, Sandis!"

Gritting her teeth, Sandis pushed her hand into Bastien's hair.

And summoned Mahk.

The enormous, whalelike creature nearly knocked Sandis over as its body ripped from a flash of light. Its long tail shot down the alleyway, breaking the fence they'd just climbed and tearing brick from the close walls. Its body blocked the red light of Kolosos, and wet air puffed from a blowhole easily the size of the six-horse carriage. It opened its mouth in a yawn Sandis could have walked into without ducking.

Mahk was easily twice the size of Kuracean, who bellowed in protest at the arrival of a new opponent. The whale's amber eyes turned to Sandis, expectant.

Sandis had no idea the scope of this beast's power. *Stop him,* she pleaded.

Mahk lunged forward. At the same time, Kolosos's knee knocked down the top half of a building.

The numen was swift for its size, and its rounded head collided into Kuracean, knocking the creature onto its back. Kuracean tried to grab Mahk in its nasty pincers, but Mahk's skin was so taut and smooth it couldn't get a grip.

"Don't kill him!" Sandis cried, running after the beast. "Pin him down. Pin him down!"

Mahk slammed onto Kuracean. Sandis thought she heard the latter's armor crack, but it might also have been the cobblestones splintering beneath them. Kuracean writhed, managing to get a hold on the edge of Mahk's lip. The whale sang in pain.

Sorry, Bastien. Sandis ran, sweating, around the numina, toward Kuracean's head. She touched the hardness of it, drawing the numen's attention to herself. Kuracean bucked, sending her onto her backside. *Tighter, Mahk!*

Mahk lifted its tail, sending more of its weight onto the other numen.

She couldn't afford to wait until Rist ran out of strength and Kuracean dismissed itself. Touching the shelled beast just above its left eye, Sandis said, *"Parte Kuracean en dragu bai!"*

Mahk, release him!

The whale floated back as Kuracean's entire body shivered and shrunk, leaving a pale, naked man on the broken cobbles. Gray hairs entwined with his dark ones. He'd been used for summoning too often. Just like her brother.

She winced as an explosion sounded behind her, the breath-stealing heat of it slamming into her like a wall. Throwing herself over Rist, she closed her eyes as bits of shrapnel assailed her skin and dress. Heat burned her. The onslaught ended, and she coughed for the smoke spilling into the air.

"Mahk," she wheezed, "help me move—"

She blinked tears and colorful splotches from her vision. Stared at the whale in wonder.

It was hovering about a foot above the ground.

She gaped. Swallowed. "You can fly."

Mahk regarded her before passing an unsure glance in Kolosos's direction. It was farther away now. Cannons no longer pierced the air, only the occasional scream.

Kolosos was destroying Dresberg's small army, even without Kazen's guidance.

"Come now. Use your fin to get him onto your back."

Mahk floated closer and turned, sliding the edge of a feathered fin beneath Rist. It lifted its fin and rolled a bit until the nude man lay prone, sideways, across its back, right where the body narrowed to form a tail.

Before she could climb up beside him, an idea struck her. Mahk was a whale—surely that meant its abilities were related to water. "Mahk, can you *make* water?" she asked.

The great beast didn't answer, of course.

"Wet the cobblestones. Just a little."

A tiny stream passed through Mahk's lips and puddled on the broken road.

Sandis grinned—"We can work with that."—and scrambled onto the whale's back, careful not to slide into its enormous blowhole. *Fly, Mahk. Toward Kolosos.* They had to stop its destruction. If Mahk could cool the demon enough, Sandis could touch it and bring back her brother, just as she had Rist. The hope that surged through her hurt.

Mahk beat its tail and rose into the air, ten feet, fifty, one hundred. It turned toward Kolosos. Hesitated. Sandis felt the numen's resistance in her veins. Was this how Kazen had felt before Kolosos broke its bond?

Only enough to distract it. I won't let you die. Go!

Sandis envisioned the whale surging forward, and it did so. The distance between them and Kolosos shrunk too quickly. Holding invisible reins, Sandis jerked the whale back, sending it skyward. She grabbed Rist's bicep with one hand, ensuring he stayed put.

Soak him, as much as you can!

Mahk moaned, a note that started high and shifted low and deep, rattling Sandis's legs. Then, opening its great maw, Mahk shot a geyser of briny water into Kolosos's shoulder, where it connected with a massive, clawlike wing.

She tried to rush in, but the steam blinded Sandis and scalded her skin. She beckoned Mahk to retreat just before a glowing red appendage zipped through the cloud.

Kolosos's hand.

"Go!" she screamed, and Mahk sailed northward, narrowly missing the lava monster's claws. Clearing the steam, Sandis saw a large patch of Kolosos had turned entirely black, cooled by Mahk's blast.

This was her chance.

"Come around!" she cried. "Do it again!" If she hit the same spot, the steam wouldn't be unbearable. If she could just reach it—

But she felt the answer in her connection as summoner. Mahk had no more water to give. Either the air was too dry or the numen's ability too weak.

Sandis's hope shattered as red veins slowly crossed over the blackened shoulder, turning it half-molten once more. *No.*

But Kolosos's time was nearly out, wasn't it? Up here, on Mahk, she could follow the beast and retrieve Anon when it vanished into the ethereal plane. She still had a chance!

Her arm strained as Rist's body began to slide. She didn't want to endanger him, but she might not get another chance to save her brother! Heaving the unconscious man back up, she gripped him hard and beckoned for Mahk to retreat a short ways. She only needed to wait a moment before her theory was proven correct; Kolosos turned abruptly northward, running for the wall.

Follow him!

She nearly lost hold of Rist as the whale shot forward, thick tail pumping through the smoky air. Her arms and fingers ached from securing Rist's weight, but she tried to ignore the pain. *Focus on Kolosos.* It would be worth the soreness in the morning if she could just—

The bull-headed monster reared around as Sandis neared, its fingernail-like wings cracking as they opened. A bright orb glowed in its hand. Liquid fire.

Jansen flashed through Sandis's thoughts.

Kolosos threw the orb straight at Mahk.

"Flee!" she cried, grabbing Rist under the arms. The whale spun and bolted, but not before the bullet of lava struck its side.

Mahk let out a long, low cry as it began to fall.

"Bastien!" Sandis cried. She and Rist became weightless. Hugging the man to her side with one arm, she lay flat against Mahk's back, gripping it with the other arm and both legs. "Bastien, please! You have to fly!" *If we crash, we all die!*

Mahk whined a high and forlorn note. Its body bucked, and it slowed its fall before shuddering and dropping to the ground. Sandis lost her grip with the impact; both she and Rist slid onto one of the numen's reedy fins and rolled to the ground.

Finding her equilibrium, Sandis stood and ran around the great beast, peering back the way they'd come. Kolosos was gone, the remaining soldiers running down the ruined street where it had fled.

Anon, forgive me. A sick feeling filled her from collar to hip.

When she turned back, two naked men lay on the street before her, one badly burnt.

Nothing. He could do *nothing* but sit in this dark, strange place and watch as Sandis took impossible risks and turned Bastien into an enormous whale beast. A glimpse here, a glimpse there, sometimes whole minutes of her running through the burning city without a single care for her safety. And he couldn't speak to her. Couldn't even try, else he'd starve.

Earlier, he'd snatched a loaf of bread from a town called Ieva, northwest of Dresberg. While some of the capital still functioned, it was easier to find food away from the destruction. Ireth, somehow, had the ability to access any location in the mortal world. Sometimes, their perspective was so close to the ground that he felt as though he stood among the men they watched. They'd found a bakery in Ieva, and despite the owner being present, Rone had managed to push through the plane just long enough to snatch a loaf.

The strain of that faint brush with the mortal world had left him dazed for hours.

She is safe, Ireth's voice fluttered through Rone's mind. *Mahk is a strong numen.*

"But not strong enough," Rone said, glancing at the half-eaten loaf of bread beside the glassy block where he'd perched. He had no appetite for it. "Is that why you wanted him bonded to Bastien? Because he's strong?" He didn't know what had become of the whale; Ireth's vision had followed Kolosos as the great numen threw fireballs at the army and bounded over the city wall.

The star-spotted world around them trembled. Ireth stretched his long neck up, looking skyward—or indigo-ward—listening. *Kolosos has returned.*

Rone chewed the inside of his cheek. Ireth didn't sound confident. Rone had cheered upon Kazen's demise, but the fire horse had merely watched on, unmoving. *"Kaj's magic is strong"* was all he'd said—enough to cut Rone's celebration short. He didn't understand the occult, but Ireth did. If the fire horse was worried, so was he.

They'd spent most of the last day walking through nothingness, not even passing another numen, to a spot Ireth thought would be safe from Kolosos. It looked like everywhere else to Rone.

Ireth's coal eyes glanced back to Rone. Flames flicked around his ears and horns. *As for your question, Mahk is an ally. He remembers a little. Not as much as I do, but he is not lost like many.*

"You mentioned that before." Rone set his elbows on his knees and picked at a loose stitch on the cuff of his jacket. He didn't need the extra clothing—this place was neither warm nor cold, unless he got too close to Ireth. "Remembers. Remembers what?"

Who we once were, Ireth answered. If a horse could look nostalgic, Ireth did. *It is what I have been trying to tell her. Sandis. But I cannot speak to her, so the learning is slow.*

Rone stiffened. Stood. After escaping Kazen, Sandis had refused to break her script because she was certain Ireth was trying to tell her something. She'd been right.

"Tell me." Rone stepped closer. "Who you once were. What do you mean?"

I was Ireth, the numen replied. *Before my body changed. I forgot for a time, but I remembered.*

Despite the lack of cold, gooseflesh trailed down Rone's arms and back. "Remembered what?"

Ireth shifted on his legs until he faced Rone fully. *That I was once human, too.*

Chapter 16

Had it not been for the soldiers, Sandis would never have gotten Rist and Bastien back to Triumvir Var's home. She should have been relieved to have her friend back, to know Kazen could no longer haunt her, but tendrils of fear coiled around her heart.

Even without Kazen's bidding, Kolosos had hidden Anon again, and the soldiers couldn't find him.

Why hide Anon if the beast didn't mean to return?

And so, while pockets of the city hesitantly celebrated, the mood in Triumvir Var's home was thick and dark. Sandis had shared her fears, and Oz before her. Everyone was too afraid to relax, even Jachim.

And as if that weren't enough, Sandis had nearly gotten Bastien killed.

Medically trained soldiers, then doctors, saw to Bastien immediately upon their arrival. The death of Kazen and the casualties the army had suffered were distracting enough that no one had yet punished Sandis for insubordination. She doubted the night would have played out much differently, were she in Oz's hands. Except Rist might be dead. At least they had managed to save *him*.

Standing in the corner of their shared bedroom, watching as men cleansed, treated, and wrapped Bastien's burns . . . she knew she'd never forgive herself. She had failed her city, she had failed Anon, and she had failed Bastien.

The burns marred the side of Bastien's head, a bit of his neck, his left shoulder and arm, and his left hip, but the doctor had said he'd recover. It was pure luck that the fiery blow hadn't also struck Sandis and Rist. Without a numen to protect them, they would have died instantly. For now, Bastien was bedridden, and Rist slumbered in the deathlike trance that followed a summoning, unscathed by their misadventure.

It was on Triumvir Var's order that Sandis left her friends for the study, hugging herself so she wouldn't fall apart in front of so many.

A familiar pressure resonated in her skull, lasting the length of a breath before fading. She clung to it and the sliver of comfort it offered. *Please take care of him, Ireth.*

If only Rone could communicate with her. Or she with him. Could she summon him the way she summoned Ireth? The idea was as tempting as it was ridiculous.

But she'd already proven to be a poor summoner. Those burns . . .

She barely registered walking into the study, once again full with the triumvirs, Chief Esgar and General Istrude, Oz, Jachim, the priests and priestess. A soldier shut the door behind her, startling her to the present.

"So it's not over," Triumvir Holwig said. He seemed to be the only rested person of the lot.

No one else moved to answer, so Sandis did, her shoulders hunched. "I don't know."

"This was what we discussed," Triumvir Peterus pointed out, his voice gruffer than usual. "Kill Kazen or take the amarinth."

But Sandis shook her head.

Triumvir Var's eyebrow twitched. "Stop moping and spit it out, woman."

Sandis curled in on herself. "Except *we* didn't kill Kazen, Kolosos did. That . . . That changes everything." She rubbed the gooseflesh sprouting on her arms. "I know Kazen. I cannot believe he would choose to end his glory with suicide, as many believe. It's unlike him, to say the least."

The chief of police folded his arms across his scarlet-clad chest, frowning.

"I admit," Oz grumbled from the corner, "that I agree with Sandis. It's out of character for him. And Kolosos . . ." He met Sandis's eyes. "It was autonomous after its summoner's death."

General Istrude said, "We're aware."

"It fought Kazen, too." Sandis knit her fingers together. "Kolosos was immobile for so long. Do you really think Kazen forced it to stand, waiting, until there was a large enough audience for his demise? I think"—she swallowed—"I think Kolosos was resisting him."

"And struck back as soon as it got the chance," Oz added.

The room was quiet for a moment. Opposite Oz, Jachim took rigorous notes, his hands smeared with ink. Sandis wondered if he'd slept at all since this had begun.

"But," Triumvir Var spoke carefully, "why would a numen, even if it is sentient, kill its summoner? To return to its resting place in the ethereal plane? Perhaps it didn't enjoy being a puppet."

Oz snorted. All three triumvirs and the general shot him a strained look.

He shook his head, as though recovering from a good joke. "Why do you think the monsters let us summon them in the first place? They have no bodies. They're mere spirits, which is why they live where they live. Think about it. Everything we feel, see, experience, is through our flesh. The numina come down to have it. None can resist it."

Jachim nearly spilled his ink vial. "Incredible theory." He flipped a page and wrote with renewed vigor.

"I must believe," said Priestess Marisa, the first to speak among the Celesians who sat nestled in chairs away from the table, "that Kazen chose to repent. That he saw the horrors of his actions and ended his life because of them."

Hunched beside her, Cleric Liddell muttered something Sandis couldn't interpret.

High Priest Dall put a hand on his shoulder. "What was that, my son?"

Cleric Liddell shook his head. "No . . . he didn't."

Priestess Marisa's brow twitched. "Must you believe the worst?"

But Cleric Liddell squeezed his hands together, his eyes on the floor.

Hesitant, Sandis said, "Sister Marisa, if Kazen meant to repent . . . why did he scream?"

A thick hush blanketed the room, suffocating them all for long seconds until Oz said, "And yet . . . Triumvir Var has a point. In killing its summoner, it condemned itself to the ethereal plane, did it not?"

"Then why run? Why hide yet again?" General Istrude asked the very questions that had plagued Sandis for hours.

Both the general and Oz looked to Sandis as though she could answer. She could summon Ireth into herself . . . but could the bond between human and vessel work the other way? Could a numen summon *itself* into the world?

"Anon," she whispered.

"How powerful is this amarinth?" Triumvir Var asked, then, leaning back in his chair, added, "Pull men from Gerech. Esgar, assemble a team to venture north. *Find* the vessel and the amarinth! Scour *everything*. Put an end to these damnable questions. Istrude, I want your militia ready, just in case we're right. Damn, I've never wanted to be wrong more in my life." He ran a hand down his face.

Hesitant, General Istrude said, "My men are weary and weak."

"They can have until noon to recover. The police can fill in until then. The rest of you remain on call." His glare shot to Sandis. "I want no one to leave unless ordered to, do you understand? The same goes for you four." He glanced at the Celesians in the corner, and the Angelic, who remained silent as stone. Triumvir Var stood, his back popping. "And I want word the moment the vessels awaken."

Rist woke first. The moment a pained groan passed his lips, Sandis leapt to his side, her summoning meditation forgotten. She couldn't focus anyway, let alone believe she could reach Rone. She had everything ready for Rist—food, water, even medicine Jachim had kindly secured for her, before she barred the door with a chair to keep the government, and Oz, out, if only for a few minutes.

"Rist?" She said his name gently, knowing summoning sickness could make one sensitive to sound. *Celestial, please let him listen to me, and recover. Please let him not hate me.*

Rist's eyes peeled open. They were so bloodshot there was more red than white. His skin was paler than usual, his nails cracked, his hair streaked gray. Kazen had been summoning Kuracean every day. It had taken a physical toll on Rist.

What was it doing to Anon?

Sandis tried, futilely, to shake the worry from her head. Chief Esgar had a party still searching for Anon. Rone had Ireth. Bastien had Triumvir Var's doctor to oversee his care. Right now, there was nothing she could do for them, and she'd do best to concern herself with what was in front of her.

If only her frail heart could agree.

"Rist?" she tried again, taking a half-full cup from the nightstand and pressing it to his palm. It took him a moment to close his fingers around it. "Rist, it's Sandis. You're with me. You're safe. Kazen is gone."

He blinked again, dark orbs shifting toward Sandis. He stared at her long enough that she noticed a few white hairs in his eyebrows and eyelashes.

Then he bolted upright, promptly spilling both the water and the meager contents of his stomach.

Sandis worked efficiently, grabbing the corners of his blanket and tying them together, whisking away the vomit and setting it by the door. She picked up the cup, which rested against Rist's foot, and refilled it from a pitcher.

"Here, drink." She put the cup in his fingers, which trembled slightly. Rist drank, slowly at first, then greedily. She refilled the cup twice, the last time slipping pain powder into it.

Pressing his palm to his forehead, Rist said, "Where am I?"

"Triumvir Var's house."

He straightened then, looking at Sandis as though seeing her for the first time. He took in his surroundings slowly, eyes wide, stopping at Bastien, who lay an arm's width away from him, still unconscious, still nude beneath his blanket, save for his bandages. Guilt trickled through Sandis like cold rain.

Rist looked at himself, taking in the scabbing bruise on the inside of his elbow, and then shifted his gaze once more to Sandis. After a moment of heavy breathing, he croaked, "How?"

"We came for you when Kolosos attacked last night," she explained, soft and slow, watching his face. He seemed solidly startled. "Bastien and I. Kazen was killed."

His lips parted. "You killed him?"

She shook her head. "Kolosos did."

Rist turned away, considering. His stomach growled, but when Sandis offered him bread and butter, he refused it with a shake of his head.

"That monster," he murmured. "I knew that monster would kill him. It's smart, Sandis. It *knows* . . ." He swallowed and looked at her again. "I . . . I wanted to make a deal with Kazen. The amarinth for emigration papers. He took everything—"

His voice squeezed off, and Sandis had the twisting feeling that it was not merely the thought of his renewed captivity that had spiked his emotion, but the memory of what had happened the last time they'd all been together.

Sandis would never forget the look of betrayal on his face when they'd told him of Kaili's brutal death. Never.

Her guilt intensified.

Rist massaged his face, then let out a sigh. "Thank you for saving me."

"You're our friend, Rist." She formed each word with care. "Of course we came for you."

His mouth tightened. He disagreed, she knew, but at least he was talking. He held out his hand, and Sandis put the bread in it. He took a small bite before saying, "I guess this is my fault."

"It's Kazen's. But he's gone now." She glanced at Bastien. Would the scars he'd sustained be too severe for him to summon Mahk after this? Would he *want* to?

Would he forgive her?

Rist shook his head. Took another bite, then a third. "He was insane, Sandis, and he was wrong, too. That monster can't be controlled like other numina. It's not over. I can't explain . . . but it's not over."

Sandis nodded, sinking onto the edge of the bed. "Anon. Is he . . . all right?"

Rist looked at her like she'd just spoken Serranese. "Who?"

Her stomach dropped. "My brother. Kolosos's host."

His eyes widened once more. "That's your *brother?*" He glanced away, shaking his head. "I . . . I never heard his name. I . . . I don't know. I think I saw him awake maybe once."

Sandis nodded, trying not to crumble at the slim, sad information. The room grew stale.

"We keep dying. All of us," Rist murmured, picking apart his bread. He glanced at Bastien, then at the door. "Where's Rone?"

Sandis's heart hit the floor, but after a drink of water, she managed to tell him.

Chapter 17

Rone's mouth was dry, and it wasn't from the heat spilling off the horse demon. He tried to speak, but words, voice, even thought failed him.

Human?

I did not remember for a long time, Ireth said, his hooves tapping faintly on the crystalline ground beneath them as he walked toward the muted light that danced through the glassy plane, a strange imitation of the sun. *I lost myself, as the others have. But I stayed near. I watched your ancestors. I learned their tongue and their ways, and I slowly came back to myself. I remembered.*

Rone accumulated enough saliva in his mouth to swallow. "Wh-Who are you?"

The horse lifted his head, black eyes shimmering. *I am Ireth. I am a captain and defender to my chief. My time was over long before yours began, Rone Comf.*

Rone's knees buckled, and his backside collided hard with the ground beneath him. "You're Noscon, aren't you?"

Ireth gave a subtle nod. *We all were. Until Kaj.*

Rone shook his head, his heart thudding. "Kaj?"

Yes. Ireth studied the stars beneath him. *He is the one you call Kolosos.*

"No," Triumvir Peterus said, looking up from the meat-heavy meal before him. He, Jachim, and a handful of soldiers ate at Triumvir Var's table. Where Triumvir Var and Oz had gone, Sandis wasn't sure. The Celesian leaders had been back and forth among local churches, trying to calm the faithful. "I have only received the one message I gave you earlier. They've found nothing in the northlands but the end of Kolosos's tracks."

Pressing her lips together until they hurt, Sandis nodded and retreated back up the stairs to her room. She hadn't told anyone other than Rist and Bastien that Anon was her brother, but she had insinuated earlier that, as a vessel, she might be of use in finding Kolosos's host. It wasn't entirely a lie—vessels *could* sense active numina, though it was an unnecessary ability when their quarry loomed as large as a tower. No one had disputed her, thankfully. She couldn't stand the idea of information regarding Anon being kept from her.

It was dusk, and Chief Esgar's team had been searching all day. They had followed a charred trail some ways outside the wall, but it had dwindled into nothing. No Anon, and no amarinth. Which meant Kolosos hadn't simply petered out.

Anon, where are you? She paused outside her room and pressed the heels of her hands into her eyes, focusing on the ache of the pressure instead of the heat that threatened tears.

This house brimmed with people, yet Sandis felt achingly alone.

She'd had Rone for so short a time. His absence shouldn't hurt this much.

Why did the world take away everything she loved?

Rone is strong, she reminded herself for what had to be the hundredth time. *Rone can take care of himself. Ireth is with him. You can't give up yet. It's not over.*

Spots appeared in her vision, but she didn't remove her hands. She couldn't, not until she got a hold of herself. Not until she could look

Bastien and Rist in the eyes and tell them, truthfully, that she believed they'd get out of this alive.

If she could look Bastien in the eyes at all.

Taking a deep breath, then another, Sandis pulled her hands from her face and blinked until her sight cleared. Then she opened the door.

Bastien sat up in bed, picking at a plate of food on his lap. From this angle, he looked perfectly normal, but the moment Sandis walked around the bed, she'd see the bandages and the angry red skin poking up from them. There was no sign of Rist.

She swallowed hard.

Bastien glanced over and offered a weak smile. His hair was unbound and flowed freely over his shoulders; he'd only lost the bit above his left ear in the blast.

Clearing her throat, Sandis approached. "How are you feeling?"

"Same as the last time you asked me." He shrugged, then winced.

She knelt on the floor and rested her elbows on the mattress. "I'm so sorry, Bastien—"

"Sandis, stop apologizing."

"But if it weren't for—"

"*Sandis.*" He put his unscathed hand on her arm. "Every t-time you apologize, I have to repeat myself. 'It's not your fault. I knew what could happen.' And I'm getting really tired of repeating myself."

Sandis tried to mimic his weak smile, but struggled to.

"Triumvir Var has a lot of fancy medicine. It honestly doesn't hurt that m-much." He speared a carrot on his plate. "If nothing else, it makes me more *char*-ming."

Sandis gaped at him. He raised an eyebrow.

She let out a long, choked breath that was almost a laugh. "How long did it take you to think of that one?"

"I've got a few saved up. But don't tell anyone—I want to use that one again."

Pushing herself upright, Sandis glanced around the room. "Where's Rist?" Fear spiked the question. Had he run off a second time?

"In the kitchen, I think." Bastien shoved the carrot into his mouth. He pushed it against his cheek and added, "I hope he doesn't *burn* anything."

Sandis's breath caught, and her throat grew tight. "I-I didn't mean to—"

"Sandis, no." Bastien set the plate aside and sat up straighter, wincing once more. "Just a joke."

When she felt steady, she crossed the room and kissed Bastien on the top of his head. "You're a good friend, Bastien." She stepped back and rubbed the discomfort building in her stomach, the guilt that had settled there like bad meat. "Do . . . you want me to braid your hair?"

He straightened. "Do you know how? It . . . hurts to do it myself." He tipped his head toward his bandaged arm.

Sandis nodded and scooted behind him, gathering the long locks in her hands. "My hair was long, before Kazen. I always wore it braided or pinned up, so it wouldn't get caught in any of the equipment."

"At the gun factory, right?"

"Mm." After helping him turn toward the window, she split his hair into two sections and began taking pieces from each and crossing them over, making the fish-bone braid she had favored when she was younger. She'd gotten a few inches plaited before Bastien spoke again.

"I-I'm sorry, Sandis."

Her hands stilled. "What for?"

"For Rone. If I hadn't woken him, he'd still be here."

Sandis shook her head, resuming her work. "And I wouldn't be." She plaited another inch before adding, "I don't know if the amarinth would have solved anything or not. I don't know what will happen tonight. But we can't move forward if we're tied down by regret."

Bastien turned just enough to see her. "You should take your own advice."

He picked at his meal as Sandis continued to braid. She had almost reached the end of his hair when Rist opened the door. He looked around, his forehead tight, before kicking the door shut and sitting on the floor in front of it.

"What's wrong?" Bastien asked, handing Sandis a tie for his hair.

"What's wrong?" Rist scowled. "Your rescue maneuver was less than subtle. Everyone knows I'm a vessel, and I've been threatened with Gerech if I try to harm my brand. I'm a slave again, just to different people."

Sandis was slow tying off Bastien's braid. "I'm sorry, Rist. Maybe it really is over, and—"

"I don't want to hear more of your nonsense, Sandis."

"Hey," Bastien snapped.

Rist smacked his head against the door. "If you'd left me alone, I would have run rampant and tired out, then woken a free man."

His words cut deep. Sandis's throat constricted. "You would have hurt people. You might have been shot," she managed.

"Maybe that would have been better."

"Shut up."

Sandis started at the hardness is Bastien's voice.

Rist's expression darkened.

"Just shut up, Rist. We risked our lives for you." He pushed his plate aside, gripped the edge of the bed, and tried to stand.

"Bastien, no." Sandis moved to grab his shoulders, then saw the bandages on his left side and reconsidered.

"We didn't choose any of this." Bastien's breath quickened.

Rist stood and strode to the bed. "And the only reason I'm choosing *you* is because it's better than being on the street. The second the food is gone, so am I—"

Bastien leapt and sent his fist into Rist's jaw.

Rist stumbled back. Bastien cried, *"Ow!"* and cradled his hand, then hissed as the action pulled on the burns on his arm.

"Bastien!" Sandis cried, easing him back onto the mattress. "You're going to tear something!" She took his left hand and checked its bandages, waiting for something to ooze through them.

"I-I'm fine." Bastien winced, opening his right hand and prodding his thumb. "Something p-popped."

Rist rubbed his jaw. "God, you punch like Kaili."

The unexpected comment tempered Sandis's worry. "Kaili hit you?"

Rist dropped his hand. "More than once. Curl your thumb on the *outside* of your fingers next time, idiot."

Bastien smirked. "Good thing I didn't try that this m-morning."

Confused, Sandis asked, "Why?"

"Because then this would be . . . break-fist."

Sandis gaped.

Rist groaned.

A laugh so raw it hurt clawed up Sandis's throat. She gritted her teeth against it, knowing that if she let herself laugh, she'd start bawling and never stop. And so, hand pressed to her stomach, she left to fetch the doctor.

He remembers, too, Ireth said, holding Rone's gaze. *I do not think he ever forgot.*

"Kolosos," Rone said carefully. "Kaj."

Ireth gave a mew of confirmation. *He has waited for someone like Kazen. Just as I have waited for someone like Sandis. Someone who can free us.*

"This is it." Rone shifted onto his knees. "*This* is what you wanted to tell her. The amarinth. The Noscon records. The dreams. You wanted her to know who you were so she could free you."

Another nod. *I have never been able to communicate with other humans. Not even when they give me their bodies as vessels. Not until her.*

Rone considered this a long moment. "Could . . . *I* tell her? I can go a day without water. If I could reach her, couldn't I tell her?"

Even if you could use words, as I cannot, it is too late now.

"Why?"

The ground rumbled beneath them.

Because Kolosos has been unleashed, Ireth said matter-of-factly. *He will either destroy or be destroyed, and that will end everything.* Ireth's ears flicked as he lifted his head. *Even now, he prepares to descend. We should move.*

"But Kazen is dead." Rone found his feet again. "We watched him die."

Ireth shook his head, sending sparks from his mane into the air. *Kaj was a master sorcerer. It was he who made the first amarinth. He who bound us here in his leap for immortality, not realizing it would destroy our bodies and lock us in this eternal prison.* Ireth began to walk, and Rone followed him. *He has tied himself to the amarinth you once called your own, and the boy who wields it. He will return to the mortal realm and try to take back what he lost.*

Shivers coursed down Rone's arms. "Take back the physical world. Take back his ability to live, as we do."

Yes, Ireth agreed. *And in doing so, he will destroy us all.*

Chapter 18

He cracked open eyelids rough as scratched glass. He shouldn't be alive. He didn't *want* to be alive. But when he wasn't a monster, he was watched, chained. Every moment, every breath guarded.

It was dark. Always dark. No light, no dreams. He tried to move leaden arms and barely managed to rake his hand across the ground. Sand? Where was he?

Blinking hurt. There were no tears left to wet his eyes, so he closed them. There was nothing left to see, besides. His stomach rolled, despite it feeling like stiff leather. Where was the water? The soup?

And then he listened. Took in the silence of the surrounding darkness. Held his breath to complete it. No voices, no footsteps. The man and the other vessel were . . . gone? But how?

He tried to push himself up and fell teeth-first into the grit. Tried again and got an elbow beneath him. Something small crawled over the back of his naked thigh. Every muscle in his body was sore. Even the hardest day on the farm hadn't left him feeling this pained, this spent, this *empty*.

If he wanted to die, now was the time to do it. He certainly couldn't run.

A dry cough escaped his throat, ripping up his neck like embers. Gritting his teeth against the pain, he reached a hand out again. Sand,

sand, more sand. He opened his eyes, but there were no candles, not even starlight. Was he underground again?

A groan escaped him as he dragged a knee beneath him, and he gasped as the muscles stretched. *Don't pass out. Don't pass out.* This might be his only chance to defy his captor. He just needed something sharp. A knife, a shard of glass, even a long nail would do. Anything to stop the summoning. *Anything* to stop it.

He pushed himself forward and fell again. Swiped out one hand to nothing, swiped out the other—there. He touched something cool and metallic. He grabbed it, pulled it close . . . Wait, was this—?

The center of the device glowed in his fingertips, burning his eyes. Illuminating the charred underground cavity around him. But something was wrong. It didn't glow white this time, but red.

And then he felt it—the heat, the pressure building in his veins and his skull.

"No . . . please," he begged.

Anon screamed.

Chapter 19

Bits of dust fell from the ceiling. It was dark anyway, so Elfri kept her eyes shut and *listened*. Strained to hear beyond the shaking earth and the groaning of her underground hideaway, currently stuffed with more civilians than mobsmen. Some of the folk had nowhere else to go. Most were too afraid to try. It wasn't like the government would do anything for them. Even in crisis, they just wanted their factories run. The people had rebelled, and no wonder, but Elfri had convinced many of them to put down their clubs and metal bars and join her men. They *needed* order, just not the government's.

Someone whispered to her left, and Elfri held up a hand, silencing them. The monster had never come this close to the boardinghouse before, but . . . yes, the footsteps were finally moving away. South. Toward the Innerchord. But that place had already been demolished, hadn't it?

She had to see for herself.

"Stay put," she ordered, her voice carrying in the stiff silence of the room. "Snuffs, Rufus, with me."

The mobsmen fell in line behind her, and the crowd parted to allow them into the maze that led back to ground level. The earth still trembled rhythmically, but it softened with each beat.

"Sherig," Rufus said. She didn't think a single man here remembered her real name. They'd used the nickname even before her husband, Grim Rig, died. She didn't mind. "Let me go first."

"Take your chivalry and shove it between your legs, Rufus," Elfri snapped, and she pushed her way to the concrete stairs.

The night sky seemed so bright compared to that dark basement, even with the extinguished lamps hanging outside the buildings of what used to be a busy street. She could even see a few stars; the drastic decline of working factories had cleared some of the haze that perpetually loomed over the city like an umbrella. But stars didn't matter.

She could see the monster's shadow, even from here. It took shape against strips of clouds highlighted by the numen's natural glow. The curve of its wings and the top of its head. It wasn't knocking buildings down this time, wasn't roaring or throwing a fit. Pat had said Kazen had been killed. Then why was the monster the grafters called Kolosos still here?

Elfri slipped into the boardinghouse, where yet more terrified citizens took up space, many pressed to windows to watch the numen trudge across the city. Elfri took to the stairs, her men close behind her. She climbed until her thighs ached, and opened the door to the roof with a smack of her large fist. This high up, she could see the monster to his shoulder blades, moving with a strange calmness toward the Innerchord.

Snuffs scoffed. "There're still lights on the wall. Even now, they won't let anyone escape."

Soldiers had been running through the city, demanding men join the army. If so much as a child slipped past the four-story wall, he'd be labeled and charged as a deserter.

They sickened her. All of them. She was recruiting her own men, preparing the Riggers for whatever the future held. But none of them would wear the blue uniform.

Elfri squinted. *What are you doing?*

She had to get closer.

"Get the horses," she ordered.

"The army will see—" Rufus began to object, but one sharp look from Elfri silenced him. He nodded and hurried back down the stairs.

Gold.

That's what the enormous fire bull had collected. She recognized the precious metal that had been stripped from the remnants of the cathedral, Degrata, and Lily Tower scattered among other bits and chunks piled in the open space in front of the demolished Innerchord. Elfri watched from atop the library. She wasn't alone; a smattering of other brave souls had climbed to watch Kazen's rogue beast. Elfri thought she saw a few soldiers below, but it was too dark to be sure. Maybe they'd finally figured out it was futile to stand around shooting cannonballs at a walking volcano.

Kolosos bent and extended a massive hand, pressing it into the pile of gold. It hissed and squealed loud enough that, even from this distance, Elfri needed to cover her ears.

A man on the far corner of the roof gasped. He had a telescope held to his eye.

Elfri made her way to him, grateful for her size in a way she never had been as a girl. She *tapped* him firmly on the shoulder. "Give that to me."

He eyed her. "But—"

Elfri snatched the telescope and shoved him aside, where her ever-faithful Riggers caught him.

Pressing her eye to the telescope, Elfri centered it on the monster as soon as it straightened. *Move, you blundering—*

And it did, revealing its creation. Was that a . . . plate? A platform of gold? But why—

Then the screaming started.

Elfri nearly dropped the telescope, and despite herself, sweat pooled in her palms and under her arms. She set her jaw and stiffened her shoulders—she hadn't *shown* fear once during all of this, and she would not relent to it now. Everything would fall apart the moment she showed fear. Her men, her efforts to keep the civilians alive, her sanity.

But the monster didn't seem to notice them on the roof. Its focus was elsewhere. Moving swiftly for its size, it whipped out its fiery arms and grabbed someone in its now-blackened claws. The person screamed and screamed, but the monster didn't crush or burn him, merely dropped him onto the plate. And waited.

Elfri held her breath. By the time she needed to gasp for air, the man on the plate simply walked off it. No screams, no hesitation. He didn't even run.

What on earth? She passed the telescope to Snuffs and squinted.

The monster lashed out at someone new, and another volley of screams filled the air. The soldiers did nothing. The scarlets did nothing.

And it was about time somebody did.

Sandis glared at the uniformed men guarding Triumvir Var's back door. Two of them, with Helderschmidt rifles slung at their sides and short swords at their hips. One ignored her. The other glared right back.

They were everywhere, at every door and in the yard. Now that Kolosos had returned, the powers that be were keeping a close eye on all the vessels.

From what Sandis could see from her distant vantage point, he was not recklessly destroying the city as Kazen had done.

The thundering of boots near the front of the house drew Sandis's attention from the men blocking her exit. "It's gone! Kolosos is gone!"

Turning so quickly it hurt her ankle, Sandis ran toward the front of the house, to the kitchen, where all three triumvirs paced across expensive tiles. A map of the circular city lay open on the dining table, with different colored pins and weights strewn across it. General Istrude and Chief Esgar had left to watch the monster with their men. Oz was on the roof with his vessels, guarded by more soldiers. High Priest Dall, along with Cleric Liddell and Priestess Marisa, had been given permission to hold vigil for the local citizens, to "keep up their morale," as Triumvir Holwig put it. But the Angelic hovered over the corner of the table, staring at the map, the lines of his face deeper than Sandis had ever seen them.

She wondered if he worried for his son at all.

Triumvir Var's narrow gaze focused on the blue-clad messenger. "Where? Is it being followed?"

The soldier saluted. "The monster headed south, sir. Leapt the wall and crumbled part of it, but it stands. General Istrude himself is in pursuit with his company."

Sandis's heart thrashed in her chest. *Anon.* She wanted them to find him. And yet fear dug its claws into her.

Would they kill him if they found him, even after reclaiming the amarinth?

He hadn't chosen this. None of them had. But life was often cruel and unfair—his lack of culpability might not save him.

She wished for the millionth time Rone were here. He'd know what to do.

Pushing her sentiments away, Sandis strained to focus on the conversation between the soldiers and the triumvirs.

"Who is controlling him?" Triumvir Var asked.

"None of the scouts found a summoner close to the numen." The soldier went on to describe a massive gold disc in the Innerchord, formed by Kolosos himself.

"It placed civilians on it, sir. It squelched their will to fight completely. We've apprehended several of them to be questioned."

"Where?" asked Triumvir Peterus.

"Gerech, sir. They . . . They won't communicate with us. Not the way they should. I don't know much; I was sent to inform you of Kolosos's vanishing. They . . . They don't *see* us. They fight against us, muttering about gold."

Gold. Sandis's brands itched. She scratched them. Fought the memory of Kaili laid out on that cursed table, her script ripped from her back. Of Alys, hers bottled and sold.

Why gold?

She thought she heard the whirring of the amaranth and turned to look, but of course there was nothing there.

Triumvir Var growled. "I want a full report by *dawn*, do you understand me? I want identification of all these people and any who weren't apprehended. I want Kolosos's vessel *found.*"

The soldier saluted and held the stance until Triumvir Var dismissed him.

Once he'd left, Triumvir Peterus said, "We should empty Gerech. Fill our ranks."

Triumvir Var clutched the countertop. "With half-starved criminals?"

"They may not all be half-starved."

The counter, which came from Jachim, startled Sandis. She'd forgotten he was there.

"The numen is altering Kazen's tactics," the scholar said, oblivious to the stress thickening the air in the room. "How interesting."

Triumvir Var grumbled and rubbed his forehead. "You find interest in stupid things, Franz."

"No."

They all turned toward the Angelic, who remained hovering over the map laid out on the table. The holy man didn't meet their eyes. "No, it *is* interesting. Because it means Kolosos is using strategy. It has a plan."

A chill coursed down the length of Sandis's body.

"Impossible," scoffed Triumvir Peterus.

But Sandis didn't agree. "The numina . . . they're not merely *animals*. They're . . . more. At least, some of them are."

All eyes bore into her, and Sandis hugged herself, as though she could shield her body from the stares. It was so strange, talking openly about the occult. Once, it would have been enough of a crime for her to be thrown into the very prison they'd just mentioned.

"Ireth is, what's the word—"

"Sentient?" Jachim supplied.

Sandis nodded. "He thinks individually. He acts on his summoner's will because of the blood bond. No blood, no bond. Some . . . Some are not the same." Hapshi's gaze held no banked intelligence, and Kuracean had gone wild as soon as Kazen's hold on it dissolved. "But Kolosos . . . I don't think a being can have that much power and not know it. I think it's using its vessel the same way I use Ireth."

Jachim brightened. "And fueling its host with the energy in the amarinth." He began sketching something.

Sandis hugged herself tighter. "But I can't summon him completely. Not into myself. What Kolosos is doing is complete."

Jachim shrugged. "It is a magic we don't entirely understand, so hypothetically, anything is possible. The monster has the vessel, and it has the amarinth. An amarinth made of the combined energy of a vessel and a numen. There may be more power in it than we understand. Still, there is hope. Kolosos does not thrive here. Its vessel is growing weak. I've been documenting its visits, and they are getting progressively shorter. If we hold out long enough, maybe the monster will burn itself out."

Sandis swallowed. If Kolosos burned itself out, it would be because its vessel died.

"And the country will burn with it," Triumvir Var snapped.

Jachim slammed a fist onto one of his books. "If only I could study it."

Sandis turned toward the Angelic. He met her eyes, then merely said, "I must pray. Alone." And departed without a backward glance.

Triumvir Var said, "We will use what we *do* have. You two should rest; there will be little time for it in the coming days. We must do whatever we can to stop Kolosos. Rip up this gold plate. Find these . . . hypnotized persons. Kill its vessel—"

Sandis could not stifle the small gasp that sucked through her lips.

"—destroy the amarinth. We will use everything we have." He passed a hard glance at Sandis. *"Everything."*

Chapter 20

"Destroy us all? How do you know?" Rone asked, nearly jogging to keep pace with Ireth. The stars beneath their feet clustered together so tightly there was more starlight than night sky. The empty heavens above them remained dark.

I am very old, and I have been watching for a very long time. He will try to merge the planes. His greed surpasses his wisdom, if he ever had any.

Ireth paused and hoofed the ground. The glassy surface swirled into an aerial view of the ruined Innerchord. A gold plate gleamed up at them. It reminded Rone of the much smaller one he'd found in the ruins.

"What is that?" Rone whispered.

Gold. It conducts magic. It is why Sandis is marked with it, why it twists around your amarinth. He said the last word with disgust. *He is making pillars with it, at the cardinal points of the city. He will use it there, and here, and destroy both our worlds.*

The vision vanished and Ireth resumed walking.

"I . . . Wait." Rone jogged again, until he stepped in front of Ireth, blocking him. His stomach rumbled, but he ignored it. He needed his senses right now. "There's nothing here but numina, right? There's no gold."

The horse shivered, which made the pale halo around his breast darken. *There are only numina. But Kaj's magic has fused with us.*

Rone stared at the coal-skinned beast a long moment, trying to understand.

The image of numina melting under Kolosos's hand sprang to his mind.

The plane shook. Ireth stiffened and lifted his long neck. A glimmer of red shone in the distance.

Quickly. Fire swirled around Ireth as he turned. *We must move quickly. And then I will show you. I will help you understand.*

Hunger forgotten, Rone peeled his eyes away from the red light that could only be Kolosos.

He ran.

In their shared bedroom, Rist slept on a pallet on the floor, and Bastien reclined on the bed. Sandis wasn't sure if he was awake or not, but he didn't start when she grabbed his shoulder.

"We need to leave," she whispered.

Her eyes were still adjusting to the dark, and she could just make out Bastien's pale irises finding hers. "What happened?"

Sandis chewed on her lip, warring with herself. *What would Rone do?*

Rone had never wanted to come here in the first place. He hadn't trusted any of them—the triumvirs, the army men, the scarlets, or the Celesians.

"I know we have to save the city. I know that. But I don't trust these people, Bastien. We know more about this situation than they do. It's in our blood, our bodies. We need to leave." Her words were accented by a sliver of fear.

Bastien pressed his lips together, contemplating. "I-I don't know, Sandis."

She squeezed his shoulder tighter. "I know you're hurt. I know it's asking a lot—"

"It's not that," he whispered. "I mean, it hurts, but my legs are fine. Mostly." Leaning forward with a wince, he turned toward her. "But leaving *them* . . ."

He made a weak gesture to the rest of the house. To the powerful men who would do everything to stop them from leaving.

She swallowed hard. "Please."

A small sigh escaped him. "I'll follow you. Wherever you go. But they have guards *everywhere*, remember?"

Sandis nodded and turned toward the window, though she couldn't see any soldiers through the gauzy covers shielding it. "Mahk could get us out, but . . ."

Bastien licked his lips. "But Mahk isn't an option anymore."

Her eyes dropped to his bandages. "Maybe." His burns were angry and blistered, with a few worse spots that no longer looked like skin. When it came to summoning, scars mattered. Scars were the reason Kazen hadn't kept Alys.

Sandis swallowed down a sore lump in her throat at the memory of her friend. "We can't summon anyway. If you're unconscious . . . I can't carry you."

"I can."

Both she and Bastien started at Rist's voice. Watched as his silhouette sat upright on his pallet.

Rist continued, "On any other day, these men would kill me. I don't trust them, either."

"W-We have other options. Besides Mahk," Bastien said, and Sandis didn't miss the quaver in his voice. "But we'd have to do it where the soldiers can't stop us."

Her heart filled with sympathy. "I want you awake, Bastien. And ready, in case we need you." She didn't want him to host, not with his injuries. Not unless they had to, and even if it worked, it would have to be with the lowest-level numen she knew.

Rist asked, "Is the basement hatch guarded?" When Sandis looked at him, he added, "I've been all over this place. I know all the doors and windows. There's a ground-level door in the basement. They're standard."

"Probably," Sandis whispered, eyeing the door. She didn't hear anyone in the hallway. Ignoring a fresh pang in her chest, she said, "If Rone were here, he could incapacitate the guards long enough for us to run."

"Rone's *not* here," Rist said. As if Sandis had forgotten. The words struck her like a dull cleaver.

"They have to sleep sometime," Bastien offered.

"They take shifts." Sandis released Bastien's shoulder and sat back on the mattress, curling her legs against her.

"I could set a fire," Rist suggested. "In the basement. Draw them away. Go out the back."

Sandis shook her head. "We can't risk hurting this house. All of Jachim's notes are here."

Rist glowered. "Do you want to escape or not?"

"I don't want to condemn the others in doing so," she retorted.

Bastien, shifting, said, "What if we can start a fire outside the house?"

Sandis turned to him. "How would we do that?"

"There's a cellar below the kitchen that has wine and stuff in it," he explained. "You can make a bottle explode. You put something flammable in it, then plug it with a strip of cloth, leaving the end hanging out of the mouth. Then you light the cloth and throw the bottle."

"Out the window?" Rist asked.

Sandis considered. "How much fire would it make?"

Bastien shrugged. "I don't know. We have to throw it where it will catch."

"But not burn another home," Sandis said.

"Much," Rist added. "Maybe they'll get a Kolosos scare, or they'll think you've called Ireth." He gestured toward Sandis. "As soon as they're distracted, we run out the other way."

Bastien squirmed. "If w-we're caught—"

"I'll summon Hapshi before we're caught." Sandis put a hand on Bastien's knee. Hapshi was a flying numen, only a level one—a creature Bastien should still be able to hold despite his injuries. It couldn't carry Sandis *and* Rone before, but Rist was lighter than Rone. Maybe it would work. Sandis didn't know the name of any other flying numina besides Isepia, and she wasn't built for burden. "I'm sorry. But I can't break my bond to Ireth, and you won't be able to carry Rist."

Bastien, prodding at the bandage on his arm, hesitated, then nodded. "You should break my bond to Mahk, just in case. It's worthless now. I'm too damaged for a level eight."

"It's not—"

"Mahk is not Ireth," he said with a faint, reassuring smile. "And I'm not you. I-I'm not heartbroken over it."

Pressing her lips together, Sandis nodded.

"Bastien's the least suspicious." Rist stood and pulled his shoes on. "He'll have to get the bottle."

Sandis nodded. "And you have the best arm, so you'll have to throw it."

***

While the fire blazed on the north side of the property, Sandis, Rist, and Bastien headed south. Sandis held Bastien's good arm as they went, helping him keep pace. His scorched hip surely bothered him, even with a thick application of the salve that Sandis had swiped from the medic. She'd also taken some light provisions from the kitchen.

They didn't go unseen; someone shouted after them. They hadn't looked back. Bastien claimed that only Inda, one of Oz's vessels, had seen *him* as he prepared the explosive, but she hadn't said anything.

"Doesn't mean she w-won't," he explained as they took off down the street. "Oz is . . . different. H-Her loyalty will be to him, n-not me."

They took a zigzagging route, not stopping until they put some distance between themselves and the gate of the elite neighborhood. Panting, Sandis carefully checked Bastien's bandages. So far, everything seemed intact, though he was paler than usual.

After their second run, they paused outside a fabric shop. Sandis couldn't see any garbage bins, but she could smell them. Trash had begun to heap up in alleyways, another sign they were a city under siege. Eyeing a nearby manhole lid, she ached for Rone. He might have led them through the underground passages and to safety. Then again, maybe the sewers weren't safe enough to travel right now, with all the road damage, not to mention what filth might sneak under Bastien's bandages.

"Where are we going?" Rist asked, hands on his knees. The question was both a worry and a relief. The first because she didn't know; the second because it sounded like Rist planned to stay with them.

"Tomorrow night, wherever Kolosos is," Sandis said. "Right now . . . away. Come on. Keep to the main roads."

She didn't know what to expect in the dark streets of the damaged city, but she swallowed her fear. Rone would have kept her close, made her feel safe. He would have known a smart place to hole up. But Sandis reminded herself that she had Bastien and Rist, along with their numina, at her side. They would be all right.

Glancing to the taller man, she said, "Rist, I . . . just in case, I need your blood."

Rist tensed beside her. "You're not summoning on me."

"I would trade you if you could summon on me," she said, though she inwardly cringed at the thought of losing what control she'd gained. "But you can't. I can."

His dark glare hit her like a whip. "I haven't forgotten what happened the last time you did."

Kaili, he meant.

"Either do it," Bastien said, leaning on a garbage bin, "or see if the afterlife exists. We don't have options right now, Rist. We all have to make selfless choices."

Sandis passed a grateful look Bastien's way, but guilt gnawed on her stomach. *Am I making selfless choices?* Bastien was capable of summoning, too, unless he hadn't kept up his exercises. Summoning was the better choice for him, being injured. And Ireth was a far more useful ally than Hapshi.

But Sandis didn't know if Bastien could think on his feet fast enough, or say the words without stuttering. And in her heart of hearts, though she was loath to admit it, she knew she was afraid to give him the reins. Afraid of losing control.

It had taken her so long to gain it.

Rist didn't respond to Bastien. They walked another block, passing a family circled around a garbage-bin-contained fire, before a low growl sounded in his throat.

"Fine," he snapped. "When the sun comes up. We'll figure out something."

He was stiff as bone and didn't meet Sandis's eyes, but she nodded, pushing down her insecurities. "Thank you."

***

"What are they doing?" Bastien whispered.

They'd wandered clear to the edge of the smoke ring, where they'd dragged their exhausted bodies up a fire escape ladder outside a cotton factory and finally slept for a few hours on some scaffolding. The nights were growing colder.

Dawn had broken over the wall, and now Sandis, Bastien, and Rist hovered at the edge of the factory's tar-covered roof, peering eastward, shielding their eyes from the morning light. Sandis had applied more balm to the side of Bastien's face and neck, which were no longer bandaged. The blisters on his ear were nearly gone, though the ones on his shoulder looked angry.

Below them, a dozen people walked as though on leashes, staring straight ahead, carrying various knickknacks, all gold. Cups, scraps, even wallpaper speckled in gold leaf. They walked single file, all moving toward the eastern wall.

"I wonder if those are the . . . minions," she said, for lack of a better word. She related what she'd overheard in the kitchen last night.

"Is it"—Rist licked his lips—"*controlling* them? But Kolosos isn't even here."

"Maybe there's something near that gold plate," Sandis offered, but her voice trembled. She didn't want to go anywhere near it. Rone would have. But Sandis . . .

"Let's follow them," Rist suggested.

Sandis shook her head. "Let's stay safe. Besides, the triumvirate is that way."

So they climbed down, helping Bastien along, and followed the back alleys through the city.

They happened upon three more minions near the cathedral, digging through the ruins. Their clothes, hands, and faces were smeared with soot, and their fingers bled, but that didn't hinder their work. Sandis tried to speak to one of them, but he ignored her. Found a golden morsel and pocketed it before digging further.

Swallowing, Sandis watched in sick fascination as one of the minions, arms full of charred gold bits, started marching north. This time, Sandis and the others followed, keeping their distance. The man walked in a straight line, taking main roads. The streets weren't empty, but most shied away from the minion, Sandis, and her friends—until Bastien offered a child half a loaf of bread. Other beggars descended upon him in a flurry, pushing one another to reach into Bastien's pockets. When they grabbed his burnt arm, making him cry out, Rist clocked the beggar and the trio ran.

They'd only traveled a few blocks when a thick arm snaked out from an alley and snatched Sandis's wrist.

The edge of a scream escaped her mouth before a dirty palm covered her lips. Rist cursed and raised his fists, but the assailant swept out a leg, knocking both him and Bastien onto their backsides.

Recognizing the fluid movement, Sandis looked back at her attacker's face. She mumbled his name against his palm. "Arnae."

Rone's old master dropped his hand from her mouth. "Sorry, lass, but I didn't want to draw attention." He nodded toward Bastien and Rist, the latter of whom had picked himself up and muttered something foul.

"You know him?" Bastien asked.

"This is Arnae Kurtz. He's a friend of Rone's." The one who had taught them seugrat, the Kolin style of fighting. Arnae's clothes were tattered, and dirt creased his skin, but he otherwise appeared hale.

"They're going to the corners of the city. Figuratively," the seugrat master said, and Sandis realized he was referring to the minion they'd been trailing. "There are about two dozen of them, give or take. Collecting gold and dumping it at the compass points. I saw some poor bloke try to steal some. It did not end well. These slaves, they're mindless, but a man is lethal when he has no care for himself."

Sandis shook her head. "But . . . why?"

"Sherig thinks Kolosos warped their minds somehow. I don't know what you've heard, but there's a golden plate near the Degrata. He—*it*—put them there, and suddenly they became mindless slaves."

Sandis blinked. "Sherig? From the mob?"

Arnae nodded. "You're acquainted? Her men have taken over a few things in these parts. Making sure folk are doing the work that matters and enforcing a sort of martial law." Then, lower, "The government has forgotten us."

Bastien, standing and favoring his left arm, said, "They're focused on eliminating Kolosos."

"And keeping casualties high." Arnae's tone was dark.

The older man's eyes whisked from her, to Rist, to Bastien, then back to her. "Where's Rone?"

Sandis felt Bastien tense. There was so much to explain that evasion was simply easier—and kinder. "We're rendezvousing with him later." *Celestial, God, please let it be so.*

Arnae nodded. "Do you know the Green Street Boardinghouse?"

It took a heartbeat for Sandis to connect the name with the building above the Riggers' hideaway. She nodded.

"If you need help, head there. I have to go"—he glanced past her—"but I hope to see you again. Take care of yourself, Sandis. And tell that boy not to get himself killed."

Cold lanced her middle. "I will."

He clasped her shoulder, then pushed past the others to the main street, where he vanished.

"Sandis?" Bastien asked.

Compass points. Sandis slinked out of the alley. Gathering courage, she said, "I want to see what he's talking about. I want to know what Kolosos is planning."

Rist said, "We'll have to watch out for soldiers."

Nodding, she clasped Bastien's hand. "Guess we'll see who knows these streets better."

Chapter 21

Touch me.

Rone and Ireth stood in a short canyon of glass painted the same indigo as the night sky. The only light came from the pinpricks of stars beneath it, and from the fire licking Ireth's dark skin like it was alive.

Rone, leaning against the cool chasm wall, said, "What?"

Touch me, and I will show you.

Confused, Rone pushed himself upright and moved toward Ireth. The fire on his back shrunk down, like it was afraid, and the heat diminished with it. Ireth stretched his long head forward, and the scent of ash and burning metal filled Rone's nose.

He touched Ireth, or tried to. His hand passed right through him, like the horse was a ghost.

The moment it did, his mind flashed elsewhere.

"It is an unexplored path, Mighty." The narrow man had a hooked nose and bluish skin, like he had been left too long in the snow. Everyone in the room looked like that. Most had thick brows and wide noses. They wore leathers and skins and favored ornaments on their shoulders. The speaker's hairline curved into a sharp widow's peak.

These are the Noscons, Rone realized, gaping.

The man called Mighty wore a headpiece not unlike the one Rone had stolen from Ernst Renad. A matching mantle hung across his shoulders and collarbone. "Kaj, it is not done."

Kaj. Rone's focus targeted the narrow man. He wasn't what Rone would have pictured as becoming an all-powerful bull god. He was thin, about Bastien's height. His hair was greasy and slicked back from his angular face. Rone wanted to move closer, but his feet remained rooted to the spot. He couldn't so much as lift a finger.

"Please, listen to me, Mighty," Kaj continued, bowing, his voice oily and pressing. "I have studied, I have sought the gods. I believe this leads to immortality. I must pursue it. Think of the glory. Think of our people!"

The heavy, accented words flowed through Rone's mind. He knew they were Noscon, yet he understood them as Kolin. His vision moved to the gilded man, the "Mighty." His broad face darkened, thick brow lowered. "It is not for man to know."

The vision blurred, changed. Rone stood outside, in a world that looked like Kolingrad . . . only richer somehow. More trees, darker earth. A funeral pyre burned hot in front of him. He could *feel* the heat on his face. Taste the smoke on his tongue.

Rone blinked, and his body returned to him. He jerked back, pulling his scorched hand from Ireth's skin. He nearly fell backward onto the glass floor.

"What was that?" He breathed heavily, desperate for water. But there was none. He'd lapped up the last drop of the puddle he'd retrieved hours ago.

My memories, Ireth said. *I can only show you what I know, and what I have remembered. It has been a long time.*

Rone took a moment to catch his breath. He studied the fire numen. He hadn't been able to move in the vision because he'd stood where Ireth, the man, had once stood.

Ireth turned away from him, his foremost set of horns pointing toward the warped sun. *One minute of immortality was not enough for him. His sorcery grew darker . . . Forgive me, I do not remember well. And I am not Kaj. His memories are not mine.*

"I think I'm keeping up fairly well," Rone offered. He rubbed a chill from his arms.

Our Mighty found out. But before Kaj could face his trials, he unleashed his magic. It swallowed us all.

"He made this place." Rone walked until he stood before Ireth once more. "The ethereal plane. He made you immortal."

He imprisoned our spirits in a semblance of immortality, yes. A puff of hot air emitted from his nostrils. *Took away our ability to touch, to taste, to smell. Took away our home, but placed it where we would always see it and yearn.*

Rone licked his lips. Slowly, he asked, "How did you forget?"

It has been a long time. Ireth straightened, his height intimidating. *We became mad as we watched a world we could not touch. With time, we forgot what we had been. Our forms changed, slowly adopting what we saw.*

"You mimicked the world you saw?" Rone ran a hand back through his hair. He thought of all the numina he'd seen. Their different and bizarre forms. All of it part animal, plant, *nature.*

When I remembered, I stopped changing. My spirit froze in the form you see now. The fire horse paused. *Even Kaj, Kolosos, regrets what he did. That is why we are here.*

Rone digested this. Turned away and paced over the starry glass. Turned back and paced in a different direction. Rubbed the back of his neck. God's tower, he was thirsty. He needed to reach into the world for more water. As much as he could get. But right now he needed to think. *Think.*

A moment later, he turned back to Ireth, itching beneath his skin. "Can you fight him?"

Ireth regarded him silently before answering. *Kaj is powerful.*

Rone rubbed his hands together. Settled them on his hips. "My people are fighting him on the mortal plane."

Feebly.

Rone glanced down at his hand, turned it over. "You can't touch me. Which means the numen that chased me before couldn't have harmed me. I'm immortal here. Minus the 'sustenance' thing."

The horse whickered, and Rone couldn't tell if Ireth was laughing at him or merely surprised. *We cannot touch you body to body, but our abilities are real.* Taking a step back, Ireth snorted, and a fist-sized fireball shot at Rone's shoe. He jumped back as the heat pushed through the leather. Stomped his foot until the small flame sputtered out.

"Point taken," he muttered as he examined his scorched boot. He met the numen's dark eyes. "I might be mortal, but the numina aren't. *Your* people could fight Kolosos, on this plane." He snapped his fingers, remembering. "Sandis said the other side of the astral sphere was the Celestial. Surely the Celestial could fight Kolosos!"

But Ireth shook his head. *Hepingya is reclusive.*

Hepingya. He'd said that name before. A cool sensation spread from Rone's chest out toward his limbs. "So it's true. The Celestial *is* a numen." And Sandis had figured it out, all on her own. "Hepingya." He couldn't say the name with the same lilt Ireth used. Shaking his head, Rone added, "What do you mean, 'reclusive'? Let's *find* it."

If I could find Hepingya, I would be at his side now. It is not possible.

Rone rolled his lips together, thinking. He paced away from Ireth, then back. "But we can find other numina, right? They could help us."

They do not remember. But this time Ireth tilted his long head, regarding him with what he guessed was interest.

"You said some do." Rone stepped closer. "Some remember. And if Kolosos faces resistance here as well as on the mortal plane, he won't have time to rest. To build whatever he's building. If nothing else, we can slow him down until we have a better option."

Ireth considered for a long moment, but Rone didn't dare break his concentration. He waited, counting his breaths. The growls in his stomach.

Perhaps. Perhaps . . . yes.

"Do you know who can help us?" he pressed.

Ireth nodded. *I know one who should be close to here. One who remembers, but not as well as I do.*

"Great!" Rone clapped. "Let's go. Who is it?"

Her name is Isepia.

***

They were making pillars.

Sandis was fairly sure. After leading the others to the northernmost curve of the wall, she had caught sight of the minion they'd followed from the cathedral. They'd watched as he and a few others stacked gold as though to make a column. Arnae had mentioned these people converging at the compass points, so it had to be the same in the south, west, and east.

Slaves. They were slaves. Sandis imagined herself among them and shivered.

She, Rist, and Bastien had returned to the Innerchord, where they'd found a perch atop a two-story sweetshop with boarded windows, seemingly abandoned by its owners. Most of the riots were happening farther out, away from easy government reach, so this was as safe a spot as any, so long as the sun was out. Sandis wondered if the bakers had managed to flee Dresberg before soldiers were appointed to keep everyone inside, or if they were hiding somewhere, waiting and praying for Kolosos to pass over them.

Sitting on the roof, they'd eaten the rest of the food Sandis had collected from Triumvir Var's house, along with nearly all their water. Sandis would have to find Sherig tomorrow for further help. But now, their bellies were partly full and they were mostly safe.

What would happen when the pillars were complete? What was the monster trying to achieve?

Warmth trickled down her spine like hot water. Sandis closed her eyes. *Ireth. What should I do?*

Pressure built at the bottom of her skull, and in it she tasted fear. This wasn't the desperate fear he'd given her earlier, but a subtle, worrying fear. Sandis swallowed and whispered, "I'll be all right."

Perhaps sensing her unease, Bastien laid a hand on her shoulder. She offered him a weak smile. Behind them, Rist paced over the slanted shingles. The roof wasn't large enough to give his long legs proper exercise.

"Soldiers." Bastien pointed up the road. "I think they're yelling at those people."

The soldiers had fallen in around a small group of men. Sandis couldn't tell what they were saying, just heard the occasional shout, spied the movement of shadowed arms. Maybe they were attempting to draft soldiers for the dwindling army.

"Let's move," she whispered, and crawled to the other side of the roof, the one facing away from the street. The moon, which was brighter and clearer than Sandis had ever seen it, thanks to so many stagnant smokestacks, ducked behind a cloud, leaving them in near darkness.

Sandis had thought she'd be prepared for Kolosos to return, for the numen's shaking footsteps and fiery aura, but nothing could prepare her for the sheer *force* that was Kolosos. A burst of heat pushed wind toward her, and on it she smelled burnt hair and something rotten. A great deal of the enormous monster was black, but the red cracks in its skin highlighted every crevice and shape of its horrid form.

It had come from the south, just as General Istrude had said.

Sandis felt both too close to and too far from the golden plate. The creature's nearness burned her eyes, and her blood ran hot and quick through her body. Its horns stretched starward like parched stakes, and for a fleeting moment, as it turned, Sandis thought its molten red eyes looked directly into her own. She grabbed Bastien's good forearm and squeezed it.

A few of the once-brave bystanders began to flee. Kolosos found them, and Sandis shrunk into herself as the monster planted them, one by one, on the gold plate. She wanted desperately to save them, yet she knew she could do nothing. Not yet. She was too weak. They all were.

It was just as the messenger had described. Sandis could barely see Kolosos's work, but the screaming ceased as soon as the chosen humans' feet hit the gold plate. Then Kolosos fetched another mortal, and then another.

One of the stupefied slaves walked down the street beside the sweet-shop. She stared forward, ignoring the bend in her right ankle. She was erect, fearless, and strange.

The world shook as Kolosos moved. Soldiers backed up the street, armed but not fighting. They also knew they were too weak. Kolosos didn't run after them, however. It moved away from Sandis, enough so that she dared to stand to get a better look.

The city trembled with the monster's steps, and the quakes knocked her back. Rist caught her shoulder. They exchanged a silent glance.

Rist slid to the edge of the roof and climbed down. Biting her lip, Sandis gestured for Bastien to follow, helping him protect his left side as he dropped to the ground.

They shied away from the soldiers, most of whom seemed to be scouting more than anything else. Was General Istrude among them, planning a new battle tactic?

Slinking against the outer wall of a silent flat, the trio crossed another road and then another, following Kolosos's glow. The numen was oddly quiet. So unlike the rage that had propelled it under Kazen's bidding.

The city shook again. Sandis barely kept her footing. The moment the ground stilled, she dashed ahead of Rist and peeked around another skyscraping building.

Kolosos was on its knees, its fire burning the concrete around it. It had dug a deep trench in the road. Continued to dig.

"I-I think," Bastien said behind her, barely audible, "I think its l-looking for the ruins. Wh-What else could be under there?"

Sandis pressed her lips together. The numina had sprung from Noscon magic. What was the monster seeking? More magic?

Gold. The word came unbidden, so much so that she wondered if Bastien, or even Ireth, had whispered it. *Kolosos wants more gold for the pillars.*

Rist's hand grabbed her upper arm. "We're too close," he murmured. "We won't miss anything if we move farther back."

Sandis's feet resisted moving. She had to stay close. Kolosos's sheer size made its strides long and fast. If she couldn't track it, she couldn't get Anon. The way the road hissed and melted beneath it confirmed what she already knew—she'd never be able to touch the monster and simply spell it back to the ethereal plane. Oh, if only it were so easy.

Rist was right. If they lingered, Kolosos could swipe out with its cleansing fire and kill them.

Nodding, Sandis allowed him to pull her away. Her brands itched, fingers twitched. Mouth dried.

Soon. Soon. Kolosos could not exist in this plane for even half an hour. It would have to run, and then Sandis would give chase. Try to do what General Istrude and the others could not.

She thought of the anguished look that had twisted Oz's face as he confessed Jansen's demise. The agony on Bastien's face as the doctor tended his burns.

But she wouldn't let Rist or Bastien die. She'd protect them. Anon, too.

She'd die doing so, if that's what it took.

———————

Rone had not missed the one-winged, savage woman in their time apart, but he was oddly happy to see her.

He and Ireth had passed two other numina on their journey to find her, both as feral as wild animals. The first had been a deerlike creature with long violet leaves growing out of its head. It had growled as they neared, but a flash of fire from Ireth had kept it at bay. The other had been what Rone could only describe as a lizard with crystalline scales in ten different colors, three long tails sweeping from its backside. Rone wondered if this was the numen that had chased him upon his arrival to the plane, but it had skittered away immediately, more prey than predator. All Ireth had said was *Forgotten*.

Isepia lingered in what Rone would call the ethereal plane's version of a mountain. It was a high, sheer cliff, similar to the one that Rone had leapt from only days ago. Square and rectangle pockets marked it like uneven windows, and Isepia rested in one of these, perhaps twenty feet up.

She hissed when they approached, human eyes flicking from Ireth to Rone. Rone thought he saw recognition in them.

He will kill us all, Ireth said. It took two heartbeats for Rone to realize the fire horse spoke to Isepia, not him, yet Rone could "hear" him still.

Maybe not the best introduction.

A low growl rumbled in the harpy's throat. Thick Noscon words filled his head. A second later, the translation from Ireth: *We cannot die.*

Rone glanced to Ireth.

The fire horse's mane and whiplike tail glowed brighter. *You have seen his destruction. He is working magic just like before.*

Isepia's growling ceased. Her brow furrowed. *Before?*

She didn't remember.

Kaj trapped us here, Isepia. You used to be as he is. Ireth gestured with his muzzle toward Rone. *We all did. Now Kaj works to destroy us to gain a mortal body.*

The half-human numen was silent a moment. She studied Rone. *He is making pillars here, too.*

"What?" Rone asked.

Ireth flicked his fire-laced tail close enough to Rone to risk burning his skin. Rone clenched his teeth together, no further message required.

Pillars? Ireth asked.

Isepia stood, but did not leave her nook. Her single wing stretched darkly behind her. *He has begun to fit the others into pillars. He seeks to match the mortal city below.*

A shiver coursed through Rone. *No gold,* Isepia continued, *but Kaj's magic is infused into the numina. We are his fodder here.*

He will kill us for his pillars, Ireth said.

Isepia glowered. Glanced at Rone. *He is stronger than even you, Ireth.*

But not us. Not if we all pull together.

Isepia growled, but nodded. *I will come.*

The city gave way to Kolosos's smoking fingers like clay to a sculptor's hands.

No one stopped it. Not Sandis, not the soldiers, not the Riggers, not God. They all watched, silent and waiting. Holding their breath. Afraid.

Every time the monster straightened and moved, Sandis's heart went wild in her chest. She pressed her nails into her arms, fighting her instinct to flee. But Kolosos didn't see her. Or if it did, it didn't care. The demon continued to dig, occasionally pulling up rocks or other objects from beneath Dresberg. Sandis never got close enough to see the exact items, but an occasional glint of gold reflected the red light emanating from the numen's body.

Kolosos dumped its finds in the Innerchord.

Then it ran.

"Go!" Sandis cried. *"Go!"*

She bolted after the giant, her gait nothing compared to its long strides. She hadn't gotten far before a wall of fire rushed toward her.

"Sandis!" Bastien shouted, grabbing her wrist. It popped when he yanked her back behind an overflowing garbage bin. The heat that encased her stole the air from her lungs and the tears from her eyes. Threatened to turn her skin to ash.

The flames passed, the light with them, encasing Sandis in darkness.

Rist cursed beside her. "No wonder they haven't found its hiding spot yet."

Bastien grabbed Sandis's hand and pressed it to his head. "Now, Sandis. We'll lose it if we don't go *now*." He met her eyes. "I'll forgive you. I promise."

Trying not to look at Bastien's bandages, Sandis offered silent thanks and summoned Hapshi.

Chapter 22

"Black ashes," Rone muttered. His footsteps slowed as he crossed the glassy, star-pocked expanse beneath his feet. All around him, the world was smooth. Dark. Like he lived inside a gem, hard and cold and eerily beautiful.

It was the pillar that ruined the effect.

The flatness of the area made it easy to see, even from far away. It had just taken a while for Rone's human eyes to be able to understand *what* he was seeing. It was a pillar. Twenty feet tall. And it was formed from numina.

He didn't recognize any of them, but they were there, stacked upon one another like bricks, twitching, writhing, yet unable to break away. At the pillar's base was a strange creature Rone had never before seen. A behemoth of a thing with a long nose sandwiched between two hulking tusks that dripped with ice. The crystalline floor of the ethereal plane wrapped up around its trunk-like legs, holding it in place. It was a bodiless spirit, and yet it had been chained as if it were flesh and blood.

Perched on the back of the lowermost numina was a rocky thing Rone would not have thought alive if not for its array of spidery eyes. Above that, two numina appeared glued together along their sides—one that looked like a rabid version of Hapshi and another with a striped, equestrian body and the head of an enormous golden flower, if flowers had fangs. Atop them, bound by its knees, was a humanoid numen like Isepia, though it had a strange-looking head that Rone wanted to call feline, and yet it distinctly wasn't. Its impossibly green eyes looked upon them, and in a heavy Noscon accent, Rone heard the word *Ireth*, followed by something that could only be pleading.

A few more creatures stood upon the shoulders of the cat-headed one, mewling and hissing at one another. Chained without chains.

"This is what you meant," Rone said softly. "It matches the pillars we saw in Dresberg, but—"

Heinous, Ireth replied. Any other day, Rone might have been impressed that the numen knew Kolin well enough to use so powerful a word. But Rone's thoughts held no mirth, only solemnity for the suffering literally piled before him.

Whether or not the numina remembered their lives before, no being should be treated thusly.

The tusked creature made a thick whistling sound as Rone approached. He lifted both hands overhead, unsure if the numen would recognize the offering of peace. "How do I free them?"

I am not sure, Ireth answered.

The tusked numen pulled against the glass enclosing its feet, but the plane didn't give. Rone reached a hand for its enormous nose. His touch passed right through it, as though it weren't there.

Images of a forest flashed through his head. Of a sparkling canopy.

Pulling his hand back, Rone blinked his vision clear. Whatever magic had shown him Ireth's past was not unique to the fire horse.

He rolled his lips together, contemplating. "If Sandis, or another vessel, were to summon one of these numina, would it still work?"

I do not know. Summoning taps into the same magic Kaj is working. I understand only a portion of it.

A sudden gust stirred Rone's hair and jacket. Isepia had launched herself into the stale air, until she was at the height of the topmost numina. If she spoke, she did so in a way Rone could not hear.

Steeling himself, Rone walked forward, passing through the tusked numen's body. It was like walking through heavy steam without heat, or water thickened by paint. More visions clouded his mind, trying to whisk him away from reality . . . but they were disjointed, confused. *A baby without a face cradled in slender arms. The forest. Running. A faceless man.* Memories eaten up by time.

Gritting his teeth, Rone forced himself to remain present. He looked up through the murky spirit engulfing him, just able to make out the shadows of the spidery rock being overhead. *A song. A lullaby with no words.* It was about ten feet from the ground; he had to jump to reach it. *Stirring a pot.* His hand brushed the bottom of the connection.

The tusked numen released a loud whistle at the same time the numen above Rone groaned, their cries followed by a sound like two slabs of granite grinding against each other. Whatever bound the two numina together vanished in the cacophony of noise.

Rone back-stepped until he exited the numen completely.

The pillar had fallen.

The glassy ground still encased the tusked numen's feet, and the other numina were still bound one to another, but the rock creature with the many eyes was no longer fused to the tusked numen.

Rone swore, more in amazement than anything else.

You are mortal, Ireth said, as though Rone had forgotten. *Your mortal touch severed them—*

The ground trembled as though God itself had grabbed its edges and shaken it. Red light split the darkness, *much* closer than the last time.

Ireth's accented voice sounded in Rone's head, but the words didn't register as Rone jolted away, then tripped over his own feet, landing hard on his backside.

Kolosos took form before him, barely one hundred feet away. Somehow, in this limitless place, he seemed even larger. Here, Kolosos was pure demon. Sheer power.

And his burning, molten eyes were focused on Rone.

Ireth's words sliced Rone's thoughts like a knife. *Move, mortal! Or you will die where you stand!*

A prompt reminder that Rone didn't have sixty seconds to spare. Not anymore.

He leapt to his feet and bounded after Ireth. Rone couldn't ride the fire horse—scorching flames aside, Ireth had no physical body here. None of them did. Isepia bolted to the left, her ability to fly helping her gain.

Rone ran faster than he ever had. He rose onto his toes, legs pumping so quickly they went numb. Heart brutally surging blood through his body. Pain flaring in his ribs.

Yes, he was a mortal—and a poorly fed one, at that.

None of the numina had corporeal forms, and yet the ethereal plane shook with Kolosos's every step. Those steps grew closer together as Kolosos gained speed. Heat pressed against Rone's back, and the smell of sulfur stung his eyes.

Ahead of Rone, Ireth reared and turned around, galloping back toward him. The pale circle of light around his breast glowed so brightly Rone had to look away or lose his sight.

Intense heat engulfed him. His skin and hair began to burn. Ash coated the inside of his nose—

The light shifted. Rone turned toward the fire horse again, watching as Ireth sent a brilliant fireball surging over his head. It collided with Kolosos's cracked, protruding face and crackled outward like lit gunpowder.

Kolosos reeled back, his steps halting. The fireball didn't seem to hurt him, only infuriate him. The glowing red between the cracks of the numen's skin burned brighter, and Kolosos let out a roar that shook Rone's eardrums.

Run, run, run! Rone huffed as he put more distance between himself and Kolosos. Ireth galloped toward him, passed him, and sent up another ball of fire. A familiar shriek split the air; Rone recognized it from Kazen's lair, the night he'd infiltrated it to rescue Sandis.

Isepia had joined the fight.

Rone risked half a glance back, spying the one-winged monster flitting around Kolosos's head, distracting him. Kolosos swung for her, narrowly missing.

Could one spirit inflict pain upon another? It had to be possible, or else the numina wouldn't be so frantic. Then again, Rone would go mad if someone forced him into that kind of chained imprisonment.

What would happen if Kolosos's burning palm met its target?

We should have been watching. We should have been watching for him. He should have kept track of when Kolosos would return. Then again, the monster might have transported back here early because he sensed Rone's manipulation of his macabre pillars.

Keep going! Ireth ordered him.

Rone faced forward, begging his body to move faster. Already his muscles ached, yearning for rest. His throat yearned for drink. His strength was waning.

And a new numen was racing toward him.

It took Rone a moment to see the body against the dark expanse before him. Its tongue hung out of its mouth, and amber eyes sparked in its wolfish face.

Rone recognized this numen. It had been bound to Dar, another of Kazen's vessels.

Drang, they'd called it.

His mind raced along with his legs, trying to sort out how the hell he was supposed to fight off another numen while running for his life. If the beast tried to tackle him, claw him, it wouldn't succeed. But for all Rone knew, Drang could summon some sort of magic to obliterate him.

Before he could reach a conclusion, Drang darted to Rone's left. Toward Kolosos.

Charlie N. Holmberg

Rone slowed, gasping for air. *He remembers,* Rone thought, watching the third numen join the fight. *He remembers, too.*

The ground quaked again . . . but wait, no. That was the *air*. It thickened and shivered around Rone, dancing in his lungs.

Kolosos looked at Rone. Addressed *him* in a voice so heavy it hurt. *Do you believe you have the power to stop me?*

Rone nearly shat his pants. Kolosos's hooves came down so hard on the glassy ground it should have cracked.

Ireth flung another fireball upward.

Clenching his hands, Rone ran.

The other way. Toward the fallen pillar. Toward the monster.

Kolosos tromped toward him again. The heat was incredible and very much *real*. So was the shaking ground and the liquid rock seeping between cracks in the monster's skin. But Kolosos was in the ethereal plane, and he was a numen, just like all the others.

Rone was about to discover if he was very smart or very, *very* stupid.

Fear pumping new energy into his legs, Rone bolted for the lava monster. Drang reached the monster first and barreled into its ankle, burning its shoulder in an attempt to knock the giant back. Isepia's wind spread the sulfuric smell of rotten eggs through the dark expanse.

Rone saw a clear path between Kolosos's legs and dashed for it. But the monster turned, swiping for Isepia, and Rone ran right through the bulb of its hoof.

It was like falling into the sun.

And then Rone *saw*.

***

"This proves it." The voice came from Rone's body, though he hadn't said a word. The language was Noscon, yet he needed no translation. Blue smoke puffed from a bowl before him. Stone walls enclosed the small space furnished with simple chairs and a table. The empty tracks

176

on the wall indicated the amarinth workshop they'd found in the sewers. "Our gods are false. *This* is the true power. There are many ways to manipulate it. We must simply discover how."

Three others in the room, two men and a woman, gaped at the bowl. One of the men grinned. The woman's face drew downward. The second man came closer and peered into the bowl.

"Teach me," he said.

"Swear to never repeat what you hear in this room," Rone's embodiment said, stirring the smoke with his hand. "Swear it. Only I can approve who joins our clan. Only *I* can reveal the secrets of this sorcery."

Kaj. Rone was watching *Kolosos's* memories.

The woman asked, "Clan? You intend to separate us from the others?"

"The others have separated from *us*." Rone felt Kaj frown. "The Mighty refuses to listen. As for this"—blue smoke danced around his fingers—"the *others* will never know."

Colors darkened. The room changed. The walls were now covered in stone tablets etched crookedly with Noscon symbols. Kaj flexed and relaxed his sore hands. Rone could feel the overused tendons, the blisters.

What is the point to power if I must one day part from it? Kaj pressed his fingertips to one of the stone tablets. He was older now. Thinner. He drew his palm across the wall, corner to corner, before stopping and tracing a symbol with an overly long fingernail.

"This," he whispered to himself. "If we sacrifice enough . . . perhaps this will let us *all* live forever."

This time the transition was more abrupt. Rone found himself standing above a large divot in the earth, where the soil grew sandy and sank into the shape of a large bowl. Within it writhed Noscons young and old, male and female, gagged and bound. Rone—Kaj—and a few others stood around the edge of the bowl, expressionless, their hands linked. Rone recognized three of them as the men and woman from the first vision.

Fear lit the bound Noscons' eyes. Some struggled. Others sobbed.

Kaj began to chant.

Rone couldn't shut his eyes. He couldn't look away. Kaj had watched it, and so he must, too.

He saw the sacrifices die, puff into wet red smoke. The smoke rose, cooled, and turned glassy against the sky.

Rone stared up in awe.

Was that . . . the ethereal plane?

"No!" shouted an older man. The one who had wanted Kaj to teach him in the beginning. The vision had shifted again, and they were in the stone room from before. Two women wept in the corner. A disc of gold glistened at Kaj's feet—the same Rone had found dented in the sewer, a miniscule version of the one Kolosos had created in Dresberg. This was that place, only thousands of years younger. "No, we will not send another! There is no point if we cannot pull them out!"

Kaj looked upward, and Rone knew his thoughts. *But are they* alive?

He'd sent his own followers into the ethereal plane. Was this his play for immortality? To create a realm where death didn't exist?

For a moment, Rone's hunger turned the vision, the *memory*, fuzzy. He felt Kolosos's heat pucker his skin.

But the magic sucked him back in.

"It will work." Kaj took the hands of two people, a young woman and young man. "The bond will keep you connected."

The woman looked doubtful. "Are you . . . sure?"

Anger flared through Kaj. "Do you question my power?"

Dropping to his knees, the man answered, "Forgive her, Kaj. We trust all that you are."

"Someone's coming," called a scout from the window. Everyone, Kaj included, froze. The young people inched toward a covered back window.

The scout relaxed. "They're gone."

"Then let us begin." Kaj guided the woman toward the gold disc on the floor. "Think of him," he gestured toward the man. Her husband, Rone guessed. "He will be your salvation."

Hugging herself, the woman stared upward. Beyond the roof that shielded her.

Kaj sent her into the ethereal plane, too.

***

The vision shifted again. It was daylight now; Rone could see it through the heavy curtains over the windows. The people in the room were fewer. The husband from before stood in the center of the gold disc, mirroring gestures Kaj made. His skin was moist, his eyes sunken. Looking closer, Rone saw brands printed down his back in gold, only half-healed. Brands just like Sandis's.

The disc flashed, making Rone's eyes water.

When the light faded, the branded man still stood there.

"Nothing happened!" snapped a man by the window.

Kaj's hands formed fists. "It makes no sense. It should have worked!"

The man by the window charged forward, lifting his hand as though to strike—

"I'm back," gasped the man on the gold disc.

Everyone froze.

The branded man studied his hands. Turned them over. Looked around the room. His eyes settled on Kaj.

"I'm here, but . . ." He touched his face, eyes wide. "This is Yetuae's body. I'm . . . I'm Yetuae."

The man began to weep.

Kaj stared. "Hoka?"

Trembling, the man nodded.

Kaj gaped and stepped onto the gold disc. "You're inside of him. *Fascinating.* And Yetuae. Is he there, too?"

Hoka—Yetuae—sobbed. "I can't hear him. I can't feel him at all."

The bond between the couple had been the key to connecting the two planes.

Yetuae could only pull his wife into his own body, but he could direct other spirits from the ethereal plane into vessels wearing the golden brands. *Within and without, above and below, fall and inhabit, I command.* It had taken Kaj weeks to formulate the words.

Though he was pleased by his success, his followers' bodies never came with them. Only their souls.

Kaj needed to change that.

"We're safe," said a scout at the window. A new one. Rone wondered what had happened to the first.

Kaj nodded. Yetuae stood in the center of the disc. His jaw was set, his skin perspiring. Like a man readying himself for pain.

If summoning was anything like Sandis had described, he was in for a lot of it.

"I'll pull her out," Kaj said, hands on the taller man's shoulders. "There is a moment where the magic burns brightest. You summon her, and I'll pull her into our realm."

This was the moment he'd been waiting for. Once Hoka came back, Kaj would find out if living in the ethereal plane had stopped her aging. If he had finally discovered the secret to eternal life.

Yetuae nodded. Braced himself. Chanted.

A familiar flash of bright light engulfed him. Kaj jerked forward and reached into it. Grabbed . . . something, and pulled it free.

Yetuae collapsed onto the gold disc, lifeless. The scout ran forward and knelt beside him, checking for a pulse.

Kaj stared in awe at the small glowing orb in his hands, oblivious to the dead man at his feet.

Rone knew exactly what it was, and what Kaj would do with it.

He'd make the first amarinth.

"It will not be you, Tagaro," Kaj said as he carefully bent thin ribbons of gold by torchlight. His hands worked with the deftness of experience. "You will stay at my side, along with the first council. You are too useful to sacrifice."

The man standing beside Kaj seemed both relieved and discomfited. "Thank you, True Mighty."

Rone recognized the Noscon word. His thoughts translated "True Mighty," but the man had spoken "Kolosos."

"I am almost ready for it," Kaj whispered, connecting the ends of one of the ribbons. Grabbing the loop with pliers, he held it over the torch fire, warming the metal.

In the distance, Rone heard shouting. It took only a few more seconds for Tagaro to stiffen and ask, "What's that?"

Kaj pulled back from the flame, turning toward the locked door. The voices grew louder. Lantern light brightened the drawn curtains.

"They've found us," Tagaro whispered as the door shook. The head of an axe pierced through the wood.

Kaj scowled. "Only you."

He pushed Tagaro toward the door and bolted for the back window.

"Give up, Kaj!" bellowed an older man at the front of the mob. His dress was familiar—he was the Mighty from Ireth's memories. He held a long staff before him, the top burning with fire. He and his men surrounded Kaj, who had his back against a sheer wall of rock. That wasn't one of the Fortitude Mountains, was it?

Kaj's nails dug into the rock behind him as the Noscon warriors slowly advanced. He'd been found out. Betrayed, perhaps. But he was so close. *So close.*

I will not die here, he thought, and it felt as though Kaj spoke to Rone directly. *I will not die here.*

There was a flash—how it happened, Rone couldn't see, but as it faded, he got a glimpse of an empty clearing. The people had disappeared, and all that remained of them were fallen torches, scythes, and swords.

This was how it happened, he realized, the vision fading. *This is how he imprisoned them all in the ethereal plane.*

Rone stumbled onto the glassy floor of the plane, gasping for air. His clothes and hair smoked, his skin burned. He felt like he'd been suspended in the monster's memories for hours, when, looking back at the ongoing battle, it had only been a fraction of a second—the amount of time it had taken him to pass from one corner of Kolosos's hoof to the other.

The images spun through his brain. Kaj had created this place, and the Noscons had vanished at his command. Leaving their world behind to decay until the Kolins found it and . . . what? Discovered Kaj's runes and tablets? Worked the magic out for themselves? But by then, the spirits had mutated, and—

The spirits. The numina.

The fallen pillar lay in front of him. He had no time to work through what he'd learned, not if he hoped to thwart Kolosos.

Shaking, Rone pushed himself upright, ignoring the tightness of skin that felt thoroughly sunburned. Limped. Walked. *Ran.*

Could he stop Kaj? Kolosos? Probably not. But the oversized numen would have to figure out what was more important: the tiny gang of numina defending Rone, or his precious pillar.

The tusked numen trumpeted as Rone neared. He didn't need to look to feel Kolosos's attention on him, despite Ireth's, Isepia's, and Drang's attempts at distraction. Kolosos's wrath raised the temperature of the perpetually mild plane to an unbearable level. The ground bucked under Kolosos's feet as he gave chase.

Rone reached the spider-rock creature and swept his arm between its rocky back and the two numina fused to it, and then freed the pair from each other. Snippets of memories poked at his mind, tangled and disjointed, none whole, but he tried to ignore them as he released the next numen, and the next.

Ireth screamed at him to run, and Rone obeyed. He ran until he thought he'd vomit all the precious morsels he'd collected from the mortal realm. Ran while the freed numina scattered, forcing Kolosos to choose between fighting and collecting. He chose the latter.

Isepia's wind beat at Rone's back, urging him onward.

Rone hissed through clenched teeth as he pulled off his ruined jacket. He felt like he'd lain out in the summer sun for a week. The skin on his back burned mightily as he moved his arms and discarded clothing that was half-incinerated.

He tried to pull off his shirt, but moving that much sent sharp stabs of pain over his skin. He craned an equally scorched neck to better see his back. Blisters. Yellow ones.

He cringed and turned toward Ireth. They had taken shelter in a blocky sort of cave, though the ceiling was far higher than in any cave Rone had ever seen in the natural world. It cut off the light from the heavens and glowed orange with Ireth's banked fire.

"I don't suppose you have anything to treat this." Rone's voice was flat.

Ireth shook his head. Behind him, Drang crouched, licking his own burns. Isepia lingered somewhere outside their protective tunnel.

You will have to find it yourself, in the mortal realm. Ireth lowered his silvery head. *But if you do, you will have to forgo sustenance. I do not think it wise. I do not believe this injury is fatal.*

No, it wasn't, but it hurt like high hell.

God's tower, what Rone wouldn't give to close his eyes and wake up back in Dresberg, despite its ravaged state. She was there, and that was enough. Rone thought he'd done a pretty good job of holding out up here. In part because everything was so new and, honestly, dangerous. It had kept his mind off things. But the novelty of the ethereal plane was wearing thin.

Drang said something in Noscon, and Ireth quietly translated, *That was foolish.* Ireth then said, *Thank you for your help.*

Trying to focus on anything besides his fire-damaged skin, Rone asked, "Why can you speak Kolin and he can't?"

Drang looked at him. Did he understand?

I have been watching mankind more closely than most, Ireth answered. *I have learned. But they understand some. Especially those who have been summoned frequently.*

Rone nodded. He touched the back of his neck, winced, and dropped his hand. He needed water, desperately. "I'm going to need you to show me the city again."

Ireth nodded and tapped his hoof on the glassy ground. Dresberg lit by morning sunlight came into view.

Rone paused a moment. "If I endured it—went a couple days, maybe three, without reaching down there—could I have enough strength to go back?"

Ireth shook his head, and the hope Rone had summoned puddled around his feet like used oil. *It cannot work that way. And you cannot be summoned, mortal as you are.*

Rone shook his head. "Then how do I get *back?*"

Ireth looked at him a beat too long for comfort. *Kaj's power holds up the ethereal plane. Destroying him will free all of us.*

Rone rolled his eyes. "Easy."

It is not.

"It's called sarcasm, Ireth." He rubbed his face. At least his hands were never dirty here. But Ireth's words sank into him, burning hotter than the blisters marring his back. He tensed, understanding.

"I'm trapped here until Kolosos dies."

Or until he destroys us, yes.

Rone flung his hands into the air, then winced as the motion pulled the tender flesh beneath his shirt. "That's not exactly *freeing!*"

Your spirit will be free.

Rone growled and turned toward the unnaturally smooth wall of the cave, smacking his forehead against it. "You sound like my father."

Ireth cocked his head, perhaps interested by the comparison. Given that he followed Sandis so closely, the numen likely knew who the Angelic was.

Keeping his forehead pressed to the dark glass, Rone considered what action to take next. He couldn't sit idly by and hope something happened. He had to continue down this path. His *only* path, as far as he could see. Knock down the pillars here, hope that Sandis and the others could do the same there. Rone could buy them time while they tracked down the amarinth and Anon. It *was* possible. It was just . . . hard.

You need to drink, Ireth reminded him, and though the fire horse was trying to be helpful, Rone really wanted to punch him.

He didn't need his hand blistered, too, so he resisted.

Find water. Water will help you think.

Rone sighed. It wouldn't help at first. He hated how much energy it took to reach into the mortal plane. The weakness made him vulnerable.

Rone turned back to the image of the city. He didn't want to risk drinking from the canals. Maybe they could move to the Fortitude Mountains. It was a little early in the year for snow and a little late for runoff, but even those barricading mountains had to have streams, right?

Footsteps outside the tunnel called Rone's attention away from the vision in the glass. He tensed for a moment before making out Isepia's silhouette. She spoke directly to Ireth, who translated, *There are others here.*

Rone's pulse quickened. "Others? Good others, or bad others?"

Ireth looked at Isepia, continuing their soundless conversation. The fire on his body danced russet and gold.

Come, he told Rone and Drang, and led the way out of the cave. Rone followed, keeping a healthy distance between himself and the wolf-lion.

When he stepped out into the muted light of the surrounding plane, he gaped.

There had to be a dozen numina there. A handful had human features mixed with those of plants or animals. There was a serpent, a cloud with tentacles, a deformed hornet. An enormous beast Rone recognized—Mahk. They clustered together, facing Rone. Studying him with curiosity.

With *knowing*.

We witnessed your fight, the cloud said in Kolin. Her mental voice was distinctly female. *And we have seen Kolosos and his intentions.*

Kaj, another echoed. And a second. *Kaj.*

"You remember." Rone's voice was little more than a croak, so he repeated himself, louder. "You remember."

Eyes—those who had them—sharpened.

"You'll help us?"

A few looked to Ireth. Perhaps not understanding. Perhaps not trusting a mortal.

It is dangerous, Ireth said in his matter-of-fact way. *But the mortals fight for their lives below. Can we not join them and fight for all that we have lost?*

A symphony of mismatching tones vibrated through the group. It sounded positive.

Rone smiled. "We can do this. We can do this."

Hepingya, one said. The serpent, maybe? The name was repeated again. *Hepingya. Hepingya.*

I do not know where the Mighty is, Ireth said, lowering his head.

Mighty? Rone looked out over the numina. So the chieftain from Ireth's and Kaj's memories was Hepingya. Rone's *god.* The revelation ignited a strange sensation in his gut, something like nervousness and dread, tainted with hope.

As though sensing his thoughts, Ireth glanced to Rone. *He fears being found by Kaj.*

The cloud numen turned . . . east? Rone could only judge by the muted sun.

187

Hepingya, someone repeated. *Hepingya.*

Ireth's flames blazed, quieting the group. He stomped his right hoof twice. *The mortal needs sustenance, and I cannot carry him. Let him drink, and we will go.*

The crowd of numina hummed.

Hope flared so strongly within Rone he forgot the pain radiating through his skin.

Perhaps they had a chance after all.

Chapter 23

Sandis had only followed Kolosos a short ways before the monster exploded in light.

It was almost like the brilliance of a summoning, but red, hot, and huge. It had flashed like lightning and boomed like thunder, swallowing the sky in its purposeful brilliance.

She and Hapshi had nearly crashed, both of them temporarily blinded, but he'd landed on a balcony at her directive. The feather-covered rodent hadn't been able to take off with Rist on its back, so it was only the two of them.

Tears streamed down Sandis's cheeks as she blinked red from her vision. By the time her eyes recovered, she faced nothing but a dark city.

No, she thought, commanding Hapshi to the edge of the balcony. Where had the monster gone?

Sandis flew, traveling in the same direction as before . . . or in the direction she *thought* she'd gone before.

This was right. Wasn't it?

She searched, feeling exposed as crowds of survivors gawked from the streets, streaming from their hovels and flats now that the demon had vanished. Sandis faced forward, hoping her hair shielded her face.

The light had disoriented her, but Sandis was close. Desperately close. And so she waited on a stairwell as Hapshi, under her blood-bound command, flew back to fetch Rist.

Beneath the pinkening sky, Sandis and Rist searched together until they found an intact but abandoned flat to hide Bastien. Sandis saw to his burns, some of which had cracked and bled, and left the medicine and remaining water with him. Then, uttering a prayer to anything that would hear it, she and Rist hurried into the city to find her brother.

This time, Kolosos had not had time to leave the city. She was sure of it.

One would think that a six-story demon with enormous wings and glowing rock skin would be hard to hide, and yet between the carnage, the fire, and the smoke . . . Sandis wasn't sure how to track it. This part of the city seemed so intact. The broken cobblestones marking Kolosos's footfalls just . . . ended. Like the monster had retracted its heat and flown to safety. To make things more difficult, they searched not for a giant demon, but a slender adolescent boy.

She and Rist barely spoke to each other as they searched street after street, peering through windows and into garbage bins, retracing their steps, and bumping into listless people who wandered the streets. In the afternoon hours, their advance was slow, thanks to scarlets and soldiers also scouting the area. Only a few of them might recognize Sandis and Rist, but the vessels didn't want to take any chances.

The uniformed patrols ventured too far north, she thought. Sandis had been *so close* before Kolosos flashed and vanished. She was sure the monster had been headed east . . .

"Maybe we should follow them." Rist pointed toward two soldiers on horseback passing through the next street.

"No. It didn't go that far."

"I watched the sky turn red, Sandis," Rist said, kicking a broken spoon on the side of the road. "It was brilliant. And *huge*. Kolosos could be anywhere in District Four."

Sandis merely shook her head. She *knew* they were close.

"Maybe one of the minions moved the body," Rist said. "Otherwise he'd be out in the open."

The back of her throat burned. "That body's name is Anon."

Rist didn't reply, but his suggestion nagged at her. If Kolosos's brainwashed victims also had instructions to hide her brother, she might never find him. Or she'd have to fight innocent people to reach him.

Her hope floundered.

Limbs weak, Sandis and Rist continued to search for Anon, occasionally checking trash bins for scraps of food, but everything had already been picked over. Sherig could help them, if she was willing, but Sandis didn't want to risk losing Kolosos's trail. The sun was already setting. Her chances of finding her brother would shrink drastically in the dark.

Even the bell towers held their breath.

She paused at a canal, scanning its depths as though its waters would grant her answers. She remembered nearly drowning in one not long ago. She'd thought Anon had suffered that fate. Shivering, Sandis forced her aching feet to move on. Cross the bridge. She and Rist were far from the smoke ring, and the flats up ahead were in better condition than many they had passed. Some still showed signs of people: hanging laundry, scents of dinner. But the windows and doors had all been closed, boarded, bolted. Some of the lower flats had broken windows. Had they been raided? Had the occupants left of their own will, or had something terrible happened?

Rist, who'd gone around back, reappeared from behind the building. He looked ragged and worn, but for once he didn't complain. When he neared her, he muttered, "Scarlet," and tipped his head back. Sandis followed his line of sight and spied two men in police uniforms. They seemed too focused on the task they'd been given to notice her and Rist.

Kill the vessel, kill Kolosos.

Get the amarinth, stop the beast, she reminded herself.

Sandis turned south, softly gesturing for Rist to follow. A man with sallow cheeks crossed their path, muttering to himself, clutching a gold candlestick to his chest. Marching east on worn shoes. Dirt lined the wrinkles of his face.

Another minion.

Sandis shied away from him, her hunger swirling into dread.

She paused at the next intersection, searching as the shadow of Dresberg's behemoth wall slowly stretched over the city, darkening it before true night settled. Rist left her side, heading for a row of shops nearby. Several had already been vandalized, but Sandis didn't stop him. She searched the shadows, a prayer in her heart. If only Rone were here. He knew the city so well. He was smart. He'd know what to do.

Rone at the forefront of her thoughts, Sandis looked up. To the roofs.

Maybe, if she looked at the city the way Kolosos did, she'd have a better chance of figuring out where the monster had gone.

***

Elfri slammed the door on the moaning, mind-numbed slave and balled her hands into fists. The Riggers had captured this one, a young woman, days ago. Treated her wounds, tried a variety of potions, talked to her . . . nothing would snap her out of her mindless crusade to serve the bull monster. Even now, eyes hollow from lack of sleep, the woman pulled against her restraints. She'd already broken a thumb in her attempts to escape.

Elfri didn't know whether to let the sad person leave, keep her out of Kolosos's clutches, or put her out of her misery.

Swallowing a growl, she trudged down the hallway and up the stairs, where tendrils of daylight poured through gaps in their metal-bar-reinforced windows. She barely got a few more steps before Rufus appeared with a middle-aged couple, thin and wide eyed.

Elfri sighed. "More?"

The man dropped to his knees and clasped his hands together as though in prayer. "Please, Sherig. Please help us. I'm still fit enough to fight. And Marg, she can cook. She don't mind physical labor—"

"Stop." Elfri waved a hand. She looked to Rufus. "See what you can find them."

The Rigger nodded and escorted the couple back whence they had come.

Changing route, Elfri took a narrow set of stairs up to the second floor and pushed open a set of double doors that led into a large space— a sort of meeting room for boardinghouse visitors. A smattering of her original men were in there, along with some of the newer, more competent recruits. One had put together a map of the city, and it was pinned to the far wall. Two others were dividing up their quickly dwindling rations. All silenced upon her arrival.

Elfri rubbed the palms of her hands into her eyes. "This is too much. Too many people."

One of the older men, Arnae Kurtz, said, "Must we begin turning them away?"

The thought made Elfri sick. Her husband, may he rest in peace, would have cut off the beggars days ago. "We're going to help them in a different way. We're going to evacuate them ourselves."

Pat stood from where he was separating rations. "Can't, boss. Just this morning word came in that the wall was still guarded."

"Then we take care of the guards," Elfri snapped. "I'd rather break a few necks to save a hundred. The sooner, the better. We'll storm the pass, or head up north to the farmlands." The latter was a better bet. Promise of food. But how long would it take the refugees to reach it?

"Might be tough," another Rigger said.

Elfri glared at him. "Remind me when any of this was easy."

He didn't dare open his mouth a second time.

193

Turning toward Kurtz, Elfri said, "With all that seugrat training under your belt, any chance you're also versed in stratagem?" Elfri couldn't maneuver this herself. There was too much to oversee already.

Blessedly, Kurtz nodded. "You give me the men, I'll make it work."

"Done." She turned toward Pat. "Release the captives and pull the guards for Kurtz. Then gather up the strongest citizens. They might need to run once we have an opening."

Pat hurried to the door, barely remembering a "Yes, sir," as he went.

<hr>

The handle of Rist's stolen lamp creaked every time he leapt between buildings, but Sandis supposed stealth wasn't absolutely necessary. Not yet. She chose only the six-story buildings, not wanting to risk a jump to anything lower. Without Bastien with them, they moved faster, though Hapshi would have been useful. She walked the perimeter of each roof, searching for signs of the monster. Once she thought she saw burnt brick, but was that from Kolosos's most recent stint through the city or a past one?

The moon was full, and the factory smoke had cleared enough for the stars to shine through the smog—a sliver of mercy from heaven. On a normal night, the city was bathed in light from homes and factories and streetlamps, but most were extinguished, save the occasional hairs of firelight that peeked through closed shutters.

Darkness aside, time was ticking. Kolosos, so far, had kept to its pattern. It wouldn't be long before the amarinth reset and the monster returned to finish whatever it wanted finished.

Fatigue weighed on her limbs like heavy mud. Even Rist was starting to wobble on his feet. If she didn't succeed soon, she'd have to repeat the chase again tonight. But would Bastien be ready to summon again? Would he *let* her summon on his weakened body?

Had she made the wrong choice again?

Yet just as she made to turn back, her eyes caught on the roof of a building slightly shorter than that on which she stood. Specifically, on the thick, black shadow engulfing the roof despite the fact that it was bathed in moonlight.

It wasn't a shadow but a hole. A *massive* hole, like the building had been cored.

"Rist," she said, some of her strength returning. She pointed.

Rist squinted, confused, but she saw the moment it dawned on him. The lifting of his features, the rounding of his mouth. "It's a pit."

"Made from above." She couldn't jump to the place, so she searched the building she stood on for a way down. Finding none, she crossed to the next one and used the butt of her rifle to break a lock on a doorway on the southern corner of the roof. It opened to stairs.

Reaching the street below took only a moment, yet it felt like eternity.

There were more soldiers in the neighborhood than there'd been during the day. Sandis and Rist hugged the wall of a narrow alley, waiting for one pair, and then another, to pass. Were they heading for the Innerchord, where they knew Kolosos was destined, or were they still searching?

Rist nudged her with his elbow, and they ran across one street, hugged an alley, and came upon a canal that separated them from their destination. It was completely dry. Kolosos's destruction might have blocked it somewhere or drained it into the sewers.

No bridges were close by, so Rist dropped into the rounded concrete basin, and reached back to help Sandis down. She marveled at the act of kindness, but didn't comment on it. Whatever motivated him, it was frail, and she dared not risk shattering it.

Climbing back out was harder. The concrete was at a steep incline and smooth. It took Rist a few runs at it to catch the lip and haul himself up, shoulders shaking. He wasn't weak, but his body was still recovering, and like the rest of them, he needed food and rest. He stretched a long arm down. Sandis ran at the wall the way he had. On her second try, she snagged his wrist, and he pulled her up.

The building they sought loomed before them, half-cast in shadow, lively as a tombstone. It was another set of flats, with wider windows and smoother brick. From the street it looked unscathed, minus a few broken windows, but no light peeked between the shutters or beneath the closed doors.

Rist chewed on his lower lip.

Sandis moved first. She tried the doors to the bottom flats, finding them all locked. Her hands began to sweat as the moon crawled across the sky. Time was running out.

Pulling out her rifle, she tried to break one of the knobs as she had before. The noise of the gun striking metal was deafening in the silence of the city. Rist grabbed the rifle's muzzle and yanked it from her hands, offering her a scowl in turn.

She knew why. The soldiers from before weren't far.

Rist, gripping the muzzle, swung the firearm at one of the windows instead, shattering it. He moved the rifle around, clearing out as much glass as he could. The window was a little high, about even with Rist's chin. He returned the gun, took a few steps back, and ran for the sill.

He grabbed it, cursed under his breath, and pulled himself up. He cursed again when he helped Sandis after him. It wasn't as easy as the canal, and a piece of glass bit Sandis's knee. When Rist released her, she noticed dark streaks smeared across her hands and forearms. He had cut himself badly.

"Are you all right?" she whispered.

There was just enough light for Sandis to see him roll his eyes. "I'll survive." He pulled out his stolen lamp and retrieved a match from their collected goods. The light blinded her and filled her nostrils with the scent of kerosene.

"Hurry." Rist turned to jump down. "Not much fuel."

Sandis leapt after him, landing smoothly on the glass-strewn floor. The flat looked abandoned, its walls empty but its rooms furnished. It smelled a little musty. She and Rist split apart, searching.

The back wall in the kitchen was burnt out.

"Rist," she called, and he appeared with the light. Sandis passed through the opening first, stepping on ash and sheet rock. She entered another flat's kitchen from the side. This one had two missing walls. Those that remained were scorched black.

Rist moved close enough that heat from the lamp burned the back of Sandis's neck. She moved inward, angling for the center of the building. She stepped through a bathroom littered with broken ceramic before entering a charcoal cavity. It was black and sooty, carved by fire. When Sandis stood in it, she could see all the way up to the moon. Lamplight followed her, highlighting the charred destruction.

"Hello?"

The word was so weak it could have come from a dying bird. Sandis whipped around, gooseflesh devouring her.

"Anon?" she croaked, running toward where she thought she'd heard the voice. She tripped on a fallen, half-burnt beam. "Hello?"

"SSSSSandis?"

She whisked to her right. The light was too slow to follow. A shadow writhed against the floor.

She didn't recognize him at first. He was covered in cinders, save for a few pale streaks on his face. His naked skin was stained black with soot. His hair was streaked heavily with gray. The whites of his eyes were dull.

He winced at the light. Shielded himself from it. Were his arms always so skinny?

"Black ashes," Rist muttered.

Sandis cried, tears pouring down her face. "Anon!" She ran to him, clasped his filthy shoulders. "Anon, we've been searching so long . . ."

She pressed her forehead against his dirty neck and washed away the soot with tears.

"Go," he whispered.

She reeled back. "What?"

His eyes, the same shade of brown as hers, widened and trembled. "Run, Sandis. *Go!*"

Sandis found her feet. "But—"

Anon squeezed his eyes shut and grabbed his head. "I can't stop it. It's c-coming—"

A soft whirring seasoned the air, and from behind her brother, a glittery light rose, surrounded by twirling gold loops. They spun faster and faster, and the amarinth's center turned a deep shade of red.

Rist cursed and dropped the lamp. He grabbed Sandis's arm and jerked her back the way they'd come.

"No!" Sandis fought him. "Anon!"

Rist shoved her ahead of him. "We will *die* if we don't get out of this building, *now!*"

Sandis hesitated. The whirring of the amarinth had turned into a keen cry. Or was that her brother?

Rist blocked her view and grabbed her by the back of her neck, yanking her toward the nearest exit. He'd barely gotten the door unlocked when red light swallowed them, bringing with it unbearable heat.

Rist and Sandis spilled out into the street, and the building behind them burst into flames.

Chapter 24

The red light pulled her back into herself, even before the heat licked her skin.

She didn't know if the next choice she made was selfish or not, but it would likely save their lives—hers and Rist's—and she could only hope it would save Anon, too.

As Rist shoved her through the door, she grabbed his hair and whispered the words. His eyes met hers when they hit the cobblestone road, and in that fraction of a second, realization and fear lit them.

The flash of light burned her eyes, but when the building exploded, the heavily armored back of Kuracean shielded her body.

We have to run, she told the enormous crustacean. The smaller of its two front claws swept down and scooped her up, but Kuracean was not gentle. Its pincers were hard and sharp, and the bony barbs dug into her ribs.

Kuracean made it about twenty feet before something—perhaps a hunk of ruined building—slammed into its back. Kuracean stumbled forward, throwing Sandis ten feet into a garbage pile. Rank, dark liquid spilled over her shoulder, but the mass of garbage had likely saved her life, for however long she would have it.

Kolosos loomed over her, larger than ever, the cracks in its obsidian skin wider and brighter. Hot, smoke-laden wind rushed from its body.

Letting out an earth-shaking roar, it lifted a hooved foot and brought it down on Kuracean—

A blur whisked down the road, colliding with the hard-shelled numen and knocking it aside the moment before Kolosos's hoof smashed the street. Cobblestones hissed and cracked under the pressure of its hoof-fall, and Sandis pushed her way out of the garbage, heat searing her skin. It had happened too quickly for her to see what had pushed Kuracean aside. *Kuracean, hide!*

A spray of water misted the air from an unknown source, cooling it down dramatically. It hit Kolosos's shin, and the enormous numen stepped back, knocking down what remained of the hollowed building behind it.

Someone was helping them, but there was no time to wonder about their allies. Kolosos roared again, stepping free of the burning ruins and trudging right through another building. Distant screams pierced the night.

It wasn't going back toward the Innerchord. It was fighting.

Embers sprayed up from Kolosos's hooves, forcing Sandis to seek shelter farther down the trash-laden alley. When the monster passed, she rushed back into the street, over the broken cobblestones. She tripped, crying out as the hot stone burned her skin. A dark mass filled the way ahead. *Kuracean! Come!*

To her shock, the creature that turned was not Kuracean, but another numen. It had an enormous feline-like head with long, twisting ears. Its skin was leathery and tight, and two massive black tusks protruded up from its wide jaw. Its enormous rounded eyes reflected light. It crouched on short but well-muscled hind legs.

"Grendoni," Bastien said in her memory. *"He's a six, I think. I've been told he looks like a goblin cat."*

This was the numen Bastien had been bound to, before Oz sold him to Kazen. But then, who . . . ?

Teppa? That would mean—

Kolosos roared behind her, pulling Sandis from her reverie. A second numen floated near the monster—not flying, precisely. She was a bare-chested woman without hair or forearms. A large, hinged fish tail protruded from her hips. She swung it, and another gust of heavy mist encircled the block. Kolosos threw its clawed hand forward, sending lava hurtling through the air. The mermaid swished away, but Sandis thought she heard her cry. The lava collided with another building, crumbling its side.

Sandis hesitated only a moment before continuing on her path. Grendoni's ears flicked, and it rushed past her. Around the corner she found Kuracean, one of its legs trapped under an enormous hunk of brick.

Use your pincer! she cried in her thoughts. *Knock it off!* Celestial above, if Rist died . . . if Rist died—

A hand grabbed her elbow. Sandis spun, the seugrat she'd practiced guiding her limbs as she twisted out of the hold and swung the side of her stiff hand into a man's neck. She made contact, and the man stumbled back, wheezing.

In Kolosos's red light, she recognized Oz.

"What are you doing here?" she cried.

Oz shook his head, rubbing his neck. "Followed you, you foolish girl." He looked up as Kolosos's light brightened and a new building caught fire.

Kolosos was going to burn down the city.

Sandis shoved her shoulder against the brick mound pinning Kuracean. It didn't budge. "We have to run—"

"We have to *fight*. We can't outrun that. Not until the army comes."

Sandis whirled toward him. "We can't fight! You don't have Jansen anymore. Rist is stuck—"

Oz whipped out a switchblade. "We can fight. Long enough to get the hell out of here. But we need all of you."

Sandis stared at his blade. A new opera of screams punctuated the night.

Hugging herself, she said, "No. I'll summon him myself."

Oz scowled. "Now is not the time for parlor tricks!"

Something exploded, and Oz jerked her forward, sheltering them behind the brick as something hot and flaming sailed into the street ahead of them. It bounced once before landing in an alley, lighting a heap of garbage on fire. The smoke was thickening the air, making it hard to breathe.

Oz winced—was his leg injured?—and looked her in the eye. "Where is Bastien?"

"Safe and asleep." Her heart pounded so hard in her throat she couldn't speak. Beside her, Kuracean whined.

Oz set his jaw and spoke through clenched teeth. "You're special, I get that. But your self-summoning gives us a few seconds of firepower, and that's it. I summon Ireth into you, and we have a chance to save our skins. Don't you hear them, Sandis?"

Tears tried to form in Sandis's eyes, but the heat steamed them away. Her knee throbbed. Her skin burned.

A new choice lay before her. Give up her control, or listen to the screams of a burning city?

But Oz . . . he was a grafter. He was just like Kazen. Just like—

Kazen is dead.

She glanced back toward Rist. Thought of Bastien. How long until Kolosos made its way to the empty flat hiding him?

Rone. What would Rone do?

Rone isn't here. The thought stung her like the tip of a lit match, though the burn radiated outward, making her whole body sting.

It hurt worse because it was true. Rone wasn't there. She couldn't lean on him, not anymore. He couldn't be her bandage, her crutch.

This was on her. Just her. She had the power to choose what happened next.

Gritting her teeth, Sandis snagged the knife from Oz's hand. Three nights had passed since their last blood exchange; it was time to renew. She shallowly pressed the tip of the blade into the inside of her elbow until dark blood bubbled beneath it. Shots fired nearby. The sky blazed crimson.

"Do it!" she barked. "Free Kuracean. With my blood, you'll control it, too. Can you handle it?"

"I can." He took the blade and carefully cut the underside of his own arm, avoiding veins, before pressing the wound to Sandis's. She forced herself not to wince.

Looking Oz in the eyes, she said, "Get us out alive."

Nodding, he placed his hand against her forehead. His words were precise, practiced, and quick. *"Vre en nestu a carnath. Ii mem entre I amar. Vre en nestu a carnath. Ireth epsi gradenid."*

Pain, scalding and bright, consumed her, shredding her flesh and grating her bones. It turned her inside out and seared her very soul. It lasted only a breath, yet stretched on for eternity, agonizing, flavored with whispers of death. It swallowed her whole and faded to black.

But when the darkness lifted, she saw Rone.

Rone jumped when the familiar white light engulfed Ireth. Their small army came to a stop, everyone turning as their general vanished from their midst. Summoned.

And yet, in his place, dull light coalesced like condensation, taking on shape and color.

Rone's legs nearly gave out when he beheld Sandis. She was murky, without definition, but he would know her anywhere. He ran to her. Tried to touch her, but just like with the numina, his hands passed right through her.

Her blurry brown eyes met his and widened. "Rone?"

God's tower, he could hear her.

"Sandis?" He spoke too loudly, his arms trembling.

A sharp sound escaped her, something between a sob and a laugh. She reached out fuzzy arms. They passed through his chest, ghostlike. She retracted them and held them to her breast. "Kolosos, it's here. It's—"

"I know."

"Oz summoned Ireth. I . . . This has never happened before. Where are you?"

Rone glanced at the two dozen numina around him. Sandis's eyes never strayed to them. He guessed she couldn't see them, only him in all his mortal glory. He also guessed they had very little time together.

So he focused on her, her faint but beautiful face, and spoke as carefully and quickly as he could.

"We're making an army of numina on this side. The ethereal plane. Kolosos is building pillars here just like in Dresberg. He needs gold for the magic. To merge the planes. We have to stop him soon, or he'll destroy us all."

Sandis hesitated only a moment. "Numina? The Celestial?"

"We can't depend on the Celestial, but we have a growing army. We have to strike him together, Sandis. Before his pillars are complete. It's the only chance we have to overpower him. We don't have a lot of time."

Her gaze never flinched. "We have to do it when Kolosos is here. In Dresberg."

"Tomorrow night."

"Without the Celestial." It was more a statement than a question. He would have told her if it were otherwise.

He dropped his head. "I'm sorry, Sandis."

"I don't . . . I don't know." Her blurry form shifted. "Bastien and Rist and I . . . we ran from the government, Rone."

"I know." He'd watched that part.

"I don't know what they're doing. What their plans are. But we can't fight without them."

"Go back."

She nodded. He could imagine her chewing on her bottom lip, though her figure was too murky for such a detail. "I'll . . . *we'll* try to knock down the pillars here. Slow Kolosos down. We'll do what we can."

"Us, too. This place . . . it's his headquarters. He's still connected here when he's there. We can still hurt him." His pulse pumped too fast. He tried to touch her again. He might as well have been grasping smoke.

Her colors began to fade, and the limited definition she had bled into the cool air surrounding them. "I'll do it. I'll tell them. Tomorrow night, midnight."

"They're the Noscons, Sandis. The numina. They're trapped here."

She paused before replying. "I'm . . . I'm fading, Rone."

Sorrow, cold and sharp, stung from his throat to his knees. He placed his hands on her, letting them hover over her intangible form. "I'll be there. I promise. Sandis." His voice strained as his throat tightened. "I love you."

The shadows of her facial features began to blur, but he could have sworn he saw her grin.

Clearing his throat, awkwardly aware of the Noscons surrounding him, he added, "It would be nice if you'd say it back."

"Oh, Rone." Her voice was little more than wind. Her form darkened, faded. "You've always known I do. I've loved you from the beginni—"

She was gone.

Chapter 25

Sandis startled awake as though doused with cold water. She sat up in a weakly sunlit room, her dry eyes shooting toward a gauze curtain. Then the walls, the ceiling, the door, the bed gradually came into focus. It took a moment for her to comprehend where she was. A moment of staring at a blue-clad guard just beyond the window, on a short balcony, while her head throbbed the rhythm of consciousness.

Triumvir Var's home. Her assigned bedroom. Besides the guard, she was alone.

She searched for water, but found none. As she rubbed her eyes, faint memories surfaced in her thoughts. It almost had the feeling of a dream, but vessels never dreamed when possessed.

Rone. The sweet flood of relief almost overwhelmed her aching head. He was alive, and although his image had been blurry, he'd appeared unharmed. Jachim had been right—he was in the ethereal plane. *With an army of numina. The . . . Noscons?*

Her lips parted, releasing all the air within her. The ancient people who'd once inhabited Kolingrad were . . . *numina*? But how? How did an entire race of people turn into—

Ireth is Noscon. Ireth is . . . human?

Was that what he had wanted to tell her all along? This changed everything. *Everything.* The occult wasn't simply summoning monsters from another world, but another time. *Noscons.*

Was Kolosos Noscon, too? Rone had called the demon "he."

Her spine stiffened. *Anon.* Celestial, save him. She'd been *right there.* If only she'd come a minute sooner. If only she had grabbed the amarinth first—

Jaw set, Sandis pressed the heels of her hands into her eyes and watched colors swirl behind her eyelids. Regret would get her nowhere. She repeated this to herself, a mantra, until she believed it. She had a plan. And she had mere hours to fulfill her end of it.

Sandis wrenched her hands away and blinked until her vision cleared. What time was it? Afternoon, but early or late? Ignoring a twinge of nausea, she got up from the bed, swaying once with fatigue. A white long-sleeved dress with silver embroidery hung from her frame. A priestess's gown? Had they taken Priestess Marisa's things to clothe her? But at least she was clothed.

The guard on the balcony must have noticed her activity, for a second later the gauzy curtains parted and he trudged into the room, tall, broad, and stoic. "You are not to leave."

Sandis winced, the pounding in her head increasing. "I need to speak to the triumvirate."

"My orders are—"

"Now. Please." Pain chipped at her resolve. She held on to it with a white-knuckle grip. "I've spoken to Rone in the ethereal plane. I know how to defeat Kolosos."

She hoped.

The soldier considered for a moment, his lips pressed into a tight line. "I'll escort you."

Sandis let him take her arm and open the door. She moved compliantly at his side as they wound through familiar halls and ventured down familiar stairs. All three triumvirs were gathered in the study. Triumvir Var's face was hollow, the skin around his eyes dark and droopy. When was the last time he'd slept?

Oz was with them, as was High Priest Dall.

Triumvir Holwig looked up first, his sword-straight hair tangling with his eyelashes. "She's awake," he said, alerting the others in the room.

The soldier saluted. "She claims to have valuable information."

Triumvir Var's red-veined gaze moved toward her. He nodded, and the soldier released her. Sandis swayed on her feet before righting herself.

Oz said, "If you want her to be useful, get her some water and something to eat." He glowered at Triumvir Var, as though this had been part of an earlier and unpleasant conversation. Sandis was still unsure how she felt about Oz, but she passed him a look of gratitude.

Var groaned softly and nodded again. The soldier scuttled off, hopefully to do as Oz had said. Sandis's stomach had begun to cramp, and her headache marched across her skull like a well-fed army.

She approached the table in the center of the room and sat in a chair before rubbing some moisture into her eyes. "What time is it?"

"Two past," the high priest answered. She'd been "dead" for fourteen hours.

Oz added, "The others aren't awake yet. Or if they are, these men won't let them out of their rooms." He gestured toward the triumvirs.

Triumvir Peterus growled. "They are deserters."

"They saved your sorry army last night," Oz spat.

"That," said Var, "is still up for debate."

Rubbing her temples, Sandis said, "Tell me what happened."

Triumvir Var took a deep breath through his nose. "Kolosos did not return to the Innerchord. It took to the wall. Crumbled the exits and rebuilt it as rubble."

Sandis's throat went dry. *It doesn't want us to escape.*

"At least it quelled the rebellion," Triumvir Holwig commented. Something else must have happened with the civilians while Sandis was gone, but she didn't take the time to ask about it. She thought of the pillars, of the mind-controlled people infected by the demon's magic.

Was that to be their destiny? To live as will-less slaves under Kolosos's eternal rule?

Thoughts of Rone's mother slipped through her mind.

High Priest Dall, who sat across from Sandis, knit his hands together atop the table. "We have volunteers trying to dig through or find a means to climb over. The devil did not have enough time to cage us completely."

"Where"—Sandis had to swallow against the dryness in her throat—"is the Angelic?"

"Seeing to the faithful," the high priest replied. Sandis shrunk beneath his hard tone. Did he still see her as a heretic?

Had her brands burned away her faith?

Was her faith relevant, anymore?

Footsteps sounded behind Sandis, and a cup of water and bread with some kind of brown spread was set before her. Sandis whispered a thank-you and grasped the cup, drinking until her belly hurt and her worries cleared. The bread was sweet, its flavor unfamiliar. After two bites, Triumvir Var said, "Now, tell us what you know."

Sandis swallowed. Rubbed her sore stomach. "Kolosos is building pillars in the ethereal plane as well." What exactly had Rone said?

"I love you."

She bit down on a smile before continuing, "It wants to . . . to merge the planes. I don't know why. He didn't have time to tell me."

Oz's brow rose. "He?"

"Rone."

The men exchanged glances. High Priest Dall spoke first. "You . . . spoke to him?"

Sandis nodded. "When Oz summoned Ireth last night, I saw him. Briefly. Jachim was right. He's in the ethereal plane. With the numina." What was it like, the ethereal plane? She had only seen Rone surrounded by swirls of color, like paint dripped into stale water. "He said Kolosos is making pillars there. That it needs gold. That it wants to merge the planes."

Triumvir Holwig shook his head. "A fever dream."

"Vessels don't dream," Sandis and Oz said in unison, both their tongues sharp. Clearing her throat, Sandis added, "Not when numina take their bodies. It's . . . hard to explain."

Triumvir Var shook his head. "This is preposterous."

Sandis stood, light-headedness be damned. "Rone will strike Kolosos tonight with an army of numina. We must strike at the same time with everything we have. This cannot be negotiated. I can't send a message to him to change our plan." Not if she wanted to be awake for the battle. She stared hard into Triumvir Var's eyes. "We have until midnight to ready your forces. *Our* forces." She glanced to Oz. "We have to be ready for Kolosos and hold nothing back."

"Attack Kolosos from both planes," Oz said softly. "I don't know . . . It might work."

"We need Franz," Triumvir Peterus murmured.

"Wake him," Triumvir Var replied, and Triumvir Peterus abandoned the table, his stride quick.

Triumvir Holwig picked at a scab on the side of his nose. "This sounds like a fancy. No one has claimed to see inside the ethereal plane before. Why now?"

"No one has summoned Kolosos before this, either," Sandis snapped. This man didn't understand any of it. He just saw monsters and vessels, black and white. Enemies and instruments to be used. But there was so much more to them. All of them.

Oz shrugged. "Rone doesn't belong there. Maybe she was able to see him because he's mortal. Maybe because of the bond he has with her." He stuck a thumb in Sandis's direction.

Sandis leaned forward. "What other choice do you have? Your army dwindles by the night. This is our best chance."

Triumvir Var didn't meet her gaze. "We have the vessels."

Sandis shook her head. "Five vessels aren't enough—"

Oz looked away, his jaw tight.

Sandis's heart sank. "You're making new ones."

The triumvirs and Oz didn't answer. High Priest Dall, scowling, said, "It was not a unanimous decision."

"*This*," spat Triumvir Var, "is not a country run by *council*. You forget your place."

Sandis might have wept, were her eyes not so dry from possession. "They'll take *weeks* to heal!" Sour memories surged forward, of her lying on a bed, her back swollen and burning, healing from her brands while Zelna wiped pus from the wounds. "Dresberg will be destroyed by then!"

Triumvir Var's palm slapped the table. "Do you think I don't know that?"

"These *people* are not your slaves!" Sandis matched his volume. "*We* are not your slaves!"

"I am using every resource I have to defeat this monster. I am giving *everything*!"

"Then trust me." Sandis's voice bent in her throat. A hard knot formed there. She held the old man's gaze, taking a few seconds to regain her composure. "Trust Rone. We've been fighting Kolosos since before you knew what it was. If we ever had a chance, this is it."

Triumvir Var's jaw clicked as it moved back and forth. Sandis felt the high priest's eyes on her. Triumvir Holwig watched Triumvir Var, and Oz stared beyond them all, his hands gripping the edge of the table.

"She's right."

The new voice startled Sandis. She turned, expecting to see Triumvir Peterus with Jachim, but it was the Angelic who stood in the doorway, his white clothes stained with ash, his face heavy with new wrinkles. A wisp of white hair poked out from his lily-crested hood.

The Angelic closed his eyes. "This war is twofold. It is not merely among mortals. Even as we speak, it rages on. And if the battle on the ethereal plane fails, we fail as well. We must be ready to strike with our allies."

High Priest Dall stood. "What are you saying?"

The Angelic opened his eyes, but he did not look at his subordinate. He focused on Sandis. She saw the strain in his face, the weariness. His emotions ran deeper than those that haunted Triumvir Var. This seemed personal. Did Adellion Comf fear for his son, or for something else?

Sandis didn't get the chance to ask.

"Get the men ready," Triumvir Var said. "Call back Istrude. I want those pillars taken down. His men can rest when the demon is dead."

Triumvir Holwig stiffened. "You'll be fighting with exhausted soldiers, Boladis."

Triumvir Var stood to his full height. "I mean to use our resources, Mirka. Not waste them. And if we are wrong in doing so . . . we die either way."

Chapter 26

Isepia was hard to see against the nothing sky, even with the demented "sunlight" glowing from Rone's far left. If not for the pale skin of her head and neck moving against the patches of shadow, he might have missed her.

She flew in a circle twice, that single wing somehow keeping her aloft, and took off toward the north, if Rone were to guess.

Two circles. She'd found a pillar, then. Navigating this place was annoyingly hard. Everything looked the same, though the numina seemed to understand it. After a couple thousand years, Rone supposed he'd begin recognizing random block formations and clusters of stars, too.

Iihedoh—the deformed hornet—took off after her, its split wings thumping more than they buzzed. Mahk's massive body floated behind. Rone would think that Pesos, the cloud with tentacles he still found hard to look at, would be able to fly as well, but it had yet to rise from the glassy ground. Instead, it—though he was fairly certain Pesos was a *she*—crawled forward like some sort of sea creature, its body half rolling with every flopping appendage. Drang moved beside Pesos, hackles raised as though impatient to use its—her?—speed.

Any numen, for the short time they had been part of Rone's life, had always been "it." Knowing what he did now, it felt strange not to know who they once had been. Ireth and Kolosos were both male. Isepia was obviously female. Unaresa—the serpent—seemed female as well. He'd asked, once, and gotten silence as a response.

He supposed it didn't matter. What mattered was slowing down Kaj and giving the mortal world a second to catch up.

The numina surged forward, following Isepia's path. Ireth lingered behind, his fire tamer than usual, emphasizing the burnt silver shape of his body. His black eyes met Rone's. *She is afraid.*

"We all are." Rone jerked his head toward the others. Ireth took off at a trot, keeping pace with Rone's jog. Rone was the slowest of the group, save perhaps for Pesos. And he stayed slow, so long as there wasn't immediate danger. His energy was low—a new normal for him, as was the buzz of the headache in his skull. He'd already lost weight, too, but his burns were less painful than they'd been.

The pillar wasn't as close as he had hoped; he was gasping for air by the time they reached it, and Rone took a moment to put his hands on his knees and scold his body into cooperating. After this, he would rest, and then he'd dip into the mortal world again. Find something meaty. Would the ethereal plane permit him to pull a whole goat through the divide? That would last him a while. All he'd have to do was cook it over Ireth's tail.

Straightening, Rone took in the sight before him and shrunk.

The pillar was enormous, tall as the Degrata, or close to it. Soft, morose sounds echoed from the creatures trapped together to form it. The faces of dozens of beasts, many of which Rone didn't recognize, watched the approaching army, a tangle of limbs both human and not. Skin, fur, scales. At the base was a great orange blob, a story high, with no other features that Rone could discern.

"I can't reach that." The first connection, between the blob and the half-human, half-bird thing atop it towered above his head. And none of the numina could give him a boost.

Iihedoh flapped its split wings at the pillar. It didn't so much as sway, but it gave Rone an idea.

214

Waving to Ireth to beg translation, Rone said to Iihedoh, "Could you and Isepia lie facedown here?" He pointed to the ground near the blob. "How fast can you beat your wings? How much air can we get?"

Ireth glanced at each of the flyers in turn, his request silent, before all three made eye contact with him.

They did as he asked, lying together, pulsing their wings. It worked surprisingly well, though Iihedoh provided the brunt of the power. Backing up, Rone ran full force toward the blob, then leapt just before reaching Isepia's head. The gusts carried him upward, nearly flipping him over. He soared through the first and second numina of the tower—*medicine bottles, mountains, a young girl's laugh*—and his mortality cut through their bond.

All six stories of the great pillar collapsed to the ground without so much as a *thump*.

Rone landed on his feet, then his knees, wincing as the skin on his back pulled. The numina behind him writhed in panic and excitement alike. Now to separate them—

The ground shuttered, the cause undeniable.

Ireth stood erect. *We must go.*

Everyone crowded into Triumvir Var's sitting room, which was the largest in the house. The furniture had been pushed back against the wall to make room for the dining table. Chairs were brought in to surround it. Teppa and Inda sat tightly together, silent, on a couch in the far corner. Rist, hands bandaged, fumed on the same furniture, pressing against the opposite arm to give himself as much space from the other vessels as possible. He had not been happy to be exiled to the back corner, but he also refused to leave. He didn't like decisions being made without him present. Decisions that could involve him.

Sandis felt very much the same. Fortunately, for now, none of that heated anger was aimed toward her. Rist had awoken sick, but more or less understanding of the actions Sandis had taken to defend them.

The triumvirs took up the head of the table, their chairs pressed so close together the arms touched, which would make it difficult for any of them to stand, let alone leave. General Istrude and Chief Esgar, both of whom had been called back from their work, sat at the opposite end of the table. Sandis sat nearest the general, with Bastien to her right and Oz to his right. Jachim sat at the corner, between Oz and Triumvir Peterus. Across from the grafters stretched the Celesian retinue: Priestess Marisa, Cleric Liddell, High Priest Dall, and the Angelic, whose tight expression very much matched Triumvir Var's.

As the last of the group seated itself, Sandis closed her eyes, trying to stretch her mind to the ethereal plane. She knew she could not reach Rone, so she sought the presence that had comforted her so many times over the last two years. *Ireth?*

She did not feel his warm response.

"The pillars?" Triumvir Var spoke first, his gaze on General Istrude.

"We've dismantled the eastern pillar." His expression was grave. "Not without casualties."

Sandis's heart thumped hard against its cage. "Casualties?"

The general glanced at her, then shifted his gaze to Triumvir Var.

Sandis didn't wait for him to receive permission to disclose his meaning. "We're meeting together because we are in this *together*." She passed a glance toward the triumvirate. "By *your* invitation. If we want to succeed, we need to trust one another."

Triumvir Var's lip curled.

To her surprise, it was Triumvir Peterus who answered. "We gave the general a kill order, should his means be hindered."

Bastien paled. "Against the . . . minions?"

The general nodded.

216

Sickness churned in Sandis's gut, but she tried not to let it show on her face.

Jachim said, "I've studied the ones we've captured, but I cannot understand the . . . spell, for lack of a better word, that Kolosos has put over them." He rested his elbows on the stack of ledgers before him. His usual excitement wasn't present today. The war was wearing down even him. "They're worse than animals. They don't sleep. They move under a will that isn't their own. They can't be dissuaded."

"We eliminated three of them," General Istrude added, hushed. "I lost two men."

Sandis nodded. What else was there to do? *Celestial, please*—

She looked toward the Angelic, who stared hard at his hands. Would it help, to pray to the Celestial? Would it even hear her?

"However," Chief Esgar butted in, "the base of the pillar won't move."

"Pardon?" Triumvir Var asked.

General Istrude rubbed his forehead. "The bases. The gold is somehow welded together."

"I've men digging as we speak," the police chief added. "But . . . it's strange. Like the foundation has merged with the earth. Like the soil beneath the cobblestones has turned to stone."

Triumvir Var sighed. "But the others are being dismantled?"

"I've men on it," the general said at the same time Chief Esgar replied, "Yes." Then, looking sheepish, Chief Esgar continued, "But the west pillar was partly demolished before we got there. Seems the . . . rebels are assisting."

He was obviously loath to admit it.

Triumvir Var made no response, merely nodded to Jachim, who bent over the arm of his chair and retrieved a large roll of paper from the floor. He laid it on the table and, with Cleric Liddell's assistance, unrolled it. A map of Dresberg lay before them. Sandis leaned forward, examining it. Black marks crossed it, seemingly at random. But

Sandis recognized them as buildings and landmarks Kolosos had already destroyed.

"Assuming Kolosos respawns at the Innerchord," Triumvir Var said without standing, "where will we place our men?"

"I have four thousand," General Istrude said, rising from his chair.

"Only four?" asked Triumvir Holwig.

The general's cheeks tightened. "Reinforcements from the border have not yet arrived, and when they do, we'll need to get them over the wall."

"When they arrive, they'll make quick work of moving the destruction, I'm sure." Triumvir Var sounded tired.

"We have Rone, as well." Sandis met General Istrude's dark eyes. "I don't know his numbers, but the numina are powerful—"

"We can't rely on that," Chief Esgar spat.

If Sandis were a cat, her hackles would have risen at the comment.

"I'm afraid we must." Triumvir Var sighed.

"This is," chimed in the Angelic, "a matter of faith." He did not look up from his clasped hands.

The chief groaned and leaned back in his chair. "I don't trust what I can't see. We don't even know what's happening . . . there. We have no means of communication."

Sandis stood, straightening her shoulders. "Then we'll do the best we can here. General, where should your men go, and how can we assist them?"

Bastien took her ring and pinky finger in his hand and squeezed.

We must go, Ireth insisted.

"Let me free them." Rone stared up at the massive pillar of numina that lay before him. He couldn't get to all of them, but a few—he rushed for the half human and the unidentifiable animal thing bound to her shoulders. His hand passed through, separating them. No vision followed—had he been too fast, or did these numina not remember anything from their time on the mortal plane? The half human took off without an iota of gratitude, but Rone didn't have the luxury of dwelling on it.

The ground shook again, harder. Red light reflected off the distant western sky.

One of the numen soldiers let out a panicked *whoop*. Ireth, hoofing toward Rone, urged him, *Quickly!*

Rone moved to the next numina pair and separated them, then the next, only half comprehending the tattered memories he saw. The fourth freed numen sputtered off in fast Noscon Rone could hear, and Ireth answered it in kind. Instead of running, the creature sidled up next to Drang, who stared at the glowing red light with watchful, intelligent eyes.

Five, six, seven. More faceless people swept through his mind as he moved between the numina. *Sharpening a spear. Kissing a child. Taming a wolf.*

Another numen joined Ireth's army. Another fled.

Were the ground true glass, it would have split on the next shake. Rone fell onto his hip. It was as though the ethereal plane resided inside a ball, and someone had shaken it with great enthusiasm.

More numina began to bleat, cry, whistle—urging Ireth to call for a retreat. But the more numina Rone freed, the longer it would take for Kolosos to reconstruct his pillar.

Idiot, he thought, *you can run through them.*

Changing his angle, Rone lined himself up with the center of the closest bound numina, then ran up the length of the pillar, passing through ghostly body after ghostly body, holding a straight line toward the top. Colors, shapes, and chunks of Noscon words swirled through his mind, making him dizzy, but he didn't slow.

An earsplitting and all-too-familiar bellow thickened the air. Kolosos's dark wings silhouetted the sky, his fire red as heart-squeezed blood.

Rone collapsed, fatigue eating up his legs. He hadn't finished, not nearly, but his energy had dwindled like flour in a sieve. His pounding heart couldn't replenish it. His mind worked to reorient itself before his stomach dumped what little it had in it.

A too-human cry ripped from one of the freed numina as it took skyward. The ground shook, then shook again, the brief pauses between the steps growing shorter and shorter until they vanished completely.

Time to go.

Rone pushed himself to his feet, passing a regretful glance to the three stories of numina still bound together, still struggling to free themselves. Their eyes shifted between Rone, their would-be savior, and Kolosos, their tormentor.

Rone nearly toppled over in the next quake. Ireth appeared beside him as though to help, but Rone couldn't lean on the fire horse. None of them. He could touch only the glass. Only the walls of the cage never intended for him.

God's tower, Kolosos moved fast.

As tall as the pillar had been, the monster rushed toward them, all black and red cracks and sulfur and *rage*.

Rone ran, but he only made it two steps before the ground bucked and threw him to his knees. He pushed himself up, muscles straining, and managed three more strides before falling backward. Even Ireth struggled to advance.

The air grew hot. Hotter.

They weren't going to make it.

Sandis, he thought, shoving himself upward once more. He would run until his body fell apart. He would. Not. Die. Here.

He took off sprinting and fell, nearly hitting his head on the quaking crystal beneath him. Overhead, Isepia and Iihedoh flew.

Ireth turned around, his fire blazing twice his height. *We cannot run!* he bellowed, even as another of his soldiers fled. Still, Drang, Unaresa, Pesos, and others took up beside him, turning toward Kolosos, who could be no less than half a mile away and gaining quickly. No, a quarter mile. It would only be seconds until—

Hepingya.

The voice was soft, feminine. Echoing in his head as though shared with anyone who could listen.

Hepingya, said another, lower. And again, *Hepingya.*

Mighty, murmured Ireth, reverent.

The quaking slowed. Eyes watering, Rone looked out across the great plain before him, to the white light growing from the east. A soft, cool glow, like starlight. It intensified, brighter and brighter, until Rone had to shield his eyes and peer through the slits between his fingers to look at it.

Everything stilled. The army, the creatures still bound into a toppled pillar, even Kolosos. The crimson cracks of his skin raged and burned, but he, too, turned toward the light, his obsidian teeth bared.

Rone stood on trembling legs, squinting, watching the light grow and take shape. It was a cloud, then loops and rings that formed the semblance of a rounded body. Nothing about it was solid or tangible. Everything was brilliant and large and—

Rone's stomach dropped. *"I can push the boundaries of this plane,"* Ireth had said. *"As far as I know, there is only one other who can do the same."*

Hepingya.

White, brilliant, enormous. Could this be . . .

. . . the Celestial?

"Black ashes," Rone muttered. He should run—limp—away as fast as he could. Kolosos was distracted.

But he couldn't turn away. And neither could any of the numina.

A horrid, choking sound emanated from Kolosos. It took Rone a moment to identify it as laughter. When the beast spoke, he did so with two voices, two languages, as though harmonizing with himself. As though he wanted Rone to hear alongside the others.

You've finally decided to face me? Now? Another chuckle. *What do you have planned, old man? You lost to me once; you will lose again.*

The reciprocating voice boomed, pushing against Rone's ears like he'd swum too deep in the canals. *You have already lost everything, Kaj. And will continue to do so.*

The air sweltered again as Kolosos's form brightened.

And lunged.

Jachim set out small blue discs as General Istrude described one plan, then another. The Angelic and all three triumvirs had pushed back their chairs and stood to examine the map.

"The first seems smarter," said Triumvir Peterus.

"I hesitate to use the buildings." Triumvir Var rubbed his chin.

"Won't see what's happening otherwise," quipped Oz. "I can send a numen with each company." He leaned forward and moved the discs back to align with the general's first plan. "Maybe two here."

Sandis's gut squeezed. *You have to let him control you. You have to sacrifice, too.*

But she was already sacrificing something important, wasn't she? Her eyes trained on the red dot at the center of the false soldiers, pulse quickening. *Anon.* In every version of the battle General Istrude had laid out, her brother died.

She really couldn't save him, could she?

Priestess Marisa, her voice delicate, said, "Can . . . Can you control them, from such a distance?"

Oz opened his mouth to retort, hesitated, and answered, "I don't know."

Swallowing against a lump in her throat, Sandis said, "You could take Inda and Teppa, and I could take Rist and Bastien."

From the sofa in the corner, Rist snorted.

"I don't think that's wise," said the general. "As you stated, a numen is worth more than a soldier. I want to fight with five, not four. And the Godobian is . . . weakened."

Bastien ran his fingers down the healing scars on his jaw.

Sandis pressed her hands to the table so she wouldn't dig her nails into her palms. "Can Oz not bear a numen? All summoners are vessels first."

Oz shot her a crooked smile. "Afraid not, dearie."

Pressing her lips into a line, Sandis nodded.

"But," Chief Esgar stepped around Priestess Marisa and Cleric Liddell to better reach the map. He pointed to the southeast corner of the Innerchord. "Your plan leaves this side wide open. Kolosos can flee, just like it always has, and come back to torment us another night. And you're also assuming it will attack from the same direction it fled."

"Then we draft more soldiers," said Triumvir Holwig.

"No," Sandis pushed. "There needs to be an evacuation."

Triumvir Holwig glowered. "We have able-bodied people in this city still."

"And how will you arm them?" Bastien asked, his good arm folded tightly across his chest. The other rested in his lap. Perspiration gleamed on his upper lip. His entire body was tense, his face paler than usual. "How will you protect them?"

"They're innocents," agreed the Angelic.

Triumvir Var's hands formed fists. "We have to use our resources—"

"The Riggers," Sandis said.

Eyes turned to her.

"The Riggers are in the city, managing a lot of the people you've . . . neglected." There wasn't a kinder way to say it.

"You're suggesting we work with the *mob*?" Chief Esgar was aghast.

Sandis nodded. "I know their leader. She's reasonable—"

"*She?*" Chief Esgar practically yelled, forcing his way between Cleric Liddell and High Priest Dall to get closer to Sandis.

"She has a network throughout the city right now," Sandis went on, ignoring the chief and focusing on Triumvir Var. "She can add to your numbers. Guard your . . ." What was it called?

"Flank," Bastien whispered.

"Flank," Sandis repeated. "But you have to recruit her quickly. Ask around. The people know. If you head toward the Green Street Boardinghouse, you'll find her. Tell her Jase and I sent you." Jase was the alias Rone had used in their dealings with Sherig.

Chief Esgar shook his head. "The likelihood of—"

"Go," Triumvir Var snapped, eyes on the chief. "Find her. *Now.*"

Chief Esgar paused, mouth agape. Several seconds passed before he fled from the table and out the door to the sitting room, which was guarded by two men in steel blue.

Sandis drew in a long breath to calm her nerves. "I think Rone can see what happens here. In Dresberg. If we make a plan, he may be able to supplement it—"

The Angelic fell back into his chair with a *thump*.

All three of his accompanying Celesians flocked to him. High Priest Dall said, "Are you well? Reverence?"

The Angelic rubbed a hand down his face, a gesture very reminiscent of Rone—enough so to make Sandis's chest ache for him.

"Fetch him some water," High Priest Dall said, and both Priestess Marisa and Cleric Liddell hurried from the room.

"I must go," the Angelic croaked.

"Are you ill?" asked Triumvir Holwig.

"I must go. Now."

High Priest Dall helped him to his feet, and he leaned heavily on the taller man's shoulder.

Sandis exchanged a concerned look with Bastien. *What?* she mouthed, but Bastien shook his head before turning his pale gaze back to Rone's father.

The Angelic and the high priest left, and the room suddenly felt very empty.

It was like watching thunder.

The two numina collided, their mass and power cracking together, emitting bursts of light that left Rone blinking spots. He felt the smooth ground beneath his fingers as his vision cleared. When had he fallen?

Rone. Ireth's voice. *Rone, we must go.*

The ground bucked as though helping him up. Rone staggered to his feet, feeling light-headed. Ireth stood before him, but Rone shifted to the side, peering toward the battle.

Another crack, loud enough to make his ears ring. If Ireth had spoken aloud, Rone would not have heard him. But the numen's firm voice sounded in his mind, clear and urgent. *We must go.*

"But . . . the Celestial . . ."

Ireth hesitated at the name. *He has come to defend us. If he loses, we cannot remain within Kolosos's reach.*

Rone blinked and finally met the numen's eyes. The ground trembled beneath him. Lights flashed against the ethereal sky. "If he loses?"

We will be the only ones left to stand against Kaj. Ireth looked over his withers as the Celestial—Hepingya—leapt into the air, bright and furious, and crashed down onto Kolosos, knocking him onto his back. The blow resounded through the ground, causing Rone to teeter backward. He tried to grab Ireth for balance, but his hand passed right through the numen. All his fingers touched was heat. A vision of blue-toned hands sharpening a spear sliced through his mind.

Ireth turned back. *He will not lose.* Then he let out a very horselike whinny and urged Rone forward. The sting of his flames licked Rone's skin, and Rone forced himself to turn, to follow the line of retreating numina he hadn't noticed before.

He glanced back at the felled pillar. "Should I—"

We must go. There are too many uncertainties. I will not risk the others.

Taking a deep breath, Rone hurried away as best he could. He moved at an uneven, pathetic jog, only now discovering pain in his right hip from his earlier fall. He swallowed, throat dry. He needed food, water, rest. Ireth's fire flared behind him, urging him on. Rone managed to pick up his pace by a hair. Drang and Unaresa were already far ahead of him.

Light flared behind him, throwing a long shadow of his body across the plane's glass floor. It faded, and Rone looked back. He couldn't help it. Kolosos glowed vividly, not so much bright as rich. The red cracks in his body expanded and beamed ghoulish light. If fire could bleed . . .

Go. Ireth's mane burned a bright white, blinding Rone to the spectacle. He focused on putting one foot in front of the other. Focused on filling his lungs with new air and expelling the old. Dark glimmers ahead revealed another symmetrical block formation. He could make it that far, couldn't he?

A quake split the ground. Rone fell forward onto knees and hands, cursing at the pain that shot up his wrists. He forced himself up and ran harder, favoring his right leg. He became so absorbed in the speed of his own pulse, the throbbing of his body, and the uneven rhythm of his steps that the battle behind him faded to the background. The farther he got, the less the ground shook. He only lost his balance once more. The burns on his back stung from Ireth's relentless, driving heat.

He reached the geometric mountain and collapsed against one of its blocks, gasping for air. He should be sweating more. That was a bad sign. He needed water.

Keep going.

Rone shook his head. It took him a moment to find his speech. "I need . . . a second."

We must keep going.

"You wouldn't say that if you were mortal." Rone pushed himself up and rolled his shoulders. His limbs felt twice as heavy as they should. He couldn't see the other numina ahead of him anymore, even Pesos. Tilting his head back, he studied the incline of the hill. Was there another close by? Could he hop these things like he did the roofs back in Dresberg?

Did he have the strength to try?

A keening cry jerked his and Ireth's attention back to the huge numina. Rone had traveled farther than he'd thought, but the monsters that marked the poles of the astral sphere were so large they were easy to see against the landscape of dark glass. Rone wasn't sure which had made the sound, but he'd never heard anything similar come from Kolosos.

The numina continued to grapple with each other, limbs of rock and limbs of light tangled together, pushing and pulling. Hepingya's legs crumpled beneath him, giving Kaj the upper hand.

A war between gods.

Something Ireth had said wormed through his thoughts. "You said you wouldn't risk the others," he managed between heavy breaths. "But you're immortal. Did you mean for the pillar?"

The fire comprising Ireth's mane and engulfing his tail snuffed down until it radiated little more heat than a struck match. Even his vibrant halo dimmed. *I do not know, with Kaj. On the mortal plane, we cannot die. But Kaj's power is that of destruction. You have held the corpse of an immortal in your hand, Rone Comf.*

227

Rone could almost feel the weight of the amarinth against his palm. Ireth's unease shuddered through the air like winter wind.

"Let's go," he whispered, forgetting for a moment his fatigue, bruises, and burns. He pushed himself along an unnaturally smooth mountain, leaning against it where he could. The sky flashed white, red, red as they hurried down the other side. Another hill loomed ahead of him. This one Rone would have to climb.

Gritting his teeth, Rone dragged himself up each block, pushing himself with whatever body part had the most strength. Ireth did not use his heat to urge him onward. If anything, the fire horse had become eerily cold.

He had nearly reached the top when Ireth galloped across the blocks to achieve a better vantage point. The sky flashed red, white, red, red. Red. A clap of thunder ripped through the ethereal plane, causing a gust of wind to spiral through the glass hills and tousle Rone's hair and clothes. It carried the scent of sulfur.

Ireth back-stepped, nearly falling off his block. He shook his large head as though accosted by bees, and a low croon ripped from his throat.

Rone pulled himself upright. "Ireth?"

It took a full minute for the numen to meet his gaze. *The Mighty has fallen.*

The voice squeezed to nothing.

Gooseflesh erupted over Rone's body. "Fallen? Ireth—" He moved closer. "Ireth, is he . . . dead?"

Ireth dropped his head toward the glass underfoot. He said nothing for a long moment. When his accented voice resurfaced, it was strained and afraid.

Move, mortal. Or we meet the same fate.

Chapter 27

There was no time. No time. And yet, as Triumvir Var brusquely adjourned the meeting and everyone ran to carry out the triumvirs' orders, Sandis remained rooted in her chair, staring beyond the wood-grain of the table before her. Would Chief Esgar reach Sherig in time? Would she be willing to help? Triumvir Peterus had agreed to start an evacuation, but the government couldn't empty the city by midnight. How many more would perish? Would this be the end, or merely the beginning of a new nightmare?

If she woke from Oz's summoning tomorrow, would her world still be here?

Did you foresee this, Kazen? she wondered. *Would you still have summoned Kolosos, if you knew?*

Her old master had known about the Celestial, but had he known about the connection between the numina and the Noscons? And how did an entire race of people become . . . this?

Warmth bloomed at the base of her skull and trickled down to her chest. She clasped her hands over her heart. *Ireth. Guide me. Help me understand.*

There was nothing for her to do until night fell. Until Oz led her, Rist, Bastien, Teppa, and Inda toward the Innerchord and readied them to fight. Oz was already selecting a new numen for Bastien, one with more bite than Hapshi.

Would she see Rone again, when Ireth took her? If she died, would Anon be waiting for her on the other side? God or no God, surely there was another side.

But what if there isn't?

The questions so consumed her that she didn't hear footsteps approaching. When a light touch fell on her shoulder, Sandis jumped, hitting her knees against the bottom of the table.

Priestess Marisa stood over her, wearing a white dress identical to the one draping Sandis. Deep worry lines formed valleys between her eyebrows.

"Sandis." Her voice was little more than a whisper. "You must come with me."

Aching knees forgotten, Sandis pushed back her chair and stood. "What's wrong?"

"The Angelic has requested an audience with you."

Her entire body tingled. "Which room is he in?"

She shook her head. "He's at the local church."

Sandis searched the other woman's eyes, trying to see her thoughts. "I can't leave. Triumvir Var forbade it, after the last time."

Priestess Marisa shook her head. "I'll guide you out. Please. It's . . . urgent." She extended a hand.

Sandis chewed the inside of her lip, then accepted the hand. Priestess Marisa pulled her from the room and down the stairs to the back door. The blue-clad guard there nodded to her with his hand over his heart. A faithful Celesian.

The sky had already dimmed, the deep blue of twilight leaking into the heavens like drops of dye. Did they have so little time? Priestess Marisa must have felt the need to hurry as well, for she quickened her step once they left Triumvir Var's property. Sandis looked over her shoulder once, wondering after Rist and Bastien.

"It's not far." Priestess Marisa squeezed her hand. "Just a small church over this way, where we've gone to worship and pray. There's been little damage to these neighborhoods, praise the Celestial." The moment she stopped speaking, she looked toward the center of the city. Sandis thought she could feel a tremor beneath Priestess Marisa's skin, but perhaps that was her own.

They walked in silence for several minutes. Many of the homes they passed were dark, but candles filled the windows of the church at the end of the winding road. The highest window was fitted with green glass, giving it the appearance of a leaf in summer light. Sandis's eyes went straight to it, watching the flames flicker against that glass until she reached the door.

Her brands ached like they were freshly printed.

"What does he want?" She kept her voice low.

But Priestess Marisa shook her head. "I admit I don't know. But I worry."

Swallowing, Sandis allowed Priestess Marisa to guide her into the small building. They stepped into a rectangular room with little decoration outside the candles in the windows. A handful of people lingered inside, sitting here and there along a single row of benches. Sandis recognized Cleric Liddell in the far corner. Half the seats faced one way, and half faced the other. She couldn't see if anything demarked the turning point, for Priestess Marisa led her up a narrow set of stairs immediately to the right. The wood creaked under their weight.

A single room occupied the top floor. High Priest Dall stood outside it with a worn set of scripture in his hands. He glanced to Sandis, nodded, and knocked softly on the door.

Sandis didn't hear an answer, but the priest grasped the knob and pushed the door open, beckoning Sandis inside.

Other than High Priest Dall, she and the Angelic were alone in the small room, its only window the green glass she had been so mesmerized by earlier. Portions of the concrete walls jutted out on two sides to form long, hard benches. A single table with two chairs rested just inside the door. One of these chairs had been turned out, and in it slumped the Angelic, looking twenty years older, with a gray cast to his skin.

She hurried to him as High Priest Dall shut the door—remaining inside—though she found herself unsure upon reaching him.

Adellion Comf opened his eyes—even the whites had darkened— and studied her. His gaze lingered on her white dress with its silver embroidery, and to her surprise, a ghost of a smile quirked his lips.

"It suits you," he murmured.

Sandis took a step back, the compliment striking her like an open hand. She looked to High Priest Dall in shock. "What's happened to him?"

But the high priest looked at the floor, forlorn.

"You know many truths, my child, but not all." The Angelic's weak voice pulled her attention back to him. "You have touched the ethereal plane, as have I. There are few who understand our bonds. Even dear Azul does not fully comprehend."

"Azul?" She glanced to High Priest Dall, but her head immediately snapped back to the Angelic. "Our *bonds?*"

The skin of her back itched.

A single, dry chuckle escaped Rone's father. "The Celestial is a powerful being, as you know. But even he cannot reach the mortal world without a connection."

Sandis only half heard what he said. The words *our bonds, our bonds, our bonds* kept echoing through her head.

Her voice as insubstantial as air, she asked, "Y-You're a vessel?"

He nodded.

She retreated another step, shaking her head. "You're a vessel. You're a vessel. And you . . . you condemn me."

"I did not know the truth until my predecessor passed on." He spoke as if he hadn't just turned Sandis's entire world upside down, as if he hadn't just unleashed a flood of utter hypocrisy on her. "But who is to say what denotes a god? What is deserving of faith?"

"I *had* faith!" Sandis shouted, and the high priest rose with his hands lifted in supplication, urging her discretion. Hot tears ran down her cheeks. Hands clenched at her sides, she said, "I had faith, but you told me it was wrong. Kazen *burned* blasphemy into my skin, and you would have killed me for it. But you . . . *you*—"

The Angelic raised a hand. "Would any apology make a difference now, Sandis?"

She pressed her lips together. A few tears dripped from her chin to the floor. No, his apologies would mean nothing to her.

Yet despite the power of his revelation, something else nagged at her. She wiped her tears away with a slap of her hand. Her voice cracked as she spoke, but she didn't care. "But you're not. There are rules for vessels." Her eyes widened. "You're not . . . You're not Rone's real father, are you?"

The Angelic looked at her, one brow askew. In that moment, he looked so much like Rone. But—

"He is my son by blood," he said. The statement shocked her more in principle than anything else. The Angelic had always rejected his connection with Rone, and yet here, in this stuffy room, in the middle of the night, while a monster tore up the city, he confessed it so easily.

Sandis had to swallow twice to clear her throat. "Only a virgin can be a vessel."

Again, the man shook his head. "That is not so. A woman who has borne a child cannot host a numen, but either sex can otherwise be appropriated, virtue notwithstanding."

Sandis's lips parted as she strained to understand. She'd uncovered another of Kazen's lies. Part of her struggled to believe it, but it made sense. He'd wanted them isolated, dependent on him. It had all been part of his plan.

Several long seconds passed.

"The early Celesians destroyed the Noscon temple so no one would discover the truth," Sandis murmured, recalling Jachim's history lesson to her.

The Angelic shook his head. "No. The Yokhosho Temple was the birthplace of Celesia."

Sandis, blood cold, opened her mouth to speak, but the Angelic held up a hand to stall her. He continued, "It never should have been done, the resurrection of Noscon magic. It is a terrible thing. I stand by that."

Sandis recalled Jachim's mention of human experimentation, but couldn't bring herself to so much as nod.

"There was a man who ended it. Who betrayed his comrades and brought condemnation down upon that horrible place. But he saw the goodness in it. Namely, in Hepingya. That is how our faith started, child. For good, not for evil." He paused. "It was meant for good."

Hepingya? She swallowed, forcing her throat to open. "And that man was the first Angelic?"

He nodded. "And he died to pass his mantle to the next. Since that time, only a few have been entrusted with the truth. Only those who could bear it."

She studied his face, as though its lines hid more secrets. "What do you mean, about the mantle?" An image of Heath, of his failed hosting of Kolosos, passed her mind's eye. She shoved it away, stomach clenched. She thought instead of the tattoo at the base of her neck, of Ireth's blood mixed with the ink.

"If you can't summon the Celestial, you can't bond to him," she tried, fearing what the Angelic would confirm.

In tones too quiet for High Priest Dall to overhear, he said, "No human can host a god. But in an attempt to summon him, we obtain the blood we need for the bond."

Chills ran down Sandis's arms. That meant . . . each Angelic died the same way Heath had, just so the bonding tattoo could be passed to the next priest. They harvested it from . . .

The *smell* rose in her nose, though the room she stood in was only scented with kerosene. She tried not to imagine a priest stooping over the ruined body of his former leader, scooping the gore into a vial of ink . . .

Gritting her teeth, Sandis rubbed a drying tear from her eye. "Anything else I don't know?"

To her relief, the Angelic shook his head. "I believe you understand the rest."

Sandis hugged herself, trying to get warm. "You're bound to the Celestial."

"To Hepingya, yes." He tried to pull down the back of his collar, perhaps to show Sandis the numen's name tattooed at the base of his neck, but the Angelic's gown was too tight around the neck. Guaranteeing his secret would never accidentally meet the eyes of a worshipper.

Hepingya. Sandis mouthed the word. So that was what the symbols on the top of the astral sphere said. He-Ping-Ya.

"What Kazen did to you and the others was wrong," the Angelic continued, pressing his hands against his knees. "That is the true blasphemy."

Sandis turned away from him, new tears tracing the paths of the old. Her heart thudded hard as a realization struck her.

Evil things had been done with her, but she had never been evil.

She breathed deeply, as though a leaden cloak had fallen from her shoulders, letting her lungs expand fully for the first time. She wasn't bad. The symbols on her back weren't bad. Ireth wasn't bad.

She had only ever been special.

She turned back to the Angelic. "Why tell me this?" She took in his deep wrinkles and off color. "You're dying."

"Not in the sense you think, child," he replied, again offering her that ghost of a smile. She didn't think she'd ever seen the holy man truly smile before now. "I tell you because you understand, and you must know the truth before this great battle commences."

Sandis waited, tense.

A long, pained sigh escaped the Angelic. "Hepingya has fought the traitor called Kolosos. And he has lost."

Sandis backed away until her knees hit the concrete bench. She sank onto it. "What?"

"In the ethereal plane. The Celestial sought to protect all of us, but his strength has failed."

Sandis's throat was raw. "The . . . Celestial . . . is *dead*?"

But the Angelic shook his head. "He is immortal, my child. There is only one way to truly kill him."

Her thoughts spun back to Triumvir Var's basement, to the men surrounding her as she chanted an ancient spell. General Istrude had held a knife, just in case.

She licked her lips. "Then . . . he will recover."

The Angelic's face grew even more ashen. "I do not know. I fear it is not so simple. Regardless"—he passed a sad glance toward High Priest Dall—"we will not."

"No." Sandis stood. "We have a chance. If you just believe in us, in Rone—"

"It is not a question of faith, my child." He met her eyes. His were so dark they looked like coal. The candlelight from the windowsill reflected in them. They were the eyes of a man who had seen much—a determined man. But determined to do what?

He continued, "I have been intimately familiar with the Celestial for many years. I understand his power. His fears and his desires."

Sandis nodded. She understood Ireth's, too.

"It was his fear of Kolosos that led me to seek out you and Rone." He sucked in a slow breath, held it, and released it all at once. "I've felt his fear ever since. I felt it when he tried to best Kolosos in the heavens. I felt it when he fell, until I didn't feel it anymore. Only resolve. Only acceptance."

Sandis brushed hair from her face. "I will not accept defeat."

"You misunderstand me. It is *his* defeat he accepts, and what must be done next. Hepingya and I are of one mind, my dear. Your battle has yet to unfold. But we will give you a chance to succeed."

Sandis might not have understood, had it not been for the soft choking sound to her right. She'd nearly forgotten High Priest Dall still lingered in the room. One of the few who knew the truth. Would he be the next Angelic, when Adellion Comf's reign ended?

It struck her then. There wouldn't be another Angelic. There could be no vessel for a numen who no longer lived.

Lightning crackled up her limbs. "No," she whispered.

The Angelic nodded. "It must be you or me, child, and the correct choice is obvious. The Celestial is weak, but he can still protect us. As can I."

New tears stung her eyes.

Adellion Comf meant to make an amarinth.

She had never been close to the Angelic, but she loved his son. And despite becoming a vessel, despite the way Kazen had used her, she'd never lost faith . . . and in a sense, she still hadn't.

"No," she repeated, clutching handfuls of her skirt. "There has to be another way."

This time Adellion Comf offered her a full smile. It changed his face completely. Made him human, brightened his eyes and cheeks. Made him look like Rone.

"My dear." He reached out a hand and took Sandis's, gently easing her fingers from the white fabric. "Sometimes we have to sacrifice what is dearest to us to save what is dearest to others. I have done it once before. I will do it again."

With some effort, the Angelic stood, releasing Sandis's hand as he did so. "I want you to have it," he said, not meeting her tear-filled gaze. "You, who comprehends its power. Who would use it for good. You, Sandis, who may understand me better than anyone else."

She trembled. "It will kill you."

"The Celestial is weak. And you will do what needs to be done before he has the opportunity to hurt my body."

A thousand protests rose in her throat, strangling her. *I can't do it. I'm not strong enough. What if I fail? We should talk to the triumvirate. You're in mourning. You're not thinking straight.*

Her gaze moved to her hands. She flexed them. Opened and closed her fingers. Remembered Bastien squeezing her ring finger and pinky in the sitting room. Sandis recalled how her hands had ached as she clutched Rist while Mahk flew through the city. The feel of Rone's hair beneath them. The way they cut through the air as Arnae instructed her in seugrat. She remembered the weight of her rifle as she lay across a rooftop with Sherig, waiting to strike Kazen's lair. Lowering her hands, she felt the material of Priestess Marisa's dress.

Her protests died, leaving her thoughts clear and her memory sharp. Her hands formed fists at her side. Strong, ready.

Lifting her head, she whispered, "I'll save them."

A familiar warmth burned in her skull. Closing her eyes, she prayed, *Ireth, help me. Give me the opening I need. Don't let me waste this chance.*

The Angelic nodded, seeming at peace. "Azul?"

The morose priest pulled from his robes several golden coils. "It's ready, as you requested."

Sandis's pulse danced. Was this really happening?

The Angelic turned toward her, again taking up her hand. This time, he clasped it between both of his own. His hands were warm, but his fingertips felt ice cold. "I want you to be the one to do it."

Her ears buzzed. "Take . . . your heart?" Her throat closed around the question.

"It should be bloodless, as our dear scholar guessed. Azul will be here to help you." He leaned in close, holding her gaze. "Sandis, you asked me to trust you, and I do. Will you not also trust me, in my last moments?"

A painful lump in her throat swelled so large she couldn't swallow it. She nodded.

"Then we have no time to waste." He motioned to High Priest Dall, who walked over and stood just behind Sandis.

"Heaven be with you always," the high priest murmured.

"Heaven be with you always," the Angelic repeated with a sad smile. He pressed his right hand to his forehead and closed his eyes. Two heartbeats later, he opened them, focusing on Sandis.

"Tell my son I love him."

Sandis nodded, and the Angelic recited the chant.

Bright-white light filled the church.

Chapter 28

Rone.

Rone glanced up from the crystal ground beneath him. He knelt on a single knee, fingertips brushing the cool glass that reflected Ireth's fiery mane and tail, his white halo.

"Is there not enough time?" Reaching into the mortal plane made him fuzzy. He didn't want to be fuzzy when Kolosos struck.

Ireth shook his dark head. *Something is wrong.*

"What?"

His tail swished. *Something has changed. The atmosphere is different. Wrong.* His dark eyes locked on Rone's. *Is your strength adequate? We must hurry to the epicenter. I believe that is where Kolosos will be.*

Rone stood. He felt . . . all right. He was hungry, but rest had done him some good. "I'll survive. The epicenter? Of the columns?"

Ireth nodded. *That is where the planes will first merge. Where Kaj will be. Where we will strike.*

Rone turned from the fire horse and looked out over their small, obscure army. It had grown again. If he counted each numen as five men, they had a decent retinue.

I cannot carry you.

Like he'd forgotten. "I can run."

And he did.

Sandis held a god in her hands.

She cradled it in her palms, the brilliance of its shining center sending sparkles of light across her skin. It reflected off her tears, no matter how many times she blinked her eyes.

High Priest Dall knelt before her. They stood just outside the room where it had happened. Where the Angelic lay lifeless, without a heart. Sandis closed her hands over the amarinth, hiding its brilliance. She thought she could feel a pulse between its golden loops.

"My child." The priest cupped his larger hands over hers. His eyes glimmered with sadness, but hope limned them, giving her strength. "Time waits for none, even God. I beg you with all that I am: don't let this sacrifice be wasted."

Sandis nodded, a final tear splashing off her cheek. "I promise."

High Priest Dall pinched his lips together and stood, moving aside to reveal her path. Sandis took the stairs down slowly. She needed to hurry, but her bones . . . they couldn't. An awed reverence had worked its way into them, her blood, her muscles.

Cleric Liddell and Priestess Marisa waited at the bottom of the stairs. Cleric Liddell opened his mouth to speak, but after seeing Sandis's face, he didn't. Sandis wondered what her countenance looked like.

Sandis pushed past them, clenching her fingers to hide the power clasped between them. She pushed toward the front of the church, out the door, and into the night.

Cool air whisked by, carrying the promise of autumn.

From the church, Sandis could see much of the city; the ground here was higher than farther west. She couldn't make out the Innerchord, but she knew how to reach it without Oz.

She'd promised to save them.

Dots of black moved against the city streets that had once glowed with lamplight. The evacuation? From here they were all shadows, merging together. Shadows that feared the monster lurking in a plane so intimately connected with theirs.

It was no wonder they hated her. *Feared* her. If the occult had been snuffed out years ago, Kolosos would not be here. He'd be trapped in that ethereal place alongside the other Noscons. Alongside Ireth, who must so desperately want freedom. Just as Sandis did.

Squeezing the amarinth, Sandis prayed. *I need your help, Ireth. I promised to save them. Save them, and you, too.*

And she would, or die trying.

She wasn't afraid anymore.

Slipping the amarinth into her pocket, Sandis undid the button holding together the collar of her dress and rent the garment down the back.

Elfri folded her arms across her chest as her men passed firearms down a line, arming Riggers and citizens alike. Elfri had promised the citizens that the act of bravery would earn them protection after the war, presuming they survived. The rest of the beleaguered city folk had joined the ongoing evacuation, which was crowded and slow, since only one exit had been cleared through the rubble that was once Dresberg's great wall. But at least Elfri needn't oversee it anymore. She just didn't have enough of her to manage it.

"Go!" she barked when a boy no older than sixteen ogled his newly received gun, lifted from Helderschmidt's firearm factory. The place was weakly guarded; it had been easy to infiltrate. The boy snapped to attention and ran with the others toward the center of the city, where Kolosos's red light burned. This would be the quickest battle of their lifetime—roughly half an hour for them to stop the monster.

Pete and Rufus galloped up, the former towing Elfri's mare behind him. He left the reins hanging for her. She grabbed them but didn't mount. Not yet. She'd see all her people off first. It might be the last she ever laid eyes on them.

She didn't like their odds, but if Sandis believed there was a chance, it was either take it or admit defeat. And a Rigger *never* cried defeat.

Admittedly, Arnae Kurtz had helped bring Elfri around to the idea. He approached her now, a gun strapped to his back. He preferred to use his hands, but every man needed to be armed. The bullets did nothing to the monster, but they'd take down its servants just fine—servants so enslaved to Kolosos's will they'd die for it.

"Move!" she shouted as the remaining men got their guns. "Go!" She followed the last one, but Kurtz stopped her with a hand clasped on her shoulder. They almost saw eye to eye; Elfri was just a hair taller.

"See you on the other side, my friend."

Elfri snorted. "I don't plan to die tonight." But there was no way to avoid watching the death. How many men would she lose? *Oh, for Celestial's sake, don't cry.*

Kurtz smiled and dropped his hand. "Then we'll reunite tomorrow."

Tilting her head to one side, Elfri said, "You don't strike me as a man interested in the mob."

"Not in the mob, no."

Elfri blinked once, smirked, and pulled her rifle from the sling on her back. "Get moving, or we'll miss our chance." She didn't clarify what she meant. She swung up into her mount's saddle and, with a jerk of her head, ordered Pete and Rufus to follow her into the fray.

Celestial speed that they survived the hour.

Sandis walked toward the center of Dresberg.

She couldn't run. There were too many people for that. Sprinting, riding, crawling through the dark. Packs on their backs. Animals on leashes. Lamps swinging in their hurry, casting dancing light across abandoned buildings. The breeze swept across her exposed back, but it didn't raise gooseflesh or invite shivers. It warmed her.

Sandis's gaze floated over them, as though it could peer through the flats and factories that surrounded them. As though she could see all the way into the charcoal heart of the city. The Innerchord. She clung to that destination like ice to an eave. She felt every dip in the cobblestones under her worn shoes. Smelled sweat and kerosene on the breeze. It tousled her hair, her skirt.

The amarinth sat heavy in her pocket and yet weighed nothing. Its concealed light burned like a hot poker against her leg. She felt it like the promise it was.

"Hey, stop!" someone called to her. A man about her age. He slowed, only to be knocked forward by another evacuee behind him. Stumbling past her shoulder, he said, "You're going the wrong—"

And then his voice cut off completely. Sandis knew why. She paused and turned toward him, not to hide her exposed script from his eyes, but to meet his stare head-on. To look into his dark gaze, so much like her own.

His gaze moved sluggishly from her back to her face, disbelief widening his features.

Yes, I'm one of them, she thought, the words cocooning her in a loose blanket. *I'm one of them. And I am not afraid.*

"Hurry," she whispered. The sounds of footsteps, murmurs, and wagon wheels nearly swallowed her voice. Someone else bumped into the man's shoulders. Oddly, no one collided into Sandis.

Eyes still round, the man nodded once, then vanished into the crowd.

It felt like a dream.

Rone ran over a world made of glass, one brick in a wall of monsters charging over the stars. Their presence gave him energy, focus. His legs pumped beside Ireth's and Grendoni's. Iihedoh flitted almost directly overhead, as though protecting him from threats from above. He could hear Drang's hot breath as the wolfish creature panted. Mahk's song floated nearby, reserved and reassuring.

We are nearly there.

Rone looked up, barely registering the change in terrain in time to jump as the ground dropped down. He blinked, and the monster was there, his red light reflecting off the hardness of the plane. His back was to them—or that's what it looked like. Rone was still too far to—

The light narrowed and brightened into a crimson pillar, and Kolosos vanished.

He has descended! Ireth called. *Surround the epicenter!*

The numina growled, sang, roared, chirped. Surged forward with renewed vigor to the place their captor had just stood.

Rone, stop.

Rone nearly kicked himself in the ankle at the command. He stopped, chest already heaving from the exercise as he turned toward the silvery beast beside him.

"What's wrong?"

Ireth tilted his head, as though listening to something. *She will need me soon.*

"You can fight until she does."

Ireth nodded. *But I want you to watch, Rone. I want you to be our eyes, to see what Kolosos does in the mortal realm. You will need to stay close to me.*

Rone nodded, trying to ignore the cold fingers of fear walking up his ribs. He pushed questions and doubts out of his mind. If he just focused, just did what Ireth said—

Come. Ireth galloped forward, nearing the circle the other numina had formed around the epicenter—a place they'd somehow recognized despite the fact that it looked no different from the rest of the ethereal plane.

Ireth's back right hoof circled the glass. The image of a starry sky swirled and parted, revealing a half-molten monster descending upon Rone's homeland.

<hr />

"Sometimes," the Angelic's voice curled in Sandis's memory, *"we have to sacrifice what is dearest to us to save what is dearest to others."*

A tear escaped her eye as she marched forward. The heavy truth bore down on her heart like a hundred grappling hands.

It had to end this way, didn't it? And she'd known. She'd always known.

To save the others, friends and strangers alike, she had to sacrifice Anon.

When she'd found him in that building, she'd been struck by the fear in his eyes, the gauntness of his body—death would be well met. She didn't know her brother as a man, only as the twelve-year-old boy who had gone missing mere days before her own capture. Where had he been? She would never know.

I'm sorry, Anon. She put one foot in front of the other. The streets had opened, only stragglers passing her. *I'm sorry I can't save you, too.*

"You!" a familiar voice barked. Sandis almost didn't turn, but a man in scarlet uniform stepped in front of her, blocking her path. "Oz needs you, blasted girl! Where have you been?"

Sandis turned her head, not to look at the scarlet in her path, but at the man who'd shouted at her. Chief Esgar jogged up from the north, surrounded by a half-dozen policemen.

His gaze dropped to the ripped back of her dress. He gawked. Why? He knew what she was. She wouldn't hide it, not anymore.

When she saved them, they would all know what she was.

Chief Esgar shook himself. "Oz is west of the Innerchord. Go! Before it's too late!"

Sandis shook her head. "My path has changed."

The ground rumbled, and all of them looked skyward, to the red light blotting out the stars.

Hissing through clenched teeth, Chief Esgar grabbed her forearm and jerked her toward him. "Insolent woman! You will—"

"Unhand her." A new voice finished the sentence for him. Low, feminine. Sandis knew it immediately.

Twisting her arm the way Arnae had taught her to do, she broke free of the chief's grip and turned around. Sherig's lamplight high-lighted the lower half of her face: a strong jaw and lips painted red. Two burly men on horseback lingered just behind her.

"Sherig!" Sandis exclaimed, and the scarlets immediately tensed. She rushed toward the taller woman. "I need to get to the Innerchord."

Sherig studied her for half a second before nodding. "Pete, take her."

Chief Esgar pulled a club from his belt and marched forward. "I must deliver her to the west flank!"

Pete offered a hand, and Sandis bolted toward his horse.

Sherig squared her shoulders. "I trust her more than you, old man. And we haven't time to bicker about it."

Pete clasped Sandis around the wrist and hauled her onto the saddle behind him.

"Don't kill my mare," Sherig snapped over her shoulder.

"Please." Sandis grabbed Pete's sides. "Hurry."

The mobsman kicked his heels into the mare's flanks, bringing her toward the sound of screams.

Rone watched in horror as Kolin fought Kolin. Whatever magic Kolosos worked, he wielded it efficiently, transforming ten men at a time into mindless minions. They dropped nearly as quickly as they rose, save for when the soldiers second-guessed their kill orders. In those cases, they died instead.

Behind Kolosos, the gold plate began to grow—and so did the epicenter in the ethereal plane. It glowed faintly at first, then brightly. The light slowly leaked outward, illuminating the crystal floor.

Drang howled, unleashing his fury against the lucent ground. All the numina did. They beat it, sprayed it, engulfed it in flames. Every numen, large and small, Ireth included, attacked the epicenter as though it were Kolosos himself.

Their attacks reached Kolosos on the mortal plane. He ticked. Winced. Every now and then, the monster would jerk and step on one of his minions or send an elbow into a standing building, lighting the interior on fire.

But the numina didn't stop him. Couldn't *hurt* him.

The epicenter and the Innerchord gleamed with power. The merge was beginning.

He searched the army ranks for Sandis, but didn't see her. He didn't know where she was, what she was doing, or how to find her. His belly tightened, and not from hunger. *Where are you?*

The epicenter reddened. Rone stepped away from his porthole to spy through the one in the center of the numina ring. It revealed the top of Kolosos's head. The center of the battle.

Some of Mahk's spray rained on Rone's head and shoulders. He barely noticed.

"He's ignoring us," Rone murmured, though none of the numina responded. "This isn't enough."

His hands formed tight fists at his side. Gritting his teeth, Rone muscled his way into the circle, pushing between Pesos and another numen.

"Kaj, you rank bastard!" he shouted. "Fight us yourself, you coward!"

Beneath the glowing glass, Kolosos tilted his horned head back and looked up with both brilliant eyes.

Chapter 29

Kolosos tilted its head back, as though distracted by something in the sky.

Whatever. Oz would take what he could get.

"Go!" Oz flung his hand forward, and Akway, the armless mermaid in Inda's body, flew forward, swimming as though the air were the sea. She couldn't get much altitude, but right now, Oz didn't need her to attack high. He wanted to keep his vessels low, beneath Kolosos's reach.

The mermaid vomited water on Kolosos's hoof, darkening the lava seeping between cracks. Steam consumed her.

"You, next!" Oz spun around and gestured to the tallest of the vessels. The resistant one with hard eyes and square shoulders. Rist. He scowled, but he came forward.

"Kill me and I'll haunt you," he spat as he lowered his head.

"You die, I probably will, too." Oz smacked his hand against Rist's head and chanted. *"Vre en nestu a carnath. Ii mem entre I amar. Vre en nestu a carnath. Kuracean epsi gradenid."*

Oz barely closed his eyes in time to avoid being blinded by the white light. The vessel grew upward too quickly to make sense, his body contorting and hardening faster than Oz could snap his fingers. He'd always envied Kazen this enormous, armored creature. Wanted it for himself, almost as badly as he'd wanted the fire horse. A creature he *still* didn't have, thanks to Sandis's ill-timed absence.

Kuracean bellowed, stretching out arms ending in claws not unlike a lobster's. One was significantly larger than the other, and when it dropped to the ground, it cracked the cobblestones.

"Go where Akway has tempered the heat on that monster's foot. Break it."

Unable to resist the command, the numen stormed forward, its pointed legs spitting up rock as it scuttled. A cannonball flew overhead, striking Kolosos in the navel. Good; the general was keeping up his side of the bargain. Distract the monster so the numina had a chance to weaken it. *Let's see how the bastard likes fighting with only one foot.*

Pulling Teppa forward, Oz summoned Grendoni into her, killing the sickly mouse he had in his pocket to do it. It followed after Kuracean. Kolosos moaned and retreated a step. That meant their dual assault was affecting it. Excellent.

Oz turned back, meeting Bastien's eyes as he did so.

The summoner let out a long breath and rested his hand on the Godobian's uninjured shoulder.

"This ain't the end yet, is it?" he asked.

The Godobian shook his head, all seriousness, his eyes watching the war and not his old master.

"You ain't shaking."

Bastien blinked. Looked at his hands. "Not much," he answered.

Oz grinned. "Now that's something." He patted the lad's shoulder once before putting his hand on his head. "You were always a shaker."

Now Bastien met his eyes. "Be smart, Oz. M-Make us win."

Oz frowned. "Now when have I ever not been smart?"

Bastien shrugged. "I w-want the chance to be."

Oz considered that a moment, then nodded. "I'll try, Bas. I'll try. We'll see the dawn together, eh?"

The slightest smile touched Bastien's lips. Oz hoped he hadn't just lied to him.

The ground shook as Kolosos lunged for the army. Screams and worse sounds soured the air.

Oz summoned Pettanatan and offered a prayer for Jansen, wherever his spirit had gone.

Perhaps they were about to join him.

General Corris Istrude gaped as he watched fifty of his men die under a single blow.

His throat squeezed tight. Bile burned in his chest. Cold numbed his legs, his hands. Sergeant Yunter was in that group. The private he'd trained himself, pretending he wasn't two years too young to enlist. That boy had fire. He had aspirations—

The general set his jaw and snagged the canteen from his belt, forcing himself to swallow the hot water within.

How many more would Corris lose?

More men, *his* men, charged at the creature's minions. Those who hadn't held on to their guns wielded knives and swords.

Nails digging into his palms, Corris shouted, "Shoot them!"

Explosions surrounded him. Bullets zinged and hit their targets.

Thank the Celestial, the light was at their backs, and Istrude couldn't see their faces.

"Load the next volley! Advance!" Kolosos had turned its attention to the numina surrounding it, namely, the armless mermaid flying nearby, slowing the monster's movements by spraying its joints with water. Corris marched with his army, moving closer to that damned glowing plate. What did that light mean, anyway?

Kolosos spun, pitching its arm through the air. It took a long moment before Istrude could tell what it intended.

He saw the cannon sailing for his men too late.

It crashed into them, instantly smashing the bodies it hit, then trampling over others as its momentum carried it through the crowd. When it stopped, lying on its side, Corris registered the spark on it—the thing had been lit before it was tossed.

And it was aimed at him.

He couldn't move fast enough. The cannon exploded, its ball clipping another soldier before sailing straight into Corris's pelvis. He felt his body shatter as his feet left the ground.

He didn't remember falling. He was suddenly on the ground, on top of something hard and rough—debris, maybe. Staring up at the sky. At the smoke that poured off Kolosos and danced across the heavens.

Celestial, won't you save us?

He couldn't feel his legs. He couldn't feel anything, except pricks of pain in the numbness. Pricks that grew sharper with each breath. It was alarmingly hard to breathe. His mouth tasted like copper.

"Forward!" a voice called. But it wasn't Colonel Wills, his replacement. No, the colonel was in the south battalion.

Corris tipped his head. That made the pain flare. He still couldn't feel his legs.

His sense of hope flickered like a candle in the wind, but then backups arrived. Hundreds of them, filling the gaps Kolosos had torn open in the army. They didn't wear uniforms, but simple civilian clothing. Many had guns. Others had clubs or pipes. Kitchen knives.

The Riggers. The citizens. They'd come to fight. Corris hadn't seen such unity since—

Since—

It wasn't enough.

Rone screamed again, calling Kolosos by his true name once more, but that tactic had lost its effect. He and the numina were like flies buzzing about Kolosos's horns. Annoying, but easily ignored.

Rone's blood turned to lead as he watched Kolosos carelessly kill person after person, often multiple at a time. They screamed, burned, bled. It made him think of a human crushing anthills in the street. Nameless, moving dots. Easily exterminated. Except Kolosos himself had been human.

Grendoni, the feline numen, vanished from the ethereal plane, summoned to join the fight down below. Moments later, Pettanatan did the same. Ireth would likely be next.

Rone turned to look at the fire horse. His flame continued to shoot at the glowing epicenter, but his eyes were distant, distracted. Was he communicating with Sandis? *Let her be all right*, Rone pleaded.

God's tower, she's one of the ants.

They had to do something. Something more. Their window was so slight, and at this rate of destruction, Dresberg wouldn't have enough resources for another fight. And if Kolosos returned to the ethereal plane . . . what would he do to those resisting him?

The epicenter glowed brighter and began to cave inward, forming a shallow bowl in the glassy floor. Rone wanted to think the plane was buckling under the numina's attack, but his gut told him the warping was a bad thing. A very bad thing.

The planes physically pulling together kind of bad thing.

Biting his lip, he looked around the numina. Those who had faces looked strained, exhausted. Turning to Ireth, Rone said, "Tell them to try harder. We need more."

Ireth's skin brightened as his fire increased by a hair. *They already give what they have. They know the stakes.*

Rone's tongue burned with curses. What more could they do? And here he was, standing by while he watched his world disintegr—

Wait.

Wait.

He could do something. Maybe. Did it work both ways?

"Tell them not to hit me," he murmured.

Ireth's dark eye slid to him, confused.

Rone ran into the circle.

Rone! What—but Ireth didn't finish. Perhaps he understood what Rone meant to do.

The floor glowed bright enough to hurt Rone's eyes, now that he stood on top of it. His shoes slid down the slick bowl that grew slowly deeper beneath him. Drang shifted away as he passed, as did a scalding beam of yellow jetting out from another numen. Rone inched as close to the center of the bowl as he could. His skin burned with both hot and cold from the power surrounding him. Hair stood on end. His stomach turned with the feeling of something *wrong*.

He pressed both hands against the bowl. He was mortal. He could push into the mortal plane.

Not for long. Seconds, really. But maybe that was all they needed.

"Here we go," he whispered, and pushed against the glass.

His last thought before it parted was to wonder who would tell his mother if he died.

Sandis grabbed Pete's sides as the horse reared. The saddle's edges bit into her thighs. Only blocks away, Kolosos crushed the top of a building. Men screamed beneath the raining debris.

"Whoa, whoa!" Pete shouted, but the mare bucked and writhed beneath them.

Sandis dug her nails into Pete's ribs and clenched her jaw to keep from crying out. The Rigger finally got the mare turned about and guided her back several yards, calming her, though her sides shook as she snorted each breath. Sandis slid from the horse, sore, and stepped away quickly, wary of the animal's dancing hooves and flaring nostrils.

"She won't go no farther." Pete pulled the reins tight, the leather whitening his fingers. The mare turned for an alleyway; he brought her back around. "I got to hurry back."

Sandis nodded. "Go."

Pete kicked the mare's flanks, and she gladly took off the way they had come.

A gush of cinder-laden wind hit Sandis, ferrying the scent of sulfur.

Clutching the amarinth in her pocket, Sandis sprinted toward Kolosos, not entirely sure what she would do when she reached it. She only knew she needed to be close. Closer than she was.

Gunshots stung her ears. Smoke dried her eyes. She heard a groan from the gutter and spied a blue-clad soldier there. She took a step toward him, intending to offer her assistance, then stopped. The gold loops of the amarinth bit into the underside of her knuckles. Time was slipping by.

She had promised.

Turning away from the injured man, she ran for the Innerchord.

It was too wide and too cluttered, its stateliness obliterated by the war. Between buildings, she could see Kolosos's wing-laden back as it crushed fighters underfoot. Sandis winced. Behind Kolosos, the gold plate glowed like a fallen sun. The sky reflected it, as though a second sun were trying to pierce through the night. She blinked spots of color from her eyes.

Closer. Closer. She looked around, spying the closest standing building to the monster.

The citizen records building.

A trickle of relief ran down her exposed back as she sprinted for it. She'd broken into this building before—she knew how to get in and where to find the stairs. That would save her time. She wasn't sure how much of it she had left.

The smell of sulfur was pungent inside, like it had collected there and festered. Sandis ran up the stairs, her footfalls echoing in the dark stairwell. Her lungs burned. Soles throbbed. For a minute the darkness blinded her, forcing her to rely on the rails for guidance, but her eyes adjusted. Her heartbeat became a song she couldn't hear the notes to.

She burst onto the roof, and the heat stole a gasp from her throat. She shielded her eyes with her arms and turned away, blinking back tears.

The city was on fire.

Still shielding herself, she crept toward the edge of the roof closest to Kolosos. The Innerchord shined with the light of the gold plate, which already burned brighter than it had mere minutes ago. She couldn't see the army, but she heard them. Someone barked orders unintelligible from this distance. Cannons exploded. Screams tore the air. She'd never stop hearing those screams, whether she lived or died tonight.

Lowering her arm, Sandis beheld the monster. She stood level with its horns. She retrieved the amarinth from her pocket.

How? How was she supposed to do this?

White light like an enormous falling star blazed overhead. Sandis staggered backward when it cut through the sky, striking Kolosos in the crown.

Rone?

Kolosos threw out his arms and arched his back, bellowing in agony. Sandis looked at his open mouth, and knew.

Pinching one of the amarinth's three loops in her fingers, she spun the device.

Then, lips moving with practiced speed, she summoned Ireth.

Rone was . . . tired.

Focus.

His mind spun. Dizzy.

From the corner of his vision, Ireth winked from existence. *Just a little longer. A little longer—*

It was blissful.

Power surged through Sandis, starting at her scalp, filling her like molten metal. It poured down her neck and filled her arms to the fingertips. Glowed in her stomach, washed down her hips and legs, burned in her feet.

Yet it didn't hurt. Sandis was on fire, but it didn't hurt.

One. Two. Three. The seconds ticked by. She had only sixty.

She turned toward Kolosos, her muscles bright and strong, her skin gleaming with flame. Beneath it all, she felt his presence. Ireth.

He was not afraid.

His courage bolstered hers, whispering of what she could do. Of what *they* could do, together.

Four. Five. Six.

Sandis ran for the edge of the roof and leapt.

She jumped with human legs strengthened by Ireth's spirit, and for a moment, she flew on wings of fire.

The beam overhead thinned.

Kolosos was a vision in a wreath of light. She focused on its mouth. Put her arms up, hands pointed, as though diving into a canal.

The heavenly power extinguished. Kolosos's cry tapered to an end.

Its black, cracked lips began to close.

Before they did, Sandis dived between them.

Ten. Eleven. Twelve.

None of it hurt. None of it could touch her.

She was fully, wholly immortal.

And she had promised.

Her light illuminated the darkness around her. She couldn't detect a tongue, but Kolosos shook, trying to dislodge her.

She dodged for the dark depth before her, heat building in her shoulders and elbows. Ireth pushed against her naked skin.

Flinging her hands forward, she opened the demon's throat with a column of flame.

Fifteen. Sixteen. Seventeen.

She leapt, fell. Red surrounded her. Red flesh, red rock, red lava. Sandis swam, attacking Kolosos from the inside out with her fiery limbs, holding her breath deep inside her, unsure whether the amarinth would let her take air from her surroundings. Keeping her pinky hooked around the amarinth's loop while it spun.

The closer she got to the monster's heart, the more damage she would do.

Twenty. Twenty-one. Twenty-two.

Even if she didn't have time to escape.

The red world engulfing her shook, belched, tremored. Fire illuminating her way, she swam deeper through the hollows of Kolosos, cutting through walls and barriers, rending flesh. She reached obsidian bone and embraced it, burning her fire, hot, hotter, until the stone began to crumble.

Thirty. Thirty-one. Thirty-two.

Sandis broke through into another cavity. For a moment she lost her way. Ireth's fire burned in one direction, so she swam the opposite way, clawing through the darkness, kicking her legs with energy that didn't wane.

Ahead, something glowed.

It wasn't the glow of lava or fire, but something soft and gentle, like a dying white ember.

Sandis dug toward it and paused. A tendril of precious air escaped her.

Anon.

He was a shadow, curled around an amarinth already spent, its center glowing with the lives it had stolen.

He was frail, thin, skin too pale and too dark at the same time. His eyes were closed as if in peaceful sleep. The roots of his hair glimmered silver in the firelight pouring from her.

She didn't dare try to speak. She didn't think he'd hear her. He dwelled in a place outside her own. Or did they both?

Forty-three. Forty-four. Forty-five.

Her eyes dropped to the spent amarinth. Rone's amarinth.

Drifting toward her brother, Sandis grasped his hand and linked his index finger through the stilled loop of her own amarinth. She took his from his limp hands.

Fitting her glowing fingers between the still loops, she grabbed the center of Anon's amarinth, flared Ireth's fire, and *pulled.*

Her attempts to wrench the core from its golden cradle sounded like steel crushing steel. Like grinding cogs. Like a distant, terrified scream.

Fifty-three. Fifty-four. Fifty-five.

Sandis blazed white, shouted, and tugged with all her might.

The core came free.

She palmed it, released the Angelic's amarinth, and ignited.

Fire swallowed her in a storm of pain and fury. Ripping, wrenching, searing her from skin to bone as the power of a god consumed her mortality whole.

Chapter 30

The glass shattered from beneath Rone without a sound. It merely was, and then wasn't.

Wind whisked about him from all directions, flipping him forward and sideways. His clothes flapped uselessly around him, whipping still-healing burns.

Then his mind snapped into place.

The sky was no longer below him, but around him. White clouds like those of deep winter. The ruined city stretched below. A city that proved hard to see, thanks to all the flipping and spinning. He was falling without descending, marooned in a strange torrent of space.

So he focused on the Innerchord below him and thought *down*.

Then, since he was a moron, he actually did fall.

He sped past sulfuric clouds, wheezing as their smoke assaulted his lungs. They parted and exposed the face of Kolosos peering up at him. The demon gaped in agony, and its crimson insides filled Rone's vision as its blackening body ripped in half. He fell through the split, as though he were the cleaver rendering the numen in two.

Ash whipped up through the air like polluted snow as the demon's body disintegrated, but at its heart burned a ball of fire. Rone recognized that flame even as he hurtled toward it. Recognized it before it winked out and took the form of a naked woman blotched red with burns.

Her name in his throat, Rone streamlined his body and dived for her, reaching to grasp her. His speed increased, but not enough. *Not enough!*

Debris and ruined cobblestones rushed at him. He squinted against the wind and the sulfur, stretching, reaching—

He grabbed Sandis's wrist. Pulled her into him as he struck the still-crumbling wall of Kolosos, riding it down like a slide. He dug his heels into the cooling rock, shooting up streams of cinders as he did so. A few feet from the ground, the last bit of Kolosos puffed into ash.

He wiped the soot from his vision. In the distance he heard the murmurings of a thousand voices. Felt the pressure of thousands of eyes. But he didn't hear it, see it. There was only her.

"Sandis?" He laid her gently among the cinders coating the ground. Ash snowflaked around them. Taking her face in his hands, he pleaded, "Sandis?"

Her shoulders were blistered, her skin reddened as though she'd been left out in the sun at the height of summer. But her chest moved. Her chest moved, and under the soft skin of her neck, Rone felt a pulse. A vibrant, panicked pulse.

Then she gasped, air rushing into her all at once. Rone grabbed her shoulders and pulled her to him, helping her sit up. She coughed violently against his chest. Her hair smelled of sulfur.

"Thank God," he whispered, holding her tightly to him, burying his face into her locks. "Sandis, thank God."

"Rone?" she croaked, fingers curling around the folds of his shirt. She shuddered against him.

He pulled back just enough to see her face. To press his forehead to hers. "I'm here. I'm here. Black ashes and hellfire, Sandis. I'm here." He kissed her cheekbone, her jaw, her lips before lifting his head and taking in the destruction surrounding them. Somehow they'd done it. They'd . . . They'd won.

It was while he tried to digest this idea that he realized he was look-ing at the destruction through a translucent shield. He blinked, noticing he was looking at a sea people. Thousands of them.

Grabbing Sandis by her elbows, Rone stood and brought her with him, then swiftly removed his jacket and draped it over her bare shoulders.

"It's them," he whispered.

Sandis clung to his arms. He put one around her, helping her stand. "Who?"

Rone swallowed. "The Noscons."

She shouldn't have been awake.

Once, only once, Sandis had managed to hold on to consciousness after a half summoning. Only for a moment, seconds . . . she wasn't sure. She'd nearly drowned.

So she shouldn't be conscious now. Her body was battered. Her burnt skin felt too tight for her body. Nausea assailed her stomach, and a familiar headache pummeled her skull.

But she was awake. Whether from the amarinth, the timing, or a sheer blessing from Ireth, she was—

The Noscons.

She turned to face them, clutching Rone with one hand, holding his jacket closed over her chest with the other. So many of them. Rows upon rows of them encircled her. They were translucent, as though formed of blown glass. Their bodies had little definition outside the markings of their limbs, but their shoulders were defined, as were their faces and hair. Their skin had a bluish hue. Through them she saw the ruined capital. Fires burning. Bodies lying still. Soldiers and civilians creeping from behind teetering buildings.

She leaned hard into Rone. Her legs trembled, and the contact hurt her singed flesh, but he was here. He was *here*, alive. And she was alive. And—

She opened her right hand. Dust like crushed diamonds fell from her palm.

"Anon." His name snapped in her mouth. "Anon. Where is Anon?"

She spun, peering through the fallen bodies. She nearly tumbled to her knees, but Rone held her steady.

"Sandis," he said, his voice strained, "if Kolosos is—"

"No." She shook her head. "No, he's here. Anon—"

"Sandis."

She looked to her left, over Rone's shoulder. Her name had a light accent attached to it. When she saw no flesh-and-blood people nearby, her eyes alighted on a spirit standing near her, who parted the heavy circle with a wave of his hand. He was an older man, perhaps in his fifties, with a broad forehead and wide nose. Despite his ethereal appearance, his eyes were wise and soulful. Round and deep set. There was something profoundly familiar about them.

"He is here." The man gestured to the gap he'd left in the circle. Sandis stumbled toward it, Rone beside her.

She didn't see him at first. The ash had grown heavier and stuck to everything like dust. She brushed it from her hair. Rone sneezed. But as she moved toward the center of the circle, she saw flashes of gold amid the rubble. The plate. Then her eyes caught a glimpse of flesh buried in the ash. She ran to it, stumbling on shaky legs. Her arms were heavy, her fingers slow to bend, but she dropped to her knees in the debris and dug. Rone appeared beside her, moving the rubble far more efficiently than she did.

Hair tickled her fingertips. She grabbed it and lifted her brother's head through the ash.

"Anon!" she cried, eyes too dry for tears. She pulled his neck free before Rone grabbed him under the arms and hauled his frail body from the cinders. He was so delicate, like a boy crafted from paper.

Sandis's muscles shook, exhausted, as she helped shift Anon to sturdier ground. The second his head touched down, she lowered her face to his.

The softest feather of breath touched her cheek.

She nearly fainted with the relief. "He's alive," she gasped. "Thank the Celestial, he's—"

Shivers coursed across her shoulders.

"Black ashes," Rone murmured, his voice light with awe. His eyes had caught on the gold coils looped through Anon's fingers.

Swallowing against her parched throat, Sandis reached forward and gently pried the amarinth from her brother's grasp. She then took Rone's calloused hand in hers and pressed the precious item against his palm.

He met her gaze, eyes wide, hair mussed and peppered with ash. Closing Rone's fingers over the amarinth, Sandis whispered, "Your father wanted me to tell you he loves you."

He snapped back. "What? How—"

"I destroyed your amarinth." Her raspy voice was a sliver above a whisper. "I destroyed it, Rone. This one is your father's. He—and the Celestial—saved us."

Deep lines carved Rone's forehead as he studied her face. "I don't—"

But then his eyes widened, and his grip tightened on the amarinth and Sandis's fingers. He mouthed, *My father,* and released her, holding the amarinth in his open palm. It looked different from his, Sandis thought. Brighter. Resplendent. Rone must have noticed, too. He must have understood. A drop of rain struck one of the gold loops . . . but no, that had come from Rone.

Sandis placed a hand against his cheek. He didn't seem to feel it at first. He hunched, unmoving, over the amarinth several moments before pushing his face against her touch. Before closing his fist around the amarinth so tightly it had to hurt.

Movement behind him drew her gaze over his shoulder, back to the spectral being with the achingly familiar eyes. He floated nearby, apart from the crowd, watching her. Through him she saw soldiers climbing toward the battleground.

Though the need for rest pulled at her joints, Sandis managed to stand, keeping her eyes on his. Studying his face.

She noticed an absence within her body at the same time a strange, warm recognition slid into her mind.

"Ireth?" She took a hesitant step forward.

The man—spirit?—smiled. "Sandis."

A dry sob escaped her. She rushed toward him, tripping once. Climbed over an unrecognizable chunk of something. Reached for him.

Her hand passed through his arm.

"My body died long ago." His accent was unlike any she'd heard before. Rounded and smooth. "But I am myself again. We all are."

Gooseflesh rose on Sandis's arms and legs. She looked at the thousands of spirits around her. Even the approaching soldiers gawked at them, unsure. "We are free." Ireth closed his eyes and smiled. It was, perhaps, the most peaceful expression Sandis had ever beheld. "We are home."

Rubble crunched nearby as Rone approached. The amarinth was no longer in his grip. His eyes flashed to Ireth.

There were so many unspoken words among them. Sandis didn't know where to start.

"I imagined you younger," Rone said. Sadness limned his voice. Sandis reached for his hand. Squeezed it.

Ireth smiled again. "Eat well, Rone. And thank you, for your assistance."

His tone ignited panic in Sandis. "You won't stay?"

The spirit shook his head. "My dear Sandis." He reached for her, but his hand passed through her shoulder. "I have waited so long for you. For someone who would understand. I am forever in your debt, as are our people. We owe many things to you, and to those who fought here. To Hepingya."

The name rang in Sandis's ears. *Hepingya.* The Celestial.

Sorrow and understanding mixed with the other emotions and sensations warring within her. Relief. Fatigue. Hope. *Anon.*

She glanced back at her brother and waited for his chest to rise before returning her attention to Ireth.

"Thank you," she whispered. "For your help. For everything."

"But where will you go now?" Rone asked, searching the faces around them.

"To the world beyond." Ireth turned toward his people, who nodded. Some smiled; some clasped their hands together; others looked confused. "We've been kept awake, trapped, for a very long time. I want nothing more than to rest." He smiled.

"So it does exist. A beyond." Sandis clutched her hands to her chest.

Ireth smiled warmly at her. "Some things are not meant to be understood, dear one. Not yet." His gaze lifted to Rone. "Take care of this land."

Rone wiped falling ash from his face. "Not much left to take care of."

Ireth closed his eyes and tipped his head backward. A soldier passed through the wall of spirits nearby and surveyed the damage. He stared at Sandis and Rone a long moment before waving the rest of his retinue forward.

"Hmmm," Ireth hummed. "Yes, it is still there."

"What is?" Sandis asked.

Ireth pointed up. "The ethereal plane. It is changed, vacant, but it is there. Your words will carry you there, Sandis, if you want to leave. It will take you where men's roads cannot."

"Leave?" Rone croaked.

He nodded. "The words to summon will open the door, and the words to dismiss will bring you back. Merely replace my name with yours. I believe"—he spoke to Sandis—"that if you hold on to him tightly enough, he will come with you."

Sandis's heart fluttered. She leaned hard on Rone.

Rone, holding Sandis close, said, "If Anon is alive . . . I thought there was only one way to kill a numen."

Ireth considered. Held out his hand. Flakes of ash passed through it. "I do not comprehend even half of Kaj's sorcery. If you are right, then he is there." He tipped his head toward the sky, as though peering into the invisible plane beyond it. "He will be trapped as before, if this did not kill him, but he will be harmless. Of this, I am sure."

Sandis swallowed, unsure.

To Rone, Ireth added, "Take care of her. I delay too long."

Finally, tears found their way to Sandis's eyes. "Thank you, Ireth. I'll never forget you."

Ireth pressed his hands together and bowed slightly. "And I you. I will see you in the beyond. But take your time meeting me, dear one."

He straightened and turned toward his people.

Then, in a flash of warm light not so dissimilar from that of summoning, he vanished.

And the other Noscons, blinking like stars, followed him.

Chapter 31

Anon Gwenwig was only sixteen. Sandis had told Rone as much. But the boy had the hair of a man near the end of his life. The tips of his short hair were nearly black, but the rest of the shafts were gray, save right at the root where they bleached white. The toll of so many frequent summonings by a monster too strong for the boy's body.

Anon was too thin to look natural. Rone hadn't seen his eyes yet—the boy had already slept longer than the usual twelve to eighteen hours a vessel took to recover from a summoning. Twenty-five hours now. Rone knew, for all the survivors—himself included—had held their breath as midnight approached. But Kolosos hadn't come. The monster was truly gone, and Sandis had destroyed the amarinth that had powered his rampage.

Rone fingered the new amarinth in his pocket as his gaze drifted to Sandis, who lay asleep on the narrow cot beside her brother. She held him in her bandaged arms, cradling him like a mother would her son. Good. She needed the rest.

Rubbing sleep from his eyes, Rone pulled the amarinth from his pocket. If he tilted it just right, rainbows danced across the diamond-like center.

His father, a vessel all this time. Once he would have barked at the hypocrisy of it, but he couldn't dredge up the contempt. Not now.

Rone curled his hand around the amarinth and tucked his fist under his chin. He struggled to comprehend the . . . what should he call it? The end of it all? But it wasn't truly the *end*, was it? Not for them. Still, the enemy was gone, and the city was in ruins. Well, a lot of it was. It would take years to clean it up. Years to rebuild.

Would he be here for it?

Ireth had said they could leave, travel in ways normal men could not. Travel in ways not *monitored* by other humans. Sandis certainly could, with those markings on her back. So could Anon. Bastien. Rist. The fire-horse-turned-man had sounded confident that Rone would be able to tag along. Rone dared to hope. He had hated this place for such a long time. Admittedly, he felt a small twinge of something—regret, nostalgia; he was bad at naming things today—at the thought of leaving for good. But the possibility gave him hope. A new beginning, with Sandis. With his mother. With his future brother-in-law.

He blinked. *That* was a new thought. But he found he didn't mind it.

Shifting in his chair, he pocketed the talisman. His tailbone was starting to hurt. Standing, Rone stretched before peeking into the bedroom. Anon's cot had been set up in an oversized closet in Triumvir Var's home, where makeshift beds and pallets had been crammed into free space on all three floors, except for the triumvir's bedroom. Var had only issued an invitation to those he deemed important: Esgar slept on the bed in the adjoining room. Sherig occupied the cot beside him, reading a romance novel. Her wounds were superficial, but she had a *lot* of them. The woman met his eye and winked before returning to her diversion. Oz, who appeared unscathed, lingered somewhere in the house, caring for the surviving vessels. Rist, Bastien, and Inda were recovering. Teppa would never wake, thanks to Kolosos. Oz had seemed so beside himself that Rone had attempted neither conversation nor condolences.

Already a memorial was in the works for General Istrude, who had also passed away in the fray. The triumvirate had survived without a scratch, of course. Peterus and Holwig were probably already scheming to get the evacuated citizens back into the city. With Kolosos gone, the factories could start up again. Rone recognized the need to get back to normal, but he hated it all the same.

Normal had never done him any good in Dresberg.

Jachim had survived, of course. He'd never gotten close to Kolosos, save for that night Rone and Sandis had rescued him. Shaking his head, Rone let out a long breath. He couldn't bring himself to be annoyed at the man. Though he'd proved a troublemaker in the past, Rone bore an odd affection, or at least toleration, for him. But maybe that was Sandis's influence.

As far as he knew, Cleric Liddell and the other white-clad Celesians had survived. But their god had not. Neither had his father. What they would do next, Rone wasn't sure. Help the people. Pursue their faith without an Angelic. Maybe find a new faith altogether.

Clutching the amarinth in his pocket, Rone offered a weak and rare prayer. *Thank you, Dad.*

Regardless of where Rone went, he had a feeling Dresberg would be transformed by siege and sacrifice.

<hr>

Bastien's head was somewhere else; he didn't notice Rone standing in the doorway. Hadn't heard the creak of the hinges as Rone peeked into their shared bedroom. He was folding the one change of clothes he'd managed to hold on to, though his pale eyes were focused on some spot between the floor and the window. He winced on occasion—his burns were bandaged, and Rone wondered if the tender skin had been ripped during the final battle with Kolosos. For a kid who often seemed scared of his own skin, the bastard could be sickeningly brave.

"I'll never host a numen again," Bastien said, raising his eyes to the window.

So he *had* noticed Rone. He stepped into the room. "Not a bad thing."

"No." His fingers absently brushed his injured arm. "Not a bad thing at all. Just unsettling. When you spend so long with an identity forced upon you, it's strange to discover your own."

Rone tilted his head at the elegant words. "And you've found yours?"

The Godobian shook his head before meeting Rone's stare. "Not yet. But soon."

Rone wondered if he should point out that Bastien hadn't stuttered once since Rone's return to the mortal realm, but he didn't want to make him self-conscious. Instead, Rone gestured to the clothes, and to the bag he now noticed at the foot of the bed. "Leaving?"

"Staying."

Rone nodded. "Sandis won't go until Anon is up. Hopefully that will be soon."

Bastien rubbed his hands together. "Staying indefinitely, I mean. Here, in Dresberg."

Rone hadn't expected that. It must have shown in his features, given Bastien's reply.

"I'm learning how to read now." He shrugged. "And . . . I don't really know Godobia. I don't remember it."

"I don't know it, either," Rone offered.

"True." He pulled his braid over his shoulder and ran his unscarred hand down its length. "But, well, Jachim says I have promise. And I think I can help here. I-I'm not sure how. But I would like to do what I can. And he's offered to teach me."

Rone snorted. "You're going to be a scholar's understudy?"

A smile tugged Bastien's lips upward. "Something like that. It's an opportunity. I . . . haven't had a lot of those. I don't want to waste it."

Rone hesitated a few seconds, then nodded. "I understand. Does Sandis know you plan on staying?"

"I'll tell her." A sad expression crossed his features, but his jaw set in resolution. "Maybe I can visit, once you're settled. Jachim is excited to study the ethereal plane."

"You told him?" That didn't sit well with Rone. He'd hoped Sandis would keep it to herself, but he wasn't surprised she'd shared the information with Bastien. Or that Bastien had loose lips.

Bastien's brows drew together. "Should I not have?"

Rone wasn't sure. "Wait until morning to tell her." He shoved his hands into his pockets. "Take care of yourself. It's been . . . an adventure, Red. Maybe I'll miss you."

Bastien beamed and shifted the bag on his shoulder. "I'll miss you, too. And good luck. Sorry to see you Go . . . dobia."

Rolling his eyes, Rone pushed off the door frame and walked away. But he couldn't help chuckling as he went.

***

Anon felt like a horse had fallen on him. And hadn't gotten up.

He struggled to open his eyes. The lids felt glued together. His insides were sand. His joints hurt. Everything hurt, but his joints especially. And his bones.

There was a weird taste in his mouth. Like . . . mint. And chicken. But he hadn't eaten in . . . how long had it been? Not since before that man died. What was his name? Kaze? Gaze?

He lifted his hand. The attempt was just a twitch at first, but he managed to get the heavy limb up to his face. Rub the glue from his eyes.

"Anon?"

That voice.

He opened his eyes. Everything was a blur. Shades of brown. Light in the corner from . . . a lamp, he thought. He blinked, urging his surroundings to sharpen. He could make out angular shadows. Walls, corners. A face loomed over him. Warm fingers touched his cheeks.

"Anon?" she said again.

Tears sprang to his eyes. How did he have tears, when his body felt so dry? But there was that taste in his mouth. Had he eaten? Drunk? Why could he not remember?

"Sandis?" he croaked. He'd dreamed she'd come to him, before. That had been a dream, hadn't it?

An *oomph* escaped him when she hugged him. She released him just as quickly.

"Sorry." She sniffed. He could see the outline of her face, her hair— it was short now—and her eyes. A blur wiped across it. Her hand? A droplet, a tear, struck his neck. "You're safe, Anon. You're safe. Kolosos is gone."

Her voice grew heavy with tears. Two more struck his neck. Anon blinked, nearly bringing his sister into focus. His heart beat hard and heavy. *Safe?*

Reaching up a hand, he touched her cheek. "Sandis?"

She grabbed his hand and squeezed it. "You've been asleep for three days. You're in Triumvir Var's home. The war is over."

War? He tried to remember . . . but everything was dark beyond glimmers of light and pain. *Such pain.* He shuddered at the memory of it.

The floor—bed?—shifted. "Here, drink this."

Cool glass pressed to his lip. Tangy liquid touched his tongue. He drank deeply until he coughed. Some of the stuff burned back up his throat, but he swallowed it down.

"That will help you feel better." She brushed hair from his face.

He tried to rub his eyes again, but his body was so heavy. His mind spun. "It . . . hurts, Sandis." His voice was raspy, but he thought the words were coherent. "There's so much that . . . hurts."

And then he slept.

Rone stalked back toward the bedroom—no, closet—where he'd left Sandis and Anon. His mind lingered on his conversation with the Godobian. *No. Bastien.* It would be odd not having him around. Sandis might be upset. Then again, she had her brother back, if he woke up. Rone hated to think what would happen if he didn't.

No, we're hoping now, he reminded himself. *We've paid our dues. We deserve hope.*

He reached the stairs and heard voices. Not loud enough to pick apart, let alone understand, but it *was* the middle of the night. Had they all become nocturnal now?

Curious, he started down the stairs instead of up them. One of the steps creaked, so he hoisted himself onto the banister and slid to the main floor. Around the stairs, down the hall, a dim light glowed under the door to the study.

A shadow lurked outside it.

Rone's muscles tensed like springs. He crept forward, but as he neared the form, the shadow took on a familiar shape.

Rist, he thought. In the dim light, the vessel's eyes met his. Rist's ear was pressed to the door.

Rone said nothing. Merely leaned close to the door and listened.

"—not much of a point."

"But if his transportation theory proves correct, this could be massive." That was . . . Peterus, Rone thought.

"Indeed." Var.

Transportation? Rone's mind spun. They didn't mean the ethereal plane, did they? *She should have waited to tell Bastien.* The Godobian had probably told the excitable scholar about the potential of the now-empty ethereal plane and the man had gotten his breeches in knots over it.

But no one could enter it without a vessel.

275

A curse popped somewhere near his larynx.

Rone missed the next speaker, but later caught, "And keep them close, until things are in order. If it works, they'll have employment."

"Do you intend to pay them?" asked another.

Rone couldn't make out the response, but he wasn't surprised by the tension rolling off Rist like summer heat.

Once a slave, always a slave.

It was time to go.

The door to the closet opened so quickly Sandis startled from the chair beside her brother's cot.

Pulse thudding in her throat, she said, "Rone."

Rone closed the door carefully behind him, twisting the handle so it didn't click. "We need to be on guard."

Gooseflesh coursed down Sandis's back. "What do you mean?"

"I mean our government is talking downstairs, and I think they want to experiment with what Ireth told us."

Sandis narrowed her eyes, trying to understand. Rone was . . . tense. "You mean the ethereal plane?"

He nodded. "*If* vessels can get nonvessels up there . . . well, you're a key to a potentially valuable lock. A key certain people won't want to lose."

Understanding washed over her like boiling water.

After all that had happened . . . would the triumvirate refuse to retract their claws?

She picked at the bandage wrapped just above her right elbow, where a burn was still healing. "Anon woke, briefly. But he's not recovered yet."

Rone tugged a hand through his hair. "We might have to carry him."

"What if it hurts him?"

Dropping his hand, Rone sighed. "For now, let's act like we don't know what the triumvirs intend. Buy Anon some time. Be all smiles and helpfulness."

Sandis nodded. "We have to tell Bastien and Rist—"

"Rist was with me. He knows. Bastien plans on staying."

A pang like a hammer struck her chest. "He's not coming?"

Rone shook his head, his shoulders relaxing. "He says he has an opportunity here with Jachim. Something about learning to read and helping and other crap."

Sandis managed a smile. "He'll be good at that. But we should tell him. At least so he doesn't give us away."

Rone nodded. "But turn off this light so we're not suspicious."

Sandis moved to the lantern. Paused. Then shifted toward Rone and circled her arms around his waist.

He embraced her tightly and pressed a kiss to the top of her head. "It's almost over," he whispered.

Sandis believed him.

Chapter 32

Sandis fell asleep on the chair, leaning against the wall. The clanking of a glass hitting the floor startled her awake, igniting a sharp kink in her neck.

"Sorry." The apology was weak and raspy. But it came from *him*.

"Anon!" She stumbled off her chair and to his side. He sat up in bed, leaning heavily to one side, propping himself up on his arm. His blanket had fallen to his hips, revealing the sharpness of his ribs against his papery skin.

Sandis moved for the pitcher in the corner, then found the now-chipped glass Anon must have knocked over. She filled it half-full and held it to his lips. He managed to take it in one hand. His grip was stronger than before.

He drank every drop.

Sandis sat on the edge of the cot. "How are you feeling?"

"Terrible." He coughed. "But . . . better." He tilted his face up, his eyes meeting hers. They were clearer this time, more focused.

Her own vision blurring with tears, she hugged him, careful not to hurt him. It was still unbelievable, him being here. Alive, all these years. And already taller than she was. She had missed his leap toward manhood completely, and—

"Sandis, *where were you?*"

She pulled back. "What?"

Anon winced and touched his skull. "Where were you? I got back from the tower, and the flat was empty. No one . . . No one had seen you. You just vanished."

A chill rolled down Sandis's arms. "The tower? Anon, where were *you*? You disappeared. I searched"—she paused, a lump forming in her throat—"everywhere for you. Kazen told me you'd drowned."

He stiffened. "Kazen." He said it like he was trying to remember.

Sandis nodded. "He's the man who took you. Who took *me*. Anon, I was his vessel for four years. Until I met Rone."

He met her eyes. "Rone?"

Sandis chewed on her lip. Her story was so long, so complicated, and Anon was so weak. "Tell me where you went."

He swallowed. Tried to sit up straighter and groaned, so Sandis helped him lie back down. He closed his eyes, and for a moment Sandis thought she'd lost him to sleep again.

"I went to the Lily Tower," he said, opening his eyes, though his dark gaze was unfocused. "I'd heard they treat acolytes well. I wanted a better—" His voice choked off, dry. Sandis hurried to give him water, which he drank slowly this time. "I wanted a better life for us. But the testing . . . it takes *days*. I didn't know." He winced again. "They said I couldn't go home . . . that it would show a lack of faith. So I didn't. And I passed. I ran home to tell you, but you were gone."

A single tear slid down Sandis's cheek. "You were at the Lily Tower."

His irises shifted back toward her.

Sandis clasped her hands together and bit her knuckle. "All this time."

"I went back. For a year," Anon said, closing his eyes again. "And then I left. I couldn't be there anymore. The tower, Dresberg. It reminded me so much of you. Of Mom and Dad. So I went north. Got a job as a farmhand. And you . . . you were here, all along."

"You never would have found me," she murmured.

Anon shook his head, then winced.

Sandis stood. "Let me find you more medicine—"

His hand snagged hers. "No. Sit."

Sandis sank back onto the cot.

Anon met her eyes again. "Tell me what happened. All of it."

Sandis pinched her lips together, taking in his gaunt features. The tightness in his forehead that belied pain. "Maybe after you rest—"

"Sandis. Please."

He tightened his birdlike grip on her hand.

Sandis rested her other hand atop his. "I was searching for you, not very far from Helderschmidt's. The sun was going down, but I wanted to check a little farther. I ran into two men. Slavers, but I didn't know it at the time . . ."

Sandis hugged Bastien tightly to her and laughed. "You smell like roses."

Pulling back, Bastien blushed and tugged on his braid. "That . . . was the only soap I could find."

Tendrils of morning light leaked through the gauzy curtains of the bedroom they had once shared in Triumvir Var's home. The sun hadn't crested the great wall yet, so the morning was still young and balmy. In a few months winter would settle in, bitter and cold. Sandis had heard it was warmer in Godobia.

Thoughts of the southern country quickened her pulse, but she smiled, hiding her nerves. Pulling a tightly folded paper from the pocket of her dress, she pressed it into Bastien's palm.

"This is where you can send letters," she whispered. "Don't show anyone, even Jachim. Just to be safe."

Bastien's blue eyes searched hers. He nodded. "I promise. You'll write back?"

Sandis took the end of his red braid and gave it a gentle pull. "Of course."

He took her hand in both of his freckled ones. The bandages were gone from the left, revealing puckered pink scars. A twinge of guilt shivered in her chest. "Be safe, Sandis. Be careful."

"We will be." Unless it didn't work. Unless Rone couldn't come, or it made Anon sick. Unless the others got word of their plan and thwarted them somehow.

She wondered if Bastien could see her heartbeat against the skin of her neck.

She kissed him on his cheek—it was soft as a babe's—and slid her hand free of his grasp. After offering him one last reassuring smile, she hurried back through the house. As fast as she dared. There were already blue-clad guards on the property, as well as scarlets. Triumvir Var had told her they would be moved to a new facility, one that would fit them better. He'd spoken of amenities and space, jobs and potential. But even if Sandis hadn't heard whispers of his intention to use her, she would have recognized the strange glint in the man's eyes. He had Kazen's confidence and Talbur's smoothness. She and the triumvir had fought together and won together, but she still didn't trust him.

And so the time to leave was now, before he decided not to trust her, either.

She moved up a flight of stairs, legs itching to run. One of the nurses came down the other way, carrying a basket of bandages. Several of Sandis's own had been discarded, leaving her with splotches of pink skin. She still wore wrappings around her left shin and midsection.

"How is he?" Sandis asked as they came together. She knew this woman. She'd been tending Arnae Kurtz's burns.

"Left at first light with the mob woman," she answered with a shrug. "Didn't even say goodbye."

Sandis nodded, hid a smile, and ascended the rest of the stairs. She wondered if Arnae would venture back to his flat with its secret room in the back or if he would remain allies with Sherig. Only time would tell, along with Bastien's letters.

Sandis wasn't entirely sure she'd ever return to Dresberg. In the end, she had very little to return to.

She strode up the hallway toward more guest bedrooms, passing a soldier as she went. She didn't miss how he shied away from her, his movements abrupt enough that his shoulder bumped one of the portraits hanging on the wall. He stopped to straighten it, and Sandis slid past him. Her brands seemed to warm as she did, almost as though Ireth spoke to her. Pressing a hand to her heart, she prayed, *I hope you are well, my friend. I hope you are at peace.*

And thank you, for this gift.

She opened the door to the bedroom where Chief Esgar slept, the curtains drawn tight to keep out the day. Light on her feet, Sandis moved to the closet and opened the door.

It was a large closet, but the three men inside it took up a great deal of room. No lamp or candle was lit, but Sandis knew them all by their shadows and sounds. The broadest one, standing still and ready, was Rone. The shortest, who shifted closer to her, oversized clothes rustling, was her brother. The one in the corner, as though part of the darkness itself, was Rist.

Their packs were ready and in hand.

"Let's hurry," she whispered. "Rone, in the middle."

Rone let out a long breath that smelled of spearmint. He shuffled to the center of the closet. Sandis and Anon stepped close to him; Rist was slow to comply.

To her brother, Sandis whispered, "Try to repeat the words as I say them."

She took his hand. Waited for Rist's. When he grabbed her fingers, his hand was dry, his grip too tight.

They surrounded Rone and pressed into him. If three vessels couldn't get him into the ethereal plane, nothing would.

Please, let this work.

"Vre en nestu a carnath," Sandis began, and Rist's voice joined her, Anon's quietly lagging behind. *"Ii mem entre I amar."*

Her skin warmed.

"Vre en nestu a carnath." She squeezed their hands tighter and pushed her forehead into Rone's chest, closing her eyes. "Anon, Sandis, Rist, and Rone *epsi gradenid.*"

For a moment, Sandis was falling. Her stomach flipped over. Her blood rose to her head. But there was no pain. No burning, no suffering.

She came back to herself. Squeezed the hands interlocked with her own. Opened her eyes.

Rone. He was still here, at least.

Rist pulled free first. Sandis turned her head.

Her lips parted.

The closet and its walls were gone, replaced by a wide-open space—grander and broader than any Sandis had ever beheld. The sky was a strange mix of dark mauve and maroon, made of clouds . . . the kind painted with brush strokes on canvas, not the kind that lived in the sky. These clouds didn't move. They glowed with a strange light, like the choking of a candle. The ground beneath her was smooth and dark as obsidian, but shaved so thin she could see through it. Not perfectly, but the shadowed shapes far beneath her looked like houses. And that curve in the distance . . . that had to be Dresberg's wall.

"It's different."

She turned to Rone, still holding Anon's hand. "What do you mean?"

Rone turned slowly, taking in their surroundings. "This isn't what it looked like before. The sky was dark, and the ground . . . it was made of glass and stars. There were random blocks . . . but everything looks level now. No mountains or caves." He knelt and ran his hand over the ground. "No portals. It's like the glass just . . . rusted."

Rist snorted. "Glass can't rust."

Rone rolled his eyes. "I know that. It's a metaphor."

Rist turned away, taking in the strange view for himself. Anon breathed heavily. Sandis pulled his arm over her neck to support him, even though he shook his head. She turned slowly, taking in the great expanse, remembering what Ireth had said about Kolosos—about *Kaj*. But she saw no other signs of life besides their small group. That was a relief. Even in a "powerless" form, she'd rather not come across the being that had haunted her for weeks before destroying half of Dresberg.

Sandis's skin tingled as though a cold breeze touched it, but the air here didn't move. Smiling, she met Rone's eyes. "We did it."

He placed his hands on her shoulder, tracing its curve with his thumb. "We did it."

⋯⋯

They walked for a long time.

The strange majesty of the ethereal plane—the place that had been Ireth's cage for so long—soon lost its appeal. It was all the same, mile after mile. The only change was the shifting of the world below them. They camped without fires, traveled without roads. This new world darkened when night fell, but not as much as Sandis thought it should. And so they walked night hours, too, resting when they needed it. For much of the way, Rone carried Anon on his back, never once complaining about the load. And Sandis loved him all the more for it.

They never came across another soul. Perhaps Kolosos truly had perished. Perhaps Kaj was merely lost, unaware that they trespassed his prison.

The Fortitude Mountains were larger than Sandis had ever imagined. She had seen them in the distance before. Pictured them like a great wall. But they were far thicker than they were tall. They walked over the pass, following the high peaks south. Sometimes they talked, sometimes they didn't. Rist, especially, was quiet. But despite the toll of traveling and the repetitive rations they'd stowed away, Anon regained a little strength each day. Though, Sandis imagined, it would be a long time yet before he was truly well. It seemed the more his body healed, the worse he slept. As they reached the end of the mountains, Anon began to wake multiple times a night, thrashing and moaning, never able to recall his dreams when he woke. Sandis soothed him. Rone assured him. Rist didn't complain.

It was early in the morning when Rone finally said, "This is it."

Sandis paused and looked beyond her feet. "Godobia?"

Rone's face brightened, lifting the dark circles that had begun to form under his eyes. He shifted Anon on his back. "It has to be. I think that's a town. Can you get the map?"

Sandis reached into his trouser pocket and grabbed the folded letter there. Many of the words were smeared, and the paper had been folded and refolded so many times it threatened to tear between her fingers. But the letter had a map sketched on it. A map to Rone's mother.

"She's not far, I think," Sandis said, hope building in her like restless butterflies.

"I'm going this way."

They all turned toward Rist, who gestured east. He shrugged under their scrutiny. "I think I'll try Serrana first."

Sandis's belly tightened. "You won't know anyone, Rist."

"I know the language. I'll get by." He shifted his pack. "Thank you, for helping me survive all . . . that. But I don't want to follow you. I don't belong."

Rone frowned. "Rist—"

"I don't. And I don't *want* to." He dipped his head to get hair out of his eyes. "I can't. You remind me of her. All of you."

Kaili. Sandis's eyes moistened, but she managed to nod. Then she opened her pack, searching for a pencil and paper. She tore a corner off Rone's expired emigration papers and scrawled the address she'd memorized onto it. Held it out to Rist.

"Write to us."

But Rist shook his head. "Sandis. I really don't want to."

She placed the paper in his palm, much as she had with Bastien. "If you change your mind."

Rist frowned, but he didn't discard the paper. And he didn't say goodbye. He merely diverged from their path, the one they'd walked together for nearly two weeks. Sandis watched him grow smaller and smaller. There was nothing in this place to block him from view.

Anon slid from Rone's back and grabbed her pack, tugging her back to them. "Let's go, Sandis," he said, weary. "We're almost there."

Swallowing a lump rising in her throat, Sandis nodded.

They walked one more day.

Their palms pressed to hers, Sandis spoke the words.

"Parte Rone, Sandis, and Anon *en dragu bai."*

She had the sensation of falling, though her feet never left the ground.

Sunlight turned her eyelids red. When she opened them, a new world surrounded her.

It was so yellow. Yellow dust on the nearby road, yellow grass waving in a cool breeze, yellow-tinged leaves on the sparse trees. It was yellow and warm and bright and wonderful.

Suddenly Rone's hands grabbed her under the arms, and she found herself flying through the air, her pack hitting the ground. She laughed, and Rone whooped, spinning her around twice before setting her down.

"We're here. God's tower, we're really here." He hugged her tightly to him, then pressed his warm lips hard against hers. Despite Anon's groan behind her, Sandis gladly reciprocated—as well as she could while smiling.

They had dropped down near a town, close enough to see it in the distance, far enough not to startle anyone. Sandis had no idea what their appearance looked like after two weeks in the ethereal plane, but she supposed it didn't matter if there were no witnesses.

Grabbing Rone's and Anon's hands, she hurried toward the town.

It was just as yellow as everything else. Storefronts and homes were built of yellow brick and wood, so much smaller than those in Dresberg. The tallest was two stories, and most were only one. The roads were wide and uncrowded and unpaved. There was something distinctly pleasing about the openness of it all.

Women with hair ranging from blonde to crimson gathered around a large well near the center of the town, gabbing to one another in a tongue completely foreign to Sandis's ears. It was quick and clipped, and she couldn't tell one word from another. As they passed by, eyes turned their way and conversation stopped. Most stared longest at Anon, a boy of sixteen with hair as silver as a newly minted coin.

Rone approached a stand selling squash and held out his Kolin money, but the merchant shook his head and turned him away. He returned slightly annoyed, running a hand back through his hair.

"You'll go bald if you're not careful." Sandis elbowed him in the ribs.

"If I do, I'll grow a beard," he teased back.

"We're not far," Anon said, leaning into Sandis. "From the border, I mean. Keep asking around for Kolins."

They did, letting Rone take the lead. "Kolin?" he asked a freckled woman by the well. "Kolin?" he asked a laundress with hair the same color as the brick behind her. All shook their heads no and turned away, only to stare at them as they passed.

They'd nearly reached the other end of the town when a man ran up to him, his hair streaked gray and his freckles so close together he looked like he had a deep tan. He darted in front of them, stopping Rone, Sandis, and Anon in their tracks.

"Kolin?" he repeated.

Rone nodded.

The man said something in Godobian.

Sandis offered her upturned hands. "We don't understand."

The man repeated himself, slower. His words were as garbled as they'd been the first time. He obviously didn't speak Kolin, as Sandis had hoped.

But he reached forward and took Rone's elbow, pointing down a road joining the one they stood on. "Kolin," he said. "Kolin."

Sandis's heart fluttered. "Kolin?" she repeated, pointing.

The man nodded, patted Rone's arm, and ran back the way he'd come.

Rone turned and met her eyes. A childlike hope sparkled in his own.

Sandis grinned and pushed them in the direction the man had pointed. Anon stumbled, so she grasped his arm and hurried him along, unable to tamper her excitement.

The road stretched south, away from the town. Half a mile out were a few small homes dotting the prairie grass. Two Godobian children played with a dog outside one of them. Another had an enormous garden behind it with a ginger-haired man swinging a scythe. The third cottage was a little farther down, with a roof in need of repair and one window boarded up. Pastel-pink flowers had been planted outside of it, and a short clothesline stretched to the side. A woman in a Kolin-style dress with dark, curly hair shook out a damp sheet and hung it to dry.

Rone stopped in his tracks, and Sandis knew they'd found the right place.

As the woman turned back for her basket, she looked up. Squinted and shielded her eyes with her hands.

Then she screamed.

Adalia Comf ran down the road, kicking up dust as she went. Rone darted toward her. When they met, he scooped her up in his arms and lifted her feet from the ground.

Wiping a tear from her eye, Sandis squeezed Anon's arm and approached.

"Rone!" Adalia cried, taking her son's face in her hands. "You didn't write! Oh, what a surprise! I'm so glad you're well. I heard about the civil war up north. I don't think any of my letters made it through." She hugged him again as tears ran down her cheeks. "Oh, Rone, I could die now and be happy."

"Please don't," he said. When she pulled back, Rone kissed her on the cheek and led her to Sandis. Adalia's dark eyes found her and widened.

Rone stood behind Sandis and placed both hands on her shoulders. "Mom, this is Sandis Gwenwig. And her brother, Anon."

"Sandis," she said the name, and recognition lit up her face. Wiping her hands on her apron, she approached and clasped Sandis's hands in hers. "I've heard much about you, Miss Gwenwig. And I admit I was hoping he'd bring you with him."

Sandis's cheeks warmed, and she laughed. "I was hoping he would, too."

"And Anon, was it?" She turned toward Anon, noticing his hair. There was a question in her expression, but she didn't ask it. "I'm very happy to have all of you." She grinned so hard her ears lifted a good half inch. "So happy."

She pulled back and dabbed her eyes with the corner of her apron. "Come in, all of you. Come in. I'll make us something to eat. And tell me everything. How did you get here? Rone, your papers—but no, tell me after we've sat down. You must be so tired. And you need a bath. Come, come."

She urged Sandis forward gently, Rone not so gently. Sandis squeezed her brother's hand, and Rone took her other one, lacing his fingers through hers and kissing her knuckles. And as they approached the house at the end of the lane, Sandis couldn't help but notice the brightness of the sun, the freshness in the air, and the promise awaiting her behind that door.

Together, Sandis and her family went home.

ACKNOWLEDGMENTS

I am so utterly grateful to those who have helped bring this book, and this series, to fruition. It's been a journey, and this is possibly the first time I've cried typing, "The End," upon finishing a manuscript. This story and its characters are so dear to me. But this isn't a one-woman show, so let's get on with it!

Thank you (again) to Marlene and Jason, whose firm encouragement planted the seed for this novel and its predecessors. Thank you to Angela for helping me polish it real shiny, and for all the editors, designers, layout-ers, etc. at 47North who put in so many hours to make my brain spew presentable.

I want to especially thank Caitlyn McFarland, who is way smarter than I am and helped me do a midbook overhaul halfway through the drafting process. It benefited the story immensely, as well as made me look better in the eyes of editors and agents alike! Go read her books. They are fantastic.

Thank you to Whitney, Rachel, and Leah, who beta read this sucker in *less than a week* so I could turn it in on time. For free. They are literally that awesome. And thank you to my alpha readers, who followed me through the entire trilogy: Rebecca, Laura, Tricia, and Cerena. And a hat tip to James, who answers all my weird medical questions.

A huge thank-you, of course, to my wonderful husband, Jordan, who should really have every book I write dedicated to him. He is so utterly supportive. He is my brainstorming champion, my critique partner, my marketing manager, and a fantastic dad to our kids. He's also incredibly good-looking, which is inspiring in and of itself.

Thanks to my kiddos, who are somehow okay with Mom locking herself in the basement every morning to invent characters and the things they do.

Finally, most gracious praises to my Father in Heaven, for my ability to create and so much more. Cheers.

ABOUT THE AUTHOR

Charlie N. Holmberg is the author of *Smoke and Summons*, *Myths and Mortals*, and *Siege and Sacrifice* in the Numina series. Her *Wall Street Journal* bestselling Paper Magician series, which includes *The Paper Magician*, *The Glass Magician*, and *The Master Magician*, has been optioned by the Walt Disney Company. Charlie's stand-alone novel, *Followed by Frost*, was nominated for a 2016 RITA Award for Best Young Adult Romance. Born in Salt Lake City, Charlie was raised a Trekkie alongside three sisters, who also have boy names. She is a proud BYU alumna, plays the ukulele, owns too many pairs of glasses, and finally adopted a dog. She currently lives with her family in Utah. Visit her at www.charlienholmberg.com.